# BLACK MARKET

**JAMES PATTERSON** is one of the best-known and biggest-selling writers of all time. His books have sold in excess of 325 million copies worldwide. He is the author of some of the most popular series of the past two decades – the Alex Cross, Women's Murder Club, Detective Michael Bennett and Private novels – and he has written many other number one bestsellers including romance novels and stand-alone thrillers.

James is passionate about encouraging children to read. Inspired by his own son who was a reluctant reader, he also writes a range of books for young readers including the Middle School, I Funny, Treasure Hunters, House of Robots, Confessions and Maximum Ride series. James has donated millions in grants to independent book-shops and he has been the most borrowed author in UK libraries for the past ten years in a row. He lives in Florida with his wife and son.

# BLACK MARKET

## JAMES PATTERSON

arrow books

5 7 9 10 8 6

Arrow Books
20 Vauxhall Bridge Road
London SW1V 2SA

Arrow Books is part of the Penguin Random House group of companies
whose addresses can be found at global.penguinrandomhouse.com.

Copyright © James Patterson 1986
Excerpt from *16ᵗʰ Seduction* © James Patterson 2017

First published in Great Britain by Hodder and Stoughton in 1986
This edition published by Arrow Books in 2017

www.penguin.co.uk

A CIP catalogue record for this book is available from the British Library.

ISBN 9781784757410
ISBN 9781784757427 (export edition)

Set in 11/15 pt ITC Berkeley Oldstyle Std
Typeset by Jouve (UK), Milton Keynes
Printed and bound in Great Britain by Clays Ltd, St Ives Plc

For Janie, who is Nora.
For Mary Katherine, who is a saint.

*For anyone who's ever dreamed about*
*some small and delicious revenge*
*against the money changers on*
*Wall Street and around the world.*

# Acknowledgements

Although *Black Market* is written as fiction, all of what follows could happen, especially the Wall Street financial parts. I would like to thank the people who helped so much in making the background information interesting and authentic.

Sidney Ruthberg—financial editor, Fairchild Publications

James Dowd—Wall Street attorney, formerly of the United States Army

Stephen Bowen—former captain, United States Marine Corps

Katherine McMahon—New York and Paris backgrounds

Joan Ennis—Irish Tourist Board

Thomas Altman—Sedona, Arizona

Barbara Maddalena—New York, Wall Street area

Mindy Zepp—New York

M. Blackstone—Soho

# PART ONE

---

# GREEN BAND

*The pure products of America go crazy.*

—William Carlos Williams

# Chapter 1

*Wall Street, Manhattan: December 1985*

THE TAWDRY YELLOW cab was double-parked at the base of Wall Street, where it intersects with South Street and the East River. Colonel David Hudson leaned his tall, athletic body against its battered trunk.

He raised one hand to his eye and loosely curled his fingers to fashion a makeshift telescope. He carefully studied 40 Wall Street, where Manufacturers Hanover Trust had offices, then 23 Wall, which housed executive suites for Morgan Guaranty. Then the New York Stock Exchange. Trinity Church. Chase Manhattan Plaza. At five in the morning the towering buildings were as impressive and striking as monuments; the feeling of history and stability was overwhelming.

Once he had it all vividly in sight, Colonel Hudson squeezed his fingers tightly together. "*Boom,*" he whispered.

The financial capital of the world completely disappeared behind his clenched fist.

*Williamsburg, Brooklyn*

Seconds before five-thirty on that same morning Sergeant Harry Stemkowsky, the man designated Vets 24, sped down the steep, icicle-slick hill that was Metropolitan Avenue in the Williamsburg section of Brooklyn. He was in a nine-year-old wheelchair, from the Queens Veterans Administration. Right now he was pretending the chair was a Datsun 280-Z, silver metallic, with a shining T-roof.

"Aahh-eee-ahh!" He let out a banshee screech that pierced the deserted, solemnly quiet streets. His long thin face was buried in the oily collar of a khaki fatigue parka replete with peeling sergeant's stripes, and his frizzy blond ponytail blew behind him like a bike streamer. Periodically he closed his eyes, which were tearing badly in the burning cold wind. His pinched face was getting as red as the gleaming Berry Street stoplight that he was racing through with absolute abandon.

His forehead was burning, but he *loved* the sensation of unexpected freedom. He thought he could actually feel streams of blood surge through his wasted legs again. Harry Stemkowsky's rattling wheelchair finally came to a halt in front of the all-night Walgreen Drug Store. Under the parka and the two bulky sweaters he wore, his heart was hammering wildly. He was so goddamn excited—his whole life was beginning all over again.

Today, Harry Stemkowsky felt he could do just about anything.

The drugstore's glass door, which he nudged open, was covered with a montage of cigarette posters. Immediately he was blessed with a draft of welcoming warm air, filled with the smells of greasy bacon and fresh-perked coffee. He smiled and rubbed his hands together in a gesture that was almost gleeful. For the first time in years, he was no longer a cripple.

And for the first time in more than a dozen hard years, Harry Stemkowsky had a purpose.

He had to smile. When he wrapped his mind around the whole deal, the full, unbelievable implications of Green Band, he just had to smile.

Right at this moment, Sergeant Harry Stemkowsky, the official messenger for Green Band, was safely at his firebase in New York City. Now it could begin.


*Federal Plaza, Manhattan*

Inside the fortress that was New York FBI headquarters in Federal Plaza, a tall, silver-haired man, Walter Trentkamp, repeatedly tapped the eraser of his pencil against a faded desk blotter.

Scrawled on the soiled blotter was a single phone number: 202-555-1414. It was the private number for the White House, a direct line to the president of the United States.

Trentkamp's telephone rang at precisely 6:00 A.M.

"All right, everybody, please start up audio surveillance now." His voice was harsh this early in the morning. "I'll hold them as long as I possibly can. Is audio surveillance ready? Well, let's go."

The legendary FBI Eastern Bureau chief picked up the signaling telephone. The words *Green Band* echoed ominously in his brain. He'd never known anything like this in his Bureau experience, which was long and varied and not without bizarre encounters.

Gathered in a grim, tight circle around the FBI head were some of the more powerfully connected men and women in New York. Not a person in the group had ever experienced anything like this emergency situation, either. In silence, they listened as Trentkamp answered the expected phone call.

"This is the Federal Bureau . . . Hello?"

There was no reply on the outside line. The tension inside the room could be felt by everyone. Even Trentkamp, whose calm in critical situations was well known, appeared nervous and uncertain.

"I said hello. Are you there? . . . Is anyone there? . . . Who is on this line?"


*Williamsburg, Brooklyn*


Walter Trentkamp's frustrated voice was being monitored electronically in a battered mahogany phone booth at the rear of the Walgreen Drug Store in Williamsburg. Inside the booth, Sergeant Harry Stemkowsky's finger combed his long, unkempt hair as he listened. His heart had gone beyond mere pounding; now it was threatening to detonate in his chest. There were new and unusual pulses beating through his body.

This was the long overdue time of truth. There would be no more war-game rehearsals for the twenty-eight members of Green Band.

"Hello? This is Trentkamp. New York FBI." The phone receiver cradled between Stemkowsky's shoulder and jaw vibrated with each phrase.

After another interminable minute, Harry Stemkowsky firmly depressed the play button on a Sony portable recorder. He then carefully held the pocket recorder flush against the pay phone's receiver.

Stemkowsky had cued the recorder to the first word of the message—"Good." The "good" stretched to "goood" as the recorder hitched once, then rolled forward with a soft whir.

"Good morning. This is Green Band speaking. Today is December fourth. A Friday. A history-making Friday, we believe."

Over a squawk box the eerie, high-pitched voice brought the unprecedented message the men and women sequestered in the Manhattan FBI office had been waiting for.

*Green Band was beginning.*

Ryan Klauk from FBI Surveillance made a quick judgment that the prerecorded track had been tampered with to make it virtually unrecognizable and probably untraceable.

"As we promised, there are vitally important reasons for our past phone calls this week, for all the elaborate preparations we've made, and had you make to date . . .

"Is everyone listening? I can only assume you have company, Mr. Trentkamp. No one in corporate America seems to make a decision alone these days . . . Listen closely, then. Everybody, please listen . . .

"The Wall Street financial district, from the East River to Broadway, is scheduled to be firebombed today. A large number of randomly selected targets will be completely destroyed late this afternoon.

"I will repeat. Selected targets in the financial district will be destroyed today. Our decision is irrevocable. Our decision is nonnegotiable.

"The firebombing of Wall Street will take place at five minutes past five tonight. It might be an attack by air; it might be a ground attack. Whichever—it will occur at five minutes past five precisely."

"Wait a minute. You can't—" Walter Trentkamp began to object vehemently, then stopped. He remembered he was attempting to talk back to a prerecorded message.

"All of Manhattan, everything below Fourteenth Street, must be evacuated," the voice track continued methodically.

"The Target Area Nuclear Survival Plan for New York should be activated right now. Are you listening, Mayor Ostrow? Are you listening, Susan Hamilton? Is your Office of Civil Preparedness listening?

"The Nuclear Survival Plan can save thousands of lives. Please employ it now . . .

"In case any of you require further concrete convincing, this will be provided as well. Such requests have been anticipated.

"Our seriousness, our utter commitment to this mission, must not be underestimated. Not at any time during this or any future talk we might decide to have.

"Begin the evacuation of the Wall Street financial district now. Green Band cannot possibly be stopped or deterred. Nothing I've said is negotiable. Our decision is irrevocable."

Harry Stemkowsky abruptly pushed down the stop button. He quickly replaced the telephone receiver. He then rewound the Sony recorder and stuffed it in the drooping pocket of his fatigue jacket.

Done.

He shivered uncontrollably. Christ, he'd done it. He'd actually goddamn done it!

He'd delivered Green Band's message, and he felt terrific. He wanted to scream out. More than that, he wished he could leap two feet in the air and punch the sky.

No formal demands had been made.

Not a single clue had been offered as to why Green Band was happening.

Stemkowsky's heart was still beating loudly as he numbly maneuvered his wheelchair along an aisle lined with colorful deodorants and toiletries, up toward the gleaming soda fountain counter.

The short-order cook, Wally Lipsky, a cheerfully mountainous three-hundred-and-ten-pound man, turned from scraping the grill as Stemkowsky wheeled up. Lipsky's pink-cheeked face brightened immediately. The semblance of a third or fourth chin appeared out of rolling mounds of neck fat.

"Well, look what Sylvester the Cat musta dragged in offa the street! It's my man Pennsylvania. Whereyabeen keepin' yourself, champ? Long time no see."

Stemkowsky had to smile at the irresistible fat cook, who had a well-deserved reputation as the Greenpoint neighborhood clown. Hell, he was in the mood to smile at almost anything this morning.

"Oh, he-he-here and there, Wally." Stemkowsky burst into a nervous stutter. "Muh-Manhattan the mo-most part. I been wuh-working in Manhattan a lot these days."

Stemkowsky tapped his finger on the tattered cloth tag sewn into the shoulder of his jacket. The patch read VETS CABS AND MESSENGERS. Harry Stemkowsky was one of seven licensed wheelchair cabbies in New York; three of them worked for Vets in Manhattan.

"Gah-gotta good job. *Real* job now, Wah-Wally . . . Why don't you make us some breakfast?"

"You got it, Pennsylvania. Cabdriver special comin' up. You got it, my man, anything you want."

9

# Chapter 2

*Manhattan*

AS EARLY AS six-fifteen that same morning, an endless stream of sullen-looking men and women carrying bulging black briefcases had begun to rise out of the steam-blooming subway station at Broadway and Wall Street.

They were the appointed drones of New York's financial district, the straight-salary employees who understood abstract accounting principles and fine legal points but perceived little else about the Street and its black magic. These unfortunates couldn't make the intuitive leap to the larger truth that on Wall Street millions were made not by accepting a fixed salary, but by taking a 10, 20, or 50 percent *vig* on somebody else's thousands, on somebody else's hundreds of millions.

By seven-thirty gum-popping secretaries were slouching off the buses arriving from Staten Island and Brooklyn. Aside from their habitual gum chewing, some of the secretaries looked impressively chic, almost elegant, that Friday morning.

As the ornate golden arms on the Trinity Church clock solemnly reached eight o'clock, every main and side street of the financial district was choked with thick, hypertense pedestrian traffic, as well as with buses and honking cabs.

More than nine hundred and fifty thousand people were being melted into less than half a square mile of outrageously expensive real estate, seven solid stone blocks where billions were bought and sold every workday—still the unsurpassed financial capital of the world.

It was too late to stop the morning's regular migration. The slim possibility had disintegrated in a frantic series of telephone calls between the commissioner's office and various powerful precinct chiefs. It had petered out into a nightmare of impossible logistics and mounting panic.

At that moment a wraithlike black man, Abdul Calvin Mohammud, was calmly entering the bobbing parade of heads and winter hats on Broad Street, just south of Wall. As he walked within the spirited crowd, he found himself noticing corporate flags waving colorfully from the massive stone buildings. The flags signaled BBH and Company, the National Bank of North America, Manufacturers Hanover, the Seaman's Bank. The flags were like crisp sails driven by strong East River winds.

Calvin Mohammud continued up the steep hill toward Wall Street. He was hardly noticed. But then the messenger caste usually wasn't. They were invisible men, props only.

Today, like every other workday, Calvin Mohammud wore a thigh-length, pale gray clerk's tunic with a frayed armband that read VETS MESSENGERS. On both sides of the words were fierce Eighty-second Airborne Division eagles.

But none of that was noticed, either.

Calvin Mohammud didn't look like it now, but in Vietnam and Cambodia he'd been a first-rate Kit Carson army scout. He'd won a Distinguished Service Cross, then the Congressional Medal of Honor for conspicuous gallantry at the risk of his life. After returning to the United States in 1971, Mohammud had been further rewarded by a grateful society with jobs as a porter at Penn Station, as a delivery boy for Chick-Teri, and as a baggage carrier at LaGuardia Airport.

Calvin Mohammud, Vets 11, slung his heavy messenger's bag off his shoulder as he reached the graffiti-covered news kiosk at the corner of Broadway and Wall. He tapped out a Kool and lit up behind a plume of yellow flame.

Slouched in a nearby doorway, Vets 11 casually reached into his shoulder bag and slid out a standard U.S. Army field telephone. Still concealed in the deep cloth bag was a sixteen-inch machine pistol, along with half a dozen 40-mm antipersonnel grenades.

"Contact." He moved back into the cold building shadows, then whispered into the field telephone. "This is Vets Eleven at the stock exchange. I'm at the northeast entrance, off Wall . . . Everything's very nice and peaceful at position three . . . No police in sight. No armed resistance anywhere. Almost looks too easy. Over."

Vets 11 took another short drag on his dwindling cigarette. He calmly peered around at the noisy hustle and bustle that was so characteristic of Wall Street on a weekday.

Broad daylight. What an amazing, completely unbelievable scene—what an apocalyptic firefight would be coming down here at five o'clock. He began to smile, exposing crooked yellow teeth. This was going to be so sweet, so satisfying and right.

At eight-thirty, Calvin Mohammud carefully wound a tattered strip of cloth around a polished brass door handle at the back entrance of the all-powerful New York Stock Exchange—a proud, beautiful green band.

Green Band started savagely and suddenly, as if meteors had been hurtled down with malevolent intensity on New York City. It blew out two-story-tall windows, shattered asphalt roofs, and shook whole streets in the vicinity of Pier 54–56 on West Street between Twelfth and Fifteenth streets. It all came in an enormous white flash of painful, blinding light.

At approximately nine-twenty that morning, Pier 54–56 was a sudden fiery caldron, a blast of flame that raked the air and spread with such rapid intensity that even the Hudson River seemed to be spurting colossal columns of fire, some at least four hundred feet high.

Dense hydrocarbon clouds of smoke billowed over West Street like huge open black umbrellas. Six-foot-long shards of glass and unguided missiles of molten steel launched themselves, flying upward, in eerie, tumbling slow motion. And as the river winds suddenly shifted, there were otherworldly glimpses of the glowing, hot-metal skeleton that was the pier itself.

The blistering fireball had erupted and spread in less than sixty seconds.

It was precisely as the Green Band warning had said it would be: an unspeakable sound-and-light show, a ghostly demonstration of promised terrors to come . . .

Inside a police surveillance helicopter quivering and bumping on serrated upcurrents of hot smoke, New York Mayor Arnold Ostrow and Police Commissioner Michael Kane were shocked beyond words. Both understood that one of New York's worst nightmares was finally coming true.

This time one of the thousands of routinely horrifying threats to New York was real. Radio listeners and TV viewers all over New York would soon hear the unprecedented message:

"This is *not* a test of the Emergency Broadcast System."

At 10:35 on the morning of December 4, more than seven thousand dedicated capitalists—DOT system clerks, youthful pages with their jaunty epaulets and floppy Connecticut Yankee haircuts, grimly determined stockbrokers, bond analysts, and supervisors with bright-green jackets were busily, if somewhat nonchalantly, promenading through the three jam-packed main rooms of the New York Stock Exchange.

The twelve elevated ticker-tape TV monitors in the busy room were spewing stock symbols and trades comprehensible only to the trained eyes of exchange professionals. The day's volume, if it was only an average Friday, would easily exceed a hundred fifty million shares.

No doubt the original forebears, the first bulls and bears, had been ferocious negotiators and boardroom masters. Their descendants, however, their mostly thin-blooded heirs, were not particularly adroit at money changing.

The heirs were a strikingly homogenous group, for the most part smug and vainglorious bean counters; they all looked blood-related and tended toward red-faced baby fat or an almost tubercular gauntness. Their pale blue eyes looked

14

like marbles, round and bulging, with a distant vagueness in them.

Moreover, the heirs were standing by helplessly while American business was losing "World War III," as the most recent fight over the world's economy had sometimes been called. They were quietly, though quite rapidly, surrendering world economic leadership to the Japanese, the Germans, and the Arab world.

At 10:57 on Friday morning, the bell—which had once actually been a brass fire bell struck by a rubber mallet and still signaled the official beginning of trading at 10:00 A.M. sharp and end of trading at 4:00 P.M.—went off inside the New York Stock Exchange. The bell sounded with all the shock value of a firework popping in a cathedral.

Absolute silence followed. Shocked silence.

Then came uncontrollable buzzing, frantic rumor-trading. Almost three minutes of unprecedented confusion and chaos on the exchange floor.

Finally, there was the deep and resonant voice of the stock exchange manager blaring over the antiquated PA system.

"Gentlemen . . . ladies . . . the New York Stock Exchange is officially closed . . . Please leave the floor. Please leave the trading floor immediately. This is not a bomb scare. This is an actual emergency! This is a serious police emergency!"

Outside the heavy stone-and-steel entranceway to the Mobil Building on East Forty-second Street, a series of personal stretch limousines—Mercedeses, Lincolns, Rolls-Royces—were arriving and departing with dramatic haste.

Important-looking men, most of them in dark overcoats, and a few women hurriedly got out of their limousines and entered the building's familiar deco lobby. Upstairs on the forty-second floor, other CEOs and presidents of the major Wall Street banks and brokerage houses were already gathered inside the exclusive Pinnacle Club.

The luxurious main dining room of the private club, which was set up for lunch with crisp white linens and shining silver and crystal, had been commandeered for the emergency meeting. Several of the dark-suited executives stood before floor-to-ceiling nonglare windows, which faced downtown. They looked dazed and disoriented. None of them had ever experienced anything remotely like this, nor had they ever expected to.

The view was a spectacular and chilling one, down uneven canyons to lower Manhattan, all the way to the pencil pocket of skyscrapers that was the financial center itself. About halfway, at Fourteenth Street, there were massive police barricades. Police buses, EMS ambulances, and a paradelike crowd could be seen waiting, watching toward Wall Street as if they were studying some puzzling work of art in a midtown museum.

"They haven't even bothered to reestablish contact with us. Not since six this morning," said Secretary of the Treasury Walter O'Brien. "What the hell are they up to?"

Standing stiffly among a small group of prominent Wall Street executives, George Firth, the attorney general of the United States, was quietly lighting his pipe. He appeared surprisingly casual and controlled, except that he'd given up smoking more than three years before.

"They certainly were damn clear when it came to stating their deadline. Five minutes past five. Five minutes past five or what? What do the bastards want from us?" The attorney general's pipe went out, and he relit it, looking exasperated. The closest observers noticed the nervous tremors in his fingers.

A somber-looking businessman from Lehman Brothers named Jerrold Gottlieb looked at his wristwatch. "Well, gentlemen, it's one minute past five . . ." He was about to add something but left it unsaid.

They were all in unfamiliar territory now, where things couldn't be properly articulated.

"They've been extremely punctual up to now. Obsessive about getting details and schedules perfect. They'll call. I wouldn't worry, they'll call."

The speaker was the vice president of the United States, who'd been rushed from the United Nations to the nearby Mobil Building. Thomas More Elliot was a stern man with the look of an Ivy League scholar. His harshest critics carped that he was a Brahmin who was out of touch with the complexities of contemporary America. He'd spent the better part of his public career with the State Department, traveling extensively in Europe during the turbulent sixties, then in South America through the seventies. And now this.

For the next few minutes everyone was quiet, tense.

This tingling silence in the club's dining room was all the more frightening because there were so many highly articulate men in the room—the senior American business executives, used to having their own way, used to being listened to and obeyed, almost without question. Now they were virtually powerless, not used to the frustration and tension that this terrifying mystery had thrust into their lives. And their awesome power had distilled itself into a sequence of small, distinct noises:

A throat being cleared.

Ice crackling in a glass.

Tapping of fingers.

Madness. The thought seemed to echo in the room.

The most fearsome urban terrorism had finally struck deep inside the United States, right at the heart of America's economic power.

There were anxious, repeated glances at the glinting faces of Rolex, Cartier, and Piaget wristwatches.

What did Green Band want?

What was the outrageous ransom for Wall Street to be?

Edward Palin, the seventy-seven-year-old chief executive of one of the largest investment firms, slowly backed away from the darkly reflective picture windows. He sat down on a Harvard chair pulled up beside one of the dining tables and, in a poignant gesture, put his head between his gray pinstriped knees. He felt faint; it was too embarrassing to watch. Were they about to lose everything now?

Twenty seconds left.

"Please call. Call, you bastards," the vice president muttered.

It seemed like thousands of emergency sirens were screaming, a peculiar high-low wail, all over New York City. It was the first time the emergency warning system had been seriously in use since 1963 and the nuclear war scares.

Finally it was five minutes past five.

The sudden, terrifying realization struck every person in the room—they weren't going to call again! They weren't going to negotiate at all.

Without any further warning, Green Band was going to strike.

"A fast recap for you," said Lisa Pelham, the president's chief of staff, an efficient, well-organized woman who'd been trained at Harvard and spoke in the clipped manner of one whose mind was used to making succinct outlines from mountains of information.

"By noon, all trading was stopped on the New York and all regional exchanges in the U.S. There is no trading in London, Paris, Geneva, Bonn. The key New York businesspeople are meeting right now at the Pinnacle Club in the Mobil Building.

"All the important securities and commodities exchanges have ceased trading around the world. The unanswered question is the same everywhere. What's the nature of the demands we are secretly negotiating?" Lisa Pelham paused and stroked a strand of hair away from her oval face. "Everyone believes we're negotiating with somebody, sir."

"And we are definitely not?" President Justin Kearney's expression was one of extreme doubt and suspicion. He had discovered the awkward fact during his term of office that one branch of government all too frequently didn't know what another was doing.

"Which we are not, Mr. President. Both the CIA and the FBI have assured us of that. Sir, Green Band has still made *no* demands."

President Kearney had been rushed, under intensified Secret Service guard, to a windowless, lead-shielded room buried deep inside the White House. There, in the White House Communications Center, several of the most important political leaders in the United States were standing around the president in a manner that suggested they intended to protect him from whatever forces were presently at work in the country.

From the White House Communications Center, the president had been put into audio and visual contact with the Pinnacle Club in New York City.

The FBI chief, Walter Trentkamp, stepped forward to appear on the monitor screen. Time and his job had given him a tough, weathered policeman's look and a harassed attitude to match.

"There's been no further contact from Green Band, other than the pier firebombing, which is the demonstration they promised us, Mr. President. It's the kind of guerrilla warfare we've seen in Belfast, Beirut, Tel Aviv. Never before in the United States . . .

"We're all waiting, Mr. President," Trentkamp went on. "We're clearly past their stated deadline."

"Have any of the terrorist groups come forward and claimed responsibility?"

"They have. We're checking into them. So far none has shown any knowledge of the content of the warning phone call this morning."

Minutes had never seemed so long.

It was now 5:09 . . . 5:10, and slowly, slowly counting.

The director of the CIA moved before the lights and cameras in the White House emergency room. Philip Berger was a small, irascible man, highly unpopular in Washington, chiefly skilled at keeping the major American intelligence agencies competitive among themselves. "Is there *any* activity you can make out on Wall Street? Any people down there? Any moving vehicles? Small-plane activity?"

"Nothing, Phil. Apart from the police and the fire

department vehicles on the periphery of the area, it could be a peaceful Sunday morning."

"They're goddamn bluffing," someone said in Washington.

"Or," President Kearney said, "they're playing an enormous game of fucking nerves."

No one agreed, or disagreed, with the president.

Speech had been replaced by the terrifying anxiety and uncertainty of waiting.

Just waiting.

But for what?

*Manhattan*

At 6:20 P.M., Colonel David Hudson was doing the only thing that still mattered—that mattered more than anything else in his life.

David Hudson was on patrol. He was back in major combat; he was leading a quality-at-every-position platoon into the field again—now the field was an American city.

Hudson was one of those men who looked vaguely familiar to people, only they couldn't say precisely why. His wheat-colored hair was cut in a short crew, which was suddenly back in vogue. He was handsome; his looks were very American. He had the kind of strong, noble face that photographed extremely well and a seemingly unconscious air of self-confidence, a consistently reassuring look that emphatically said "Yes, I can do that—whatever it is."

There was only one thing wrong, and a lot of people didn't notice it right away—David Hudson had no left arm. He had lost it in the Vietnam War.

His Checker cab marked VETS CABS AND MESSENGERS rolled forward cautiously, reconnoitering past the bright-green pumps at the Hess gas station on Eleventh Avenue and Forty-fifth Street. This was one of those times when Hudson could see himself, as if in an eerie dream ... as if he could objectively watch himself from somewhere outside the scene. He knew this uncomfortable, distorted feeling extremely well from combat duty.

He'd felt it like a second skin ever since he'd stepped off a crowded USMC transport and watched himself encounter the one-hundred-and-seven-degree heat, the gagging, decaying, sweet-shit smell of the cities of Southeast Asia. He'd known this awful sensation of detachment, of distance from himself, when he'd realized that he could actually die at any given beat of his heart ...

Now he felt it again, this time in the sharp wintry wind blowing through the snowy gray streets of New York City.

Colonel David Hudson was purposely allowing the Green Band mission to wind out just one highly important notch tighter. It was all moving according to the elaborate final plan.

Every second had been rigidly accounted for. More than anything else, David Hudson appreciated the subtleties of precision, the detail and the fine-tuning involved in getting everything absolutely right.

He was back in full combat again.

This strange, strange passion was alive again in David Hudson.

He finally released the hand microphone from the PRC transmitter built into the cab's dashboard.

"Contact. Come in, Vets Five." Colonel David Hudson spoke in the firm, charismatic tones that had characterized his commands through the late war years in Southeast Asia. It was a voice that had always elicited loyalty and obedience in the men whose lives he controlled.

"This is Vets One . . . Come in Vets Five. Over."

A reply immediately crackled back through heavy static over the transmitter-receiver. "Hello, sir. How are you, sir? This is Vets Five. Over."

"Vets Five. Green Band is now affirmative. I will repeat—Green Band is now affirmative . . . *Blow it all up* . . . and God help us all."

# Chapter 3

*Brooklyn*

"YOUGOTAQUARTER, SIR? PLEASE! It's real cold out here, sir. You got two bits? . . . Awhh, thank you. Thanks a lot, sir. You just saved my life."

Around seven-thirty that evening, on Brooklyn's Atlantic Avenue, a familiar bag man called Crusader Rabbit was expertly soliciting loose change and cigarettes. The bag man begged while he sat huddled like a pile of soiled rags against the crumbling red brick facade of the Atlantic House Yemen and Middle East restaurant. The money came to him as if he were a magnet.

After a successful hit, forty-eight cents from a trendy-looking Brooklyn Heights teacher type and his date, the street bum allowed himself a short pull on a dwindling half-pint of Four Roses.

Drinking while begging change was counterproductive, he

knew, but sometimes necessary against the raw cold wintertime. Besides, it was his image.

The deep slack cough that followed the sip of whiskey sounded convincingly tubercular. The bag man's lips, bloated and pale, were corpse white and cracked, and they looked as if they'd bled recently.

For this year's winter wardrobe, he'd carefully selected a sleeveless navy parka over several layers of assorted, colored lumberman's shirts. He'd picked out open-toed high-topped black sneakers, basketball player snow bird socks, and painter's pants that were now thickly caked with mud, vomit, and spit.

The tourists, at least, seemed to love him. Sometimes they snapped his picture to bring home as an example of New York City's famed squalor and heartlessness. He enjoyed posing. Asked them for a buck or whatever the traffic would bear. He'd hold his two puffy shopping bags and smile extra pathetically for the camera. Pay the cashier, sport.

Now, through gummy, half-closed eyes, Crusader Rabbit stealthily watched the usual early evening promenade along Atlantic Avenue's Middle Eastern restaurant row.

It was a constant, day-in day-out noisy bazaar here: transplanted rag-headed Arabs, college assholes, Brooklyn professionals who came to eat ethnic. In the distance there was always the clickety-clack of the subway.

A troop of counter kids from McDonald's was passing by Crusader Rabbit, walking home from work. Two chunky black girls and a skinny mulatto boy around eighteen, nineteen.

"Hey, McDonald's. Whopper beat the Big Mac. Real tough break. Gotta quarter? Something for some McCoffee?" Crusader coughed and wheezed at the passing trio of teens.

The kids looked offended; then they all laughed together in a high-pitched chorus. "Who asked you, aqualung? You old geek sheet-head. Kick your ass."

The kids continued merrily on. Rude little bastards when Ronald McDonald wasn't watching over their act.

If any of the passersby had looked closer, they might have noticed certain visual inconsistencies about the bag man called Crusader Rabbit. For one thing, he had impressive muscle tone for a sedentary street bum. His shoulders were unusually broad, and his legs and arms were as thick as tree limbs.

Even more unusual were his eyes, which were almost always intently focused. They scanned the teeming avenue over and over again, relentlessly watching all the street action, everything that happened.

There was also the small matter of the quality of the dirt and dust thickly caked on his ankles, on his exposed toes. It was all a little too perfect. It was almost as if it might actually be black Kiwi shoe polish—shoe polish carefully applied to look like dirt.

The conclusion was obvious after a careful and close look at the street bum. Crusader Rabbit was some kind of undercover New York cop on a stakeout . . .

Which Crusader Rabbit truly was.

His real name was Archer Carroll, and he was currently the chief terrorist deterrent in the United States. He had been on a stakeout for five weeks, with no end in sight. Meanwhile, across the busy Brooklyn street, inside the Sinbad Star restaurant, two Iraqi men in their early thirties were sampling what they believed to be the finest Middle Eastern cooking available in New York City. They were the objects of Arch Carroll's long and painful stakeout.

The Iraqi men had purposely chosen a rear alcove of the small, cozy restaurant, where they noisily slurped thick carob bean soup. They gobbled up mint-flecked tabbouleh and cream-colored hummus. They eagerly munched greasy mixtures of raisins, pine nuts, lamb, Moroccan olives, their favorite things to eat in the world.

As they savored the delectable food, Wadih and Anton Rashid were also immensely enjoying their official American immunity from criminal prosecution and harassment, something guaranteed them by the FBI. On the strictest orders from Washington, the two brothers, admitted Third World terrorists, were to be treated like foreign diplomats on UN duty in New York. In return, three marines, convicted "spies," were soon to be released from a Lebanese jail.

New York and federal police authorities were permitted to act against the Rashid brothers only if the Black September killers actually moved to endanger property or life in the United States. These, of course, were two of their favorite avocations in past residences: Tel Aviv, Jerusalem, Paris, Beirut, and most recently London, where they had cold-bloodedly murdered three young women, college-age daughters of Lebanese politicians, in a Chelsea sweetshop.

Back out on Atlantic Avenue, Arch Carroll shivered unhappily in the probing, icy-cold fingers of the rising night wind.

At times like these Carroll wondered why it was that a reasonably intelligent thirty-five-year-old man, someone with decent enough prospects, someone with a law degree, could regularly be working sixty- to seventy-hour weeks, invariably eating stone-cold pizza and drinking Pepsi-Cola for dinner. Why was he sitting outside a Middle Eastern restaurant on a Friday night stakeout?

Was it perhaps because his father and two uncles had been pavement-pounding city cops?

Was it because his Mickey Finn grandfather had been a rough-and-tumble example of New York's finest?

Or did it have to do with incomprehensible things he'd seen a decade and a half ago in Vietnam?

Maybe he just wasn't a reasonable, intelligent man, as he'd somehow always presumed. Maybe, if you got right down to it, there was some kind of obvious short circuit in the wires of the old brain, some form of synaptic fuck-up. After all, would a really bright guy with all of his marbles be standing here freezing his dick off like this?

As Arch Carroll pondered the tangible mistakes of his life, his full attention began to wander. For several minutes at a clip he'd stare at his sadly wiggling toes, at the equally fascinating burning ember of his cigarette, at almost anything mildly distracting.

Five-week-long stakeouts weren't exactly recommended for their entertainment value. That was exactly how long he'd been watching Anton and Wadih Rashid, ever since the State Department had let them come into New York for their sabbatical.

Suddenly, Carroll's attention snapped back.

"What the . . ." he mumbled as he stared down the congested street. Is that who it looks like? he asked himself. Can't be . . . I think it is . . . but it can't be.

Carroll had noticed a skinny, frazzle-haired man coming directly his way from the Frente Unido Bar and Data Indonesia. The man was scurrying up Atlantic Avenue, periodically looking back over his shoulder. From a distance he looked like a baggy coat walking on a stick.

Carroll squinted his eyes for a better look at the approaching figure.

He just couldn't believe it!

He stared down the street, his eyes smarting from the bite of the wind. He had to make sure.

Jesus. He was sure.

The fast-walking man had a huge puffy burr of bushy, very wiry, black hair. The greasy hair was combed straight back, and it hung like a limp sack over the collar of his black cloth jacket. The man's clothes were soberly black; if he hadn't known better, Carroll would have taken him for a minister of some obscure religious sect.

Carroll knew the man by two names: one was Hussein Moussa; the other was Lebanese Butcher. A decade before, Moussa had been recruited by the Russians; he'd been efficiently trained at their famed Third World school in Tripoli. During the late seventies he'd worked in the European network under the guidance of the supreme terrorist himself, Juan Carlos.

Since then Moussa had been busily free-lancing terror and sophisticated murder techniques all over the world: in Paris, Rome, Zaire, New York, in Lebanon for Colonel Qaddafi. Recently he'd worked for François Monserrat, who had taken over not only Juan Carlos's European terrorist cell, but South America, and now the United States as well.

Hussein Moussa halted in front of the Sinbad Star restaurant. Like a very careful driver at a tricky intersection, he looked both ways. Twice more he looked up and down Atlantic Avenue. He even noticed the bag man camped out on the other side of the busy street.

Apparently he saw nothing to fear, nothing of real concern

or interest, and he disappeared behind the gaudy red door of the Sinbad Star.

Arch Carroll sat up against the crumbling brick wall of the restaurant. He was stiff, half-frozen.

He groped inside his jacket and produced a stubby third of a Camel cigarette. He lit up and inhaled the gruff tobacco.

What an unexpected little Christmas present. What a just reward for endless winter nights trailing the Rashids. The Lebanese Butcher on a silver platter. His bosses in State had told him not to touch the Rashids without extremely strong physical evidence. But they'd issued no such orders for the Lebanese Butcher.

What was Hussein Moussa doing in New York, anyway? Carroll's mind was reeling. Why was he here with the Rashids?

The firebombing of Pier 54–56 went quickly through his mind. He had picked up strands of information from gossip he'd heard all day long on the street—somebody had taken it into his head to blow a dock and the surrounding West Side area, it seemed, and for a moment Carroll pondered a possible connection between Hussein Moussa and the events on the Hudson River.

He'd heard nothing definitive, though. Gossip, whispers, street rumors, nothing more substantial. Somebody had finally said it was some kind of natural gas explosion. Another street rumor had offered the opinion that the city of New York was now being held for ransom. Mainly the speculations he'd heard were vague. Until he knew more, he couldn't begin to link the Lebanese Butcher to the West Side firebombing.

Arch Carroll had been ramrodding the Antiterrorist Division of the DIA for almost four years now. During that time only a few of the mass murderers he'd learned about had gotten to him emotionally and caused him to lose his usual policeman's objectivity. Hussein Moussa was one.

The Lebanese Butcher liked to torture. The Butcher liked to kill. The Butcher enjoyed maiming innocent civilians . . .

As he studied the Sinbad Star restaurant, Carroll reflected that he didn't particularly want Moussa dead. He wanted the Butcher locked away in a maximum-security cage for the rest of his life. Give the animal lots of time to think about what he'd done, if he did think.

From underneath newspapers and rags inside one of his shopping bags, Carroll began to slide out a heavy black metal object. Very carefully, peering down close, he checked the firing chamber of a Browning automatic. He quickly fed in eight shells with an autoloader.

A stooped, ancient Hasid was passing by. He stared incredulously at the street bum loading up a handgun. His watery gray eyes bulged out of his sagging face. The old man kept walking away, looking back constantly. Then he walked faster. New York street bums with guns now! The city was beyond all prayers, all possible hope.

Arch Carroll stood up. He felt stiff, ice cold all over. One globe of his rear end was completely numb.

He was getting too old for extended street duty. He had to remember that in the future: it might be very important for staying alive and intact one of these days.

Weaving through the thick, fuzzy night traffic, Carroll only half heard the bleating car horns and angry curses directed at him.

He was drifting in and out of reality now; there was a little nausea involved here, too. The same thing, the same absolutely identical feeling, came to him every time—just the possibility of killing another person was so foreign and absurd to him that it left a bitter taste in his mouth.

A middle-aged couple was leaving the Sinbad, the fat wife pulling her red overcoat tight around bursting hips. She stared at Crusader Rabbit, and the look said "You don't belong inside there, mister. You know you don't belong in there."

Carroll pulled open the ornate red door the departing couple had slammed in his face. Hot, garlicky air surrounded him. A muffled *snick* of the Browning under his coat. A deep silent breath. Okay, hotshot.

The tiny restaurant was infinitely more crowded than it had looked from the outside. Arch Carroll cursed. Every available dining table was filled to overflowing. Every one.

Six or seven more people, a group of boisterous friends, were waiting in the front to be seated. Carroll pushed past them. Waiters wearing black half-jackets hurried in and out of the swinging kitchen doors in the rear.

Carroll's eyes slowly drifted along the back of the crowded dining room.

Hussein Moussa had already seen him. Even in the packed, bustling restaurant, the terrorist had noticed his entrance. The Lebanese Butcher had been watching every person who came in from Atlantic Avenue.

So had the restaurant's owner, an enormous two-hundred-and-fifty-pound man. He charged forward now, an enraged bull guarding his herd at mealtime.

"Get out of here! You get out, bum! Go now!" the owner screamed. The diners were suddenly silent.

Carroll tried to look lost, dizzily confused, as surprised as everyone else that he was inside the small neighborhood restaurant.

He stumbled over his own flopping black sneakers.

He weaved sideways before moving suddenly toward the right rear corner of the dining room.

He hoped to God he looked cock-eyed drunk and absolutely helpless. Maybe even a little funny. Everybody should start laughing. If he did this exactly right, he'd have Hussein Moussa and the Rashids without firing a shot.

Carroll groped down his body with both hands, graphically scratching between his legs. A middle-aged woman turned away with obvious disgust.

"Bayt-room?" Carroll slobbered convincingly, rolling his eyes. "Gotta go to the bayt-room!"

A young bearded man and his girlfriend started laughing. Bathroom humor got the youth crowd every time. This was the success lesson of modern Broadway and Hollywood.

Hussein Moussa had stopped eating and was smiling. His teeth were a serrated blade of shining yellow. He looked like an animal, a brutal scavenger. He apparently thought this scene was pretty funny, too.

"Gotta go to the bayt-room!" Carroll continued a little louder, sounding, he thought, like a drunken Jerry Lewis. But, Jesus, you had to be a decent actor in this line of street work.

"Mohamud! Tarek! Get bum out! Get bum out now!" the owner was screeching hysterically at his waiters.

Pandemonium had completely overtaken the Sinbad Star when suddenly, fluidly, expertly, Arch Carroll wheeled hard to his left. He whipped the Browning automatic out of the ratty, cumbersome parka. It was completely out of place in the family restaurant. Women and children began screaming at the top of their voices.

"Freeze! Don't move! *Freeze*, goddamn you!"

At that same moment, one of the Lebanese waiters hit Carroll hard from his blind side, spinning him in a fast half-circle to the right. He ruined the drop Carroll had on the three terrorists, and he turned everything into a complete, instantaneous disaster.

Moussa and the Rashids were already scattering, rolling sideways off the red vinyl dining chairs. Anton Rashid yanked out a silver automatic from under his brown leather car coat.

Movies sometimes show particularly violent scenes in very flowing slow motion. It wasn't like that at all, Carroll knew. It was a jumpy collage of loud, shocking still photos. The disconnected photos clicked at him now in random order. They stopped. They started. They stopped. They started again. It was as if someone with the palsy were operating a slide projector.

"Everybody hit the floor!" Carroll screamed as he fired the Browning.

The first bullet brutally uncorked the right side of Anton Rashid's throat, spilling his blood in pools on the floor.

Hussein Moussa's gun flashed; it roared as Carroll dove across the backs of a couple already down.

Seconds later Carroll peered over the table. He fired off three more quick shots. Two of the bullets drove stocky Wadih Rashid hard against a hollow partition wall decorated with black skillets. Twin rat holes opened in the terrorist's chest. The heavy skillets clattered noisily to the tile floor.

"Moussa! Hussein Moussa! You can't get out! You can't get past me!" Carroll screamed.

There was no answer.

Somewhere in the front of the restaurant, an old woman was wailing like an imam. Several people were crying loudly.

Outside, distant police and ambulance sirens screamed through the night.

"Give up now, and you live . . . Otherwise I'll kill you. No matter what, Moussa. I swear it!"

He was breathing hard. One, two, three. Carroll chanced another fast look.

He saw nothing of the Lebanese Butcher this time. Moussa was also under the tables, hiding and crawling, looking for some advantage. He was moving toward either the front door or the kitchen.

Carroll guessed it would be the kitchen. He began to scramble toward it.

"I have antipersonnel grenades!" The Butcher suddenly let out a piercing, high scream. "Everybody dies in here! *Everybody dies* in this restaurant! Everybody dies with me! Women, children, I don't care."

Carroll stopped moving; he almost didn't breathe. Straight ahead, he stared at a shaking, very frightened woman curled like a snail on the floor. She looked about thirty years old. She didn't want to die in the middle of her big night out with her husband.

Carroll peeked above the dining tables again, and a gunshot rang out to his immediate left. Things didn't look good.

Moussa was in the far right corner.

Did he have grenades? It could be a bluff, but the worst was always possible with the Lebanese Butcher. He had been known to bring a machine pistol to a child's birthday party.

Carroll had to make a quick decision, and he had to make it for everybody trapped in the restaurant.

The people sprawled on the floor were inching toward panic; they were close to rising en masse and bolting for the

35

door. This would be perfect for Hussein Moussa. In the inevitable confusion, Carroll wouldn't run the risk of shooting. Moussa would have his best chance of escape.

Food was spattered everywhere on the dining room floor. Carroll finally reached for a platter holding an unfinished meal of pungent lamb and rice. With a sudden wrist snap, he hurled the dripping plate hard against the kitchen door, then shifted instantly into a professional shooting crouch—a two-handed pistol grip with both arms rigid. He was ready. He was as confident as he could be right now.

Moussa came up again, shooting. The Butcher fired twice at the slapping noise against the kitchen door. Son of a bitch had a grenade in his left hand! Arch Carroll squeezed the trigger.

Moussa looked incredibly surprised.

Blood gushed from Hussein Moussa's forehead. He slid down against a table still covered with mounds of food and tableware, dragging the cloth, plates, wine, and water glasses with him. He spit out a throaty curse across the room.

Then the terrorist's gun rose again.

Carroll shot Hussein Moussa a second time, and the bullet exploded his right cheek. The Lebanese Butcher fell heavily onto the back of a fat diner lying on the floor.

Carroll shot Moussa again as the man trapped underneath wiggled like a beached fish. The top of the terrorist's head flapped off like loose skin.

There was an eerie, terrible silence inside the Sinbad Star. A second or two passed like that. Then loud crying started again. There were angry shouts and relieved hugging all over the restaurant.

His gun thrust stiffly forward, Arch Carroll moved awkwardly across the chaotic room. He was still in a police school crouch. It was as if he were locked into that position. His hands and legs were trembling.

He carefully examined the Rashid brothers. Wadih and Anton were still alive. He looked at Moussa. The Butcher was dead, and the world was instantly a better place in which to live.

"Please call me an ambulance," Carroll spoke softly to the astonished restaurant owner. "I'm sorry. I'm very sorry this had to happen in your establishment. These men are terrorists. Professional killers."

The restaurant owner continued to stare with disbelief at Carroll. His black eyes were small, shiny beads stuck in his broad forehead, and he gave Arch Carroll a piercing look.

"And what are you? What are *you*, please tell me, mister?"

# Chapter 4

GREEN BAND STRUCK the Wall Street financial district at 6:34 P.M. on December 4.

There had been no demands, no further warning or attempt at justification of any kind. There was no reason given why the massive attack came an hour and twenty-nine minutes past the deadline. When it happened, it was like a volcano of heat. One small, essential corner of New York seemed for a moment to tilt, then spin out of balance. And the black Manhattan sky, which had been settling down in wintry sullenness, came abruptly alive with flares of chaotic light, much like a battlefield at night.

Under towering, half-mile-high plumes of roiling black smoke, the canyons of Wall Street suddenly blazed with fierce individual fires.

The flames were like a blitzkrieg raging out of control on Wall and Broad streets, on Pine, South William, and Exchange Place. The scene of sudden random destruction reminded some news observers of Beirut; others thought back to banished memories of Berlin, to London during World War II, to North and South Vietnam.

Shrill, deafening choruses of police and hospital emergency sirens screamed through the glowing darkness. The streets were thick with uniformed police, hospital medics, forensic vans, detectives' and commanders' vehicles. Army, network news, and New York Police Department helicopters chattered overhead, barely avoiding tragic collisions among themselves.

A well-known and respected eyewitness TV reporter stood, without hat or coat, on what had recently been the stately corner of Wall and Broadway, right under Trinity Church spires. He spoke solemnly into a gaping ABC videotape camera lens. Genuine awe was softening his usually thespian voice.

"Thus far this is our definite information, and more is coming in all the time . . . The following sites in the Wall Street area were either partially or completely destroyed tonight: the Federal Reserve Bank of New York, where over one hundred billion dollars in foreign-owned gold bullion is stored . . . Salomon Brothers, one of the country's largest traders in government securities . . . Merrill Lynch at One Liberty Plaza . . . the Depository Trust Company, which handles debits and credits for brokerages via computer . . . Lehman Brothers, an old-line investment house . . .

"Also reportedly struck during the siege of unexplained bombings were safe deposit and storage vaults at Chase and the U.S. Trust Company; the New York offices of NASDAQ; the venerable New York Stock Exchange Building; Three Hanover Square, which is where Manufacturers Hanover and the European American Bank were located.

"The full extent of this awesome damage, the complete toll,

will not be known tonight. Probably not for days, from the look of this incredible chaos. First estimates of the actual number of explosions range from a dozen to as many as forty separate blasts ... It is an awful, awful scene here in what remains of the once proud and lofty financial district of New York."

Green Band had struck like an invisible army.

Two justifiably nervous New York City patrolmen, Alry Simmons and Robert Havens, were carefully threading a path through the smoldering ruins of the Federal Reserve Bank located on Maiden Lane. The two men were attached at their belts to five-hundred-yard-long safety lines snaking back toward the street.

The patrolmen were now deep inside what had once been the Fed's massive and richly ornamental public lobby. Indeed, the gray-and-blue limestone, the sandstone bricks of the Federal Reserve, had always impressed visitors with a sense of their durability and authority. The fortlike appearance, the stout iron bars on every window, had reinforced the image of self-importance and impregnability. The image had obviously been a sham.

The destruction that officers Simmons and Havens found downstairs in the coin section was difficult to comprehend and even more difficult to assess. Mountainous coin-weighing machines had been blown apart like a child's toys. Fifty-pound coin bags were strewn open everywhere.

The marble floor was easily three feet deep in quarters, dimes, and nickels. Building support columns had been knocked down everywhere on the basement floor. The entire structure seemed to be trembling.

In the deepest basement of the Federal Reserve Bank was the largest single accumulation of gold stored anywhere in the world. It all belonged to foreign governments. The Fed both guarded the gold and kept track of who owned what. In an ordinary change of ownership, the Fed merely moved gold from one country's bin to another's. The gold was transported on ordinary metal carts, like books in a library. The security system in the deep basement was so highly elaborate that even the bank's president had to be accompanied when he ventured into the gold storage area.

Now patrolmen Havens and Simmons were alone in the cavernous basement. Gold was everywhere around them. Rivers of shining gold ran through the dust and rubble. Gold bars, more than they could possibly count, surrounded them. There was well over a hundred billion dollars at the day's market price of three hundred and eighty-six dollars an ounce, all within their reach.

Patrolman Robert Havens was hyperventilating, taking enormously deep breaths. His broad, flat face was expressionless.

Suddenly both emergency policemen stopped inching forward. Robert Havens let out a sharp gasp. "Christ Jesus! What the hell is *this*?"

An armed Federal Reserve Bank guard was sitting on a caned wooden chair, directly blocking their path from the gold section into the Fed's main garage. The cane chair still smoldered.

The guard was staring directly into Robert Havens's eyes, but he was beyond words. He was horribly burned, charred a blistering charcoal black. The ghastly sight made them so sick, they almost missed the most important clue . . .

Wrapped around the bank guard's right arm was a shiny, bright green band.

As Archer Carroll carefully maneuvered his battered station wagon along the Major Deegan Expressway, the words of the Atlantic Avenue restaurant owner came back to him with the persistence of an unanswerable philosophical question: *And what are you? . . . What are* you, *please tell me, mister?*

He glanced at his tired face in the rearview mirror. Yeah, what are you, Arch? The Rashids and Hussein Moussa are bad people, but you're some kind of okay national hero, right?

He was drained, completely numb. He wanted everything to be quiet and still inside his throbbing head.

And what are you, mister?

"Nothing worth a shit," he finally answered in the general direction of the station wagon's fogged windshield. He felt as if he were traveling inside a sealed capsule. The world he could see beyond the grimy car windows had retreated one step farther away from him.

He turned on the car radio, looking for a diversion from his mood.

Immediately he heard the news about Wall Street, delivered by a voice edged in the hushed hysteria so favored by newscasters when they describe events of national importance. Carroll turned up the volume.

Along with the newscaster's tensely delivered reportage were a couple of man-on-the-street interviews recorded against a brassy background of screaming sirens. The people spoke in shocked tones.

Carroll tightened his hands on the steering wheel. His mind was crowded with realistic images of urban guerrilla destruction. He understood that Wall Street was a perfect target for any determined terrorist group—but he couldn't make the jump from his thoughts to the horrible reality of what had just happened.

He didn't want to think about it. Not tonight, anyway. He was almost home, and he didn't need to drag the world inside the last sanctuary left to him.

Moments later Carroll swung his stiff, aching body inside the familiar, musty front hallway of his house in the Riverdale section of the Bronx. Automatically he hung his coat up on the hook under an ancient totem—the snoopy-eyed Sacred Heart of Jesus. Turn out the night-light. Home from the wars, at last, he thought.

As he slumped into the living room, Carroll sighed.

"Oh, *poor* Arch. It's almost eleven-thirty."

"Sorry. Didn't see you there, Mary K."

Mary Katherine Carroll was sitting neatly curled up on one corner of the couch. The room was only dimly illuminated by an amber light from the dining parlor.

"You look like a skuzzy Bowery bag man. Is that *blood* on your sleeve? Are you all right?" She stood up suddenly.

Carroll looked down at his torn, dingy shirtsleeve. He turned it toward the dining parlor light. It was blood all right. Dark, dried blood, but not his own.

"I'm fine. The blood isn't mine. At least I don't think it is."

Mary Katherine frowned deeply as she came forward to examine her brother's arm. "The bad guys get banged up, too?"

Arch Carroll smiled at his twenty-four-year-old "baby" sister. Mary Katherine was the keeper of his house, the substitute mother for his four children, the uncomplaining cook and chief bottle washer, all for a two-hundred-dollar-a-month

43

stipend, a "scholarship." It was all he could afford to pay her right now.

"I had to kill one of them. He won't be bothering people with his plastique bombs anymore . . . The kids all asleep?"

The kids, in order of arrival, were Mary III, Clancy, Mickey Kevin, and Elizabeth. All four of them were far too Irish-American cute for their own good: outrageously tow-headed and blue-eyed, with infectious smiles and quick, almost adult wits. Mary Katherine had been their house mother for nearly three years now. Ever since Arch's wife, Nora, had died on December 14, 1982.

After Nora's funeral, after just one desolate night at their old New York apartment, the six of them had moved into the Carroll family homestead in Riverdale. The old house had been closed and boarded up since the deaths of Carroll's mother and father back in 1980 and 1981.

Mary Katherine had redecorated immediately. She'd even set up a huge light-filled painting studio for herself in the attic. The kids were out of New York City proper, at least. They suddenly had acres of fresh air and space in which to ramble around. There were definite advantages to being up in Riverdale. They had almost everything they needed up here . . . everything but a mother.

Carroll had held on to their old rent-controlled apartment on Riverside Drive. Sometimes he even stayed there when he had to work weekends in New York. It wasn't ideal, but it could have been a lot worse. Especially without Mary K.

"I have several important messages for you," Mary Katherine announced brightly.

"Mickey says, if I might paraphrase, that you work too hard and don't make enough skoots. Clancy says if you don't play catch with him this weekend—and not video game baseball—you're a dead man. That's a *direct* quote. Let's see . . . oh, yes, I almost forgot. Lizzie has decided to become a prima ballerina. Lessons for the spring semester at the Joliere School start at three hundred per, Dad."

"That's all?"

"Mairzy Doats left you a humongous kiss, and a hug of equal magnitude and intensity."

"Uncomplicated young woman. Shame she can't stay six years old forever."

"Arch? What about this Wall Street thing? The bombing? I was worried."

"I don't know. Too late to talk."

Carroll wanted to box off Wall Street in a dark, private corner until he was ready to deal with it. It would still be there in the morning, you could bet on that. He massaged his eyelids, which were heavy with fatigue. His mind was crowded with unwelcome pictures—the Lebanese Butcher, the face of the Atlantic Avenue restaurant owner, fire trucks and EMS ambulances flashing all over Wall Street . . .

Carroll bent and loosened his flopping high-topped sneaks. He peeled off a discolored satin Tollentine High School jacket. His fatigue now yielded to a kind of peaceful, ethereal, waking slumber.

In the large bathroom on the second floor, he turned on the water full blast. Curling hot steam rose toward the ceiling from the chipped and scratched white porcelain tub. He took off the rest of his squalid street-bum ensemble and rolled a fluffy bath towel around his waist.

Quick mirror check. Okay. He was still around six two, solid, durable, and sturdy. Pleasant face, even if it was a little pug ordinary, like some friendly mutt people generally took in out of the rain. Generally.

While the hot water was running, Carroll stiffly padded back downstairs to the kitchen and popped the top of a cold Schlitz. Mary Katherine had bought the Schlitz beer as a "change of pace." Actually, she was trying to stop him from drinking so much.

Carroll took three chilled cans and headed back to the bathroom. Stripping off the soft bath towel, he slowly, luxuriously, entered the hot, sweet-smelling tub.

As he sipped the cold beer, he began to relax. Carroll used a bath the way some people used psychiatry—to get back in touch, to sort it all out. Hot water and soap, the only therapy he could afford.

Carroll began to think about Nora. *Damn.* Always at night when he got home from work . . . their time. The emptiness he felt then was unbearable. It pulsed against him and filled him with a terrible, hollow longing.

He closed his eyes, and he could *see* her face. Oh, Nora, sweet Nora. How could you leave me like this? How could you leave me alone, with the kids, fighting against this crazy, crazy world?

She had been the best person Carroll had ever met. It was simple, no more profound than that. The two of them had made a perfect fit. Nora had been warm, and thoughtful, and funny. That they had found each other convinced Carroll such a thing as fate might indeed exist. It wasn't all randomness and whim and unseeing chance.

Strange, the ways of life and death.

Growing up, all through high school in New York, at college (South Bend, Notre Dame), Carroll had been secretly afraid he'd

46

never find anybody to love him. It was a curious fear, and sometimes he'd imagine that just as some people were born with a talent for art or music, he'd been given the gift of solitude.

Then Nora had found him, and that was absolute magic. She'd discovered Carroll the second day of law school at Michigan State. Right away, from their very first date, Carroll simply *knew* he could never love anybody else, that he would never need to. He'd never been more comfortable around another person in his whole life. Nothing even close to the feeling he had for Nora had ever existed before.

Only now Nora was gone. Nearly three years back, in the cancer ward of New York Hospital. *Merry Christmas, Carroll family. Your friend, God* . . .

"I'm just a kid, Arch," Nora had whispered to him once, after she'd found out she was dying. She'd been thirty-one then, a year younger than he.

Carroll slowly sipped his can of watery beer. A song played through his head: " . . . The beer that made Milwaukee famous, made a loser out of me." Ever since she'd died, he understood he'd been trying to commit slow, sure suicide. He'd been drinking too much; eating most of the wrong things; taking stupid chances on the job . . .

It wasn't as if he didn't understand the problem, because he did. He just couldn't seem to do a damn thing to stop his steep downhill slide. He was like some daredevil skier determined to destroy himself on the most treacherous slopes. He didn't seem to care enough anymore . . .

Arch Carroll, supposed tough-guy cop, well-quoted cynic around town—sitting in the tub with one of his kid's rubber toys floating next to him. The kids delighted and astonished Carroll. So why was he screwing up so badly lately?

He was tempted to wake them up now. Maybe go sleigh riding at midnight on the back lawn. Play catch with Mickey Kevin. Teach Lizzie how to do a plié and become a hot-shit little ballerina.

Arch Carroll's ears suddenly tuned in sharply. He thought he heard voices. A door slammed. There were loud steps in the hallway and the familiar creak of the floorboards.

The kids were up! Exactly what he needed, Carroll thought, and he began to smile broadly.

There was a light tap on the bathroom door. That had to be Lizzie or Mickey trying to be cute. Soon to be followed by Dolby Stereo kid screams and uncontrollable belly laughs.

"*Entrez.* Come right in, you little assholes," he called.

The bathroom door opened slowly, and Carroll cupped his hands, ready to splash them with water.

He managed to control his impulse just in time.

The man framed in the doorway was wearing a black London Fog raincoat, wire-rimmed eyeglasses, a white button-down shirt, and a striped rep tie. Carroll had never seen him before.

"Excuse me, sir," the man said.

"How did you get up here? Who the hell are you?" Carroll asked.

The stranger looked like a banker, maybe an account executive at a brokerage firm.

The man spoke with Ivy League formality, pretending not to notice the little yellow duck. Nothing even close to a smile crossed his pale, thin lips. "Your sister let me come up. Sorry to barge in on you, to trouble you like this at home. I need you to get dressed and come with me, Mr. Carroll. The president wants to see you tonight."

48

# Chapter 5

*Washington, D.C.*

AS EARLY AS the hot and steamy summer of 1961, John Kennedy had confided to close advisers that the stressful work of the presidency had already aged him ten years. He said it would do the same to anyone who wanted, or needed, the job of chief executive in the most powerful free country in the world.

As he hurried down the plush, half-darkened corridors on the second floor of the White House, Justin Kearney, the forty-first president of the United States, was realizing the same inescapable truth that Kennedy had put into words. He had recently begun to question the motives that had driven him to his present residence at 1600 Pennsylvania Avenue. Indeed, he had begun to question the intrinsic value of the office itself—he had become acutely aware of the limitations of his power, and this greatly disillusioned him.

Justin Kearney was only forty-two years of age; by one month, he was the youngest American president ever elected and the first Vietnam War veteran to reach the White House.

At one-fifty on Saturday morning, President Kearney took what he hoped would be a calming breath and entered the National Security Council conference room. Those already gathered there rose respectfully, Archer Carroll among them.

Carroll watched the president of the United States take his customary place at the head of the heavy oak conference table. In the course of his three previous visits to the White House, he'd never seen Kearney so nervous, so clearly uncomfortable.

"First of all, I truly thank you for getting here on such very short notice." The president sloughed off his wrinkled navy blue suit coat. "I think everyone knows everyone else. One, maybe two exceptions . . . Down there, sitting between Bill Whittier and Morton Atwater, is Caitlin Dillon. Caitlin is the chief enforcement officer for the SEC. She just might be the toughest enforcer since James Landis himself . . .

"Down at the far right corner, gentleman in the tan corduroy sport coat is Arch Carroll. Mr. Carroll is the head of the DIA's Antiterrorist Division. This is the same group that was created following Munich and Lod." The president licked his lips nervously as he gazed around the assembly.

Commissioner Michael Kane from the New York Police Department was asked to report first.

"Right now we have men down inside the rubble of all the buildings that were hit. We have explosive-arson squads underground. They've already reported that Thirty Wall, as well as the Fed, is badly damaged and extremely dangerous. Either building could conceivably collapse tonight.

"Based solely on a raw visual impression of the explosions,

gentlemen, the people who did this are at the highest levels of their trade. The plan was brilliantly executed. It was all carefully, *obsessively* worked out in advance."

Claude Williams of the U.S. Army Engineers was called to speak next.

"There's a disturbing attention to detail in every area—that's what is particularly frightening about this. The river pier, the initial setup with the FBI, the elaborate study of Wall Street itself. I've never seen anything like this, and I'll tell you, I'm not standing here exaggerating for effect. It's as if a well-organized army hit Wall Street. It's as if a war's been started down there."

Walter Trentkamp from the FBI spoke next. Trentkamp had been an old and dear friend of Arch Carroll's father. He'd even helped talk the younger Carroll into his first police job. Arch Carroll leaned forward to listen to Walter's report.

"I agree with Mike Kane," Trentkamp said in a gravelly, imposing voice. "Everything has the veneer of an expert paramilitary operation. The explosives on Wall Street were placed for maximum damage. Our ordnance boys actually seem to admire the bastards. The whole operation was brilliantly organized, very thoughtfully devised. I haven't seen anything like it, either. The closest would be Munich.

"The plan must have taken months, maybe years, to develop and execute with this high a level of success. PLO? IRA? Red Brigade? I assume we'll know more on that score before too long. They have to contact us eventually. They must want something. Nobody goes to this extreme without having some kind of demand in mind." Trentkamp shrugged and looked around at the puzzled, solemn faces in the room. "In other words, gentlemen, I've got nothing right now."

Each of those present was called upon to give a report, from the secretary of defense to SEC representative Caitlin Dillon. All spoke briefly. Although Caitlin Dillon didn't have a great deal to add, she spoke with remarkable fluency, the kind where you could see the semicolons in her speech. Arch Carroll couldn't take his eyes away from her face. Only when she fell silent did he glance elsewhere.

"Arch? Are you with us?"

Carroll gave the room an embarrassed smile as he rose to address the group. The mostly recognizable faces that turned his way were dark and impassive.

Carroll was characteristically rumpled. His long brown hair and street clothes brought to mind underground witnesses and policemen called in drug-related grand jury trials. His face was strong. His brown eyes were bright and alert, even though he was exhausted. He'd thought about wearing his one good Barneys warehouse sale suit, but then had changed his mind. What was it Thoreau had advised? Beware all enterprises that require new clothes . . . something like that.

Several of the principals attending the emergency session knew Carroll by reputation, at least. As a modern-day policeman, Carroll was thought to be appropriately unorthodox and extremely effective. The team he supervised was credited with helping to make the world's terrorists think twice about raiding forays into the United States.

Arch Carroll had also occasionally been characterized as a troublemaker: too much of a perfectionist for the Washington politicians to handle, too off-Broadway theatrical at times. Moreover, he was becoming increasingly known as an Irish drunk. It was a reputation that might not have hurt him too much in the old days of New York police work, but it wasn't doing him any good in these more rarefied circles.

"I'll try to be brief," Carroll began softly. "For starters, I don't think we can make the assumption yet that this *is* an established or known terrorist group.

"If it is, then it probably means one of two groups: the Soviets, through the GRU—which could include François Monserrat and his network—or a second possibility, a freelance group, probably sent out of the Middle East. Financed there, anyway.

"I don't believe anyone else has the organization and discipline, the technical know-how or money to manage something this complex." Carroll's intense brown eyes roamed the room. Why did his own remarks sound so hollow? "You can cross out just about everyone else as suspects." He sat down.

Walter Trentkamp raised a finger and spoke again. "For everyone's general information, we've set up an investigative unit down on Wall Street. The unit is inside the stock exchange building, which suffered limited damage during the raid. Somebody from the NYPD already released number Thirteen Wall to the press. So that's what we'll call headquarters.

"There's no such address, actually. The stock exchange *is* on Wall, but the actual address is Broad Street. *That* may be significant. See, we've made our first mistake, and we haven't even started the investigation."

Almost everyone laughed, but the important irony was lost on none of them. There would be more mistakes—a lot more serious mistakes—before anything was resolved. Number 13 was surely an omen of things to come.

President Kearney stood once again at his end of the massive conference table. His face registered the day's extreme stress. He was no longer the good-looking, energetic young senator who'd successfully hit the national campaign trail two years before. Now he seemed cruelly drained.

Kearney said, "I need to clear the air about something else. Something that must never go beyond this room." The president paused, looked up and down the rows of his closest advisers. Then he went on.

"For several weeks now, the White House, Vice President Elliot, and myself have been receiving reliable intelligence leaks, steady information about a dramatic counterinsurgent plot. Possibly a scenario involving the elusive François Monserrat."

The president paused again, deliberately pacing himself. Arch Carroll turned the name Monserrat over in his mind. "Elusive" didn't quite do Monserrat proper justice. There were times, indeed, when he had seriously doubted the man's existence, times when he'd considered Monserrat as the nom de guerre of several different individuals acting in collaboration. He was in France one day, Libya the next. He might be reported in Mexico even as somebody else claimed to have seen him at the same time stepping aboard an unmarked plane in Prague.

President Kearney continued. "Our intelligence people have learned that Middle Eastern and South American oil-producing countries have been seriously considering a run on the New York Stock Market.

"This action was to be 'just' retribution for what they considered broken promises, even outright fraud practiced by U.S. banks and the New York brokerage houses. At the very least, the oil cartel hoped to initiate a short-term panic, which they alone would be in a position to take advantage of. Is this rumored scenario related to tonight? At this moment, I don't know . . .

"I have serious fears, though, that we're at the beginning of a grave international economic crisis. Gentlemen, it would not be an exaggeration to postulate, to prepare ourselves for the possibility, that the Western economy could effectively collapse on Monday, when the market will conceivably reopen."

President Kearney's intense blue eyes continued to make contact around the crisis table. "We might find out who initiated the attack on Wall Street last night. We have to find out how they did it. We have to find out why . . . What is the meaning of this insane, unthinkable thing?"

Arch Carroll's head was buzzing and his eyes stinging as he filed out of the White House conference room at 2:55 A.M. The other participants were subdued and silent; they looked reflective, exhausted.

Carroll had already started down the flight of creaking, thickly carpeted south White House stairs when he felt a hand rest lightly on his shoulder, startling him. He turned to see Walter Trentkamp, impressive as ever at three in the morning.

"Trying to run out on me?" Trentkamp shook his head like a father about to chastise his son in the friendliest terms possible. "How have you been? I haven't seen you in a while. Have a minute to talk?"

"Hello, Walter. Sure, we can talk. How about going outside? It might clear our heads a little."

Moments later Carroll and one of his earliest mentors were walking side by side through the early morning mist shrouding Pennsylvania Avenue. The sky was a heavy gray slab covering the capital like the roof on a mausoleum. In the distance Carroll could see the Washington Monument.

"I haven't seen enough of your homely face lately. Probably not since you and the kids moved back to the old homestead."

"We miss you, too. It was kind of odd, going back there at first. Now it's good, absolutely the right choice. The kids call it their 'country house.' They think they live on a Nebraska farm now. Riverdale, right?" Carroll grinned.

"Wonderful kids. Mary Katherine's a gem, too." Trentkamp hesitated a moment. "How are *you* doing? *You're* the one who concerns me."

Carroll began to feel as if he were talking to a rabbi on the police force. "Holding up pretty well. I'm all right. I'm actually doing fine." He shrugged.

Trentkamp shook his closely cropped silver-gray curls. His eyes held a knowing look, and Carroll felt suddenly uncomfortable. The cop part of Walter had a knack of wheedling his way inside you, so that you were left feeling transparent, like thin paper held up to a bright light.

"I don't think so, Archer. I don't think you're doing fine at all."

Carroll stiffened. "No? Well, I'm sorry. I thought I was all right."

"You're not so fine. You're not even in the general ballpark of fine. The late night drinking bouts have become legend. Risks you're taking with your life. Other cops talk too much about you."

It was the wrong hour for this kind of talk, even from the man he'd grown up calling "Uncle Walter." Carroll bristled. "That all, Rabbi? That all you wanted to see me about?"

Walter Trentkamp abruptly stopped walking. He laid a

56

hand on Carroll's shoulder and squeezed it lightly. "I wanted to talk to the son of an old friend of mine. I wanted to help if I could."

Arch Carroll turned his bleary eyes away from those of the FBI director. His face reddened. "I'm sorry. I guess it's been a long day."

"It has been a long day. It's been a long couple of years for you since Nora. You're close to being broken out of your unit in the DIA. They like the results, but not your working style. There's talk about replacing you. Matty Reardon's one name I've heard."

It was a verbal punch. Arch Carroll knew, somewhere in the back of his mind that this was coming. "Reardon'd be a good choice. He's a good company man. Good man, period."

"Arch, please cut the crap. You're playing games with someone who's known you thirty-five years. Nobody can replace you at the DIA."

Carroll frowned, and he began to cough in the manner of Crusader Rabbit. He felt like a real shit. "Aww, hell, I'm sorry, Walter. I know what you're trying to do."

"People understand what you've been through. I understand. Please believe that, Archer. Everybody wants to help . . . I *asked* for you on this one. I had to ask."

Carroll shrugged his broad, sloping shoulders, but he was hurt. He hadn't known his reputation had slipped so badly, maybe even in Walter Trentkamp's eyes.

"I don't know what to say. I really don't. Not even a typical Bronx Irish wisecrack. Nothing."

"Talk to me on this one. Let me know what you find out. Just talk to me, okay? . . . Don't go it alone. Will you promise me that?" said Trentkamp.

"Promise." Carroll nodded slowly.

Walter Trentkamp turned up the collar of his overcoat against the early morning mist. Both he and Carroll were over six feet tall. They looked like father and son.

"Good," Trentkamp finally said. "It's real good to have you. We'll need you on this nasty son of a bitch. We'll need you at your best, Archer."

# Chapter 6

*Manhattan*

AT SIX O'CLOCK on Saturday morning, December 5, a bleak Seventh Avenue subway train, its surface covered with scars of graffiti, lackadaisically rocked and rattled north toward the Van Cortlandt Park station. The New York subways were generally a bad joke. This particular train wasn't so much public transportation as public disgrace.

Colonel David Hudson sat in an inconspicuous huddle on an uncomfortable metal seat. As always, he was wearing clothes no one would look at twice. Uninteresting clothes that created a street camouflage of drab gray and lifeless brown. He realized it wasn't a very successful disguise because people had looked at him, anyway. Their probing eyes invariably discovered the missing arm, the empty flap of his coat.

Hot-and-cold flashes coursed through his body as the train dutifully hurled itself north. He was drifting in and out of the present, remembering, trying to accurately replicate long hours spent at a Vietnam firebase perimeter listening post . . . Every one of his senses had been at its sharpest back then. Head cocked—listening, watching, trusting no one but himself . . . He needed exactly the same kind of brilliant clarity right now, the same kind of absolute self-reliance—which was probably the greatest high he'd known in his lifetime.

From Fourteenth Street, where he'd boarded the inhospitable subway train, up past Thirty-fourth, Forty-second, and Fifty-ninth streets, Hudson objectively contemplated the first days of his capture in Vietnam. An old Doors song, "Moonlight Drive," drifted through his mind. A period piece.

He was vividly remembering the La Hoc Noh prison now. Above all else, Colonel David Hudson was remembering the one known as the Lizard Man . . .


*La Hoc Noh Prison, North Vietnam: July 1971*

Captain David Hudson, his nervous system a mass of fire, felt each bruising, jarring bump, even the smallest stones underfoot, as four prison guards half carried, half dragged him toward the central thatch-roofed hut at the La Hoc Noh compound.

Through the flat white glare of the Asian sun, which resembled a bleached penny, he squinted at the pathetic hootch, with its tattered North Vietnamese flag and sagging bamboo walls.

The command post.

What an incredible, existential joke this all was. What a cruel joke his life had recently become.

Well muscled once, clean-cut and always so perfectly erect, so proper, the young U.S. Army officer was pitiful to behold now. His skin was wrinkled and sallow, almost yellow; his blond hair looked as if it has been pulled out in great, diseased clumps.

He understood and accepted the fact that he was dying. He weighed less than a hundred and fifteen pounds; he'd had the dreaded yellow shits literally for months without end. He'd gone beyond mere exhaustion; he lived in a shifting, hallucinatory world where he doubted even his own sensations and ordinary perceptions.

All Captain Hudson possessed now was his dignity. He refused to give that up, too.

He would die with at least some essential part of himself intact, that secret place deep inside that nobody could torture out of him.

The SNR officer, the one they had called Lizard Man, was waiting expressly for him inside the dread command hootch. The North Vietnamese leader sat in awful silence, crouched like some feral animal, behind a low, lopsided table.

He almost seemed to be posing for a photo beneath a twirling bamboo fan that barely stirred the hundred-and-five degree air.

North Vietnamese cooking smells—green chili, garlic, litchi, durian, and spoiled river prawn—made David Hudson suddenly gag. He clutched violently at his mouth. He felt himself begin to faint. But he wouldn't allow that. No! Honor and dignity! That was everything. Honor and dignity kept him alive.

He stopped at his own mental command, drawing on the scant resources, the human spirit, that remained in him.

The North Vietnamese guards held him up. He collapsed, a weightless puppet in their tangle of bony arms. A guard punched David Hudson's jaw with a hard bare fist. Hot blood filled his mouth, and he gagged repeatedly.

"*You Cap-tan, ah Hud-son!*" the senior officer suddenly screeched, cawing like a heat-crazed jungle bird. He peered at the wrinkled notepad he always carried. His fingers struck hard into the page to emphasize certain words.

"Ho-Ho. Twen-six yea-ah old. Veetnam, Lah-ose since nine-teen six-nine. Yow spy six yeah. Ho-Ho. You's sain! 'ssassin! Convic to *die*, Cap-tan."

The prison guards let Captain David Hudson fall to the dirt floor, which was littered with gaping fish heads and rice.

Hudson's fragile mind was reeling, crashing, exploding with sharp-pointed lights. He'd understood only a few of the Lizard Man's fractured English words."Vietnam . . . spy . . . assassin . . . convicted to die."

Hudson's eyes absently ran over the highly polished board surface. Games? Why did they all love games?

The Lizard Man snorted obscenely. A distorted smile appeared across his face. His jaw moved slowly, seemingly unattached to the rest of his skull. David Hudson imagined he could see, just behind the loose lips, a flicking, reptilian tongue in the man's mouth. He shook his head, trying vainly to find a clearing, a little area of reality, within his wildly confused thoughts.

"Yow play game? Yow play game me, Hud-sun?"

David Hudson's eyes were riveted to the game table, trying to focus. Play a game with Lizard Man?

The board appeared to be real teak. It was precious wood, exotic and beautiful, incongruous in this sodden armpit of a place. Even more striking were the hundreds of polished black and white stones, exquisite playing pieces. They were circular in shape, convex on each side.

For a lucid moment, Hudson remembered a marble collection. Something magical and forgotten from his youth in Kansas, on his father's farm. Collecting solids and cat's-eyes. Had he actually been a boy in this same lifetime? He honestly couldn't seem to remember. Die with dignity! Dignity!

"Play game for your life? Ho?" the Lizard Man asked.

The game board was divided into vertical and horizontal lines, creating hundreds of intersections. There were 180 white stones, 181 black.

Beside the pile of black stones, the Lizard Man's hand rested on a bulky Mosin-Nagant military rifle. One of his long yellowed fingers tapped the table relentlessly.

"Yow play. Play game me! Loser die!"

Captain David Hudson continued to stare hard at the game board. Focus, he thought. Concentrate. Die with dignity.

What did this man want from him now? It was an obscene joke, Hudson knew. One more way the Lizard Man had of torturing him.

The black and white stones seemed to be moving by themselves. Spinning, crawling like insects, in his blurred vision.

Finally Hudson spoke up. His voice was surprisingly strong, angry, even defiant.

"I have never lost at the game of Go," Captain David Hudson said. "You play, asshole!" Dignity!


*Manhattan: December 1985*

The New York subway train braked noisily at a station stop. The soiled platform was bathed in eerie blue.

A few passengers on the sleepy, early morning train were

staring absently at David Hudson. Even at a casual glance, he seemed like someone quietly in control of his environment. Beneath the drab street clothes, there was about him a sense of purpose. He was a man accustomed to taking command.

Hudson stared back at the other passengers. He peered into their hollow, pathetic eyes until most glanced away. The majority of American people were devoid of any real basic integrity, any sense of themselves. Civilians tended to disappoint David Hudson again and again. Maybe it was because he expected too much from them—he had to remind himself constantly that he couldn't apply his own high standards to others.

More listless passengers struggled onto the subway train at the West Eighty-sixth Street stop. There were mostly older whites, time-bent men and women, small-business merchants, ciphers who managed or owned the rip-off clothing stores, the rip-off food markets, in Harlem and the Bronx. One of the men boarding, however, was completely different from the rest.

He appeared to be in his mid-thirties. His striking black hair was brushed straight back. He wore a tan cashmere overcoat with a paisley scarf, pressed navy dress slacks, super-WASP duck boots. The impression he gave was of someone boarding a subway for the first time in his life and finding something amusing in the phenomenon of a slum on wheels.

He sat beside David Hudson and immediately snapped open Saturday's *New York Times*, coughing idly into his fist. As the subway rumbled forward, he crisply folded the newspaper into quarters.

"You made the front page. Congratulations," Laurence Hadford finally offered in a guarded, casual whisper. His voice was exquisitely controlled and as smooth as his expensive silk scarf. "I watched the intriguing spectacle on the six o'clock, the seven o'clock, the ten, and the eleven o'clock news shows. You've succeeded in totally baffling them."

"We've done reasonably well so far." Hudson nodded in agreement. "The difficult steps are still ahead, though. The true tests of the plan's legs, Lieutenant."

"You brought me a present, I hope? Christmas present?" As Laurence Hadford slid closer, Hudson could smell the man's citric cologne.

"Yes. Exactly as we agreed the last time."

David Hudson looked sideways for the first time. He stared into the pale blue eyes and mocking half smile of Laurence Hadford. He didn't like what he saw. Never had. Not now and not back in Vietnam, either, when Hadford had been a smug young officer.

Laurence Hadford was impassive, cool. The well-shaved face might have been a door closed on private rooms. Hudson had a sudden impression of icy places locked away inside the man. Hadford was already a partner at one of the larger Wall Street investment firms and was said to be climbing to even higher rungs on the corporate ladder.

Reaching deep inside his coat, Hudson handed over a thick, overstuffed manila business envelope. The package bore no external marking, nothing to identify it in case there was any problem, an unlikely slipup on board the subway.

The envelope disappeared inside the rich softness of cashmere.

"There's one small hitch. A tiny problem has come up. The amount here isn't enough." Hadford smiled so easily. "Not considering what's happened. What you've gone and done now. You've made this a very dangerous business arrangement for me. If you'd told me what you actually planned to do—"

"You wouldn't have helped us. You would have had too many doubts. You would have been scared shitless."

"My friend, I *am* scared shitless."

The subway train buckled slightly but only slowed minimally as it charged into the 110th Street station.

Angry graffiti was scrawled on all the walls. It shouted at anyone who cared to look up from his early-bird edition of the *Daily News.* Most didn't look up.

"We agreed on a figure before you did any work for us on Wall Street. Your fee, half a million dollars, has now been paid in full." Hudson felt a familiar alarm sounding inside him. His control was slipping away. "Any information you've supplied us, any personal risks you took, were infinitesimal, considering your enormous financial gain."

Hadford's perfectly capped white teeth gritted very slightly. "Please. Don't tell me how well I've been paid. I know what you're all about now. You've got so much money, you couldn't possibly know what to do with it. Another half million is virtually meaningless. What's another million, for that matter? Don't be so uptight."

Colonel David Hudson finally managed a smile. "You know, perhaps you're right. Under the circumstances—what *is* another half million? . . . Especially if you're willing to do a little more investigation for us. We still need your help on Wall Street."

"I suppose for the right price I could be convinced, Colonel."

The next station David Hudson noticed was 157th Street. Between 110th and there, he and Laurence Hadford talked of

66

the next steps to be taken on Wall Street, the kinds of additional information needed for Green Band.

Stenciled numbers announced the train stop on mottled, pale blue standposts. A sullen black face slowly slipped past the spray-painted train windows. The brakes screeched, then let out a loud, gaseous *whump*.

The last few passengers exited at the 157th Street stop. The black face didn't get on board. The subway doors slammed shut. They were completely alone. David Hudson felt himself tense. The blood coursed rapidly through his veins. All his senses were suddenly alert, and his perceptions had an astonishing clarity. Everything around him on the train stood out as if illuminated by a harsh arc light.

"I'm sorry, Hadford."

"Excuse . . . *Oh, God, no!*"

As the train rumbled loudly out of the station, the flashing knife appeared from nowhere. What made David Hudson's parlor trick completely unexpected was that the blade was so very long, six inches, at least, and the handle perhaps another four.

The sharp blade jabbed hard and disappeared into Hadford's underbelly. It shredded the cashmere coat, tearing fibrous material and parting soft flesh and clenched muscle with virtually no effort. Almost instantly the long blade reappeared, dripping red.

As Laurence Hadford was sliding face up off the subway bench, Colonel Hudson relieved him of the weighty envelope. Hadford's rolling eyes were now staring sightlessly at the ceiling. His body underwent a series of racking convulsions, then went completely limp. He died somewhere between the 157th and 168th Street stations.

Hudson quietly slipped off at the next stop. He was shaking now. His mind was filled with tiny white explosions, with dark flowing streaks much like Hadford's blood. It was the first time in his career that he had ever harmed a fellow officer. But Hadford's greed had represented a weakness in the Green Band plan. And when you encountered greed, Hudson understood, instinctively, you ran into the likelihood, somewhere down the line, of betrayal. He could take no chances now, because there was no margin for error or for human weakness later.

Once he was out on Broadway, David Hudson struggled onto a city bus headed south. The Lizard Man screeched at him like a jungle monkey as the bus lurched forward. The Lizard Man screamed so loudly, Hudson had to grit his teeth. The Lizard Man laughed and laughed as David Hudson escaped into the awakening daytime city. *Revenge!*

A little more than an hour later, his composure intact once again, David Hudson climbed off the grunting, growling bus at the last stop—Columbus Circle and the New York Coliseum. Bundled inside his plain brown greatcoat, he walked farther south. He was almost sure people were staring, and that worried him.

Anonymity, he thought. He needed the cover of beautiful anonymity. He craved it. Especially now, he had to hold on to his New York cabdriver image. He had to be consistent. He also had to keep firmly in mind that he had been one of the very best Special Forces commanders in the world.

He reached the Washington-Jefferson Hotel, where he had a room at the far end of a depressingly drab second-floor hallway. He'd had this particular room for almost five weeks, and that was pushing his luck, perhaps. But the northern Times

Square district was so perfectly anonymous, uncaring, and so convenient for the specialized work he still had to do. He specifically hadn't wanted a place too close to either the Vets garage or the Wall Street financial district.

Hudson sat on the edge of his hotel room bed for a moment. His thoughts turned idly back to Laurence Hadford, but he knew he couldn't dwell on the death of the man. He stared at the nearby telephone. Finally he decided to forget Hadford and reward himself for Friday night's success. Some well-deserved, maybe even spectacular, R&R was in order. His only vice, really—David Hudson's only remaining human connection, he sometimes thought.

He picked up the telephone and dialed a familiar local number in Manhattan.

"Hello, this is Vintage." The connection was terrible. He could barely hear the words over the static.

"Yes. This is David . . . I've used Vintage Service before. My number is three twenty-three." Hudson spoke in his usual soft but firm voice. "I can tell you exactly the kind of escort I'm looking for. She's between five feet six and five feet ten. I'd like her between the ages of nineteen and twenty-six. I'll be paying cash."

Colonel Hudson waited, then he received a time and name for his "date." He spoke into the telephone again. "In thirty minutes at 318 West Fifty-first. Thank you very much. I'll be expecting . . . Billie."

It was just past eleven o'clock when Billie Bogan, her eyes raised to a winking neon hotel sign, stepped from a Checker cab on West Fifty-first Street.

The Washington-Jefferson? Now here was an odd one.

It certainly didn't look like the kind of place where Vintage clients usually stayed. Not the kind of successful men who could afford a hundred fifty dollars and up for an hour with some of the most exquisitely beautiful escorts in New York.

Billie finally shrugged and entered the paint-peeling hotel lobby. She had been told the client would be paying cash. As she walked down the dimly lit second-floor hallway, she shut off her Vintage beeper. It would be unbelievably tacky to get an electronic message while she was in the middle of a session with a client.

But the Washington-Jefferson? She shivered involuntarily.

Billie tapped on the door, and it swung open almost immediately. She was surprised to see someone so good-looking. His smile was open and pleasant. He was quite tall, slender, and . . .

Then she saw the flaw. The left sleeve of his mufti was empty—he had only one arm.

Billie couldn't feel too sorry for the man framed in the doorway. There was nothing about him that inspired pity; quite the opposite. He was certainly attractive, and his disability didn't seem to trouble him. He did not appear at all self-conscious as he gazed at her. He had the kind of face she somehow associated with the outdoors. Probably he was one of those self-reliant types who loved camping and knew the right knots to tie and the best place to pitch a tent.

"Hi. I'm Billie. How are you today?" She smiled courteously. "You're David?"

Colonel David Hudson stared at her for a few seconds longer before answering.

She was one of the best-looking prostitutes he'd ever seen. Her hair was an unbelievably rich, ash blond with thick

70

bouncy curls. She was long-legged and thin in the manner cultivated by high-fashion models, but without the glossy emaciation Hudson didn't care for. Her breasts were firm under a pricey silk blouse. She wore a flattering straight skirt, dark stockings, and high heels. Her face managed to combine an exotic loveliness with an innocent quality that excited him.

"I'm sorry," he finally managed with another smile. "I was staring, wasn't I? Come in. You're very pretty. Very beautiful. I didn't expect so beautiful a girl."

Billie smiled—as if she'd never heard any of this before. The hint of a blush rose along her high, elegant cheekbones. The sudden color sloped down her neck to the deep hollow of her throat.

"I'm sorry. I wasn't paying attention. It was Billie what? Your last name?"

"Just Billie," she smiled again. All of her gestures were very natural.

For the first time he noticed her accent. She was British. Maybe even upper class from the clipped sound of her phrases.

Hudson gestured around his Spartan hotel room. "I know, it isn't exactly the Plaza. Not just yet . . . You see, I'm writing a play. I hope this qualifies as an artist's garret?"

For some reason Billie found herself slowly relaxing with this one. He was easy to be with, and he sounded halfway intelligent. The bit about writing a play, whether it was true or not, had come out naturally enough. She sat down tentatively, almost demurely, on the edge of the unmade day bed. As if she were a real date and they hadn't discussed exactly why she'd come up to his room.

Staring at her face, Hudson thought she was twenty-five at the most. She was extremely elegant, even for Vintage.

71

"I like the theater a great deal. When I first came to New York to live, every single Wednesday I went to a Broadway matinee," she said. "I'd get these half-price tickets at Times Square. Sometimes at hotel desks. I saw *Death of a Salesman* with Dustin Hoffman, *Torch Song, Cats, Glengarry*. Everything I could get into."

Very nonchalantly, as she talked about the theater, she unfastened the top button of her silk blouse, then the next.

"Sit down by me?" A very innocent-sounding question.

Hudson did, and she kissed his cheek lightly. Her perfume was hypnotic, an expensive scent that captivated him. It drifted luxuriously up into his face.

"You said I was beautiful. I'd like to repay the compliment—you're very handsome. I hope you write a good play."

Still innocently, Billie unbuttoned the middle two buttons of his shirt and lightly slid her hands inside. The hair on his chest was downy soft, and his body was muscled and hard.

Her touch was light and warm. Then something extraordinary happened, something unusual. Hudson began to feel.

A severe warning bell went off deep inside.

Yet she was so natural and relaxed. The lightest touch of fingers. She was massaging him tenderly as she undressed. First the silk blouse delicately *shushed* off. Then the straight black skirt. At last she stood over him—only sheer dark stockings, garters, and high heels. There was a glistening droplet on her golden patch of hair. He felt as if he were sinking right through the mattress.

The inner warning alarm sounded again.

He watched her breathe—so unexpectedly beautiful—and she smiled when she realized what he was doing.

"You *are* beautiful."

72

"*You're* beautiful."

Her breasts were swelling in anticipation. Hudson touched them gently, exploring their perfect roundness, exploring each light pink aureole.

She slid on top of him, and her blond hair glowed in the light from the overhead lamp. She rocked back and forth, a peaceful, swaying motion. Everything seemed so easy. The warning signals quieted, like a siren fading in the distance.

He was breathing faster and faster. Her eyes shut, then opened, seemed to smile, shut again.

Faster and faster, faster and faster. He thought of dance rhythms.

He played with her as she gently rocked on top of him like a cresting sea wave. He manipulated her lightly with his hand as she moved to her own rhythm. Then her whole body stiffened, and she began to fall forward against his chest. She arched dramatically backward and jerked forward again. It was as if currents of electricity were passing through her long, slender body.

He was almost certain . . .

She was coming, her whole body shuddering.

This expensive escort from Vintage . . . this beautiful prostitute was having an orgasm.

Billie. Just Billie.

Warning signals were going off like a hundred piercing police sirens in his head. He didn't come. He never did.

# Chapter 7

ARCH CARROLL WAS flying on People Express to Miami that morning. It wasn't the most enjoyable experience he'd ever had. People Express happened to be the day's first scheduled Florida flight out of Washington. The light through the jet's tiny windows was dark and ominous for most of the trip, which had begun at the highly uncivilized hour of 4:45 A.M.

The airline service crew was young and inexperienced. They giggled inanely during the seat belt and airbag pep talk. They sold cellophane-wrapped Danish in the aisle for a dollar. Was this the hotshot outfit that had TWA and American shaking in their cockpits?

Carroll shut his eyes. He tried to make everything about the morning, especially about the night before, Black Friday, vanish, vanish far, far away. But nothing went away.

This scenario of terror was more like the state of siege people had learned to live with in the political capitals of

Western Europe, all through the teeming urban ghettos of South America—but never inside America, until now.

Until now.

The back of Arch Carroll's eyelids became a crisp white screen for a thousand flashing images: Wall Street ablaze; the frightened faces of ordinary people running amok through New York City's streets; the way President Justin Kearney had looked at the White House. Why did he keep returning to that same disturbing image of the president? Christ, he had more than enough to occupy himself right now.

Like this sudden trip to Miami . . .

The first possible break in the Green Band mystery had come quickly. Almost too quickly, Carroll thought. He'd spotted the clue himself on the FBI sheets for the nights before and left as soon as he could for Florida to check it out.

He opened his eyes briefly and stared the length of the aisle at two stewardesses talking in conspiratorial whispers. Then, the next thing he knew it was about halfway through the two-hour-and-forty-minute flight, and he got up wearily and trudged to the plane's bathroom.

The people on the early-bird flight looked thoroughly depressed and groggy, as if they'd risen way too early and their constitutions hadn't had time to catch up. But some of them had early-edition newspapers with stark headlines announcing the Wall Street bombing. The intense black letters burned into Carroll's mind as he moved up the aisle. Beyond the simplistic language, he could sense something else—something that reverberated beyond Wall Street, a far-off thunder that threatened a way of life— nothing less than the free enterprise systems of the Western world.

Inside the small bathroom, he cupped water in his hands

and splashed it over his eyes. He took a tiny red plastic case out of his pants pocket.

When Nora had been sick, she'd used this container to hold her day's supply of Valium and Dilantin and a few other prescriptions to help control seizures. Carroll slugged down a small yellow pill, a light upper to keep him alive. He would have preferred a drink. An eye-opener Irish whiskey. Double Bloody Mary. But he'd promised Walter Trentkamp.

Carroll continued to stare at himself in the clouded mirror. He thought some more about Green Band as he examined the puffed, purplish bruises sagging under each eye. He rifled through his mind as if he were sifting through a library's massive index card system. When it came to terrorists and their various specialties, Carroll had a long, reliable memory. During his first year with the DIA, all he'd done was catalog terrorist activities. He'd learned his early lessons well. In some ways, he was an incredibly orthodox and thorough policeman.

The hard evidence so far suggested ... what? Maybe Soviet-inspired GRU activity. Why, though? Qaddafi? A very long shot there. The Wall Street plan showed far too much patience for the usual Third World types, especially Middle Eastern hit men ...

Cubans? No. Provos? Not likely. Crazed American revolutionaries? Doubtful. Who, then? Most of all—*why*?

And how did the latest sketchy report from the Palm Beach Police Department fit? ... A south Florida drug dealer had been talking about the Wall Street attack the day before it happened. The local hood had even dropped the unannounced code name—*Green Band!*

How would a south Florida drug dealer by the name of

Diego Alvarez know anything about Green Band? What possible connection could there be?

Like everything so far, it didn't make much sense. It didn't seem to lead anywhere Arch Carroll particularly wanted to go. Certainly he didn't want to be in southern Florida at this ungodly hour of the morning.

He rubbed his eyes, splashed more cold water on his face, and looked back at his reflection. Death warmed over, he thought. It was like one of the photographs on Wanted posters inside post office buildings, the kind that seemed always to have been taken in dim lighting.

Carroll turned away from the mirror. It would soon be time to come down in the fantasyland of orange juice, Walt Disney World, multimillionaire dope dealers, and, he hoped, Green Band.

The local FBI chief, Clark Sommers, accompanied by an assistant, was there to meet Carroll at the makeshift People Express arrival gate. As usual, Miami International Airport was experiencing an electrical brownout.

"Mr. Carroll, I'm Clark Sommers of the Bureau. This is my associate, Mr. Lewis Sitts."

Carroll nodded. His head ached from the flight and the effects of the upper he'd swallowed, which was just kicking in now, buzzing through his bloodstream.

"Walk and talk?" Sommers suggested. "We've got an awful lot of ground to cover this morning."

"Yeah, sure. Tell me something, though. Every time I come through this airport the lights are half out. Am I just imagining that?"

"I know what you mean. It can seem that way. Dope dealers claim the bright lights hurt their eyes." Clark Sommers flashed a low-key, cynical smile. He was definitely FBI all the way—a neat, buttoned-down man with the body of someone who might have lifted weights years ago and still occasionally hit the bench.

Sommers's assistant, Mr. Sitts, was wearing a lightweight blue sweater, tan golfing slacks, and a matching Ban-Lon shirt. The only thing missing were some espadrilles. Probably getting a promotional fee from Jantzen, Carroll thought. He tried to picture himself as a successful Florida police officer, but he couldn't make the right visual or emotional connection.

As they walked down the corridor, Carroll glanced at the cheery posters depicting surf and sun. They seemed to assault him personally. The sea was a shade too blue, the sun a touch too garish, the people having fun in the photographs a little too all-American beautiful for Carroll's taste. He yearned for New York, where at least there was a sense of reality to the gray, wintry halftones of the familiar streets.

Sommers, fidgeting with a pair of sunglasses, spoke in a quiet, assured voice. "Mr. Carroll, one thing you probably should understand about this territory down here. For reasons of morale, in order to keep my men fully efficient and organized, this bust has to be mine. I have to make the key calls. These are my men, after all. You can understand that, I hope?"

Carroll didn't break stride. His face showed nothing. Almost all policemen were fiercely, irrationally territorial—something he knew from personal experience.

"Sure thing." He nodded. "This is your bust. All I want to do is talk to our drug-dealer friend afterward. Ask him how he likes the nice Florida weather."

The South Ocean Boulevard neighborhood was pretty much Spanish and Mediterranean in style, a six-block cluster of pastel blue and pink million-dollar estates. Carroll had the impression of everyone and everything lying dormant around him. People still sleeping peacefully at twenty past eight, flagstone patios sleeping, red clay courts sleeping at the bath and tennis club, putting-green lawns and candy-striped cabanas and swimming pools—all sleeping, as if everything had been placed under a pleasant narcoleptic spell.

Clark Sommers spoke in a steady drone as they rode alongside the glittering, bluish green ocean. "Real estate dealings here on South Ocean aren't exactly handled by Century 21. Most sales are actually arranged by Sotheby's, the big antiques outfit. Owners in Palm Beach, they think of their homes as valuable works of art. Maybe you can see why."

"Reminds me of my neighborhood in New York," Carroll said.

Agent Sitts pointed from the backseat suddenly, his long, well-tanned arm between Carroll and Sommers. "That's our people up ahead there, Clark."

At one of the quiet intersections lined with palm trees and sea-grape, six nondescript blue-and-green sedans were gathered together. The cars were parked in clear sight. Several of the FBI men were checking pump-action shotguns and Magnums right out in the street.

"There goes the neighborhood," Carroll muttered. "I hope Sotheby's is not showing any houses real early this morning."

"Don't be fooled by the suburban ambiance," Clark Sommers said. "The Mizeners, the real big shots, they don't live around here. This is Palms ghetto. Drug dealers and South American pimps. These people here are rich, but they're all street scum."

Arch Carroll shrugged and began to check his own gun. He

was wondering more than ever how a Florida hood would know about Green Band the day before it happened. Could that mean a connection with South American terrorists? Which ones? The Cubans? If the Cubans were involved, he could already foresee some impenetrable network of clues that could lead all the way back to Fidel himself, which wasn't a prospect he liked to consider. Castro had always managed to stay aloof from conspiracies, at least the ones that involved his name.

Sommers suddenly snatched the car's microphone. "All units! We will proceed with extreme caution up South Ocean now. Watch yourselves. These people are probably heavily armed."

The seven-vehicle caravan began to drift slowly up South Ocean Boulevard. Carroll glanced at the peaceful neighborhood. Every house was set back from the street, isolated by closely cropped, bright green lawns that looked as if they'd been spray-painted by gangs of meticulous handymen.

A *Miami Herald* paperboy rode by in the opposite direction, mounted on a chugging moped the same impossible blue color as the sky. He braked to a stop, scratched his crewcut, and stared.

One of the FBI men frantically signaled for him to keep going.

"That's it. Number six forty," Sommers said. "That's where our friend Diego Alvarez lives."

Carroll tucked the loaded Browning back into his shoulder holster. His stomach was rocking and rolling, and the speed was lighting fires throughout his nervous system.

The FBI cars turned single file down an impressive side street of South Palm. They lined up in front of two Spanish-style estates.

Car doors clicked open and shut very quietly.

Carroll slipped into step with a dozen or so gray-suited FBI agents. They trotted back toward the Alvarez place.

"Remember what I said back at the airport, Mr. Carroll. I give all the orders, okay? I hope the capture of this guy's going to help you get what you want, but don't forget who's running the show, okay?"

"I remember."

Handguns and shotguns caught the hard, bright glint of the early morning Florida sun. Carroll listened to bolt-action apparatus slamming into ready. The FBI agents looked like young professional athletes as they fanned out in the manner of a marathon team.

Combat was full of visual paradox.

Carroll could see peaceful gulls rising from the sea, lazily sliding west to check the sunrise party at the Alvarez house. Being a seagull seemed like a pretty good idea right now, but he had never been much for vocational planning.

The ocean wind was pleasantly warm. It carried a curious scent of salty fish and orange blossoms. The sun was already intense, too blinding to look at without shading your eyes with your hand.

"Elegant house Diego has for himself. Run about two, two point five million with Sotheby's. When I give the signal we're going to put men in every wing of the villa. We'll shoot anything that moves to threaten any of our lives."

Arch Carroll remained silent. These were Sommers's men. This was his little planet, where he reigned supreme. Carroll looked at the FBI man for a moment, then took out his handgun again. He pointed the massive black barrel upward as a safety precaution. As he knelt in a sniper shooter's crouch, the heavy wooden door of the Alvarez house flew open and banged hard against the pink stucco front wall.

"What the fuck?" Clark Sommers whispered loudly.

First a blowsy white-haired woman in a tattered Maranca shirt stumbled outside. Close behind came a dark, well-built man, bare-chested, in white flare-bottomed trousers. All across the front lawn automatics and revolvers clicked off their safeties.

Diego Alvarez began to scream at the FBI men. "You motherfuckers! I shoot this old lady, man. She jus' innocent old lady. My fuckin' cook, man. Put down all those motherfucker guns!"

Sommers became deathly quiet. His beach-hero tan seemed to be fading fast. The surprised expression on his face was that of a man who saw his private domain slipping out from under his control.

Carroll studied the south Florída drug dealer. The dark eyes of the man were frantic, desperate. There were flecks of saliva at the corners of his mouth. He was well muscled, like a pro fighter. Carroll turned to Sommers and said, "We have to take him. No matter what, we have to take him. You understand that?"

Sommers remained deathly quiet. He didn't even look at Carroll.

"We *have* to take Alvarez now. There are no other options."

Sommers glanced quickly at Carroll. His look said "You're a New York City cop; this is my backyard, we do things my way down here." Carroll had a vision of Alvarez escaping, and it was an exasperating vision. That was a possibility he had to prevent. Sommers didn't know what was involved here. The FBI was concerned about the dope bust, nothing more.

Diego Alvarez was awkwardly pulling the enormously fat cook toward a red Cadillac parked outside the garage. The cook's eyes were as wide and as round as two saucers.

Carroll tried to sort through the surprise and sudden, chaotic confusion of the moment. He controlled his breathing the way he was taught during his combat days in Southeast Asia. It helped him regain his focus.

One possible solution came to mind.

He'd actually seen a New York detective demonstrate this particular approach during a robbery in progress in Manhattan's Greenwich Village.

Carroll waited for Alvarez to eye-check the FBI agents on the far left. As he did so, Carroll smoothly slid behind a flower-decked wall that concealed him from the drug dealer. He waited a few seconds to see if he'd been missed, then continued hustling down behind the flowered wall, back through the side yard between Alvarez's house and the one next door.

A green watering hose snaked up the walkway to a swimming pool with a floating rubber horse that looked ludicrous to Carroll at that moment. He broke into a run, stopping only when he was back out on the street where the FBI team had parked their cars.

A very disturbing thought entered his mind as he climbed into Sommers's Grand Prix.

He never would have done this if Nora were still alive . . . Never in a thousand years would he have tried this stunt.

Even as the thought cut deeply, Arch Carroll eased the FBI sedan to the corner, where he made a sweeping right turn, then a quick left onto South Ocean.

A block ahead he saw Diego Alvarez backing into the

Cadillac. He was still holding the white-haired cook and screaming wildly at the FBI men, his words lost now in the sea breeze.

Carroll kicked down hard on the accelerator. The sedan twitched from first into third gear. The car licked forward with a screech from the expensive radial tires put on for precisely this kind of breakneck situation.

Don't think about this. Get it over with now.

His gun lay on the car seat beside him.

The speedometer read thirty, forty, fifty. Then the front wheels struck the concrete curb loudly with a jolting crunch. The car's front end leaped at least three feet in the air. All four wheels were off the ground, and the vehicle moved in slow motion, the speed at which a car flies.

Carroll double-pumped the sedan's brakes at the last possible moment.

"*What the hell—!*" an FBI man yelled, and dove to one side of the lawn.

"Holy *shit!*" came another high-pitched shout from one of Sommers's men.

Diego Alvarez fired three wild shots at the careening Pontiac. The sedan's windshield shattered, spitting glass fragments into Carroll's face.

The car was back on all four wheels again, bouncing over the lawn and over a red-tiled walkway. Suddenly it was skidding helplessly on the turf.

Carroll's foot stomped down full force against the gas pedal again. Just before contact, he tucked his head down. He held the steering wheel in a viselike grip, held on as tightly as he possibly could.

The bounding FBI car crashed broadside into Diego

Alvarez's cherry-red Cadillac. The convertible crumpled. It slid sideways like a hockey puck floating on ice and smashed into the side of the garage.

Half a dozen FBI officers were instantly sprinting across the front lawn. They got there before the two interlocking cars had stopped moving.

Revolvers, riot shotguns, and M-16 rifles were thrust inside the Cadillac's open front windows.

"Don't move, Alvarez. Don't move an inch!" an FBI man screamed. "I said *Don't move!*"

Carroll grunted, then pushed himself painfully out of the wrecked Pontiac. He roared out Diego Alvarez's name, surprised by his own intensity. He was still yelling when he grabbed the shirtless drug dealer out of the hands of the FBI agents, who stared at him with astonishment.

"Arch Carroll, State Department Antiterrorist Division! You have *no rights!* You hear me? . . . How did you know about Green Band? Who talked to you? You look at me!"

Diego Alvarez said, "Fuck you!" and spat into Carroll's face.

Carroll shuffled a little to his left, then hit the drug dealer with a sharp right hand delivered to the mouth. Alvarez fell to the ground, already out cold.

"Yeah, fuck you, too!" said the former Bronx street kid still lurking somewhere inside Carroll. He wiped the dope dealer's saliva from his cheek.

Clark Sommers's mouth fell open, creating a surprised *O* at the center of his suntanned face.

At the FBI office on Collins Avenue in Miami, Diego Alvarez was taken to a small interrogation room, where he told Carroll everything he knew.

"I don't know who they are, honest, man. Somebody jus' want you down here to Florida," he said with almost believable sincerity. Because he had been busted with three hundred and fifty thousand dollars' worth of cocaine, and because his prospects of freedom looked grim, he didn't have much to gain by lying. Carroll studied the man as he spoke.

"I swear it. I don't know nothin' more, man. But I got a feelin' somebody playin' some kind of games wit' you. They set me up, my big mouth. But somebody playin' wit' you . . . Somebody jus' want you come here 'stead of someplace else. They playin' wit' *you*, man. They playin' wit' you real good."

Carroll wanted to put his head down on the interrogation table. He'd been used, and he had no idea why. All he knew was that whoever was doing it was extremely smart. They were sending a message: See, we can manipulate you—any which way we like.

Carroll eventually wandered outside the FBI building and leaned heavily against the warm white stucco wall.

He tried to let the Florida sun soothe his weary brain. He thought that Miami might be a better climate for playing Crusader Rabbit than New York.

He was relatively certain about a couple of disturbing things. The Green Band group, whoever they were, knew who he was and that he would be assigned to the investigation. How did they know? What should that tell him about who they might be? . . . They seemed to want him to know how superior, how well organized, they were. They wanted him to be a little in awe—and frankly, right now he was.

How did they know he'd be assigned to the investigation? Who was trying to send him a cryptic message? Why?

On the plane home, Eastern—the wings of man—Arch

Carroll had two beers, then two Irish whiskeys. He could have gone for another two Irish, but he'd promised Walter Trentkamp—promised Uncle Walter something he couldn't quite remember. Finally he slept the rest of the way home to New York.

He had a real nice dream on the flight, too. Carroll dreamed that he quit his job with the DIA's Antiterrorist Division. He and the kids and Nora went to live on the nicest sugar white beach in Florida.

And they all lived happily ever after.

# Chapter 8

*Manhattan*

BEFORE BREAK OF dawn on Sunday morning, Caitlin Dillon waded through a becalmed river of ice and slush that rose four inches above her ankles. Once she successfully emerged on half-deserted Fifth Avenue, the director of enforcement for the SEC's Division of Trading and Exchange hailed a yellow cab, which ferried her down to the Fourteenth Street Police and National Guard barricades. From there she was transferred by a snazzy police blue-and-white down into the smoldering chaos and confusion of the financial district itself.

The ride went by amazingly fast. There were no working traffic lights below Fourteenth and almost no other traffic on any of the downtown streets.

The sergeant driving the police car was as good-looking as any young actor in a Hollywood cop show. He had long blue-black hair curling over his uniform collar. His name was Signarelli. Caitlin figured he definitely watched "Hill Street Blues."

"Never seen anything this bad." The police sergeant revealed a nasal Brooklyn accent when he spoke. His eyes kept darting in and out of the rearview mirror.

"Can't even call in to your normal communications desk. Nerve center they set up is always busy, too. Nobody knows what the army's doing. What the FBI guys are doing, either. It's completely nuts!"

"How would you handle it?" There was nothing patronizing in the question. Caitlin was always curious about the rank and file. That was one reason she made a good boss at the SEC. A second reason was that she was smart, so knowledgeable about Wall Street and the workings of business that most of her associates legitimately held her in awe. "If this was your show, what would you do now, Sergeant?"

"Well . . . I'd hit every terrorist hangout we know about in the city. We know about a hell of a lot of them, too. I'd blow into their little maggot nests. Arrest everybody in sight. That way we'd sure as hell get some information."

"Sergeant, I believe that's what teams of detectives have been doing all night. Over sixty separate squads of NYPD detectives. But the maggots are just not cooperating on this one."

Caitlin arched her eyebrow, then smiled gently at the cop. Predictably, he asked her for a date, and just as predictably, Caitlin turned him down.

With police and army helicopters constantly whirring overhead, Caitlin Dillon stood still and numb on the northwest corner of Broadway and Wall. She allowed her eyes to roam across the most chilling, surreal scene she ever hoped to view in her lifetime.

What appeared to be billions of tons of granite block, shattered glass, and concrete and mortar had crashed down onto Wall Street and Broad Street and Pine and all the narrow, interconnecting alleyways. According to the latest army intelligence estimate, as many as sixty separate plastique bombs had detonated at 6:34 Friday evening. The police theory was that the bombs had been exploded by sophisticated radio signals. The signals could have been transmitted from as far away as ten or twelve miles.

Caitlin craned her neck to gaze up at nearby 6 Wall Street. She winced as she observed the sheared, swinging clumps of wiring: thick elevator cables dangling between the highest floors of the office building. Here and there patches of sky shone through great yawning holes in the building's walls. The overall effect reminded her of a doll house utterly destroyed by a child's temper tantrum.

She stood all alone, shivering and cold, on the stone portal of the New York Stock Exchange. She couldn't stop herself from staring at the abysmal destruction, the incomprehensible damage, on Wall Street. More than anything, she wanted to be sick.

She saw an oil painting, a Yankee sailing clipper, hanging in a distant office with two of the room's walls blown away. It looked absurd. In the foyer of an adjacent building, an overturned copier had collapsed through several floors before striking the unyielding marble in the lobby. She could see the shattered screens of computer terminals and the melted remains of keyboards that reminded her of some nightmare art form. All over the littered, desolate street, police and hospital emergency vehicles were flashing bright red-and-blue distress signals.

Caitlin Dillon could feel a cold dead weight pushing down on her. Her body was numb. Her ears buzzed softly, as if there were a sudden drop in air pressure. She couldn't stop a feeling of nausea, of sudden weakness in her legs. She understood what many of the others still didn't—that an entire way of life had quite possibly been destroyed here on Friday night.

Inside number 13, Caitlin was confronted immediately by noisy squads of secretaries typing frantically in the marble-and-stone entryway corridors. Stock exchange clerks milled around with a kind of busy uselessness, carrying clipboards with a hollow show of self-importance, carting files from one office to another.

Caitlin took in the command post scene and then, as she stepped nimbly around the broken glass and debris that had been shaken loose from the ceiling, she was surrounded by heavily armed policemen who demanded to see her identification.

She smiled to herself as she showed her ID. No one knew who she was; no one recognized her here in the stock exchange foyer.

How very typical that was. Damn it, how typical.

For the past three years the SEC's director of enforcement had been a most unlikely Wall Street figure: Caitlin Dillon was clearly a major force yet a person of supreme mystery to almost everybody around her.

Women in general had only been permitted on the floor of the stock exchange since 1967. Nevertheless the idea hadn't particularly caught on. In fact, in the visitors' gallery of the exchange one infamous sign still retained a position of prominence:

WOMEN MAKE POOR SPECULATORS.
WHEN THROWN UPON THEIR OWN
RESOURCES, THEY ARE COMPARATIVELY
HELPLESS. EXCELLING IN CERTAIN LINES,
THEY ARE FORCED TO TAKE BACKSEATS
IN SPECULATION. WITHOUT THE
ASSISTANCE OF A MAN, A WOMAN ON
WALL STREET IS LIKE A SHIP WITHOUT A
RUDDER.

Caitlin Dillon had actually inherited her job because of her predecessor's bad luck in the shape of a sudden fatal coronary. Caitlin knew that insiders had predicted she wouldn't last two months. They compared the fateful situation with that of a politician's wife taking over for an unexpectedly invalid husband. Caitlin was called by some "the interim enforcer."

For that reason, and some strong personal ones from her past, she had decided that—for however long she might last in the job—she was going to become the sternest, hardest SEC enforcement officer since Professor James Landis had been doing the hiring himself. What did she possibly have to lose?

She was, therefore, stubbornly serious. Some said Caitlin Dillon was unnecessarily obsessed with white-collar criminal investigations, with skillfully prosecuting malfeasance by senior officers of major American corporations.

"I'll tell you something off the record," Caitlin had once said to a dear friend, Meg O'Brian, the financial editor of *Newsweek*. "The Ten Most Wanted men in America are all working on Wall Street."

As the "interim" enforcement officer at the SEC, Caitlin Dillon made a lot of news very fast. The mystery of Caitlin Dillon—how she had surfaced virtually from nowhere— grew each week she held on to the important job. The power brokers on the Street still wanted to replace her, but suddenly they found they couldn't do so very easily. Caitlin was simply too good at what she did. She'd become too visible. She was almost instantly a strong symbol for the disenfranchised in America's financial system.

At seven forty-five that morning, Caitlin finally reached her office inside 13 Wall. It was respectably large, even elegant. She removed her coat and took a deep breath as she sat down. On her desk lay a damage report prepared for her the previous night. As her eyes scanned the page, she felt a deepening despair at the sheer amount of destruction done:

> The Federal Reserve Bank
> Salomon Brothers
> Bankers Trust
> Affiliated Fund
> Merrill Lynch
> U.S. Trust Corporation
> The Depository Trust Company

The list went on to detail fourteen downtown New York buildings that had been partially or completely destroyed.

She closed her eyes and placed her hands on the report. If only it could give her a hint, a clue. Fourteen different buildings in the Wall Street financial district—the whole thing was beyond her, out of control by any measure.

She opened her eyes.

It was the start of the second day of her formal investigation of Green Band, and she knew no more than she'd known before. It was going to be a long, long Sunday.


Arch Carroll strode briskly from a comfortable State Department limousine toward the ominous gray stone entranceway to 13 Wall Street. At least Green Band had left this building mostly intact—a fact that caused him to wonder. If a terrorist cell was going to strike out hard at U.S. capitalism, why wouldn't they destroy the New York Stock Exchange?

Carroll had on a knee-length, black leather topcoat that Nora had given him the Christmas before her death. At the time she'd joked that it made him look like a tough-guy hero in an action movie. The coat was now one of his few personal treasures; that it was a little too tight under the arms didn't matter. There was no way he'd have it altered. He wanted it exactly as it was when Nora had given it to him.

Carroll was smoking a crumpled cigarette. Sometimes on the weekends he wore the coat and smoked crumpled cigarettes when he took Mickey Kevin and Clancy to the New York Knicks or Rangers games. It made both kids laugh hysterically. They told him he was trying to look like Clint Eastwood in the movies. He wasn't, he knew. Clint Eastwood was trying to look like him—like some nihilistic, tough-guy city cop.

Hurrying down the long, echoing corridors, Carroll pulled his way out of the leather coat. For a few hefty strides he left it capelike over his shoulders. Then he folded it over one arm, in the hope that he'd look a little more civilized. There were lots of very straight businesspeople in the hallowed halls of 13 Wall.

Carroll pushed open leather-covered doors into a formal meeting room thick with perspiration and stale tobacco smoke. The room where the New York Stock Exchange professional staff usually met was the size of a large theater.

The scheduled meeting was already in progress. He was late. He was also weary from his flight, and his nerves—kept moderately alert by an infusion of amphetamine— were beginning to complain. He glanced at his watch. There was another long day ahead of him.

Carroll scanned the shadowy room. It was filled with New York City police and U.S. Army personnel, with corporate lawyers and investigators from the major banks and brokerage houses on Wall Street. The only seats left were way in front.

Carroll groaned and crouched low. He clumsily climbed over gray-and-blue pin-striped legs, and over someone's abundant lap, toward the front row. He thought everybody in the room must be staring at him.

The speaker was saying, "Let me tell you how to make a hell of a lot of money on Wall Street. All you have to do is steal a little from the rich, steal a little from the middle rich, steal a lot from the lower rich . . ."

Nervous laughter cascaded around the vast meeting room. It was a muted, mirthless outbreak that sounded more like a release of fear than anything else.

The speaker went on: "The Wall Street security system simply *doesn't* work. As you all know, the computer setup here is one of the most antiquated in all of the business world. That's why this disaster could happen."

Carroll finally found a seat. He lowered himself onto it until only his head peeked above the theater's gray velvet seat back and pressed his knees against the wooden stage in front.

"The computer system on Wall Street is a complete disgrace . . ."

Carroll looked up and took in the meeting's speaker. Jesus. He was completely taken aback by the sight of Caitlin Dillon on the podium. Her hair, a sleek chestnut-brown color, was bobbed at the shoulders. Long legs, slender waist. Tall—maybe five feet eight. She looked, if anything, even more intriguing than she'd seemed that first night in Washington.

She was staring down at him. Her brown eyes were very calm, measuring everything they saw. Yes, she was staring directly down at Carroll himself.

"Are you expecting trouble during my briefing, Mr. Carroll?" Her eyes had fastened onto his Browning, his beat-up leather shoulder holster. He was suddenly embarrassed by her question and the way his name had sounded through her microphone. Those pale red lips seemed to be lightly mocking him.

Carroll didn't know what to say. He shrugged and tried to sink a little deeper onto his seat. Why didn't he have one of his usual wisecracks to throw back at her?

Caitlin Dillon smoothly switched her attention back to the audience of senior police officers and heavy-duty Wall Street businessmen. Without missing a beat, she resumed her briefing at exactly the point where she had interrupted herself.

"In the past decade," she said, and her next chart efficiently appeared on the screen at her back, "foreign investment in the United States has skyrocketed. Billions of francs, yen, pesos, and deutsche marks have flowed into our economy to the sum of eighty-five billion dollars. The Midland Bank of England, for instance, took full control of the Crocker National Bank of California. Nippon Kokan purchased half the National Steel Corporation. The list goes on and on.

"At this rate, I'm sorry to say, the Japanese, the Arabs, and the Germans will very soon control our financial destiny."

As she recited exhaustive facts and numbers that defined the present situation in the financial community, Carroll listened attentively. He also watched attentively. Nothing could have drawn his eyes away from her, short of a second Wall Street bombing raid.

There was a disarming twinkle in her eyes, an unexpected hint of sweetness in her smile. Was it really sweetness, though? Coyness? How could she hold down the job she had if she was shy and retiring and sweet? "Sweet" was not in the Wall Street lexicon.

She was chic—even in a conservative, salt-and-pepper tweed business suit. She looked stylish and somehow just right.

Most of all, though, she looked untouchable.

That was the single word, the most precise idea floating through Carroll's head, that seemed to sum up Caitlin Dillon best.

Untouchable.

In Carroll's experience, neither he nor anybody he knew ever actually got to meet the spectacular-looking women you all too frequently saw in midtown New York, in Washington, in Paris. Who the hell *did* get to know them? . . . Was there a matching species of untouchable men whom Carroll never bothered to notice? . . . What sort of man woke up with this Caitlin Dillon woman next to him? Some superwealthy Wall Street lion? One of those buccaneers of the stock arbitrage game? Yes, he'd bet anything that was the case.

His attention drifted back to her speech, which was a succinct description of the Green Band emergency, of the current state of Wall Street's insufficient computer records, and of the stoppage of all international transfers of funds. She had some sobering and scary material up there on the podium.

"Surprisingly, there's still been no further contact by the terrorist group, whatever kind of group they are. As you may know, no actual demands were made. No ultimatums. Absolutely no reason has been given so far for what happened on Friday.

"There'll be another meeting after this, for my people and for the analysts. We have to get something going with the computers before the market opens on Monday. If not . . . I would expect major unpleasantness."

The meeting room became still. The scraping of feet, all paper shuffling, stopped.

"Are we talking about a stock market panic? Some kind of crash? What sort of major unpleasantness?" someone called out.

Caitlin paused before she spoke again. It was obvious to Carroll that she was choosing her next words with extreme care and diplomacy.

"I think we all have to recognize . . . that there is a possibility, even a likelihood, of some form of market panic on Monday morning."

"What constitutes a panic in your mind? Give us a for instance," said a senior Wall Street man.

"The market *could* lose several hundred points very quickly. In a matter of hours. That's if they decide to open on Monday. In Tokyo, London, Geneva, the subject's still under discussion."

"Several hundred points!" Quite a few of the brokers groaned. Carroll watched them envision their comfortable lives eroding. The stretch Mercedeses, the Westchester estates, the fashionable clothes—everything gone. It's so fucking fragile, he thought.

"Are we talking about a potential Black Friday situation?" asked someone from the back of the auditorium. "Are you saying there could actually be a stock market crash?"

Caitlin frowned. She recognized the speaker, a stiff, stuffy bean counter from one of the larger midtown New York banks. "I'm not saying anything like that yet. As I suggested before, if we had a more modern system of computers down here, if Wall Street had joined the rest of the twentieth century, we'd know a lot more. Tomorrow is Monday. We'll see what happens then. We should be prepared. That's what I'm suggesting—preparedness. For a change."

With that, Caitlin Dillon stepped down from the stage. As Carroll watched her leave the room, he became conscious of another figure approaching him: Captain Francis Nicolo from the New York City Bomb Squad, a cop who liked to think he was something of a dandy with his sleek, waxed mustache and his three-piece pin-striped suits.

"A moment, Arch," Nicolo said, and gestured rather mysteriously for Carroll to follow.

They hurried out of the room and along various dimly lit stock exchange corridors, Carroll trailing behind. Nicolo opened the door to a small inner office tucked directly behind the trading floor. He closed it with a secretive gesture when Carroll was inside.

"What's happening?" Carroll asked, both curious and slightly amused. "Talk to me, Francis."

"Check this," Nicolo said. He pointed to a plain cardboard box propped on the desk. "Open it. Go ahead."

"What is it?" Carroll hesitantly stepped toward the desk. He laid the tips of his fingers lightly against the box lid.

"Open it. Won't bite your widget off."

Carroll removed the lid. "Where the hell did this come from?" he asked. "Christ, Frank."

"Janitor found it behind a cistern in one of the men's rooms," Nicolo answered. "Scared the living piss out of the poor guy."

Carroll stared at the device, at the length of shiny green ribbon that was wound elaborately around it. Green Band.

"It's harmless," Nicolo said. "It was never meant to go off."

Arch Carroll continued to stare at the makings of a professional terrorist's bomb. It was never meant to go off, he thought. Another warning? "They could have totaled this place," he said with a sick feeling.

Nicolo made a clucking sound. "Easily," he said. "Plastique, like all the others. Whoever did it knew what the hell he was up to, Arch."

Carroll wandered over to the window and peered down into the street, where he saw New York cops standing all over the place, where he saw the incomprehensible war zone.

# Chapter 9

USING A TINE of his fork, Sergeant Harry Stemkowsky punctured each of the three sunny-side-up eggs staring at him from his breakfast platter that Sunday morning. He lathered on a thick wave of ketchup, then buttered and spread strawberry preserves on a row of four hot toasted bialy halves. He was ready to rock and roll.

The superb greasy-spoon meal was his usual breakfast: corned beef hash, eggs, and bialys. The place was the Dream Doughnut Coffee at Twenty-third Street and Tenth Avenue. The meal arrived at the table approximately three hours into his day shift. Stemkowsky had been looking forward to the food all through his first dreary hours on the road.

Harry Stemkowsky almost always went through the same exact thought process while he was devouring breakfast at the Dream . . .

It was so unbelievably good to be out of that Erie VA

hospital, that piss-and-shitting hole. It was just so goddamn tremendous to be alive again. He had a valid reason to keep going now, to get really psyched about his life.

And it was all thanks to Colonel David Hudson. Who happened to be the best soldier, the best friend, one of the best men Stemkowsky had ever met. Colonel Hudson had given all the Vets another chance. He'd given them the Green Band mission to get even.

Later that same morning, as he slalomed through the deep slush of Jane Street in the West Village, Colonel David Hudson thought he might be seeing apparitions. He leaned his head out of the half-rolled window of the Vets taxi. His green eyes sparkled intensely against the street's murky gray.

He shouted ahead into the cold driving rain, the dripping winds ripping and grabbing at his face. "You're going to rust out there, Sergeant. Get your pitiful ass inside." Harry Stemkowsky was perched solidly on his familiar, battered aluminum wheelchair. He was huddled zombielike in the drowning rain, right in front of the entrance of the Vets garage.

It was an incredibly moving sight, probably more sad than weird, Hudson thought. A true retrospective on what was ultimately accomplished in Vietnam. There was Harry Stemkowsky, as poignant as any journalist's picture taken of the wounded in the Southeast Asia combat zone. Hudson could feel his jaw muscles tighten and the beginnings of an old rage. He fought against it successfully. This wasn't the time to allow himself the luxury of personal feelings. This wasn't the time to wallow in old, pointless anger.

Stemkowsky was grinning broadly by the time David Hudson jogged to the weathered door of the Vets garage.

"You're section eight for life, Sergeant. You're out of your mind," Hudson said firmly. "No explanations accepted."

But he was beginning to smile. He knew why Stemkowsky was waiting outside, knew all the Vets' sad sack stories by heart now. He was betting everything on knowing the Vets at least as well as he knew their military histories.

"I—I wha-wanted to be ri-right he-here. When, when you got in. That—that—that's all it was, Cah-Cah-Colonel."

Hudson's voice softened. "Yeah, I know, I know. It's real good to see you again, Sergeant. You're still an asshole, though." With an audible sigh, Colonel David Hudson bent low and easily scooped up the hundred-and-thirty-seven-pound bundle of Harry Stemkowsky with his powerful right arm.

Since the spring offensive of 1971, Stemkowsky had been a helpless cripple. He had also been a violent, totally incurable stutterer ever since he'd been splattered with seventeen rounds from a Soviet SKS automatic rifle. A pitiful wreck, right up until a few months ago, anyway.

As he pushed his way to the top of the cramped, musty stairway inside Vets, Hudson decided not to think about Vietnam anymore. This was supposed to be an R&R party. Green Band was a rousing operational success so far. George Thorogood and the Destroyers' "Bad to the Bone" blared loudly from the room above. Good tune. Good choice.

"It's the colonel himself!"

As he stalked inside a large, drab yellow room on the second floor, David Hudson heard shrill hollers and shouts all around him. For a moment he was embarrassed by the clamor. Then he thought about the fact that he'd given these twenty-six veterans another lease on their lives, a purpose that transcended the bitterness they had brought back from Vietnam.

"The colonel's here! Colonel Hudson's here. Hide the girls."

"Well, shit. Hide the good Johnnie Walker booze, too . . . Just kidding, sir."

"How the hell are you, Bonanno? Hale? Scully?"

"Sir . . . we goddamn did it, didn't we!"

"Yes, we did. So far, anyway."

"Sir! It's great to see you. Went just like you said it would."

"Yeah. The easy part did."

The twenty-six men continued to cheer. Hudson shielded his eyes as he stared around at the dingy room where they'd been plotting together for almost a year and a half. He scanned the rows of familiar faces, the scraggly, home-cut beards, the unfashionably long hairstyles, the drab green khaki jackets, of the Vets. He was home. He was home, and he was obviously welcome. He could feel the vibrations of unadulterated warmth that these men felt toward him. And for one brief moment Colonel David Hudson almost lost control. There was a tightening in his throat, a feeling of moisture in his eyes.

Finally he offered a wry, conspiratorial smile. "It's good to see you all again. Carry on with your party. That's an order."

He ambled on, gripping hands, greeting the rest of the Vets group: Jimmy Cassio, Harold Freedman, Mahoney, Keresty, McMahon, Martinez—all men who hadn't been able to fit back into American society after Vietnam, all men he'd recruited for Green Band during the past sixteen months.

As he walked, he thought deeply about his men, his final combat command—the final mission.

The twenty-six Vets were antisocial, chronically unemployable; they were dramatic losers by the standard American measurements of success and accomplishments. At least half of them still suffered some form of PTSD, the post traumatic stress disorder so common among war veterans, an illness that, start-lingly, had tripled after Vietnam. PTSD involved constantly reexperiencing combat trauma in an endless series of flash-backs, nightmares, extremely intrusive memories. Among other things, PTSD seemed to cause emotional numbing, a kind of paranoid-schizy withdrawal from the external environment, sometimes compounded with the guilt of having survived.

David Hudson knew this from personal experience: he still suffered from PTSD himself. He suffered more pain than anyone would ever be permitted to know.

The twenty-six men packed into the cabdrivers' locker room had performed spectacularly in Vietnam and Cambodia. Every one of them had served under Hudson at one time or another. Each man was a highly trained technical specialist; each had a unique skill no one other than Hudson seemed to want or need in civilian society. Steve "the Horse" Glickman and Paul "Mr. Blue" Melindez were the finest rifleman-sniper team Hudson had ever commanded in the field.

Michael Demunn and Rich Scully were experts at ordnance, at assembling and creating complex plastique explosives in particular.

Manning Rubin could have been making a thousand a week for either Ford or GM. *If* his skill at fixing automobiles had been matched by patience, just a little ability to handle sub-urban bullshit . . .

Davey Hale had an encyclopedic knowledge of just about everything, including the Wall Street Stock Market.

Campbell, Bowen, Kamerer, and Generalli were high-caliber professional soldiers and mercenaries. Since Vietnam they'd soldiered for pay in Angola, in San Salvador, even in the streets of Miami. The combat group was particularly lethal at close-quarter, hand-to-hand urban street fighting. That single fact would be their key advantage entering the second stage of the Green Band mission.

"All right, gentlemen. We have to do some homework now," Hudson said. "This is the last time we'll have the chance to review these details and any of our final operating schedules. If this sounds like a formal military briefing, that's because it damn well is."

David Hudson paused and methodically took in the circle of assembled faces. Each was turned toward him with intense concentration. There was a bond in this intimate war room, he knew, that went beyond Green Band. It was a bond of blood and hopefulness, forged out of a shared, tragic history.

"Personal anecdote, gentlemen . . . At the highly-thought of JFK Special Warfare Center and School at Fort Bragg, they repeatedly told us that 'genius is in the details.' When the truth of that finally sank in, it held like nothing I've ever learned before or since.

"So I want to go over the final details one last time. Maybe two last times with all of you. Details, gentlemen . . . if we master the details, we win. If the details master us, we lose. Just like in 'Nam."

Vets 1 had purposely modeled his presentation after the concise and always very technical Special Forces field briefings. He wanted these men to vividly remember Vietnam now. He wanted them to remember precisely how they'd acted—with daring and courage, with dedication to the United States, with honor at all times.

Hudson could feel his body pulsing and tingling lightly He spoke to the men without any written notes—everything was committed to memory.

His personal grasp of minutiae and military theory was riveting that afternoon in early December. For nearly two and a half hours Colonel David Hudson painstakingly reviewed every foreseeable scenario, every likely and even unlikely change that might occur up to, and including, the end of the Green Band mission. He used combat-proven memory aids: reconnaissance topographical maps, mnemonics of memorizing, army-style organizational charts.

A deep graveled voice sounded from the shadowy rear of the Vets locker room. One of the combat mercenaries, a southern black named Clint Hurdle, had taken the floor.

"Why you so sure there won't be no attacks of conscience? This going to heat up now, Colonel. Who says nobody going to fuck up and run?"

There was a startled hush around the small room.

Hudson considered the question very carefully before answering. He had, in fact, posed almost the same question hundreds of times in his own head. He always assumed the worst, then created a number of alternative ways to effectively deal with, and avoid, disaster.

"*Nobody*, not a single one of you men, broke during combat . . . Not even in a war none of you wanted or believed in. Nobody broke in POW camps! Not one of you! . . . None of you will break now, either. I'm fully prepared to bet everything we've worked for on that."

There was an uncomfortable silence after the difficult question and emotional answer. David Hudson's intense green eyes slowly surveyed the Vets' dressing room one more time. He wanted them to feel in their guts that he was sure about everything he'd just said. The way he *was* sure. Even though it might not look it, every man in the room had been carefully hand-picked from hundreds of possible vets. Every soldier in the room was special.

"If any one of you wants to leave, though, this is the time . . . Right now, gentlemen. This afternoon . . . Anybody? . . . Anybody who wants to leave us? . . ."

One Vet slowly started to clap. Then the rest of them. Finally all the Vets were solemnly clapping their hands. Whatever was going to happen, they were in it together now.

Colonel Hudson slowly nodded; the cocksure military commander once again took control.

"I've saved the foreign travel assignments, the specific assignments, until last. I'm not going to entertain any discussion, any disagreement at all, over these assignments. The operational environment is already confused. We will not be confused. That's another reason we're going to win this war."

Hudson walked to a long wooden table, from which he began to pass out thick, official-looking portfolios. Each one had a white tag pasted carefully on the front. Inside the envelopes were counterfeit U.S. passports and visas, first-class airplane tickets, extremely generous expense monies, and copies of elaborate topographical maps from the briefing. The genius was in the details.

"Cassio will go to Zurich," Hudson began to announce.

"Stemkowsky and Cohen have Israel and Iran . . . Scully will go to Paris. Harold Freedman to London, then on to Toronto. Jimmy Holm to Tokyo. Vic Fahey to Belfast. The rest of us stay put right here in New York."

A schoolboy's groan went up. Hudson silenced it instantly with a short, chopping hand motion.

"Gentlemen. I'll say this one time only, so you have to remember it . . . While you're in Europe, in Asia, in South America, it is absolutely essential that you act, that you groom and dress yourselves, in the particular style we've laid out for you. Remember the catch phrase: Nothing succeeds like excess . . .

"All of your air travel arrangements are first class. All of your clothing and restaurant expense money is meant to be spent. Spend that money. Throw it around. Be more extravagant than you've ever been in your lives. Have fun, if you can under the circumstances. That's an order!"

Hudson eased up. "For the next few days you have to be self-assured, successful American business types. You have to be like the people we've been studying on Wall Street for the past year. *Think* like a Wall Street man, *look* like one, *act* like a high-powered Wall Street executive.

"At oh-four-thirty, you'll be given self-respecting corporate haircuts, shaves, and—believe it or not—manicures. Your wardrobes have been carefully selected for you, too. They're Brooks Brothers and Paul Stuart—your favorite shops, gentlemen. Your shirts and ties are Turnbull & Asser. Your billfolds are from Dunhill. They contain credit cards and plenty of cash in the appropriate denominations you'll need in your respective countries."

He paused, and his eyes roamed slowly across the room. "I think that's all I have to say . . . except one important thing. I wish you all the very best luck possible. I wish you the best, in the future after this mission . . . I believe in you. Believe in yourselves."

Colonel David Hudson shut his eyes briefly, then opened them. It was impossible to tell what he was thinking. His face gave nothing away. It was a blank mask staring at the handful of men gathered in the dressing room.

He raised his arm, and in a tone that sounded almost religious, he said, "Now, our rendezvous with destiny."

# Chapter 10

IT WAS TWO-THIRTY on Sunday afternoon when Arch Carroll kicked both weathered Timberland work boots up on his desk inside number 13. He yawned until his jaw cracked; it felt as if it had just been dislocated.

He'd already finished four absolutely draining and futile interrogations. He'd been lied to by the very best—the most dangerous provocateurs and terrorists from all around New York.

Carroll had purposely chosen a cramped office for himself, tucked away at the back of the Wall Street building. His small but hearty DIA group, a half-dozen unorthodox police renegades and two efficient and extremely resilient secretaries, surrounded the uninspiring office in a satellite of Wall Street–style cubicles.

Like burned skin, paint peeled from the walls of Carroll's office. The windowpane had been shattered, courtesy of Green Band. He'd tacked a square of brown paper to the hole, but rain soaked through, anyway. It was a depressing working space for a depressing task. Even the light that managed to fall inside was oppressive, mangy brown, dim, and hopeless.

The first four suspects Carroll had interviewed were known terrorists who lived in the New York City area: two FALN, a PLO, and an IRA fund-raiser. Unfortunately the four were no more knowledgeable about the Wall Street mystery than Carroll was himself. There was nothing circulating on the street. Each of them convincingly swore to that after exhaustively long sessions.

Carroll wondered how it could be possible. *Somebody* had to know something about Green Band. You don't calmly blow away half of Wall Street and keep it a state secret for over forty hours.

The scarred and rusted wooden door into his office opened again. He watched the door over the steamy lid of his coffee container.

Mike Caruso, who worked for Carroll at the DIA, peeked inside. Caruso was a small, skinny, ex–office cop with a black fifties pompadour pushed up high over his forehead. He habitually wore wretched Hawaiian shirts outside his baggy pants, attempting to create a splash of colorful identity in the usually drab police world. Carroll liked him immensely for his dedicated lack of style.

"We got Isabella Marqueza up next. She's already screaming for her fancy Park Avenue lawyer. I mean the lady is fucking screaming out there."

"That sounds promising. Somebody's upset, at least. Why don't you bring her right in?"

Moments later the Brazilian woman appeared like a sudden tropical windstorm. "You can't do this to me! I'm a citizen of Brazil!"

"Excuse me. You must be mistaking me for somebody who gives a shit. Why don't you please sit down." Carroll spoke without getting up from his cluttered work desk.

"Why? Who do you think you are?"

"I said sit down, Marqueza. I ask the questions here, not you."

Arch Carroll leaned back in his chair and studied Isabella Marqueza. The woman had shoulder-length gleaming black hair. Her lips were full and painted very red. There was an arrogant tilt to her chin. Her hair, her clothes, even her skin looked expensive and cosmopolitan. She had on tight gray velvet riding pants, a silk shirt, cowboy boots, a half-length fur jacket. Terrorist chic, Carroll thought.

"You dress like a very wealthy Che Guevara." He finally smiled.

"I don't appreciate your attempt of humor, senhor."

"No, well, join the crowd." His smile broadened. "I don't appreciate your attempts at mass murder."

Carroll already knew this striking woman by reputation, at least. Isabella Marqueza was an internationally renowned journalist and newsmagazine photographer. She was the daughter of a wealthy man who owned tire factories in São Paulo, Brazil. Though it couldn't be legally proved, Isabella Marqueza had sanctioned at least four American deaths in the past twelve months.

She was responsible, Carroll knew, for the disappearance, then the cold-blooded, heartless murders of a Shell Oil executive and his family. The American businessman, his wife, and their two small girls had vanished that past June in Rio. Their pitiful, mutilated bodies had been found in a sewer ditch inside the *favelas*. Isabella Marqueza reportedly worked for the

112

GRU through François Monserrat. According to rumors, she had also been Monserrat's lover. A classic spider woman.

She tossed Carroll a cold, indignant look. Her dark, sullen eyes smoldered as she stared him down in practiced silence.

Arch Carroll shook his head wearily. He set aside the steaming coffee container. The impression he got from Isabella was that of a tempest about to unleash its force. He watched as she leaned forward and thumped her hands on the desk—the fiery light in her dark eyes was really something.

"I want to see my lawyer! Right now! I want my lawyer! You get my lawyer. *Now*, senhor!"

"Nobody even knows you're here." Carroll spoke in a purposely soft, polite voice. Whatever she did, however she acted—he would do the exact opposite, he'd decided. Step one of his interrogation technique.

He said nothing further for the first uncomfortable moments. He'd learned his interrogation technique from the very best—Walter Trentkamp.

Carroll knew that two of his DIA agents had illegally intercepted Isabella Marqueza as she'd walked down East Seventieth Street after leaving her Upper East Side apartment that morning. She'd screamed out, struggled, and fought as they'd grabbed her off the street. "Murder! Somebody please help me!"

Half a dozen East Side New Yorkers, with the anesthetized look of people observing a distant event that interested but didn't particularly involve them, had watched the terrifying scene. One of them had finally yelled as Isabella Marqueza was dragged, fighting and sobbing, into a waiting station wagon. The rest did nothing to help.

"You people kidnap me off the street," Isabella Marqueza

complained angrily. Her red mouth pouted, part of her routine interrogation act.

"Let me confess to you. Let me be honest, and kind of frank," Carroll said, still going gently. "In the last few years I've had to kidnap a few people like yourself. Call it the new justice. Call it anything you like. Kidnapping's lost most of its glitter for me."

The louder Isabella Marqueza got, the softer Carroll's speaking voice became. "I kind of like the idea of being a kidnapper. I kidnap terrorists. It's got a nice ring to it, you know? Don't you think?"

"I demand to see my lawyer! Goddamn you! My lawyer is Daniel Curzon. You know that name?"

Arch Carroll nodded and shrugged. Daniel Curzon worked for both the PLO and Castro's Cubans in New York.

"Daniel Curzon's a piece of sorry shit. I don't want to hear his name again. I'm serious about that."

Carroll eyed a manila package on his littered desk, a plain-looking folder wrapped in brown string. Inside was his moral justification to do whatever he needed to do right now.

Inside the envelope were a dozen or so black-and-white and color 35-mm photographs of the Shell Oil executive, Jason Miller, and his family, formerly of Rio, all of whom had been murdered. There were also grainy photographs of an American couple who had disappeared in Jamaica, pictures of a Unilever accountant from Colombia, and a man named Jordan who had disappeared last spring. Isabella Marqueza was suspected of murdering all eight individuals.

Carroll continued softly. "Anyway, my name's Arch Carroll. Born right here in New York City. Local boy makes good . . . Son of a cop who was the son of a cop. Not a lot of imagination at work in our family, I'll admit. Just your basic poor working slobs."

Carroll paused briefly and lit up the stub of a cigarette Crusader Rabbit style. "My job is to locate terrorists who threaten the security of the United States. Then, if they're not too strongly politically connected, protected, I try my best to put a stop to them . . . Put another way, you could say I'm a terrorist for the United States. I play by the same rules you do—no rules. So stop talking about Park Avenue lawyers, please. Lawyers are for nice civilized people who play by the rules. Not for us."

Carroll slowly untied the string bow on the manila envelope. Then he slid out the handful of photographs. Casually he passed them to Isabella Marqueza. The pictures were the most obscene pornography he'd ever seen. Still, he remained calm.

"Jason Miller's body. Jason Miller was an engineer for Shell Oil. He was also a financial investigator for the State Department, as you and your people in São Paulo know. A fairly nice man, I understand . . . Information gatherer for State, I'll admit. Basically harmless, though. Another poor working slob."

Carroll made soft clicking noises with his tongue. His eyes briefly met those of Isabella Marqueza.

She was quiet suddenly. His putting-green voice was throwing her off. She obviously hadn't expected to encounter the deck of photographs, either.

"Miller's wife, Judy, here. Alive in this photo. Kind of a nice midwestern smile . . . Two little girls. Their bodies, that is. I have two little girls myself. Two girls, two boys. How could anybody kill little kids, huh?"

Carroll smiled again. He cleared his throat. He needed a

beer—a beer and a stiff shot of Irish would go real good right now. He studied Isabella Marqueza a moment. He had an urge to get up from his desk and whack her. Instead he kept speaking gently.

"In July of last year, you ordered and then participated in the premeditated murders, the political assassination, of all four Millers."

Isabella Marqueza instantly shot up from her seat. "I did nothing of the sort! You prove what you say! No! I did not kill anybody. Never. I don't kill children!"

"Bullshit. That's the end of our friendly discussion. Who the fuck do you think you're kidding?"

With that, Arch Carroll slapped the wrinkled portfolio shut and jammed it back in his lopsided desk drawer. He looked up at Isabella Marqueza again.

"Nobody knows you're here! Do you have that memorized? Nobody's going to know what happened to you after today. That's the truth. Just like the Miller family down in Brazil."

"You're full of shit, Carroll—"

"Yeah? Try me. Push me a little and find out for sure."

"My lawyer, I want to see my lawyer—"

"Never heard of him—"

"I told you his name, Curzon—"

"Did you? I don't remember—"

Isabella Marqueza sighed. She stared at Carroll in silence, her expression one of exquisitely cold hatred. She folded her arms, then sat down again. She crossed and uncrossed her long legs and lit a cigarette.

"Why are you doing this to me? You're crazy."

This was a little better, Carroll thought. He could sense she was melting a little, cracking at the edges.

"Tell me about Jack Jordan down in Colombia. American business accountant. Machine-gunned to death in his driveway. His wife got to watch."

"I never heard of him."

Carroll clucked his tongue and slowly shook his head back and forth. He seemed genuinely disappointed. Sitting behind the bare, bleak office desk, he looked like someone whose best friend had just inexplicably lied to him.

"Isabella . . . Isabella." He gave an exaggerated sigh. "I don't think you get the total picture. I don't think you really understand." He stood up, stretched his arms, fought back a yawn. "You see, you no longer exist. You died suddenly this morning. Taxi accident on East Seventieth Street. Nobody bothered to tell you?"

Carroll was feeling dangerously overloaded now. He didn't want to finish this brutal interrogation. He walked out of the questioning room without saying another word. He'd done his best, he thought as he idly patrolled the long, blurry hallway outside, passing busy secretaries who were tapping away at purring typewriters.

He walked with his head down, talking to no one. Blood pounded furiously in his temples. He was drained and bleached, and his throat was dry. The vision of a cold beer and a shot had rooted itself firmly in his mind, and the image was roaring for attention.

He paused at a water fountain, pressed the button, and let the cold water splash across his face. It was better than nothing. He wiped his puckered lips with the back of his hand, then leaned against the wall. Isabella Marqueza. Green Band. A green ribbon tied neatly, almost cheerfully, around a plastique bomb in a cardboard box.

Questions. Too many disconnected questions. He didn't have any answers. He doubted whether Walter Trentkamp himself could have cracked Isabella Marqueza.

Ordinarily Carroll might have felt bad about the harshness of the Marqueza interrogation. Except he kept seeing the creased snapshot faces of the two senselessly murdered little Miller girls. Those two innocent babies helped put Isabella Marqueza in perspective for him. Beautiful Isabella was a worthless piece of shit.

He finally trudged back to his office, where Isabella Marqueza was waiting.

She looked like a wilting flower. He'd read in her files that she'd joined a GRU terrorist cell in 1978, after which she'd worked for François Monserrat in South America, then in Montreal and Paris, and finally here in New York. Her supposed weakness was that she had little tolerance for discomfort and pain. She'd never had to suffer any in her life. Carroll considered that momentarily, then moved in for the kill.

An hour and a half later Carroll and Isabella Marqueza were finally beginning to communicate. Carroll sipped the day's hundredth coffee. His stomach had begun to scream at him.

"You *were* François Monserrat's mistress here in New York. Come on. We already know about that. Two summers ago. Right here in Nueva York."

Isabella Marqueza sat with her head hanging. She wouldn't look up at Carroll for long stretches of time. Dark sweat stains had spread under her arms. Her right leg kept tapping the floor nervously, but she didn't seem aware of it. She looked ill. Carroll decided to keep up his staccato attack. Stage three of his interrogation.

"Who the *hell* is Monserrat? How does he get his information? How does he get information that no one outside the United States government could possibly get? *Who is he?* Listen . . . listen to me very carefully . . . If you talk to me right now, if you tell me about François Monserrat—just his part in the bombing on Wall Street—if you do that much, I can let you leave here, I promise you. No one will know you were here. Just tell me about the Wall Street bombing. Nothing more than that. Nothing else . . . What does François Monserrat know about the firebombing? . . ."

It took thirty minutes more of cajoling, threatening, and screaming at Marqueza, thirty grueling minutes in which Carroll's voice grew hoarse and his face turned red, thirty minutes during which his shirt stuck to his sweaty body. Finally Isabella Marqueza stood up and shouted at him.

*"Monserrat had nothing to do with it!* He doesn't understand it, either . . . Nobody understands what the bombing is all about. He's looking for Green Band, too! *Monserrat is looking for them, too!"*

How do you *know* that, Isabella? How do you *know* what Monserrat is doing? You must have seen him!"

The woman clapped her hand across her hollow, darkened eyes. "I *haven't* seen him! I *don't* see him. Not ever."

"Then how do you know?"

"There are telephone messages. There are sometimes whispers in private places. *Nobody* sees Monserrat."

"Where is he, Isabella? Is he here in New York? Where the hell is he?

The South American woman shook her head stubbornly. "I don't know that, either."

"What does Monserrat look like these days?"

119

"How should I know that? How should I know anything like that? He changes. Monserrat is always changing. Sometimes dark hair, a mustache. Sometimes gray hair. Dark glasses. Sometimes a beard." She paused. "Monserrat doesn't have a face."

Now conscious of having said too much, Isabella Marqueza had begun to sob loudly. Carroll sat back and rested his head against the grimy office wall. She didn't know anything more; he was almost certain he'd gone as far with her as he could possibly go.

Nobody had anything concrete about Green Band. Only that wasn't possible. Somebody had to know what the hell Green Band wanted. But who?

Carroll looked up at the interrogation room ceiling before he shut his sore and heavy eyes.

Faded, yellowing newspapers, at least a dozen different ones dated October 25, 1929, were spread haphazardly across a heavy oak library-style worktable. The thirty- and forty-point headlines were as jarring now as they must have been fifty-odd years before.

WORST STOCK CRASH EVER; 12,894,650-SHARE DAY SWAMPS MARKET; LEADERS CONFER, FIND CONDITIONS SOUND.

WALL STREET PANIC! RECORD SELLING OF STOCKS! HEAVY FALL IN PRICES!

STOCK PRICES SLUMP $14,000,000,000 IN NATIONWIDE STAMPEDE TO UNLOAD; BANKERS TO SUPPORT MARKET TODAY.

PRICES OF STOCKS CRASH IN HEAVY LIQUIDATION, TOTAL DROP OF BILLIONS.

TWO MILLION SIX HUNDRED THOUSAND SHARES SOLD IN THE FINAL HOUR IN RECORD DECLINE!

MANY INDIVIDUAL ACCOUNTS WIPED OUT
COMPLETELY!

WHEAT SMASHED! CHICAGO PIT IN TURMOIL!

HOOVER PROMISES BUSINESS OF THE COUNTRY
IS STILL SOUND AND PROSPEROUS!

Caitlin Dillon finally stood up from the worktable and its musty newspaper clippings. She stretched her arms high over her head and sighed. She was on the fifth floor on 13 Wall Street, with Anton Birnbaum from the New York Stock Exchange Steering Committee.

Anton Birnbaum was one of America's true financial geniuses, a wizard. If anyone understood that precarious castle of cards called Wall Street, it was Birnbaum. He had started, Caitlin knew, as an insignificant office boy at the age of eleven. Then he'd worked his way up through the market hierarchy to control his own huge investment house. Caitlin respected him more than any other man in the money business. Even at eighty-three his mind remained as sharp as a blade, and a mischievous light still burned in his eyes. She knew that now and then Anton Birnbaum looked her over appraisingly, delighted to be in the company of a young, attractive, and undeniably sharp-witted woman.

Once, there had even been a bizarre rumor on Wall Street that Birnbaum might be having a final fling with Caitlin Dillon. The relentless, often ridiculous gossip on the male-dominated Street was perhaps the most difficult business reality for any woman to face or stomach. If a woman broker or lawyer was seen having drinks or dinner with a man, it was assumed they were having a romance. Early on, Caitlin had realized that the sleazy, degrading practice was the way some men reduced the threat women posed to their power base on Wall Street.

Actually, Caitlin had met Anton Birnbaum years before, while she was still at Wharton. Her thesis adviser had invited the financier for a guest lecture during her final year. After one of his characteristically iconoclastic talks, Birnbaum had consented to private sessions with a few of the business school's brightest students. One of them turned out to be Caitlin Dillon, about whom Birnbaum later told her adviser: "She is extremely intense, and quite brilliant. Her only flaw is that she is beautiful. I mean that quite seriously. It will be a problem for her on Wall Street. It will be a serious handicap."

When Caitlin Dillon graduated from Wharton, Anton Birnbaum nevertheless hired her as an assistant at his brokerage firm. Within a year Caitlin was one of his personal assistants. Unlike many of the people he hired, Caitlin would disagree with the great financier when she felt he was off base. Early in 1978 she correctly called the market bottom and then the top right before the bloody October massacre. Anton Birnbaum began to listen even more closely to his young, and still very intense, assistant after that.

During that period, Caitlin also began to make the Wall Street and Washington connections she needed for the future. Her first job with Anton Birnbaum provided an education she couldn't have paid to receive. Caitlin found the financier totally impossible to work for, but somehow she worked for him, which proved to Birnbaum that she was as outstanding as he had initially thought she was.

"Anton, who would benefit from a stock market crash right now? Let's make ourselves a complete list, a physical list, as some kind of starting place."

"All right, let's explore that avenue, then. People who would benefit from a market crash?" Birnbaum took a legal pad and pencil in hand. "A multinational that has a huge discrepancy to hide?"

"That's one. Or the Soviets. They'd possibly benefit—in terms of world prestige, anyway . . ."

"Then perhaps one of the Third World madmen? I believe Qaddafi is psychologically capable of something like this. Perhaps capable of getting the necessary financing as well."

Caitlin looked at her watch, a functional, ten-year-old Bulova, a gift from her father one Christmas back home in Ohio. "I don't know what to try next. What are they waiting for? What in God's name happens when the market opens on Monday?"

Birnbaum took off his horn-rimmed eyeglasses and rubbed the bridge of his bulbous nose, which was reddened and deeply indented. "Will the market even open, Caitlin? The French want it to. They're insisting they will open in Paris. I don't know, though. Perhaps it's one of their typical bluffs."

"Which means the Arabs want their French banks open. Some toady in Paris wants to take advantage of this awful situation—or hopes to get some of the money out before there's a complete panic."

Birnbaum replaced his glasses and gazed at Caitlin for a moment. Then he gave one of his characteristic shrugs, a huffy gesture of the shoulders that was barely perceptible. "President Kearney is at least talking with the French. They've never appreciated him, though. We haven't been able to placate them since Kissinger."

"What about London? What about Geneva? How about right here in New York?"

"They're all watching France, I'm afraid. France is threatening to open its market, business as usual on Monday. The French, my dear, are being carefully, carefully orchestrated. But by whom? And for what possible reason? What is coming next?" He placed his fingertips together, making a small cathedral of his ancient hands. He narrowed his eyes and looked thoughtfully at Caitlin.

Caitlin and the old man were quiet for several moments. Over the years they had become comfortable with long periods of silent thought when they were examining a problem together. Caitlin watched as the financier took out a cigar, his only remaining vice, and stroked and lit it methodically.

Within moments the room was filled with a soft blue fog. Birnbaum studied the glowing tip of the cigar, then set it down in a well-worn brass ashtray. "I'll tell you something, my dear. In all my years on the Street, I have never felt this apprehensive. Not even in October of 1929."

Bendel's on Fifty-seventh Street had been open all day Sunday for the usual neurotic rush of Christmas shopping. Store sales were dramatically down, however, affected by the Wall Street panic and the financial uncertainty reigning not only in New York, but all across the United States.

François Monserrat entered the very chic and expensive department store at a little past five that evening. Another snowstorm was darkly threatening outside. Winter skies had descended like a heavy curtain over the entire East Coast.

Monserrat was wearing thick wire-rimmed glasses and an unmemorable gray tweed overcoat. He also wore a matching hat and black gloves, all of which created a monochromatic impression. The wire-rimmed glasses magnified his eyes for observers but didn't distort his view of the world. He'd had them especially made by a lens grinder on the rue des Postes in Bizerte, a city in Tunisia.

Monserrat quietly marveled as he got off a crowded elevator onto one of the upper floors. There was nowhere else, no city he knew of, in which one consistently saw quite so many provocative and stunning women. Even the store's perfume demonstrators were dreamily sensual and exotic. A stylishly anorectic black girl approached and asked if he'd like to experience the new Opium.

"I've already experienced it. In Thailand, my dear," François Monserrat answered with a shy smile and an effete wave of the hand.

The demonstrator smiled back, slinking off politely, but seductively, to try the next customer.

A thick gallery of shoppers hugging glittering shopping bags from other famous department stores moved slowly before Monserrat's wandering eyes. "Winter Wonderland" played gaily from a hidden stereo system. It was taxing and exceedingly difficult to move through the crowd; it was more like visiting a New York disco than a store at Christmastime.

François Monserrat cautiously made his way toward the rear of the store. With some amusement he wondered how Juan Carlos would have reacted to the blatant outrage of capitalism that was Henri Bendel's . . . In 1979—because his flagrant need for publicity had finally rendered him ineffective—Ilych Sanchez, "Juan Carlos," had been quietly retired by the Soviet GRU. Carlos had, in fact, been brought to live in the one capital city where he was reasonably safe from political assassination—Moscow itself.

That same year François Monserrat expanded his tight-fisted

control of North and South America to include Western Europe. Carlos's protégés, Wadi Haddad and George Habbash, reluctantly came under Monserrat's widening sphere. A completely new philosophy for Soviet terror had begun: strategic and controlled terror; terror more often than not programmed by Moscow's sophisticated computers.

By its very nature, the world of the terrorist was a foggy, vaporous place, and information had a tendency to be either sketchy or hyperbolic. The sinewy avenues of communication and news were vague at times; at other times they were overloaded with rumor and innuendo. Given these conditions, it wasn't long before all manner of terrorist acts were being attributed to Monserrat and his people. The murder of Anwar Sadat, the attempted assassination of Pope John Paul II, the Provo bombings in central London . . .

As he strolled through the store, Monserrat reflected on his reputation with a measure of pride. What did it matter if he'd been responsible for this act or that one—when his only real goal, his sole driving force, was the total disruption and eventual fall of the West? A dead Egyptian president. A wounded pope. A few Irish bombs. These amounted to nothing more than a few grains of sand on a beach. What François Monserrat was interested in changing was the direction of the tide itself . . .

The bubbling crowd inside Bendel's ebbed and flowed. The predominantly female shoppers milled anxiously in all directions around François Monserrat. Finally he saw the woman he'd followed. She was sifting through a long rack of cocktail dresses, always thinking of her appearance, always defining her existence through her beautiful reflection.

Monserrat concealed himself behind a display case of

sweaters and continued to watch. He felt a certain coldness in the center of his head, as if his brain had become a solid block of ice. It was a feeling he knew in certain situations. Where other men would experience the uncontrollable rush of adrenaline, Monserrat experienced what he thought of as "the chill." It was almost as if he'd been born with a chemical imbalance.

Every man who passed checked out Isabella Marqueza carefully. So did several of the chic, well-dressed women shoppers. Her fur jacket was left casually open. As she turned, swiveled left or right, a tantalizing glimpse of her breasts floated deliciously into the cleavage. Of all the striking women in the department store, Isabella was the most desirable, the most visually dramatic, by Monserrat's personal standards.

Now he observed Isabella slink off toward a dressing room. He put his hands in the pockets of his overcoat, caught a reflection of himself in a mirror as he moved, then paused outside the dressing room.

He walked past the closed door, studied the throngs around him pursuing Christmas gifts with forced gaiety, and then darted back the way he had come.

Pretending to examine a silk shirt, like a wealthy East Side husband picking out a stocking stuffer, he listened outside the dressing room. Coming closer, he could hear the whisper of clothing as it peeled away from Isabella's body.

In one swift move he stepped inside the tiny room. Isabella Marqueza swung around in astonishment.

Why did she always look so utterly beautiful? Warmth that might have been desire flowed within him. He took his hands from his coat. She was wearing only panties, tight and sheer and black. The cocktail dress she intended to try on hung limply in one hand.

He thought she would have looked very exciting in it.

"François! What are you doing here?"

"I had to see you," he whispered. "I heard you had a little trouble. You must tell me everything."

Isabella Marqueza frowned. "They let me go. What were they going to hold me for, anyhow? They had nothing but a stupid bluff, François." She smiled, but the expression couldn't conceal a look of worry.

He pressed one gloved hand lightly against her breasts. He could smell Bal a Versailles, her favorite perfume. His as well. Inwardly, inaudibly, he sighed.

"Are you being followed, Isabella?"

"I don't think so."

"Are you sure?" Monserrat asked.

"As sure as I can be. Why?" A troubled look clouded her dark eyes again. He could see her wince. From beyond the door of the dressing room he heard the Christmas Muzak, relentlessly bland and empty of all meaning.

"Good. Good," he whispered soothingly.

Isabella's mouth fell open and she quickly stepped back against the wall. There was really no place to go in the tiny dressing room. "François, don't you believe me? I told them nothing. Absolutely nothing."

"Then why did they let you go, my love? I need an explanation."

"Don't you know me any better than that? Don't you? Please . . ."

I know you only too well, François Monserrat thought as he moved closer.

The tiny handgun made an inconsequential, guttural spit. Isabella Marqueza moaned softly, then collapsed on the shiny black-and-white tiles. Monserrat was already out of the dressing room and walking quickly, inconspicuously, toward the nearest exit.

She'd talked. She'd told them too much. She had admitted knowing him, and that was enough.

She'd been broken during the interrogation, skillfully, in a way she might not even have truly recognized. Monserrat had heard the news not ten minutes after Carroll had finished with her.

He burst into the cold wind that was raking West Fifty-seventh Street. He turned a corner, to all intents and purposes an ordinary man losing himself in the crowds that hunted the spirit of Christmas with red-faced eagerness.

# Chapter 11

SHINY WHITE CABIN cruisers and myriad other expensive ships had begun to haunt the perimeter of lower Manhattan. More than one inflatable rubber boat was tied to the railing of the seawall at the Battery Park City esplanade. In fact, a considerable number of individuals were willing to use the most unorthodox means to return to their Wall Street offices, whether or not such a return was authorized.

Anton Birnbaum appeared live on the "Today" show. The face of the financier was highly familiar, though few could have matched it with an equally familiar name they'd come upon scores of times in newspapers and magazines.

"Neither the American nor the New York Stock Exchange will sell a single share this Monday. NASDAQ, the over-the-counter market automated quotation system, will be down as well. The commodities exchange in New York will not open, nor will the metals exchange. This is complete madness," he told the early morning viewers.

It got worse.

The regular Monday auction of the United States Treasury bills wouldn't take place. Among the chipped and pocked tombstones of Trinity Church cemetery, no drug dealers would palm out their usual glassine envelopes of cocaine.

No messengers would trudge the streets with even more valuable envelopes filled with securities, valuable stock certificates, multimillion-dollar checks, and legal documents.

None of the all-male luncheon clubs would serve up their bland, overcivilized fare at Monday noon.

All the usual activities of the Wall Street community would be stillborn. It would be as if the modern money world had not yet been invented. Either that, or it had been completely destroyed.


"I want you to have lunch with me, Mr. Carroll," Caitlin Dillon had said over the telephone. "Is twelve-fifteen today possible? It's important."

It was a call that took Carroll completely by surprise. He'd been going through his elaborate back files—sifting through the various terrorist organizations in his search for some clue to Green Band—when the call came. The idea of a civilized lunch with a beautiful woman was the last thing on his mind.

"I want you to meet somebody," Caitlin had told him.

"Who?"

"A man called Freddie Hotchkiss. He's important on Wall Street."

She had a rich telephone voice. Music in a tuneless world, Carroll thought, little symphonies coming out of the impersonal Bell system. He put his feet on the desk and tilted his head back against the wall. With his eyes shut, he tried to bring Caitlin Dillon's face firmly into his mind. Untouchable, he remembered.

"Freddie Hotchkiss is connected with a man called Michel Chevron," Caitlin said.

"The name rings a bell," Carroll said, trying to place it. "Several bells."

"The information I have is that Chevron's a wheel in the stolen securities market and—this is what should *really* interest you, Mr. Carroll—there are rumors of a link with François Monserrat."

"Monserrat?" Carroll opened his eyes. "So why can't we go direct to Chevron? Why go through this Hotchkiss?"

"Do I detect impatience?"

"When it comes to Monserrat, I'm impatient."

Carroll could hear Caitlin exchange quick words with somebody, and then she said, "The point is that we can't get a direct connection with Michel Chevron unless—and this is a big unless—Hotchkiss is prepared to confirm some of our information. When he does, O'Brien will set up a meeting for you and Chevron just as soon as you can get to Paris— he's got the clout. But, Chevron is a French citizen—unless we get some hard data on him, we'll never get the cooperation of the French police." Caitlin paused. It made sense, Carroll was thinking. "What I'm saying is that you may have to lean on Freddie Hotchkiss a little. Isn't that the expression the police use?"

"Something like that," Carroll said, laughing as if there were some intimate conspiracy between them. "I guess I'll see you for lunch."

Now Carroll loosened his favorite crimson-and-blue school tie before he took the first inviting sip of Sam Smith Pale Ale in the dining room of Christ Cella on East Forty-sixth Street. He found ties uncomfortable, which was one of the reasons he rarely wore them. Actually, he thought neckties pretty much without a purpose, unless you impulsively wanted to hang yourself or get inside some overpriced New York steakhouse.

The restaurant required a dress jacket and respectable tie. Otherwise it was comfortable enough, with something of the atmosphere of a men's club. Besides, it felt damned good to be sitting here with Caitlin Dillon.

Christ Cella's steaks were sixteen ounces at a minimum, choice prime, and aged properly. The lobsters started at two pounds. The waiters were immaculate and subservient, city cool to a fault. For the moment, Carroll was enjoying the hell out of himself. For this moment only, Green Band had receded from his mind. Wall Street might have been on another planet.

"One of the first things I learned in New York is that you have to make the steakhouse a ritual if you're going to survive on Wall Street." Caitlin smiled across the fading white linen. She'd already told Carroll that she was originally from Lima, Ohio, and he could almost believe it, listening to her unusual perspective of New York City living.

"Even to survive in the SEC, you have to know the conventions. Especially if you're a young 'gal,' as a particular brokerage house CEO once called me. 'I'd like you to meet the new young gal from SEC.'"

She said the last phrase with such casual, twinkling malice, it almost sounded nice.

Carroll started to laugh. Then they both laughed. Heads turned at other tables, staid faces looked around. Was somebody daring to have fun here? Who?

Carroll and Caitlin were waiting for the arrival of Duncan "Freddie" Hotchkiss, who was fashionably late despite the fact that Caitlin had specifically asked him to be on time.

A shrimp cocktail eventually found its way to Carroll's place. The shellfish was perfect and overpriced by at least three hundred percent.

Carroll asked Caitlin about Wall Street—what it was like from her vantage point at the SEC. In answer, Caitlin began regaling him with a few of her favorite horror stories about the Street. She happened to have a treasury of absolutely true, mind-bending stories that circulated in the inner sanctums but were usually not shared with outsiders . . . for reasons Carroll soon began to fully understand.

"Embezzlement has never been easier on Wall Street," Caitlin said. Her brown eyes sparkled with dark humor. Carroll thought how easy it would be to fall over the imaginary edge, to drown in those eyes—a very pleasant end indeed.

"The computer makes 'cooking the books' an exciting challenge to anyone modestly gifted in the area. Of course, the potential thief has to know the program code and have access to the data bank. In short, he or she must be in a position of absolute trust.

"One young economist we prosecuted worked at the Federal Reserve Bank of New York. At twenty-seven he went off and bought a summer house in the Hamptons, then a new Mercedes convertible *and* a Porsche, then a sable coat for his dear mom. Along the way he managed to get in debt close to three-quarters of a million dollars."

"He's still working for the government?" Carroll finished the second shrimp. "In your story, I mean?"

"He quits Treasury right about this time—for a much

better-paying job. Only he takes with him the security access codes that allow him to find out enough to buy or sell on the credit and stock markets. A very, very profitable bit of knowledge. He's got the ultimate on insider trading information . . . You know how it fell through? His mother called the SEC. She was worried that he was spending all this money without any job she could see. His mother turned him in because he gave her a sable fur.

"There was an outfit called OPM Financial Services—that stood for other people's money, I swear to God. In the seventies, Michael Weiss and Anthony Caputo opened their company over a Manhattan candy store. Along their merry way, Michael and Anthony managed to defraud Manufacturers Hanover Leasing, Crocker National Bank, and Lehman Brothers for about a hundred and eighty million. Don't ever feel bad if you lose a little money on the market. You're in very good company."

"I'm real lucky in that respect—I don't have any money to lose. Why is it allowed to happen? What about the SEC?"

Carroll was already beginning to feel slightly incensed, though he'd never personally lost a dime on Wall Street. Stocks and bonds and securities had always seemed Olympian things to him, arcane matters in which other classes of people dabbled.

"It's fairly simple, really. As I said in the beginning, these kinds of stories are rarely told outside Wall Street."

"I'm honored."

"You should be . . . The Wall Street banks, the brokerage houses, investment bankers, even the computer companies—they know that the success of their marketplace depends on confidence and trust. If they prosecuted all the embezzlers, if they ever admitted how easy it was, how many stock certificates are actually stolen each year, they'd *all* be out of business. They'd have about the same reputation as used-car salesmen—which some of them *ought* to have . . . The point is, Wall Street is more afraid of bad publicity than of the actual thefts."

Suddenly Caitlin was silent.

"Caitlin, will you forgive me? I'm so very sorry."

Freddie Hotchkiss had finally arrived. It was one o'clock. He was forty-five minutes late for their business lunch.

Carroll looked up and saw a man with thinning blond hair and a ridiculous, innocent grin on his face. He had pale, water-blue eyes and a face as round and as expressionless as a pie tin. He would have looked eight years old if it hadn't been for the lines on his face.

What did they do down on Wall Street? Carroll wondered. Were there genetic laboratories dedicated to the preservation of the pure-blooded, uncontaminated WASP strain? All of them turning out plump little Freddie Hotchkisses?

Caitlin had told Carroll that Hotchkiss was becoming legendary on Wall Street. He was a very hot partner at his firm, a frequent emissary to both the West Coast and Europe—where he had extensive dealings with key European bankers as well as movie moguls.

"Truly sorry about the time." Hotchkiss looked anything but sorry. "I completely lost track. Roughing it out in the pied-à-terre on Park since the trouble on Friday. Kim and the kids are staying down in Boca Raton, her mom and dad's place. Ah, what exquisite timing you have, sir."

A Christ Cella waiter had spotted Hotchkiss arriving and had scurried to the table for the all-important drink order. Carroll stared at Hotchkiss. This was a type he wasn't comfortable with and didn't particularly like. Poor bastard had to rough it on Park Avenue. Carroll thought his heart would break.

"I'd like a Kir. Anyone for seconds?" Hotchkiss asked.

"I'll have another Sam Smith." Carroll was *trying* to be good: no hard liquor, no neat shots of Irish. He was also trying not to say something impulsive, something that might lose him the advantage of surprise with Freddie Hotchkiss. It might be fun, he decided, to lean on this character.

"No, thank you, nothing for me," Caitlin said.

"Freddie, this is Arch Carroll. Mr. Carroll is the head of the United States Antiterrorist Division. Out of the DIA."

Freddie Hotchkiss beamed enthusiastically. "Oh, yes, I've read *volumes* about you specialized police folks. The sooner someone can bring a little order and reason to this whole unfortunate affair, the better, I say. I heard yesterday, or maybe I read it somewhere, that there is a Libyan hit team right here in New York. Actually *residing* in Manhattan."

"I doubt it's the Libyans we're looking for," Carroll remarked casually. His darker eyes held Hotchkiss's pale blue ones for an extra beat as he sipped his Sam Smith. He was going to attack.

He leaned forward, softly nudging a finger into Freddie's pale blue shirt, seeing a faint expression of surprise float across the man's puffy face. It amazed Carroll that such a face was capable of expression.

"I'd like to cut out the chitchat bullshit, okay? You're an hour late, and we're pressed for time. I have absolutely no personal interest in you, Freddie, you understand that? I don't think I like you, but that doesn't matter. I'm only interested in a man named Michel Chevron."

"He's not one for small talk, Freddie." Caitlin threw a quick glance at Carroll, and he thought it was the most intimate thing he'd experienced in years.

Freddie Hotchkiss, meanwhile, seemed to have stopped

breathing. He looked down at Carroll's finger sticking in his chest. "I'm not sure . . . I don't think I understand. I mean, I've heard of Michel Chevron, of course."

"Of course you have," Carroll said.

"Tall, austere-looking French gentleman," Caitlin intervened. "Plush Louis Quatorze offices on rue de Faubourg in Paris. Very affluent digs in the heart of Beverly Hills."

She flipped open a leather-bound notebook.

"Let me see if I can jog your memory. Mm, oh, yes . . . on February nineteenth of last year, you visited Michel Chevron's Beverly Hills office. You stayed for approximately two hours. On March third, you visited the Los Angeles offices again. Also on July ninth, July eleventh, July twelfth. In October you visited Chevron's Paris office. You had dinner with Chevron that night at Lasserre. Remember? Can you place him yet?"

Freddie Hotchkiss had slowly begun clasping and unclasping his plump, hairless hands. The watery eyes were even more watery.

"We've known for over two years that Michel Chevron is the largest stolen securities and bond dealer in Europe and the Middle East. We also know he has a personal relationship with François Monserrat," Caitlin continued. "We know a great deal about your own security-trading abilities as well. Right now we need to know exactly *who* else Chevron deals with, and we need a rough idea of the nature of these deals, a general feel for the Euro-Asian black market. That's why I thought we all should have lunch." Caitlin Dillon smiled.

Right then, Freddie Hotchkiss found the strength to frown derisively. He began to snap back, to rally strongly.

"Really. You don't expect me to talk about private *and* absolutely legal business dealings here in this restaurant? You had

138

better have all your subpoenas and your Justice Department lawyers ready, if you believe that will happen. I can assure you, it won't be *done* over lunch . . . Good afternoon, Caitlin, Mr., uh, Carroll."

Arch Carroll sat up very straight. He leaned across the dining table and flicked his finger three times very hard against Freddie Hotchkiss's starched white shirt collar.

*Thwack.*

*Thwack.*

*Thwack.*

"Just sit tight now, okay? Just put your nice soft ass back down on the chair, Freddie. Try to relax. Okay?" Hotchkiss was so astonished, he obeyed.

In a soft voice, which to Carroll's ears sounded mildly seductive, Caitlin said, "February twenty-first—you deposited one hundred and twenty-six thousand dollars in Geneva, Switzerland. February twenty-sixth—you deposited another one hundred and fourteen thousand. April seventeenth—you deposited . . . is this a typo? . . . four hundred and sixty-two thousand? April twenty-fourth—thirty-one thousand . . . Small potatoes, that one . . ."

"What Caitlin has been politely trying to point out to you, Freddie, is that you are a second-rate thief!" Carroll leaned back and smiled at Hotchkiss, who now sat as expressionless as a ventriloquist's dummy.

Carroll raised his voice above the restaurant's usual buzz. "Poor Kim, the kiddies, wintering down in Boca Raton. They have no idea, I'll bet. Tennis pals at the club. The boys at the yacht club. They don't know, either . . . *You ought to be in jail.* You shouldn't be allowed to eat here, you're such a sad piece of shit."

Other diners in the expensive restaurant had stopped

eating. In a state that resembled a communal hypnotic trance, they stared across the room.

Carroll finally lowered his voice. He pointed toward a corner table where two men in dull gray suits were seated. "Those two guys? See them? They can't even afford to eat the nibbles here. See, they're sharing a three-dollar ginger ale. That's the FBI for you . . . Anyway, they're going to arrest you, right here and now . . . *or*, Fred, you're going to tell us a long and very convincing story about Michel Chevron. It's absolutely your move. And yes, it's going to happen right here in the restaurant.

"*Then*, in that second case I mentioned, you get to go home absolutely scot-free to the pied-à-terre on Park Avenue. No problems, 'cause then you're my main man, see."

Arch Carroll dramatically crossed his two fingers. "We're tight, like that. Except, of course, you're the finger on the bottom."

Freddie Hotchkiss slumped pathetically at the table. He hesitated, then slowly began to tell yet another Wall Street horror story

This one was about Monsieur Michel Chevron. It was a truly fascinating story of the most exclusive rat pack of thieves in the world. All of them very respected bankers, high-priced lawyers, successful stockbrokers. Every single one of them was in a position of absolute public trust.

Was this Green Band? Arch Carroll couldn't help wondering.

Was Green Band a powerful international cartel of the richest investment bankers and businessmen in the world? What would be their motivation?

Carroll finally signaled to the two FBI guys patiently waiting at the corner table.

"Read him his rights and arrest this guy now . . . Oh, and

Freddie? I told a white lie about letting you go scot-free ... Have your lawyer call my lawyer in the morning. Ciao."

Mike Caruso was outside the restaurant when Arch Carroll finally appeared. Carroll's lieutenant, a devotee of summer who never embraced the winter season, was wearing a garish beach shirt beneath his overcoat. He beckoned to Carroll. Both policemen huddled at the far edge of the sidewalk.

"I just got a report on our friend Isabella Marqueza," Caruso said. "Somebody murdered her in Bendel's. She was shot four times. At point-blank range," he added in the offhand manner of someone immunized against murders. "It freaked out all the Christmas shoppers."

"Yeah, I'm sure it would." Carroll was silent a second. He tried to imagine Isabella Marqueza dead. "Somebody thought she talked too much. Somebody was keeping close tabs on her."

Caruso nodded. "Somebody who knew all of her movements, Arch. Or *yours*."

A ragged wind blew down East Forty-sixth Street, whipping discarded newspapers around. Carroll plunged his hands inside the pockets of his coat and stared at the cold, grim city surrounding him. He liked this investigation less and less.

He pointed to the doorway of Christ Cella. "Nice place to eat, Mickey. Next time you want to blow a couple of hundred on lunch."

Caruso nodded. He tucked in a flap of his flowered shirt. "I already had a Sabrett."

# Chapter 12

THE FOLLOWING MORNING, eighty-three-year-old Anton Birnbaum, appearing on a special edition of the PBS show "Wall Street Week," explained why the destruction of Manhattan's financial district did not exactly signal the end of the civilized world.

"The *major* American market was indeed knocked out this past Friday. More markets exist out there, however—believe it or not—and they may just possibly become the beneficiaries of this disaster ... These markets are the midwestern, the Pacific, and the Philadelphia exchanges. They handle local issues as well as certain board listings. If Joe Investor has to sell fifty shares of A T and T to meet the balloon payment on his mortgage, his local broker may well be able to make a deal for him outside New York. Of course, he may not find a buyer at a price even close to what he's asking.

"Obviously," Birnbaum went on, "Chicago is where the significant action is this week. Between the midwest exchange and the two premier commodity exchanges, there are still plenty of opportunities for everyone to lose a lot of money."

Even as he gave this purposely calming and reassuring speech, Anton Birnbaum knew that the existing situation was more tragic than he dared admit. Like almost everyone intimately connected with the market, he fully expected a crash.

In a way, somewhere deep in the recesses of his mind, he almost welcomed the purification rite, so very long overdue. As of Tuesday morning, the venerable financier had no idea how large a part he himself would play in Green Band.

# Chapter 13

*Paris, France*

PARIS . . . a powerful man named Michel Chevron . . . Green Band . . .

The idea of the magnificent city filled Carroll with something akin to dread. Even as he sat inside a dark blue State Department limousine, riding down the rue Saint-Honoré, Carroll didn't want to look out at the streets. He didn't want to acknowledge that he was truly back in the splendid French capital.

The street sounds he heard pressing against the limousine were like the rattling of old bones. For Carroll, this Paris was a city of sharply painful memories. This Paris was Nora and himself in another age and time. This Paris was a fading decal imprinted with the spectral shapes of two young, carefree honeymooners who wandered all the boulevards, holding hands, who stopped to kiss impulsively every so often, who couldn't keep from touching each other constantly even in the most casual of ways.

Carroll stared at the two American flags that flapped regally on the bumpers of the luxury car. Make believe you're somewhere else, he told himself.

Christ, though, the memories kept coming back like a forceful tide. Nora sipping café au lait on the crowded boulevard Saint-Germain. Nora smiling and laughing as they made all the tourist stops—the Eiffel Tower, Montparnasse, the banks of the Seine, the Latin quarter.

Carroll felt a tightening around his throat. It was a sense of the unfairness that had ended Nora's life, and it crowded him uncomfortably now.

Near the Sorbonne, a man with a reptilian face crouched and pretended to hurl a spoiled grapefruit at the smooth, cruising symbol of American wealth and power.

Seated in the gray velvet rear salon of the car, Carroll flinched at the sight of the man. But when the prospect of the grapefruit assault had passed, he relaxed a little and tried to shake his head free of the fog of overseas jet lag. He opened his bulky Green Band file and began to look over his scribbled notes. He knew work would be a salvation from the memories of this town. If he dug into his material on Green Band, he could make himself a foxhole safe from the scenes that passed by.

How could Green Band have isolated itself so well from the terrorist underground? How could there be no rumor, no concrete leads, anywhere out on the street? And what was the ultimate reason for the New York financial district bombing?

Something else occurred to Carroll: What if he was still looking in all the wrong places?

"Société Générale bank, monsieur. *Vous êtes arrivé*. You

have arrived safely, comfortably, I hope . . . This is le Quartier de la Bourse."

Arch Carroll climbed out of the limousine and slowly walked inside Société Générale.

The bank building itself, the cavernous lobby, the hand-operated elevators, were all carved stone and exquisitely gilded. Everything was regal and impressive, the kind of background against which American tourists would take pictures to later put in albums.

The prestigious French financial institution reminded Carroll quite powerfully of another era. Compared with Wall Street, it was visually softer and more civilized to behold. It was as if money were not the major game being played here. The aim was something less vulgar, something even spiritual, perhaps. In actuality, le Quartier de la Bourse occupied the former site of a Dominican convent. No matter the history of the place, no matter the artistic appeal, it was the same religion you found on Wall Street. Gentility and manners, these were only illusions.

Michel Chevron, Carroll thought, remembering why he was there. Chevron and the massive, secretive European black market.

The question was whether Chevron really fit into the frustrating Green Band puzzle and whether there was a bridge, even a frail one, linking Chevron with François Monserrat.

The bank executive's personal assistant was a thin, sickly-looking man of perhaps twenty-eight. He had white-blond hair, closely cropped, almost punk in style. He sat stiffly behind an antique desk, which in New York would have seemed inappropriate for anyone except a chief executive. He wore a double-breasted pin-striped suit, a funereal, mauve four-in-hand tie.

Carroll tried to imagine applying for a loan from this chilly character, something for home repair, maybe, a room extension, or an underground sprinkler system. He could just see the bank assistant sniffling over the application papers with an expression of mild disgust. He knew this particular assistant would turn him down flat, possibly even laugh at him.

"My name is Archer Carroll. I'm here from New York to see Monsieur Chevron. I spoke to someone yesterday on the telephone."

"Yes, to me." The bank assistant addressed him as a country gentleman would address a stable hand on the subject of a gelding's health. "Director Chevron has provided fifteen minutes . . . at eleven forty-five."

Observing the bank assistant's manner and tone, Carroll had the impression that only a very few names could have been substituted for "Director Chevron" in the assistant's reply—names like de Gaulle or Napoleon. Maybe even the Lord God Almighty.

"Director has an important lunch at twelve. You will please wait. The sofa for waiting is there, Monsieur Carroll."

Arch Carroll nodded his head slowly. Reluctantly he wandered over to a tight nest of art deco couches. He sat down and clenched his hands together. He was trying to fight back anger now, seething anger. On the telephone the bank assistant had set up a meeting firmly for eleven o'clock. He was right on time, and he'd traveled several thousand miles to be here.

Michel Chevron was right behind those heavy oak doors, he kept thinking, probably laughing up his well-tailored sleeve at the ugly American outside in reception . . .

He steadily drummed his fingers on his knee. His right

loafer tapped against the elegant marble floor. At fifteen minutes to twelve, the bank assistant set down his slender silver fountain pen. He looked up from a thick sheaf of paperwork. He smacked his purplish lips before he spoke.

"You may see Director Chevron now. Will you please follow me?"

A moment or so later, Director Michel Chevron, a tall man with an equine face and shock of ink-black hair that stood up on his head like a fuzzy yarmulke, said, "Mr. Carroll, so good of you to come to Paris," almost as if this transatlantic journey were something Carroll did every other day of the week.

Carroll was ushered into an intimidating, old-world chief executive's office. Tall, glass-enclosed bookcases filled with antiquarian books crowded one paneled wall. Along the other, there were crimson-draped casement windows looking out onto a narrow gray stone terrace. The ceiling was at least twelve feet high, beautifully sculpted, ornamented with grinning bronze cherubs. A glass chandelier hung down like the world's heaviest key chain.

Michel Chevron remained standing behind his massive desk. He was obviously impressed with himself, his position, and all the trappings of success that surrounded him. A regal Fragonard hung directly behind the bank executive.

The Frenchman began to speak rapid, excellent English as soon as his assistant left the room. His tone remained cool and superior, and Carroll felt inferior all over again.

"There is a slight problem, Monsieur Carroll. A regrettable circumstance, beyond anyone's control. I'm very sorry, but I have an important engagement at Taillevent. The restaurant, monsieur? The rest of my afternoon is equally bad . . . I can spare these few moments with you only."

Arch Carroll could suddenly feel a very hot place in his stomach. He knew the sensation well, and he tried to ignore it, but a familiar fuse was burning. When the spark reached close to his emotional arsenal, there was very little he could do to stop the explosion.

"All right, then just shut the hell up now," Carroll said, raising his voice suddenly. "I don't have time to be civil anymore. You kept me waiting through my polite and civil period."

The French bank executive broke into a disdainful smile. "Monsieur, you don't seem to understand whose country you're in now. This is not America. You have no authority whatsoever here. I freely consented to see you, in the spirit of international cooperation only."

Carroll immediately reached into his coat pocket and sent a light tan envelope spinning across Chevron's handsome desk.

"Here's your spirit of international cooperation. A warrant for your arrest. It's signed by the commissaire de police, Monsieur Blanche of the Sûreté. I met with him before I came here. The formal charges include extortion, bribery of public officials, fraud. I'm honored to be the one to deliver the good news to you."

Arch Carroll couldn't help smiling. His only regret was that Chevron's huffy assistant wasn't there.

Michel Chevron sat down heavily on his chair.

He covered his face, now drained of all color, with his long, elegantly manicured fingers. His features appeared to have imploded, so that the face looked crinkled, like a concertina devoid of air. Carroll loved the look.

"All right, Mr. Carroll. You've made your point. Why exactly have you come here? What information is it that you wish to extract from me?"

Carroll eased himself onto the chair across from Michel Chevron. The Frenchman's voice was still cool and controlled, even if his features had undergone an unflattering transformation.

"For starters, I'd like to know about the European and Middle Eastern black markets. I need specific names, places, specific dates. *How* the black market is structured, the principals involved. And I want to hear all about François Monserrat."

Chevron cleared his throat hoarsely. "You have no idea what you're saying, what you're asking of me. You have no idea the predicament you're placing me in. We are speaking of billions of dollars. We are speaking of participants of a less than savory nature . . . The French Corso . . . the Italian Cosa Nostra."

Chevron seemed to wipe imaginary crumbs from his fingertips now. He sat back in his chair, and Carroll could see tiny stars of perspiration glistening on the man's forehead. Even the impressive black hair seemed to have lost its color. Carroll felt relaxed and confident for the first time since he'd arrived in Paris.

"I'm listening," he said. "Keep going. I love stories about the Cosa Nostra."

But Michel Chevron had already spoken the last words of his life. The oak doors into the executive suite splintered and crashed open.

For one frightening, incomprehensible moment Carroll imagined that what had happened on Wall Street was repeating itself in Paris. He jumped from his chair and turned to face the shattered door.

Three heavily armed men in trench coats had come from the director's reception area. Each had a machine pistol drawn.

In the narrow corridor behind them stood Michel Chevron's blond assistant, armed with a small black Beretta.

Carroll's lingering jet lag suddenly left him. He was already diving across the floor. Glass and expensive wood were everywhere around him. Machine pistol explosions slashed through the previously secure and elegant office suite.

The terrifying volley nailed Michel Chevron against the wall. His body arched spastically, then spun to the floor. His blue suit was instantly blood soaked. Particles of bone and flesh floated through ghostly spirals of gunsmoke in the office suite.

The professional assailants now switched their attention to Carroll. Hollow-headed slugs thudded like hammer blows into the oak-paneled walls all around him.

His heart pounding, Carroll crawled beyond the heavy drapes, which fanned the air as bullets ripped through the fabric. Sharp needles of glass and wood pierced his hands.

He scrambled to his feet, the glass slivers slicing deeper with every movement. The outside terrace was a narrow stone catwalk, sixteen stories above the Paris street. The walkway seemed to stretch around the entire length of the floor.

Carroll inched toward the nearest corner of the building, bloodying the ancient stone. He could hear the deafening gunshots, followed by screams of incredulous terror and agony inside the bank offices. Machine pistols coughed and fired repeatedly, insanely.

French terrorists? The brigade? François Monserrat?

What was happening now?

Who had known he was going to be here?

Bullets were whistling past his head, nicking the brooding stone body of a crouching gargoyle. Behind him and to the left, he registered the direction of the gunfire and glanced over his shoulder.

Two of the assassins were closing fast, their leather trench coats flapping. They were the kind of European thugs he thought existed only in French movies. Painfully, Carroll raised his own gun. He fired, hearing the slightly unreal, muted spit of the silencer in his ears.

The man running in front grabbed his chest, then stumbled and fell over the stone wall, somersaulting sixteen stories to the street.

"Oh, goddammit!" Carroll suddenly clutched his shoulder. Blood spread instantly where he'd been shot. He felt sick and afraid. These could be the final seconds of his life. He could hardly breathe as he stumbled around the next stone corner of the building.

He moved now as if he were in a bad dream.

He weakly moved to another clear stretch of stone terrace. The walkway ended abruptly at a gray brick wall topped by severe iron fencing.

He was dizzy. He could taste warm blood in his mouth. Piercing chest pains came with each breath. The wounded arm ached with a deep, searing pain such as he'd never felt before.

To die suddenly here in Paris seemed ironic and appropriate.

To die here surrounded by memories of Nora.

He watched the sky slip away from him. The wintry sun was a hard uncaring disk.

Carroll used his good arm on the restraining wall and vaulted over the side. He saw a spinning flash of cars sixteen floors below. And cold concrete, as gray as a tombstone.

As he landed safely on the terrace six feet below, he struck his wounded shoulder hard against a slab of granite. The pain that exploded was a savage, biting agony. Blinded by it, he forced himself toward a casement door that opened as he leaned into it.

He was bleeding badly now. He could see a package-crowded stockroom, and he stumbled in. Crouched on trembling legs, he waited. Airborne Express mail was stacked all around. There was no possible place to hide if they came through. If they found him now.

He couldn't think clearly. Everything was blurry. His forehead, his cheeks, and the back of his neck throbbed from the splinters of glass embedded in his flesh. He felt dizzy and sick. And he was filled with rage.

Gunshot explosions and horrible screams continued to echo through the Société Générale building. Then warbling police sirens shrieked and howled outside. They filled the air with the sudden news of terrifying disaster. Carroll finally took off his shirt and wrapped it tightly around his bleeding arm.

Michel Chevron would be telling nothing about the powerful black market in Europe and the Middle East now. Nothing about what Green Band might be.

Who was behind this horrifying noonday massacre? What could the French banker Michel Chevron have possibly known?

Carroll was too weak to stand. He slumped against a plaster wall, his head down between his knees.

What could Chevron have possibly known?

What could be worth this terrifying massacre?

What in the name of God could justify this?

# Chapter 14

*Queens, New York*

IT WAS A magical moment, one that Sergeant Harry Stemkowsky knew he would never be able to forget. It was like a fantastic movie scene he'd been dreaming about for as long as he could remember.

As dawn edged through soiled, slate-gray skies, Stemkowsky rolled his wheelchair down the concrete ramp he'd built to get in and out of his house in Jackson Heights, Queens. His wife, Mary, a former nurse who was ten years older than Harry, sauntered close behind him.

"This is it, sweetheart," she said in a whisper.

"This is definitely it," Harry said brightly.

Mary Stemkowsky carefully set down Harry's two new Dunhill travel bags. She glanced at her husband. She couldn't believe how impressive and businesslike he looked in his dark pin-striped suit. His blond hair and beard were neatly trimmed and shaped. He held a soft leather attaché case that looked as if it cost big money, impossible money.

"Excited, Harry? I'll bet you are." Mary Stemkowsky couldn't control a shy, softly blossoming grin as she spoke. She believed that Harry was truly a saint. You could ask any of his friends at the Vets Cab Company, any of the physical therapists who worked with him at the VA hospital, where she and Harry had originally met.

Mary Stemkowsky didn't know how he'd done it, but Harry seemed to completely accept what had happened to him more than a decade before in Vietnam. He almost never complained about the wounds or the constant pain. In fact, he seemed to live his life for other people, for their happiness, especially her own.

"Tell the truth, I'm a li-li-little scared. Nuh-nuh-nice scared."

Harry tried to smile, but he looked pale around the gills, Mary thought. She immediately bent and kissed him on both cheeks, then on his slightly bloated lips. It was strange the way she loved him so much, what with his infirmities, his physical limitations. But she did. She truly loved Harry more than she loved the rest of the world combined.

"Sa-sorry *you* can't go, Muh-Mary."

"Oh, I'll go next time, I guess. Sure, sure. You better believe I will." Mary suddenly laughed, and her broad, horsey smile was close to radiant. "You look like the president of a bank or something. President of Chase Manhattan Bank. You do, Harry. I'm so proud of you."

She stooped and kissed him again. She didn't want him to ruin one minute, not a single heartbeat, of his European trip just because she couldn't go with him this time.

"Oh, here he comes! Here comes Mitchell now." She pointed up along the row of dull, virtually faceless tract houses.

A yellow cab had turned onto their street. Mary could make out Mitchell Cohen at the wheel, wearing his usual flap-eared Russian fur hat.

She knew that Mitchell and Harry had been working on their business scheme for almost two years. All they would tell her and Neva Cohen was that it had to do with arbitrage—which Mary loosely understood as trading currencies from country to country, making money on discrepancies in the exchange rates—and that this arbitrage scheme was their ticket out of hacking cabs for the rest of their lives.

"He takes two Dilantins before bedtime," Mary said as she and Mitchell Cohen helped load Harry into the Vets cab.

Harry absolutely cracked up at that remark. He loved the way Mary continually worried about him, worried about dumb things like the Dilantin, which he took regularly every night and three times during the day.

"You have a wonderful trip over to Europe, Harry. Don't work *too* hard. Miss me a little."

"Awhh, cah-cah-mon. I muh-muh-miss you already," Harry Stemkowsky muttered, and he sincerely meant it.

He'd never really been able to understand why Mary had decided to live with a cripple in the first place. He was just happy that she had. Now he was going to do something for her, something that both of them deserved. Harry Stemkowsky was going to become an instant winner in life. And fuck everybody who didn't believe in him.

Tears suddenly welled in his red-rimmed eyes. They continued to roll down his cheeks as the Vets cab slowly bumped up the deserted early morning Queens street. He had wanted desperately to take Mary along—it just wasn't possible. Among other complications, he wasn't going to Geneva, Switzerland, as he'd told her. He and Mitchell Cohen were flying to Tel Aviv, then to Tehran . . . They were going to be in considerable danger for the next thirty-six hours, danger they hadn't seen since Southeast Asia. But there was another side to the trip, too. There was a whole other perspective both men couldn't help considering . . .

Harry Stemkowsky and Mitchell Cohen were feeling alive for the first time in almost fifteen years.

The Green Band mission had brought them back to life.


While Stemkowsky and Cohen drove to Kennedy Airport, another of the chosen couriers, Vets 7, was already on board Pan Am flight 311, winging its way toward Japan.

Jimmy Holm was entertaining a first-class stewardess, skillfully recounting the true stories of how he had survived three years in a North Vietnamese prison, then two more years in a Bakersfield, California, VA hospital. Bakersfield, he said, had been much, much worse.

"And now, here I am. This high-and-mighty clipper-class life-style. Europe, the Far East." Holm smiled and drained his glass of Moët & Chandon. "God bless America. With all the ugly warts we hear so much about, God bless our country. Isn't this the greatest?"

At approximately the same hour, Vets 15, Paul Melindez, and Vets 9, Steve Glickman, were enjoying similar first-class treatment on another Pan Am flight scheduled for Bangkok's Don Muang Airport. Both Melindez and Glickman had recently worked as private rent-a-cops in Orlando, Florida. Today, December 9, they were personally in control of something over sixteen million dollars . . .

"Samples."

Vets 5, Harold Freedman, had already arrived in London. Vets 12, Jimmy Cassio, was in Zurich. Vets 8, Gary Barr, was settled in Rome—where he was sitting on a classically beautiful stone terrazzo terrace that overlooked the dazzling Tiber.

Barr had most recently been a comedy nightclub bouncer for over four years on Sunset Drive in Los Angeles. Now he was thinking that this had to be a dream. Vets 8 finally closed his eyes. He blinked them open again . . . and Rome along the Tiber was still there.

So was the twenty-two million for his upcoming negotiations.

More "samples."

*Manhattan*

In the West Village section of New York, Vets 3 wasn't flying or even living very first class. Nick Tricosas had no four-hundred-dollar Brooks Brothers suit. He had no leather Dunhill wallet full of fancy credit cards. Vets 3 was wearing a cut-off USMC T-shirt, a greaser's head bandanna, and faded khaki-drab fatigue trousers.

He was playacting that he was in 'Nam again. In a weird way, he figured that he was. Green Band was the unofficial end of Vietnam, wasn't it? It was something close to that.

Tricosas stared around the cramped radio room and felt a rush of claustrophobia tighten his chest. The broom closet was tucked up on the third floor of the Vets garage. The place was bare but for a gray metal card table and matching folding chair, the PRC transmitter-receiver, and a *First Blood* movie poster taped to the greasy walls.

"Contact. This is Vets Three." Tricosas's finger finally clicked on the PRC again.

"All right, all you brave veterans of foreign wars, you Purple Heart and Medal of Honor winners . . . who can handle a pickup at Park Avenue and Thirty-ninth Street? . . . A Ms. Austin and her day nurse, Nazreen . . . Ms. Austin is a very sweet lady with a fold-it-up wheelchair. Fits very nicelike in the trunk of a Checker. She'll be going to Lenox Hill Hospital for her weekly chemotherapy. Over."

"Over. This is Vets Twenty-two. I'm at Mad Ave. and five two. I'll pick up and take Ms. Austin. I know the old chick. Be there in approximately five minutes. Over."

"Thank you kindly, Vets Twenty-two . . . Okay, here's another hot one. I have a corporate account at Twenty-five Central Park West. Account T-Twenty-one. Mr. Sidney Solovey is headed for the Yale Club at Fifty Vanderbilt. Mr. Solovey used to work for Salomon Brothers. Before somebody blew the living shit out of Wall Street, that is. Over."

"Over. Vets Nineteen. I'm CPS and Sixth. I'll take Mr. Solovey to Yale. Listen, Trichinosis, who you like, Knicks and the Philly Sixers? Knicks laying two and a half *at home*. Over."

"Contact. Bet your life on the powerful shoulders of young Mr. Moses Malone. Knicks are point three nine one lifetime against the Sixers and the spread. Over and out."

Nick Tricosas stood up. He stretched another three inches into his body and rubbed the small of his back. He needed a break from the taxi-dispatcher radio clatter, the constant radioman duty since five that morning.

He lit up a cigar, rolling it gently between his thumb and

index finger. Then he wandered down the winding back stairs of the Vets building, trailing clouds of expensive smoke. He climbed down another twisting flight of stairs to the main garage.

The basement floor was thick with collected filth and debris. It was a typically rat-infested New York cellar. There was a second dispatcher's office flanked by cabbie waiting benches. Off to the left were rusted candy and soda machines and an unpainted gray metal door.

Tricosas squinted and started down the serpentine, dungeon-type hallway. He sighed, Colonel Hudson had said nobody was to go inside the locked basement room under any circumstances.

Tricosas produced a key, anyway. He turned it into the stout Chubb mortise lock and heard the releasing click-click-click. He pushed the creaking door open. Then he peeked inside Colonel Hudson's forbidden holy of holies . . .

Nick Tricosas couldn't help smiling, almost laughing out loud. He sucked in his breath. His deep brown eyes doubled in size. His head tensed, felt as if it might actually explode, blow off his shoulders. Right back up three flights of stairs to the claustrophobic radio-dispatcher room.

He had never actually seen so much money! What he was looking at just didn't seem possible.

Billions of dollars. *Billions!*

Colonel David Hudson did a highly unusual thing—he hesitated before acting. He reconsidered one final time as he waited in the phone booth at the southeast corner of Fifty-fourth Street and Sixth Avenue and stared at the condensation on the glass panes. He understood that he was taking an unnecessary chance here, asking for the same girl again.

He lightly tapped a quarter against the black metal box and listened to it drop.

*Ding. Ding.* Connection made.

Yes, he wanted to see Billie again. He wanted to see her very much.

Less than an hour later she glided into the buzzing and crowded O'Neal's on West Fifty-seventh and Sixth. Hudson watched her from a stool at the bar. His head began to swim.

Yes, he wanted to see her again. Billie . . . just Billie.

She had on a long, speckled charcoal-gray coat and black leather boots to her thighs. A soft gray beret was placed carefully on the side of her flowing blond hair. She stood out in the tide of young and middle-aged businesswomen crowding into the popular bistro.

She smiled when she finally saw him and smoothly moved his way.

"I see you're coming up in the world. Finished and sold your play already, have you?"

"That's a possibility. Or maybe I robbed a bank so I could afford to see you again." His smile was quiet, genuine.

Billie bowed her head slightly at the mention of payment for their time spent together. The unusual blush he'd seen at the hotel once again streaked her forehead and cheeks. He had the feeling she hadn't been in the business very long—though perhaps that was what he *wanted* to feel. Perhaps it was her best skill as an escort—to seem so innocent, such an ingenue.

"They set an hour for your appointment. Should we go someplace? An hour isn't that long."

"I'd like to have a drink here with you. We have time. One drink."

Hudson signaled for the bartender, who came immediately, in his crisp white shirt and black bow tie, like a man answering an urgent summons. Hudson seemed to have a way of getting whatever he wanted, Billie had already noticed. He was very much in command for the Washington-Jefferson Hotel type.

She ordered the house white, finally smiling and shaking her head at Hudson—as if he were a little hopeless, bewildering certainly.

A hundred and fifty dollars an hour, plus the bar tab, seemed extremely steep for the honor of tipping a drink with an attractive call girl. He certainly didn't look as if he could afford it—but she knew enough not to put a lot of faith in appearances and superficial impressions.

"You don't have to pay. I'll say you didn't show." Then she seemed instantly flustered and embarrassed again.

Now Hudson was quite certain she hadn't been doing this kind of work very long. Sometimes it happened to young actresses, to up-and-coming New York models.

"I like you. I don't think I understand you, but I like you," she said.

They looked into each other's eyes, and it was if they were all alone in the hectic, buzzing barroom. Hudson could feel a strong desire for her growing again. In his mind, he saw her rose-tipped breasts. He remembered her fast breathing as she came.

He leaned forward and kissed her cheek—he kissed her as gently as he'd ever kissed anyone. He had the desire to get close, to try to open up a little with her. At the same time he felt a soldier's warning, an instinct powerfully holding him back.

"Tell me something about yourself. Just one small thing . . . It doesn't have to be anything important."

She smiled again, seeming to be enjoying herself. The missing arm, the way he carried himself, made him quite dashing. "All right. Sometimes I'm too impulsive. I shouldn't be offering you what's commonly called a freebie. I could be fired from Vintage. Now tell me something about yourself."

"I don't even have enough money to pay this bar tab," Hudson said, and laughed.

"You really don't?"

"Really. Now tell me one *true* fact. Anything, just something true."

She hesitated, then shrugged. "I have two older sisters back in Birmingham. Back in England."

"They're both married. Successfully married. And your mother won't let you forget it," Hudson said with a smile.

"No. They're both married all right. Right on the button there. That's what you do if you're a sensible girl in Birmingham. But neither marriage is successful. And, yes, my mother won't let me forget I'm still single. Are you honestly writing a play in that awful hotel? Your so-called garret?"

"I have one particular story I have to get out about Vietnam. It's a factual story about what happened over there. Once that story is told, I think I can go on with the rest of my life. Not until then, though."

He sipped his beer, cautiously watching her blue, almond-shaped eyes, her lips slightly wet with wine. He found himself wondering what was going on inside her head right now.

She laughed then, nicely. "I'm completely losing it! I *don't believe* what I'm doing right now. I really don't believe this."

"Having a drink of white wine? At midday? Not that unusual in New York."

"I think I have to go. I really should go. I have to call and tell them you didn't keep your appointment."

"That's a problem. If you did that, they wouldn't let me see you again. I'd get a bad reputation as somebody completely unreliable. And we wouldn't want that, would we?"

"No, I guess we wouldn't. But I really have to go."

"Well, that's not acceptable to me. No. Just hold on a minute."

Hudson reached inside his weather-beaten, drab brown overcoat. He placed three fifty-dollar bills on the bar.

"Billie what? Tell me your last name, at least."

"You can't afford this. Please, David. It really isn't a good idea."

"Billie what? I thought you liked me."

She looked as if she'd been slapped, as if someone in her lower-middle-class English family had caught her at this escort work in New York. She hesitated, then finally spoke up again.

"It's Billie Bogan. Like the poet Louise Bogan . . . 'Now that I have your face by heart, I look . . .'"

"You look extremely beautiful to me. Let's get out of here, now."

David Hudson hadn't felt this way in fifteen years. It was inconvenient, and the timing was terrible—but there it was.

Feeling—where there had been none for so many years. Intense feeling. And the warning signals were going off all at once.

# Chapter 15

THE MORNING OF December 9 was a gloomy day in Washington, where even the stark, bare trees seemed to be gasping for light and life. A second emergency meeting was being held at the White House for members of the National Security Council and other officials associated with the Green Band inquiries.

As he waited patiently for the president to arrive, Arch Carroll was thinking about pain.

It was hard for him not to. His right arm, which was cradled in bandages and a temporary sling, would flare up every now and again. He'd flinch and curse before he had time to remind himself he was lucky just to be alive. Despite the Tylenol 4 he'd swallowed, his nerve endings felt as if they were being gnawed on.

Lucky to be alive, Carroll thought again. There were four fewer orphans in the world.

A morbid little syllogism clicked in his head.

A cat has nine lives.

I am not a cat.

Therefore I don't have nine lives.

So how many lives do I have? How many more chances if I keep playing the game this hard?

President Kearney finally entered the room, and everyone stood up.

The president of the United States was dressed casually. He had chosen a navy Lacoste shirt and slightly wrinkled, knockabout khakis. He looked like a kind of regular guy, Arch Carroll thought to himself. You could imagine him, in better times and another season, puttering around the backyard, poking the center of a sirloin on the barbecue. Carroll remembered that Kearney had two young boys. Maybe he played ball with them. But there wouldn't be much leisure for that these days. President Kearney had taken the brunt of press criticism over Wall Street, a case of the press creating a convenient scapegoat for the public. Suddenly, in just a few days, his political moon had lost almost all its former brightness.

The participants inside the White House conference room avoided formal handshakes this time. They'd all brought bulging leather briefcases and portfolios for the early morning meeting; the physical proof of the relentless investigations were there to be reviewed and acted upon.

Judging from the impressive look of the paperwork, someone had to have discovered something about Green Band, Carroll thought as the meeting began. He looked across the room at Caitlin Dillon, who smiled back at him. She, too, had an overstuffed briefcase. Today she looked businesslike and efficient in a tailored navy blue suit and an unadorned white shirt. She wore a navy necktie in the form of a large bow. For some reason Carroll found all this severity of style attractive.

"Good morning to all of you—although I don't know what might be especially good about it. To be perfectly blunt, I'm even more concerned than I was on Friday night."

President Kearney certainly did nothing to relieve the strain as he delivered his opening remarks. He remained standing stiffly at the head of the long wooden table.

"Every reliable projection we have says that a stock market panic, a full-scale crash, may soon be on us . . . Some of the more manipulative bastards around the world have actually figured out how to make this tragedy work to their advantage . . .

"I will tell all of you this in strict confidence—the Western economy cannot survive a major crash at this time. Even a minor market crash would be catastrophic."

The president had raised his voice, and there was the palest flash of his old campaign style, the inspirational voice, the characteristic firmness of the jaw—but then, as suddenly as the echo had come, it vanished. Justin Kearney looked like a man whose spirit had sagged entirely.

The president once again solicited information, and new data from around the table. Each adviser gave a succinct report on any findings relating to Green Band.

When his turn arrived, Carroll inched his chair closer to the conference table. He tried to make everything very quiet inside his head. He was still hazy. His body was numb and cold at times since the shooting in Paris. And his arm was throbbing again, a palpable pain.

"My news isn't good, either," he began. "We have some concrete facts, some statistics, but not a lot that's worth-while. The raw information about the bombing is complete, anyway. Five packages of plastique would be required per building. They could have leveled lower Manhattan if they'd wanted to. They didn't want to . . . They wanted to do exactly what they did. New York was a controlled, a tightly disciplined, demonstration. My team has spent forty-eight hours going through every terrorist contact that exists. There are no connections to this group.

"There *was* a somewhat unclear but promising connection with the European black market," Carroll continued, flipping a page on his notepad. Somewhat unclear, he thought. Maybe it would have been promising if Michel Chevron had survived, if some ID had been found on the man he'd shot in Paris. There were too many ifs and maybes, twice as many as in the usual police case. One thing was certain, you couldn't build an arrest around conditionals.

"Unfortunately, so many Wall Street computers and broker-age house records were destroyed, we have no way to determine the true stock market picture. We don't know if securities were taken, or if there's been a computer scam."

The vice president, Thomas More Elliot, interrupted Carroll. Of all the men seated in the room, the stern New Englander seemed the sharpest, the most in control of himself. That morning, at least, Vice President Elliot looked more like the group's leader than the president.

"You're saying we still have *no idea* who it is we're dealing with?"

Carroll frowned and shook his head. "There haven't been any further demands. No bargaining. No contact whatsoever. They seem to have invented a completely new and terrifying game. It's a game where we don't even get to know what game we're playing! They move—then we have to try to react."

168

"Comments?" Vice President Elliot asked, his tone clearly acerbic. "On Mr. Carroll's contributions."

The blank faces staring at Carroll certainly weren't encouraging or supportive. The heads of the enforcement agencies were especially cool and distant. The cabinet members were mostly business-management types who didn't understand the problems of police work in the field. They were indifferent to the trials and demands of a start-from-scratch street investigation.

The Senate majority leader finally spoke. Marshall Turner's familiar voice was southern and boomed like an echo. "Mr. President, I'm afraid this simply will not do. All of what I'm hearing is unsatisfactory. Late last week we came *that* close to a full economic collapse in this country."

"That's what we're told, Marshall."

"Now you tell us we're still in serious danger, maybe even worse danger. A second Black Friday is being discussed. I feel it's our responsibility to make certain we have our best investigative apparatus in place. Now, as I understand it, the Federal Bureau and the CIA are both being underutilized in the current manhunt for terrorists."

The tone in the senator's voice was offensive to Carroll. He stared at the political leader, who had the kind of swollen pink face you might encounter in the sawdust-filled back room of a country store.

Phil Berger, the director of the CIA, stepped into the uncomfortable silence. He was a small, lean man whose head, starkly bald and shining under the lights in the room, came to a domed point. He reminded Carroll of a hard-boiled egg sitting in an eggcup.

Berger said, "The FBI and the CIA are working

twenty-four-hour shifts. There's no question of underutilization." He turned his eyes toward Carroll. "And I'm sure Mr. Carroll is giving it his very best, even if he hasn't managed to come up with anything."

"All right. Let's not fight among ourselves." President Kearney abruptly rose from the conference table.

Justin Kearney looked at Carroll and said, "I made a hard decision late yesterday. I would have called you, but you weren't in New York, Archer."

"Right. I was in Paris, getting shot at."

The president ignored Carroll's remark. "Effective immediately, I'm ordering the following changes. I want you to continue to run the part of the operation that deals directly with known terrorist groups. But I want Phil Berger to supervise the overall investigation of Green Band, including the investigation of terrorists inside the United States. You're to report directly to Phil Berger. You're also to give the CIA a complete record of your personal contacts, all of your files."

Carroll stared incredulously at President Kearney. He was almost certain it wasn't legal for him to give his record files to the CIA. He also had the feeling he'd just been floated down the Potomac on a leaky raft. Thanks for all of your past help, but your team's working methods leave something to be desired.

He turned his face away from the president, who seemed, in his Olympian wisdom, to have reached this decision single-handedly. That fact troubled and perplexed Carroll. But there was something else, one thing that disturbed him even more.

It was the general boardroom coldness, the sterile big

business atmosphere that was growing up everywhere in the government. It was the supersecrecy, the superdeceit usually under the misleading cover of "national security" and "need to know." *They* made the command decision, and *they* no longer felt they had to explain themselves to anybody.

"I guess I understand, Mr. President, and I'm afraid I have to quit under those circumstances. With all due respect, I resign, sir. I'm out of this."

Arch Carroll got up and walked out of the conference room, out of the White House entirely. It was over for him. Washington was a bureaucratic company town, and he just didn't want to work for the company anymore.

Approximately an hour later, Arch Carroll was in an Eastern shuttle jet destined for New York.

Outside, an electrical storm whipped the sky. From his window he could see dramatic black clouds. He stared at the gathering storm, and he felt overwhelmed by a curious loneliness.

It was at times like these he missed Nora most. Nobody he'd met before or since was as good at making him feel whole; nobody else seemed able to make him laugh at himself. And that was the real trick, being able to laugh when you needed to—and right now, Arch Carroll needed to laugh at something.

He felt Caitlin Dillon's hand on his arm. Turning, he gave her a weary half smile. She was trying her hardest to be sympathetic, to be kind.

"You must know it isn't your fault. Everybody's frustrated, Arch. Green Band didn't just do a number on Wall Street, it created an atmosphere of panic. Our president, who is turning out to be even less decisive than I imagined he'd be, made a panicky decision. That's all."

She patted his arm, and he felt like a kid with a scarred, bloody knee. This warm, almost maternal, streak in Caitlin surprised him.

"It isn't your fault. You've got to keep that in mind. Washington is loaded with scared men making inadequate decisions." She paused before asking, "What will you do? Go into legal practice? Draw up wills? Deed of trust? Maybe something like corporate law?"

Carroll drifted back from somewhere distant inside his mind. Her light sarcasm didn't escape him. He even welcomed it. Law, he thought. The reason he'd never used his degree was because he couldn't stomach the idea of law tomes, of hunting down precedents in the dust of unreadable books, of having to fraternize with other lawyers. They were a breed that depressed the hell out of him.

He was quiet for a time. Then he said, "Can you honestly imagine me reporting to that CIA clown Phil Berger?"

Caitlin shook her head. A puff of smoke surrounded her face a moment, and she blinked. "He's an egghead in more than one sense of the word. The man must have been hatched."

Carroll suddenly roared. The storm rocked the plane a moment. "When I was a kid, my mother used to give us hard-boiled eggs for breakfast. Some tradition from the old country. All of us kids would beat the tops open with our spoons. That's what I should have had back there in the White House. A goddamn big spoon to beat on Phil Berger's head."

Carroll turned his head toward Caitlin Dillon. She was laughing, too. It was a musical laugh, like some quirky tune you couldn't forget, one that ran through your mind in a tantalizing way but you couldn't put a name to. "You surprise me. You really surprise me."

"Why is that?"

"You look so damn straight and businesslike, but you've got this weird sense of humor underneath all that—"

"Weird for a Wall Street business type, I guess. For a dyed-in-the-wool midwesterner. A Presbyterian."

Arch Carroll laughed some more, and it felt pretty good. Tension knots in his neck were finally loosening up. "Yeah. Of course. For a country hick from Ohio."

"My father taught me that you need a good sense of humor to survive on Wall Street. He survived it, though just barely."

She gazed at him, saying nothing more. She had stopped laughing, and her expression was serious; her eyes searched his face. She looked as if a small, important gear had just shifted in her mind.

Carroll watched her, conscious of something happening in his body, the unsettling motions of desire. For a moment he had the uncomfortable feeling that he was betraying Nora, betraying a sacred memory.

Christ, it had been a long time since his body had reacted like this; he was suddenly aware of how deprived he was, how hungry he'd become. He raised one hand, his fingers trembling slightly, and placed the palm against Caitlin's cheek.

Gently, tenderly, he kissed her.

And then the moment was over, suddenly, as if it had never happened.

Caitlin Dillon was looking from the window at the theatrical cloud display and talking about how soon they'd be back in New York—and what Arch Carroll wondered was whether he'd really kissed this woman. Or if it had been nothing more than a passing hallucination.

*Manhattan*

When Carroll returned to 13 Wall Street, all that remained was for him to clear out his desk and leave the world of pointless stakeouts and twenty-hour workdays. It was easy and mostly painless, he thought. Something he probably should have done a long time ago. He'd had enough cops and robbers for one lifetime.

He was interrupted by a knock on the door. Walter Trentkamp came in. The FBI man walked slowly across the room. He leaned against the cluttered desk and sighed loudly.

"I'd quit, too, if I had an office like this." Trentkamp frowned. He stared around the room. "I mean, I've seen bleak before."

"What can I do for you, Walter?"

"You can reconsider the decision you made in Washington."

"Did somebody send you up here? Did they tell you to go talk some sense into Carroll?"

Trentkamp pursed his lips. He shook his head. "What'll you do now?"

"Law," Carroll lied. It was something to say.

"You're too old already. Law's a young mart's game."

Carroll sighed. "Quit, Walter. Quit it right now."

Trentkamp continued to frown. "Nobody knows terrorists the way you do. If you leave, lives will be lost. And you know it. So what if your goddamn pride is a little wounded right now?"

174

Carroll sat down hard behind his desk. He hated Walter Trentkamp just then. He hated the idea that another person could see through him so easily. Walter was so goddamn smart. There was an impressive superiority that peeked through his policeman's facade every now and then. "You're a manipulative son of a bitch."

"Do you think I got where I am without some small understanding of human foibles?" Trentkamp asked. He held out his hand. "You're a cop. It's in your blood. Every day you remind me a little more of your father. He was a stubborn bastard, too."

Carroll hesitated. With his own hand in midair, he hesitated. He could choose—right now he had a choice.

He shrugged and shook Trentkamp's hand.

"Welcome back on board, Archer."

On board what? Carroll wondered. "One thing I want you to know. When Green Band is settled, I quit."

"Sure," Trentkamp said. "That's understood. Just keep in touch until Green Band is settled."

"I want to be a free man, Walter."

"Don't we all?" Walter Trentkamp asked, and finally smiled. "You're so fucking cute when you pout."

# Chapter 16

*Manhattan*

ON THE SECOND floor of 13 Wall, meanwhile, Caitlin Dillon sat in dark silhouette on a high wooden stool. Most of the overhead lights in the room known as the crisis room had been dimmed. She listened to the soothing electronic whirr of half a dozen IBM and Hewlett-Packard computers, complex machines she was entirely comfortable around.

It had been Caitlin's original idea to collect and evaluate all the available newspaper information and police intelligence flowing in over the word processor consoles. The news arrived in sudden, urgent bursts, streams of tiny green letters that came from both the financial sectors and the police agencies all around the world. As she sat there, her eyes hurting from the glare of the screens, she pondered two things.

One was the scary and real possibility of a total international financial collapse.

The other was the intricate and almost hopeless puzzle of her own private life.

Caitlin was aware that she had lived her thirty-four years subject to two strong and contrary urges, two radically different pulls on her energies and emotions. Part of her wanted to be a traditional woman: feminine, desirable, the kind of woman who loved to dress in expensive things from Saks, or Bergdorf Goodman, or Chloe and Chanel in Paris.

The other separate and equal part was independent, highly competitive, and ambitious, possessed of an unusually fierce will.

Many years before, Caitlin's father, who was a deeply principled and intelligent investment banker in the Midwest, had tried to stand up to the large Wall Street clique of firms. He had lost his battle, lost an unfair fight, and been thrown into bankruptcy. Year after year Caitlin had listened as he'd lectured bitterly against the injustice, the unfairness, and sometimes the utter stupidity built into the American financial system. In the same way that some children grow up wanting to be crusading lawyers, Caitlin had decided that she wanted to help reform the financial system. She had finally come east as a kind of avenging angel. She was fascinated and repelled by the self-contained world of big business and by Wall Street in particular. In her heart of hearts Caitlin wanted the financial system to work properly, and she was fierce, almost obsessed with the application of her moral position as the SEC enforcer . . .

It was likewise the independent, nontraditional part of Caitlin that enjoyed other mild eccentricities—like wandering the streets of New York in tight-fitting Italian jeans, crumpled oversize T-shirts, leather boots that came almost to her butt.

She might happily devote a particular Sunday afternoon to some exotic Italian recipe from Marcella Hazan—but she could easily go weeks abhorring the idea of doing any cooking at all, avoiding all housework in her East Side apartment. She was proud of earning almost six figures a year at the SEC, but sometimes she wanted desperately to throw it all over and have a baby. Sometimes she was afraid she might never have a child. She *ached* with the idea the way one ached from a real loss. And she had no idea, absolutely none, whether these opposing impulses could ever peacefully coexist.

She had been thinking along these lines ever since that surprising kiss on the Washington–New York plane. It had been quick, casual, yet she had the instinctive feeling she wanted to go beyond that first kiss with Archer Carroll. But where?

What was she thinking of, anyhow?

She hardly knew Carroll. His kiss had been the kiss of a stranger. She wasn't even sure if it had meant anything to him or whether it had been something thrown up by the peculiar circumstances of the flight, his way of relieving tension, and disappointment, and more than a little justified anger.

I don't really know the first thing about him, she thought.

A shuffling noise made her turn, and she saw Carroll in the doorway. She was embarrassed, as if she suspected he'd been standing there, reading her thoughts.

He had his arm in a fresh white sling, and he looked pale. She smiled. She'd already heard about the success of Walter Trentkamp's personal appeal, and she was relieved—decisions made under duress were almost always the wrong ones, she knew. Carroll's impetuousness was part of his charm. But one day, she thought, one day he might run into the kind of serious trouble from which there was no escape.

"I had Michel Chevron all ready to talk about the European black market," he said.

"Don't keep blaming yourself."

"Somebody knows all of our moves. Christ, who knows what Michel Chevron could have told me?" He shifted his weight from one foot to the other. She was reminded of a restless, agile prizefighter warming up.

"How's the arm? Hurt?"

"Only when I think about Paris."

"Then don't think." She slid off the wooden stool. She wanted to go across the room and somehow ease his discomfort, his embarrassment. "I'm glad . . ."

"Glad?"

She stared at him. Carroll had a vulnerable quality that inspired her to strange sympathies and concerns, but also to anxieties she couldn't quite articulate. He had a lost-boy quality; maybe that was it.

"Glad you didn't get yourself killed," she said.

There was a breathless silence in the room.

She turned to one of the computer screens, studying the mass of crawling green letters. The spell between them was broken again.

"Another Baader-Meinhof member was shot and killed in Munich." Caitlin looked up from the screen message. She watched him, wondering again what the kiss on the plane had meant.

Carroll merely nodded. "The West Germans are using Green Band as an excuse to solve their local terrorism problems. The BND is very pragmatic. They're probably the toughest police force in Western Europe."

Caitlin perched herself atop the high wooden stool again and hugged her knees. Another message started to blip over the nearest computer. She turned to watch the computer screen closely.

And froze.

"Look at this, Arch."

MOSCOW. THE KGB HAS INTERCEPTED
PYOTR ANDRONOV. IMPORTANT
UNDERWORLD BLACK MARKET SPECIALIST.
ANDRONOV HOLDING U.S. SECURITIES,
PRESUMED STOLEN. ANDRONOV LINKS
STOLEN BONDS TO GREEN BAND.
AMOUNT: ONE MILLION TWO HUNDRED
FIFTY THOUSAND DOLLARS. REFERRED TO
AS "SAMPLES."

Moments later another equally curious item began to appear on the screen.

The second entry was from the Swiss in Geneva.

INTERPOL. RELIABLE LOCAL INFORMER
HAS REPORTED "FLOODING" OF GENEVA
MARKET WITH STOLEN BOND OFFERS.
SELLER LOOKING FOR "SERIOUS BUYER."
AMOUNT SUGGESTED AS HIGH AS FIVE TO
TEN MILLION AMERICAN DOLLARS.
SOURCE VERY RELIABLE.

Carroll gnawed at his lip. "I think this might be the moment of truth."

"Something's definitely happening. But why is it happening all at once like this?"

For the next hour and a half, during which the various screens virtually exploded with new information, as many as a dozen U.S. Army and police officials rushed down to look at the messages inside the crisis room. News was being transmitted from all over the world, all at once.

As bad as it seemed, there was the sense of relief that *something* was happening. Was Green Band finally moving?

ZURICH. PREVALENT RUMORS HERE
TONIGHT OF STOLEN U.S. SECURITIES
AVAILABLE. VERY LARGE AMOUNTS.
HIGH SEVEN-FIGURE THEFT INDICATED
BY SOURCES.

LONDON, SCOTLAND YARD. DURING
ROUTINE SEARCH IN KENSINGTON,
AMERICAN STOCK CERTIFICATES FOUND.
SERIAL NUMBERS TO FOLLOW. SUSPECT
NOT IN FLAT WITH CACHE. SUSPECT IS
JOHN HALL-FRAZIER, A KNOWN FENCE IN
EUROPE BOND MARKET. SUSPECT KNOWN
TO MICHEL CHEVRON.

BEIRUT. AHMED JARREL ARRESTED THIS
EVENING HERE. TRADED THE FOLLOWING
INFORMATION . . . JARREL HAD BEEN
ATTEMPTING TO SELL U.S. SECURITIES IN
BEIRUT. ASKING PRICE THIRTY-FIVE
CENTS ON A DOLLAR VALUE. VERY
HIGH-QUALITY BONDS. SOME *BLANK
CHEQUES* ALSO. JARREL CLAIMS AMOUNT

AVAILABLE UP TO ONE HUNDRED
MILLION AMERICAN.

Half an hour later, using an ordinary hand calculator,
Caitlin added up the amounts indicated on the display screens
so far.

The final sum came to just under a hundred million U.S.
dollars.

"Samples . . ."

Next she made a quick printout of the Fortune 500, America's largest individual corporations, to check against the stolen
securities reported thus far.

Nearly all the thefts were in the top one hundred companies. Those reported to date created an unusual, elite universe.
Was there a clue or potential lead in that?

| Rank in Company Fortune 500 | Stockholder Equity |
|---|---|
| 1 Exxon (New York) | $29,443,095,000 |
| 2 General Motors (Detroit) | 20,766,600,000 |
| 3 Mobile (New York) | 13,952,000,000 |
| 5 International Business Machines (Armonk, N.Y.) | 23,219,000,000 |
| 6 Texaco (Harrison, N.Y.) | 14,726,000,000 |
| 8 Standard Oil (Indiana) (Chicago) | 12,440,000,000 |
| 9 Standard Oil of California (San Francisco) | 14,106,000,000 |
| 10 General Electric (Fairfield, Conn.) | 11,270,000,000 |
| 15 U.S. Steel (Pittsburgh) | 11,270,000,000 |
| 17 Sun (Radnor, Pa.) | 5,355,000,000 |
| 20 ITT (New York) | 6,106,084,000 |

| | | |
|---|---|---|
| 26 | AT&T Technologies (New York) | 4,621,300,000 |
| 28 | Dow Chemical (Midland, Mich.) | 5,047,000,000 |
| 34 | Westinghouse Electric (Pittsburgh) | 3,410,300,000 |
| 39 | Amerada Hess (New York) | 2,525,663,000 |
| 42 | McDonnell Douglas (St. Louis) | 2,067,900,000 |
| 43 | Rockwell International (Pittsburgh) | 2,367,300,000 |
| 45 | Ashland Oil (Russell, Ky.) | 1,084,824,000 |
| 50 | Lockheed (Burbank, Calif.) | 826,200,000 |
| 52 | Monsanto (St. Louis) | 3,667,000,000 |
| 55 | Anheuser-Busch (St. Louis) | 1,766,500,000 |
| 67 | Gulf & Western Industries (New York) | 1,893,924,000 |
| 69 | Bethlehem Steel (Bethlehem, Pa.) | 1,313,100,000 |
| 77 | Texas Instruments (Dallas) | 1,202,700,000 |
| 84 | Digital Equipment (Maynard, Mass.) | 3,541,282,000 |
| 89 | Diamond Shamrock (Dallas) | 2,743,327,000 |
| 92 | Deere (Moline, Ill.) | 2,275,967,000 |
| 97 | North American Philips (New York) | 883,874,000 |

By nine-fifteen the crisis room was filled with officials from the White House and the Pentagon. They scrutinized the computer screens like gamblers nervously watching the outcome of their bets. The secretary of the Treasury and the vice president were both present. Phil Berger of the CIA had been flown in by special air force helicopter from Washington.

At eleven o'clock urgent reports were still chattering in over the computer terminals. The president had been kept informed; another National Security conference had already been called for late that night.

This time, however, neither Arch Carroll nor Caitlin Dillon was invited to travel down to Washington.

"What did *I* do?" Caitlin complained angrily when she found out.

"You've got the wrong friends," Carroll said. "You're traveling in some bad company."

"You?"

"Yeah. Me."

# Chapter 17

*Zavidavo, Russia*

AT FOUR-THIRTY THAT morning, three sets of yellow headlights lanced a dense gray wall of fog. The lights stopped suddenly, making circles on a twelve-foot-high electrified gate that dripped snow and ice.

The oppressive gate was meant to help protect the Russian version of Camp David, a heavily fortified hunting lodge called Zavidavo.

Two militiamen from the Internal Security Division immediately waddled out into the bracing cold. They were dressed in bulky coats and carrying machine guns. It was their job to check the identification of all visitors.

In a matter of seconds, with highly unusual dispatch, a Cheka and two hand-tooled Zil limousines were cleared to proceed up the icy lanes winding to the main hunting lodge.

The automobiles, side blinds drawn, carried six of the most

important decision makers in Soviet Russia. The military guards hurried back into their gatehouse and immediately called for emergency security for the woodland resort compound.

Both men had been shocked by the identity of the six people they had just seen at the front gate. They exchanged looks and muttered quietly to each other, their breath hanging like thick clouds of smoke on the chill air. All at once the peaceful atmosphere of the compound had changed; the guards were nervous and alarmed.

Inside the main dacha, meanwhile, Major General Radomir Raskov of the GRU Secret Police was feeling apprehensive as well, but he was also heady with excitement and heightened expectation. Raskov had commissioned an elegant country breakfast to be served in a sun parlor, which was heated by a blazing log fire. Everything was ready.

Right after breakfast, Major General Raskov would drop his private bombshell on the six visiting leaders.

At a little past 5:00 A.M., the Politburo steering group sat down to steaming platters heaped with duck eggs, country sausage, and freshly caught fish. The breakfast group included Yori Ilich Belov, the Russian premier; a Cossack, Red Army general named Yuri Sergeivtch Iranov; the first secretary of the Communist party; General Vasily Kalin; and the heads of the KGB and GRU.

Raskov spoke informally over the clacking noise of forks and knives. His smile, which was usually tight and superficial, was surprisingly warm. "In addition to the main business of our meeting, I am delighted to report the wood pheasant are back on the north ridge."

Premier Yori Belov clapped his huge, hamlike hands. A

stiffly formal man wearing thick bifocals, he raised his dark, fuzzy eyebrows and smiled for the first time since he'd arrived. Premier Belov was an obsessive hunter and fisherman. One of the things he liked best about General Raskov was that Raskov was a dedicated and intelligent student of human nature—a classic and unabashed manipulator—something he undoubtedly fine-tuned during his frequent stays in America.

Raskov continued in a more serious, sober tone. "On December sixth, as you all know, I spoke with our friend and comrad François Monserrat about the dangerous and now potentially uncontrollable economic situation developing in the United States. At that time he informed me he had been contacted by persons claiming responsibility for the unprecedented Wall Street attack ... During the past two days, Monserrat's representatives have actually met with representatives from the so-called Green Band faction. In London . . ."

Premier Belov turned sharply to Uri Demurin, director of the KGB. "Comrad Director, has *your* department been successful in discovering anything further about the provocateur group? How, for example, were they able to originally contact François Monserrat?"

"We have been working very closely with General Raskov," General Demurin lied with unctuous sincerity. A network of veins ran across his sallow face. "Unfortunately, at this time we have been able to come up with nothing definitive about the precise makeup of the terrorist cell."

General Radomir Raskov clapped his hand harshly, ostensibly for a servant.

Demurin was his only real rival in the highly competitive Soviet police world. Demurin was also a capital shit, a petty bureaucratic turd without a single redeeming characteristic.

Whenever Raskov was in a staff meeting with Demurin, his blood would automatically boil; his eyes would bulge out of the broad slab that was his forehead.

A busty blond maid appeared, hovering nervously like a moth. The peasant maid's name was Margarita Kupchuck, and she had served at Zavidavo since the early 1970s. Her quiet, earthy humor had made her a personal favorite with all the important Soviet government members.

"We're ready for more coffee and tea, my dear Margarita. Some preserves or fruit would be nice as well. Would anyone prefer a stronger libation? To thicken the blood against the cold of this miserable morning?"

Premier Belov smiled once again. He had placed a navy blue packet of Austrian cigarettes in front of himself. "Yes, Margarita, please bring us a bottle of spirits. Some Georgian white lightning would be appropriate. In case some of our engines don't start so easily in this arctic cold."

Belov laughed now, and his various chins shook, giving everyone the impression that his face was about to slip through layers of his neck and vanish into his body.

General Raskov smiled. It was always politic to smile, at least whenever Premier Belov took it upon himself to laugh. "We now believe we know the reason for the bombing in America," he said, finally dropping his bombshell on the group.

General Raskov gazed silently around the handsome, rustic breakfast parlor. The important men sitting at the table had stopped lighting cigars, stopped taking sips of Russian coffee.

"This Green Band group has made a somewhat frightening proposal to us. Through François Monserrat's terrorist cell, actually. The offer was made last evening, in London . . . *This* is why I've called all of you here so early in the morning."

General Raskov drummed his fingers on the dining table as he spoke the next words. "Comrades, the Green Band group has requested a payment. A total of one hundred twenty million dollars in gold bullion. This sum is in exchange for securities and bonds stolen during the December fourth bombing on Wall Street.

"The securities were apparently removed during the seven-hour evacuation. How this incredible robbery actually took place, I do not know . . . Comrades, the net worth of the stolen goods offered to us . . . is in excess of two billion dollars!"

The men, the elite who ruled Soviet Russia, were uniformly silent; they were obviously reeling at the massive numbers they had just heard. There was no way anyone could have been prepared for such an announcement.

At first, no word at all from Green Band. And now *this*. Two billion dollars to be ransomed.

"They plan to sell to buyers other than ourselves as well. The total amount would seem to be enough to cripple the Western economic system," General Raskov went on. "This could easily mean a cataclysmic panic for the American stock market. An opportunity for control such as this has rarely been presented to the leadership of the Soviet Union. Either way, we must act now. We must act quickly, or they will withdraw their offer."

General Raskov stopped speaking. His very round, widely spaced eyes circled the table, pausing at each perplexed face. He nodded with satisfaction; he had everyone's full attention, and more.

At 5:30 A.M., the highest-ranking Soviet leaders began heatedly to discuss the issues, the unbelievable decisions suddenly at hand.

*

Less than ten miles away from Zavidavo, a Russian delivery truck marked *Muka* (flour) fishtailed, then regained moderate control. It was barreling down a narrow country road that seemed little more than an ice-slicked toboggan track.

The truck finally plowed to a stop in front of a dilapidated cottage in the country village of Staritsa. The Russian driver leaped out and began to crunch his way through bright new snow that reached to his knees.

The cottage door opened, and a woman's arm, in a drab gray bathrobe, took an envelope. The driver then high-stepped back to his truck and drove away.

From the village of Staritsa, the contents of the envelope were relayed in telephone code to a young woman working at the GUM Department Store in Moscow. There the clerk used a special telephone and another complex code to make an urgent transatlantic call to the United States, specifically to the city of McLean, Virginia.

The original message had been sent by Margarita Kupchuck, the peasant housekeeper at Zavidavo. For nearly eleven years Margarita had been one of the most important operatives of the Central Intelligence Agency working in Russia.

The message provided the American team with the first substantial break in the Green Band investigation.

It consisted of just sixteen words:

Ritz Hotel, London. Thursday morning. Two billion dollars, stolen securities to be finally exchanged . . . Green Band.

# Chapter 18

*Manhattan*

IT WAS PROBABLY a dream, and a very bad one.

He was standing in an unfamiliar room where the walls met the ceiling at angles that would have been impossible in anything other than dream geometry. Through the half-open door, a pale pearl light created a slat of dull color.

A shadow moved into the light and stood there, just beyond the door. He knew that the figure was Nora. He wanted to move forward, to step out of the room; he wanted to see Nora and hold her. But something held him back, rooted to the floor. He cried her name aloud.

And then—

A bell was ringing. And he imagined it rang in Nora's hand.

Disturbed, sweating, Arch Carroll sat up and rubbed his eyes.

Then he realized that the bell was real. Someone was

ringing the doorbell, and this was the sound his dream had absorbed. He swung his legs over the side of the rumpled covers on his bed and wandered from the bedroom. He squinted into the spy hole of the Manhattan apartment he'd once shared with Nora.

"Who is it?"

He could see nothing except swirling blackness where the hallway had definitely been last night.

Years before, he'd lucked into the West Side apartment, a sprawling three-bedroom with a river view. The apartment was still rent-controlled at two hundred and seventy-nine dollars a month, an impossible bargain. After Nora died, Carroll had decided to hold on to the place and use it nights when he worked late in the city.

"Who is it? Who's out there?" Doorbell goddamn ring itself, or was he still dreaming?

Whoever was out in the hallway didn't answer.

Carroll went back for his Browning and then unlocked the Segal, leaving the heavy link chain secure. He opened the door about four inches, and the chain snapped against the sturdy wooden jamb.

Caitlin Dillon was peering in at him through the crack. She looked frightened. Her eyes were hollow and dark.

"I couldn't sleep. I'm sorry if I disturbed you."

"What time is it?"

"I'm embarrassed to say it's before six. It's about twenty to six."

"In the morning?"

"Arch, please laugh at this or something. Oh, God. I'm going." She suddenly turned to leave.

"Hold it. Wait a minute. Hey, stop walking!"

She half turned at the elevator. Her hair was wildly wind-blown and her cheeks were flushed, as if she'd been riding horses in Central Park.

"Come on in . . . Please come in and talk. Please?"

Inside the apartment, Carroll whisked clean the kitchen table. He made coffee. Caitlin sat down and twisted her long fingers together nervously. She opened a box of cigarettes and lit one. When she spoke her voice was husky, strange.

"I've been chain-smoking for hours, which is uncharacteristic of me. I couldn't sleep, I couldn't stop pacing around, either. All that information about the stolen securities kept spinning through my head . . . "

Carroll shook the last remnants of the bad dream from his mind, jerking himself into the present. "Green Band's moving at last. Only I can't figure out the direction they're taking."

"That's one thing that bothers me," Caitlin said. "And then I start to wonder how much has been stolen and how far this whole incredible thing goes. I calculated an amount in the region of a hundred million, but God knows how much more has actually disappeared."

She sighed and crushed her cigarette impatiently. "Also, I'm still really ticked off at not being invited to that meeting in Washington. Do they honestly think I've got nothing to contribute? *None* of them understands the financial world. They really don't."

Carroll had never seen her in quite this frame of mind. It was like watching her from a whole new set of angles—she was angry, she was worried, and she seemed confused. Her usual business-world professionalism couldn't help her now; she was reduced to asking wild questions that neither of them could answer. Suddenly Caitlin Dillon wasn't quite so untouchable. If he was the son of two generations of New York cops, she was a ruined banker's daughter, and equally serious about her obligations to her past.

Around seven-fifteen they put some Sara Lee Danish in the oven, the only moderately edible items in Carroll's kitchen.

"When I was thirteen or so I actually won a Bake-Off. This was at an Ohio country fair," Caitlin admitted as she pulled the steaming pastries out of the oven. She kind of looked the part at the stove, too—pure Lima, Ohio.

They moved out to a windowed nook that overlooked the river and the New Jersey Palisades. One whole wall of the room was covered with 35-mm pictures of the kids. A single, fading picture was of Carroll as a sergeant in Vietnam. He'd taken down the last pictures of Nora only a few months before.

"Mmmfff. Tremendous." He licked sticky crumbs off his fingers.

Caitlin rolled her eyes. "I'm not impressed with your kitchen supplies, Arch. Your cupboard's stocked with four bottles of beer and a half jar of Skippy peanut butter. Haven't you heard—the contemporary man in New York is a gourmet cook."

Maybe *her* boyfriends were, Carroll thought to himself. None of the "contemporary men" he knew could cook anything more complicated than Campbell's tomato soup. "What can I tell you? I'm basically an ascetic. Skippy peanut butter happens to be cholesterol free."

A different kind of look crossed Caitlin's face. A private-joke smile? He wasn't sure he'd read it correctly. Was she laughing at him now?

Then came a quick reassuring smile that was warm and even more comfortable.

194

"I think we're going to need at least an hour," she said some-what mysteriously. "Uninterrupted time. Phone-off-the-hook seclusion and quiet. You didn't have any big plans for the morning, I hope?"

"Just sleep."

"Boring. Also not very ascetic."

Carroll shrugged his broad shoulders; his eyes burned with curiosity. "I'm a boring person. Daddy, sometimes mom, of four, straight job with the government, occasional terrorist contact."

There was a dense silence as he and Caitlin finally walked out of the windowed nook. They cleared their throats almost at the same moment. Caitlin reached for him, and then they were lightly, just barely, holding hands.

Arch Carroll was suddenly very aware of her perfume, the *shh-shh* of her jeans, the soft silhouette of her profile . . .

"This is one of the more impressive New York apartments I've been in. I really didn't expect this. All the hominess, the charm."

"What did you expect? Hunting rifles on the wall? Actually, I sew. I can knit. I do iron-on patches for four little kids."

Caitlin had to smile.

It was the first time he'd seen this particular smile. Irony but also a nice warmth glowed in her eyes at the same time. He felt as if they'd crossed some invisible barrier, made some slightly more solid connection. He wasn't sure what it was, though.

They started to kiss and touch each other lightly in the nar-row hallway. They kissed chastely, gently, at first. Then the kiss became harder, with urgency and surprising strength on Caitlin's part.

They kissed all the way to the front bedroom, where amber morning light was flooding the room. Huge, curtain-less windows faced the Hudson, which was a flat, slate blue lake that morning.

"Caitlin? . . . Is this really wise?"

"It *is* really wise. It doesn't mean the end of the world, you know. It's just one morning. I promise not to get hurt, if *you* do."

She put a gentle finger to Carroll's lips, softening the blow of her last statement. She then lightly kissed the back of her own finger.

"I have one small favor. Don't think about anything for ten minutes or so. No Ohio jokes, either. Okay?"

Carroll nodded. She was smart about this kind of thing, too. A little scary smart. She'd been here before: I won't get hurt; don't you get hurt.

"All right. Whatever you say can be the official rules."

For a moment they sat together, hugging, on the low-slung, quilt-covered double bed. Then, very slowly, they began to undress. A shivery draft slithered in from the casement windows; the cold air seemed to blow right through the tall black windowpanes.

Carroll was physically and spiritually entranced. Also frightened. He hadn't been with anybody for over three years. There hadn't been anything like this for so very long. He felt a little guilty, automatically comparing Caitlin with Nora, though he didn't want to.

Caitlin's hands had the lightest imaginable touch. Extraordinary control and gentleness as she tugged off his trousers. He felt everything beginning to relax inside. Her fingers were like elegant feathers over his upper back. Tickling. Dusting his neck.

Then her palms. Rotating in easy circles. Into his temples. Gently pulling on the curls of his dark hair.

Carroll was inspired to remember that he was ticklish down both sides of his stomach. He had been since he was a little kid getting baths from his mother up in the west Bronx.

More feathery fingers. Teasing Carroll up and down the insides of his legs . . .

On to the callused balls of his feet, his bony toes, his soles . . .

Then everything was moving slightly faster; up another whole notch in tempo.

His body suddenly, involuntarily, spasmed. *Jesus Christ.*

Caitlin was doing some completely unexpected things to him.

She blew softly on the insides of her hands. She cupped warm fingers over his eyelids, then over his ears. She spoke in a voice that was nearly as gentle and sensual as her touch. "This is called a thrill massage. Believe it or not, it was the fad at little Oberlin College."

"Yeah? You're very good at it. At this. You're wonderful, in fact."

"Awh gee blush . . . Wild youth in long-forgotten mid-western cornfields."

He was beginning to like her. Maybe an awful lot. He didn't know if he should, if this truly *was* wise.

She brushed his legs again . . . his upper back again . . . neck, scrotum. Only much faster, even lighter, now. Turning him into jelly, no container.

There was no real impression of fingers, he was noticing. Quite amazing. More like the softest combs of air.

How had she gotten this good? . . . A little unbelievable in a way . . . being who she was . . . Who was she, really?

Her lovely face came down very close. "Smile for the camera, Arch." Faint, smiling whisper from Caitlin. "My heart is pure, but my mind is occasionally kinky."

At some time, somewhere in all the light touching, brushing, tickling, Caitlin had taken off her jeans and blouse. She still wore pink underpants, wool knee socks. Her breasts had the loveliest, delicate, shell pink nipples. They were hard now, totally aroused. She touched one erect nipple, then the other, to the head of Carroll's penis.

She was a classic feminine masterpiece, Carroll couldn't help thinking, completely filling his eyes. She was so elegant to look at, to drink in like the finest wine. He remembered what she'd said before in the kitchen, and it made him smile: *We're going to need at least an hour.*

There was no longer such a thing as time; no Green Band urgencies existed right now. Carroll had the comfortable, wonderful idea that he trusted Caitlin Dillon ... How could he so easily trust her already?

"Tell me all about yourself. Whatever comes out. No editing, okay, Carroll?"

To the continuing rhythm of her fingers, to the slightest crooning of the bed springs, to the dancing morning sunbeams, Carroll spoke the truth, as he knew it.

"Whole life story, about thirty seconds ... As a little kid I always wanted to play for the Yankees, maybe, maybe for the football Giants. I settled for the Golden Gloves— Arch 'White Lightning' Carroll. Son of a New York cop. Very good, honest, poor cop. Typical Irish-Catholic family from the west Bronx. That's my youth. Notre Dame on scholarship ... Law school at Michigan State, then drafted. I didn't try to dodge it, for some crazy reason.

"Four great, absolutely terrific kids. Kind of a perfect marriage until Nora passed away. That's middle American for she died . . . I'm, I think I'm a very different person when I'm with my kids. Childlike and free. Maybe a little retarded . . . um . . . boy . . . that's very nice . . . Yes, right there. Ohio, huh?"

"What else? You were telling me your life story. *Reader's Digest* condensed version."

"Oh, yeah . . . I have this recurring problem. Big problem . . . with *them*."

"Who's *them*?"

Arch Carroll suddenly felt a sharp twist of tension. Not now. He made it go away.

"Just *them* . . . ones who make all the most important decisions . . . ones who rob people, without caring one way or the other. On Wall Street, down in Washington. Ones who trade terrorist murderers for innocent, kidnapped businesspeople. The ones who kill people with brain cancer. The bad guys. As opposed to . . . *us*."

Caitlin gently kissed Carroll's curly brown hair, she kissed his puffed cauliflower ear. She finally found his mouth, which tasted very nice, she thought. Fresh and clean and sweet.

"I don't like *them*, either. I think I like you. I think I like *us*. Please like me a little."

"All I can do is try, Caitlin. You're beautiful. You're witty. You seem to be nice as hell. I'll *try* to like you."

Somewhere else that morning . . .

"Now me. Your turn to . . ."

"This an' that, the next thing."

"Really softly, Arch . . . with you that name's more like the verb. To arch. Anybody ever call you Archie?"

199

"Not more than once."

"Tough guy," she purred.

"Grrr. I'm a street cop."

Carroll slowly rose onto his hands, then his knees. He was very hard, almost painfully hard.

At his first touch, Caitlin tightened her stomach. Then slowly she let herself relax. She tightened the abdominal muscles in her long flat stomach, then let herself relax again. She controlled her breathing magnificently, holding effortlessly for several seconds. Her pulse was slow, that of a long-distance runner . . .

Where did she learn this stuff? he wondered. Not in Ohio; not at Oberlin College.

Her eyes closed softly. She was unbelievably easy to be with.

Carroll's pulse was thumping so damn hard. He'd never in his life held off this long, never felt excited in quite this way. His head grew light.

"Please wait. Okay?" Caitlin whispered to him. Her body spasmed lightly.

"Trying . . . "

"Just . . . wait . . . please . . . Arch?"

Carroll's brain was screeching, burning up. His body was a million raw exposed nerves—as he floated down, floated down, floated down. Finally—he went inside Caitlin, both of them hyperventilating.

Her mouth opened. Wider and wider, an unbelievable soft, delicately pink mouth.

Her face was generous, so surprisingly sweet in passion. She actually seemed to be smiling all the time . . .

Then Caitlin's eyes opened—looked at him—and she made him feel so good. Wanted again. So necessary to somebody.

"Hi there, Arch. Nice to have you here."

"Hi yourself. Nice to be had."

They moved faster together. Her hair slowly danced backward and forward. Her thick curls spread across the pillow, brushed, flowed majestically across his face—hid her eyes.

Carroll arched dramatically. He spasmed, shuddered, called out her name so loudly that it embarrassed him.

"*Caitlin*."

It was a new way of saying . . . trust.

Completely new feelings were coming so fast . . . Old familiar feelings were returning.

Again: "Caitlin."

"Oh, Arch. Sweet, dear Arch."

He felt as if she knew him—instantly saw through his defenses, his poses . . . Finally, somebody . . . Jesus.

When it was over, when it was finally, finally over, neither of them could move at all . . . Nothing anywhere in the universe could possibly move. Not ever again.


Carroll and Caitlin slept in each other's arms. Carroll was able to sleep deeply for the first time in days. He had a dream, and it wasn't a bad one this time; it wasn't a dream haunted by past losses and old wounds. He and Caitlin were in a quiet French seaside village. They were walking hand in hand on a deserted, rock-strewn beach. They met his four kids along the way. The kids had been playing and swimming . . .

A soft ringing sounded in his ears.

He was suddenly looking all around the beach, searching for the sound. Caitlin and the kids were searching as well.

Telephone.

Carroll flung out his arm across a tangle of quilt and bed-sheets. He groped for the unseen phone receiver, finally picked it up.

"Yes, who is it?"

It was Phil Berger of the CIA. He had something that might interest Carroll.

Berger's voice was characteristically cold. It was obvious he didn't care to pass along information to Carroll, but at the same time he realized he was under an obligation to do so. The investigation of Green Band was still a team effort, right?

The call was about Margarita Kupchuck's coded letter from Zavidavo.

The call was about the Russians.

About an upcoming meeting in London.

About two billion dollars. At least that much.

About Green Band happening again.

"How soon can you leave, Carroll?"

"I'm on my way."

Carroll put the receiver back in place and turned to look at Caitlin, who was watching him through half-open eyes, her look one of pleased satisfaction—as if she'd at least solved one of the puzzles in her life.

"Four minutes?" She smiled outrageously. "Uninterrupted time? Phone-off-the-hook seclusion and quiet?"

# Chapter 19

*Outside Dublin, Ireland*

THOMAS X. O'NEIL, chief of U.S. Customs at Dublin International Airport, Ireland, habitually walked with his weight ponderously thrown back on his boot heels. As he walked, his toes splayed out as if he were wearing ill-fitting bedroom slippers. His size 47 waist protruded obscenely, as did his customary nine-incher Cuban cigar. Chief O'Neil looked like an unflattering caricature of Churchill, and he couldn't have cared less. He had a public image, and he enjoyed it. He didn't give a good goddamn what anyone thought.

At noon O'Neil casually waddled across the frozen gray tarmac toward North Building Three at the Irish airfield located outside Dublin. As he walked, O'Neil could smell fresh peat settling in the air. Nothing quite like that blessed aroma, he was thinking. He looked up and saw a majestic 727 from America just gliding in through a blowing fog. Seven years before, he'd come over from New York himself. He never ever planned to return to that syphilitic rat's asshole. He had even tried to alter his accent so that he'd sound Irish. It was a ludicrous attempt, and he came off sounding like a ham in some third-rate touring company doing George Bernard Shaw.

Inside Building Three there were literally hundreds of various-size wooden crates marked with the usual faded corporate logos. A carrot-haired Irish inspector stood with a red marker and clipboard beside a bare wooden desk in the center of the cluttered warehouse room.

"This the lot of it, Liam?" Chief O'Neil asked the inspector. "This Pan Am 310 from this morning?"

"Aye, sir. These particular boxes're from the Catholic charities in New York. Clothes and such for sendin' up north. Givin' us all their old Calvin Kleins, their Jordache jeans, so they are. Look very smart and chic on the provos, I'll bet."

Chief Inspector O'Neil grinned broadly and nodded. He was trailing grand clouds of smoke all around the freight-inspection shack. He chewed and puffed his Cubans, to get his full money's worth.

Thomas O'Neil had been born and raised in New York's Yorkville section. He'd worked as an inspector at Kennedy International, nearly nine years before his fortuitous transfer as head of the U.S. service at Shannon. Before that, he had been a master sergeant in general supply in Vietnam. Over in 'Nam, he'd managed to look like a junior Patton, instead of Churchill.

He was also Vets 28.

"Looks fine and dandy to me, lad. Let the hearty boys load it up for the trip north. Spiffy new clothes for the women and wee children. A very good cause."

Chief Inspector O'Neil laughed for no apparent reason. He was in a chipper mood that afternoon.

And why not? Had he not just succeeded in getting one billion four worth of freshly stolen stock certificates and securities into Western Europe? Had he not just become an instant multimillionaire himself?

*London, England*

Why were there suddenly so many 4:00 A.M.'s crowding into his life? Arch Carroll wondered. For a foggy moment he was disoriented. He felt like a man on a treadmill, sent spinning off into space, where time zones collapsed, where clocks had no meaning.

This, he remembered, was the heart of London.

But that didn't matter because 4:00 A.M.'s were mostly alike. A bleached-out, dour hour of the day when cities slept and only cops and criminals wandered around, following some curious ancient chronology of their own.

Everything always started as the same intense four-bell-alarm emergency, but nothing ever happened after you broke every imaginable speed and safety law getting to the supposed crime scene. Not right away . . .

First you wait.

Always you wait.

And wait.

You drink drums of bitter black coffee; you smoke countless stale cigarettes; you pay your full dues every single time on a police case.

His fingers gently massaged his warm, throbbing temple.

He felt weirdly numb as he watched Caitlin, who catnapped across the room in the stuffy Ritz Hotel. For the past few hours she had been drifting in and out of a restless sleep. Her pale lips parted slightly as she swallowed. The scooped hollow in her throat made her look particularly sweet and vulnerable. Her long legs were neatly curled under her.

They'd been on emergency alert for twenty straight hours now. They were one of several police/financial teams that had been rushed to London following Margarita Kupchuck's warning transmission from Russia.

It was exactly like the tense and chaotic Wall Street deadline on December 4.

Nothing happened when it was supposed to happen.

No Russians with an extraordinary one-hundred-and-twenty-million-dollar payment.

No Green Band with their enormous pilfered hoard of stocks and bonds.

First, you wait.

"How in hell did they manage to make contact with François Monserrat? Monserrat is completely unknown. Without a face. Damned fellow's an enigma to every intelligence agency I know of in the world."

A chief inspector from Britain's MI6, the secret intelligence service, sat on a leather club chair opposite Carroll in the London hotel suite. Patrick Frazier was a tall man with thinning pale blond hair and a pencil-thin mustache. He wore his clothes in the rumpled manner favored by Oxford dons, and he spoke in a cultivated drawl, every word deliberately shaped. Frazier, however, was one of Britain's resident experts on urban terrorism.

Pain was coursing through Arch Carroll's body as he listened. Yes, you paid your dues every single time.

Too much tension, not enough sleep. Too much confusion. And the arm still ached like hell.

Hours later, the telephone rang and Patrick Frazier snatched it up eagerly. "Ah, Harris. How are you, old man? . . . Oh, we're holding up. I suppose we are. It's for you, Carroll. Scotland Yard."

Perry Harris on the other end was speaking very loudly. Harris was from the Yard's serious crime squad. Carroll had worked with Perry Harris twice before in Europe, and Carroll respected the man, who was thorough and honest and who spoke to criminals in a voice that effectively bludgeoned them. A hard man of the fast-disappearing old school.

"Carroll, listen to what we've just found. You're not going to believe it, I'll wager. There's been an incredible turn. The IRA . . . the IRA has just contacted us . . . They want a meeting set up with you in Belfast. You specifically. They're in the game now, too. The Russians seem to be out."

"In what way? How are the provos involved, Perry?"

Blood was suddenly pounding in Carroll's forehead. Green Band came at you hard, then they pulled away just as fast. They came at you—then they disappeared again. They were like cardsharps. Carroll was assailed by the same exasperating thought as before—they're still playing games. He sighed wearily.

Come to Florida, Mr. Carroll.

Go see Michel Chevron, Mr. Carroll.

And now the provos.

"They've come into some securities, some U.S. bonds. Over a billion American dollars' worth, according to the boyos . . . They listed names and serial numbers for us to check in New York. They check."

"Hold on, wait a minute," said Carroll. "The IRA has taken over all the stolen securities?"

"I don't know. They're definitely in possession of some stolen goods."

"But how?"

"Who knows. They must have met with Green Band, maybe with François Monserrat's people. They're telling us as little as possible, of course."

"Son of a bitch." They'd come so far; they'd seemed so close to some kind of break in the Green Band puzzle. "All right, all right. We'll be back in touch as soon as we sort out some things here. Thanks for calling. We'll get back to you, Perry."

Carroll slammed down the phone receiver. He glared across the hotel room at Chief Inspector Frazier, at Caitlin, whose eyes were now wide open and alert.

"*Somehow* the IRA has made a move into this thing. More chaos orchestrated by Green Band ... It seems the provos want to talk about selling some securities back to us. Over a billion American dollars' worth. They know we're in London. How could they know?"

The question shrieked in Carroll's brain.

He couldn't answer it. He hadn't been able to answer it. What was the point of it all now? Something was deflating in him. He wanted to sleep.

*How could they know everything ahead of time? Who was keeping them informed?*

The man called François Monserrat, who was wearing a black nylon anorak and a dark beret and who now walked with a pronounced limp, moved down Portobello Road in the west of London.

He passed through the open market for which this street was famous; now and then he would pause at this stall or that and examine an antique. There were some very fine pieces to be had here. There were also some obvious fakes.

You needed a good eye, a practiced eye, to tell the real article from the false. In the palm of his hand, he turned over a small jade lynx. He curled his fingers around it, squeezing hard . . . He was not a man who gave way to his emotions easily. But at any given moment an emotion could all too easily explode.

Like now.

Cold anger was coursing through Monserrat. If the lynx had been real, he would have squeezed the life out of it. He didn't like clever games, when they were played by someone else's rules.

Green Band had become a threat.

They said one thing. They did another.

They suggested important meetings. The meetings never took place.

They were phantoms. Monserrat had grudging admiration for them.

He set down the jade lynx and closed his eyes. He retreated into a dark, cool place in the deepest part of his mind. In this place he always had control. Nothing slipped away from him in that hidden recess.

This time, though, it failed him. He opened his eyes and the bustling market assaulted his senses.

Green Band was somewhere close by. What did they want?

Perhaps very soon, he would know.


*Belfast, Ireland*

They had to wait at the tiny, fastidious Regent Hotel in Belfast.

Arch Carroll tried to accept the helpless feeling that they

had no control over anything that was happening. The Green Band strategy was working flawlessly.

Well-coordinated economic terror.

Massive psychological disorientation designed to create escalating chaos and worldwide terror.

Patrick Frazier kept up a cheery pep talk under the unusually trying circumstances. The British Special Branch man was almost tirelessly gung ho, but understated, too.

Frazier slid off his wire-rimmed glasses and rubbed his eyes briskly. "You'll be outfitted with an internal transmitter, Caitlin. Absolute state of the art. Designed for the military. Armalite Corporation. You swallow the damn thing.

"If we ever do meet up with them, Caitlin, you must verify that the securities are genuine," Frazier said.

"*If* we ever meet up with them."

Six more hours droned by in painful, slow waltztime. The only perceptible change was the morning sliding into afternoon, the day turning to the steel blue shades of the Northern Irish cityscape.

A red-haired serving girl, no more than sixteen or seventeen, brought in steaming tea and hot Irish soda bread. Carroll, Frazier, and Caitlin ate nervously, more out of boredom than of anything else.

Carroll remembered to check in with Walter Trentkamp's office in New York. He left a message for Walter: "Naught, zero, bopkes, zip, goose egg . . . as in wild goose egg chase."

Ten hours passed slowly in the Regent Hotel suite.

It was exactly like the night of December 4 in New York, when the final deadline for the bombing had passed.

From the fourth-floor window of the hotel suite, Carroll saw an antiquated bicycle bumping over the cobblestoned street. The man on the bike looked to be about seventy, and his thin frame didn't look as if it could survive the shuddering motions of the bike. Carroll leaned closer to the window.

The rider parked his bike almost directly below the hotel window.

"Could this be our contact?" Carroll asked in a hoarse voice.

Patrick Frazier moved to the window and studied the old man. "Doesn't look the terrorist type. That's a good sign. They never do in Belfast."

The rider hobbled into the hotel, then disappeared from Carroll's sight.

"He's inside now."

"Then we wait and see," Patrick Frazier said, muttering to himself.

Carroll sighed. He looked toward Caitlin, who smiled bravely at him. How did she always stay so calm? The journey, the tension, the awful waiting. The sense, all around them, of imminent danger. Belfast, after all, was a fully declared war zone—a tragic city where innocent people died daily, pursuing confusing beliefs that had their roots in a conflict begun hundreds of years before.

Less than ninety seconds after he went in, the old man came marching out again. He rigidly climbed back on his bike. Immediately there came a solid rap on the hardwood door of the suite.

Caitlin opened the door with a sharp pull.

"An old man just delivered this message," a young British detective crisply reported. He went to his commander, passing both Caitlin and Carroll without so much as a nod.

Patrick Frazier ripped open the envelope and read without any discernible expression. Finally his red-rimmed eyes peeked over the wrinkled note at Carroll. He seemed nervous and concerned.

He read the message aloud to Carroll and Caitlin: "There's no salutation or date . . . It reads as follows: 'You are to send your representative with the proof of transfer of funds. Your representative is to be at Fox Cross Station, six miles north-west outside Belfast. That's the railroad. Be there at oh five forty-five. The precious securities will be safely waiting nearby . . . The messenger is to be Caitlin Dillon. No one else is acceptable to us. There will be no further contact."

# Chapter 20

AT FIVE-THIRTY, THE morning air was misty in suburban Belfast.

It was the kind of day in which objects had no hard definition. The railway platform at Fox Cross was silent. All the trees were stripped and bare and looked arthritic in the wintry absence of clear light. Up beyond the mist the sky was dark gray and the cloud cover low.

Caitlin shivered slightly and folded her arms around her chest. She could definitely hear the drumming of her own heart. She wasn't going to let herself be frightened. She vowed not to act the way a woman would be expected to act under the difficult circumstances. She wouldn't give in to the rising sense of hysteria she was feeling.

She sucked in a raw, cold breath. She shifted impatiently from one boot to the other.

No one was visible yet, not anywhere up and down the weathered railway platform.

Was it all going to be over after this?

Would they learn the identity of Green Band? . . .

What possible part did the North Irish play? And what could have happened between the Russians and Green Band back in London?

A black leather briefcase hung down from her wrist. Inside were codes to release the enormous sums now on deposit at a Swiss bank, and which were to be paid outright this morning. The ransom of the century was to take place here at historic Fox Cross Station.

Caitlin imagined she looked like a successful business-woman with the fine black leather briefcase. Some regular commuter heading into downtown Belfast. Another day at the bloody office. She thought she was playing the part fairly well.

She glanced at her watch and saw it was a few seconds before five forty-five. The time they'd indicated for the exchange had come. She cautioned herself that they were not necessarily punctual.

What did their lack of punctuality mean now? What did it mean in terms of any emergency police action planned at Fox Cross?

Caitlin tensed. Every muscle, every fiber in her body, tightened involuntarily.

A faded blue panel truck had appeared and was approaching the deserted station from a thick row of pine trees.

The slow-moving truck steadily loomed larger and larger. Caitlin saw that there were three passengers, all of them men.

Then the truck passed by her. A gust of frozen wind swept back her hair, and Caitlin let out what must have been the deepest sigh of her life.

Carroll and the British detectives were less than a mile

away, according to the plan. It was a comforting thought, but there was nothing they could do if trouble suddenly bloomed—if someone panicked, if someone made a simple, foolish mistake. Was Green Band nothing more than an outrageous robbery?

A car, a nondescript sedan, approached moments after the panel truck. Caitlin tried to observe everything about it as it rolled forward over the parking lot gravel. Very possibly it was just dropping off a passenger for the first scheduled train at 6:04.

It was a late-model Ford, grayish green, with a slightly smashed-in front grille. There was a tiny chip in the wind-shield. Four passengers inside—two in front, two in back,

Irish working men? Thick, heavyset types, anyway. Maybe farmworkers?

But the second car passed by her, too.

Caitlin was tremendously relieved and disappointed at the same time. She was trying desperately to keep her wits about her.

Then the car suddenly stopped and the tires screeched as it reversed. The two burly men in back jumped out; both were wearing black cloth masks, and each carried a machine pistol.

They ran to Caitlin, work shoes splatting hard against concrete.

"You're Caitlin Dillon, missus?" one of the masked men asked. He thrust forward his menacing gun muzzle.

"I am." Caitlin's legs had begun to buckle.

"You were born in Old Lyme, Connecticut?"

"I was born in Lima, Ohio."

"Birth date—January 23, 1950?"

"Thanks a lot—1951."

The masked IRA terrorist laughed at Caitlin's automatic response. He apparently appreciated a modicum of coolness and humor. "All right, then, dearie, we're going to put one of these hangman masks on you. No eyeholes for lookin' out. Nothing to be afraid of, though."

"I'm not afraid of you."

The other man, the silent partner, looped a black hood over her head and pulled it tightly over her face. He was careful not to bump or touch any other parts of her body. How very Irish Catholic, Caitlin couldn't help thinking. They'd put a bullet into her without blinking, she knew that. But no impure thoughts, no accidental touching of a female breast.

"We're going to lead you back to the car now. Nice and easy . . . Easy does it . . . All right, step up, step inside. Now down in back. On the car floor here. There we go, all comfy."

Caitlin was feeling numb; her body didn't seem to belong to her. She found herself saying, "Thank you. I'm fine right here."

"Your mum's name is Margaret?" Cleverly timed.

"My mother's name is Anna. Her maiden name is Reardon."

"No tracking device anywhere on your person."

"No."

Caitlin had answered a little too quickly, she thought. Her skin became clammy, cold. She couldn't breathe.

There was no apparent reaction, nothing she could perceive as wrong, from the Irishmen. They seemed to believe her, not even to question what she'd said about the tracking device.

"I have to check you all the same. Pat you down. All right, here goes."

Clumsy male hands (mechanic? some kind of working man?) groped all over her body. Caitlin tensed her stockinged legs as a man's hand wedged up between. The intruding hand felt very harsh and rude. The worst part so far. Probably not the worst she was going to experience today, though.

"If you have a transmitter, we have orders to kill you . . . If you don't, tell us right now. Don't lie about this, dearie. I'm quite serious. Do you have any tracking device? We'll check you thoroughly as soon as we're out of here. Please tell me the truth."

"I have no tracking device on me." Inside me. Could they really find that?

There was no more talking after that. The horrible body search ended abruptly.

The car's engine coughed and came alive.

Someone wiped her face with a dripping wet cloth.

*Jesus.* The fumes were everywhere. The fumes wouldn't let her breathe.

"No, I—"

Chloroform!

"Oh, bugger it. Look at this hopeless mess," Patrick Frazier exclaimed.

Torrents of water jackhammered the black Bentley that Carroll and Inspector Patrick Frazier were riding in. Rain blasted the steamy windshields, hitting with the solid force of a fire hose.

It had begun to spit rain at five minutes to six. Then suddenly it was coming down heavily, piercing the mist, making it nearly impossible to see the road ahead. "They're on the Falls Road now. That's in the rough-and-tumble part of Belfast," Frazier said. "The Provisional Irish Republican Army owns it . . . It's your basic urban ghetto, where they regularly ambush our soldiers. Hit-and-run snipers in there, mostly. Urban guerrilla warfare at its best."

Carroll and Frazier were hunched forward on the front seat of the Bentley. The transmitter-beeper tracking Caitlin was coming over frighteningly loud and clear. It sounded a little like a sequence of radar blips, all originating somewhere deep in Caitlin's stomach.

Carroll couldn't help thinking of a heart-monitoring device in an intensive care unit, something that registered one's hold on life. Poor Caitlin. But he couldn't have done anything to stop her from going—he couldn't have offered himself as a substitute messenger; the instructions had been specific and final.

The monitoring *blip blip blip* was becoming louder now, more stubbornly insistent.

The car with Caitlin was apparently slowing down. Maybe it had temporarily stopped at a streetlight? In heavy traffic? What now?

"Range closing fast, sir," reported the driver.

"Hang it. They're at the home base," Patrick Frazier pronounced. His driver immediately stepped on the gas, and the car leaned forward with a thrusting surge of power.

"Either that, or they're switching transportation," Carroll said.

Carroll's mind cocooned tightly around the thought of Caitlin in serious danger. He was angry and afraid for her. "Let's get in closer. Come on! Come on, let's move it now!" he snapped at the driver.

Less than two miles away, the hood was removed from Caitlin's head; she reeled away as acrid smelling salts were briskly passed under her nose. Her watering eyes rolled backward.

*Focus.* There were dull-edged silhouettes rather than faces clustered around her. Three of them.

Behind the looming shapes stood excessively bright lamps.

Behind the lamps were still more shadowy, unidentifiable figures. Green Band?

She couldn't see who the others were . . . not yet, anyway.

"Welcome back among the living. You're a brave one to accept our invitation. Probably a little scared right now. That's natural enough."

"You *do* have authority to transfer the agreed-upon sum of money? You have the necessary bank codes, Ms. Dillon?"

Caitlin nodded. Her neck was stiff, her throat dry and itchy. When she spoke her voice sounded hollow and lifeless to her, the words clumsily formed.

"Would you mind showing me . . . some of the stolen securities? I need some reassurance as well. I need to see what we're getting in the exchange."

"You'll be able to estimate the true value by yourself, aye? And you can tell counterfeit from the genuine article? You've that finely trained an eye?"

"*Touch* is more important than the eye," Caitlin said calmly, hiding any anger she felt. "I can tell a great deal by touching the securities. Enough to release the money in Geneva. Please? May I examine them?"

They finally brought her the "sample" stock certificates and bonds. She held in a tiny gasp of amazement. The look of the securities was certainly authentic. She quickly read off the top names: IBM, General Motors, AT&T, Digital, Monsanto.

She played with the outrageous numbers in her mind. It was several thousand times the amount of the great train robbery. And who knew how much of the total stolen amount this was? What was coming still?

"You can touch the documents all you like, darling. They're real enough. We wouldn't bring you all the way here for nothing. Just to chat and admire your fine all-American boobies."

The black Bentley sedan Carroll rode in barely slowed as it squeezed around a crumbling white brick wall in the inner city. The wall was blackened in places from petrol bombs. The car's radial tires screeched above the bustling city noises.

Suddenly a flatbed was in the same narrow, twisting lane as the Bentley. The truck's engine roared and its horn blared loudly.

A blast of gunfire erupted from the cab of the onrushing truck. Spits of gunfire came from the flat tenement rooftops to the right of the thread-needle roadway.

"Ambush!" Inspector Patrick Frazier grunted. He slumped back against the door as a jagged black hole appeared at the center of his forehead.

Carroll opened the door quickly and followed the driver of the Bentley out. Then he lay pressed tightly against the side of the car. He looked up, staring at Patrick Frazier's wound through the open Bentley doorway. The MI6 inspector was dead, his eyes registering a final glassy surprise.

Carroll angrily swung his gun barrel in the direction of the flatbed. Without any accompanying sound, the weapon opened rapid fire. Gaping bullet holes appeared everywhere on the truck's already mottled surface.

One of the Irish gunsels, astonished because there had been no gun sound, blew back, away from the faded red hood of the truck. Blood spurted from his black-bearded face and throat. And then the body rolled and rolled across the road like a barrel.

Carroll's machine pistol had been developed and perfected by the Israeli army in 1981. It fired automatically, up to two

220

hundred and fifty rounds in six seconds. The bullets were attracted by body heat. "Silent death," the Israelis and their enemies called it.

A stout redheaded man's forehead was angrily stitched straight across with bullet holes. The man performed a brief two-step, then spun off a steep-shingled rooftop. He plummeted onto the street with a hollow, crunching sound.

Carroll was aware of movement on each side of him.

Crowds, mostly women and children, were streaming out of crumbling, low-slung tenement buildings. They mobbed forward instead of hiding in the safer shadows. They had deep red faces filled with anger.

The two remaining gunmen from the truck immediately dodged back among the women in their plaid bathrobes and tattered men's jackets. They crouched among the dirty-faced children, many of whom were still in their pajamas, dragged out of the innocence of sleep and made to confront still another horror in their sad young lives.

Carroll clicked the machine gun off automatic so it wouldn't fire into the converging crowds.

"British spies!" the Irish people had suddenly begun to jeer, protecting their revolutionary soldiers, some of whom were immediate family members, some less close relatives and friends.

"Damn British spies! Damn you British!"

"Ga home, damn Brits!"

Carroll cautiously ran forward, anyway. He threw himself directly into the fierce, snarling faces, the threatening, murderous shouts. His machine pistol jutted out, the ugly black snout just menacing enough to keep them off him. Who was the real terrorist here? his mind rambled.

"Big man with yer gun," someone taunted.

"Fookin' coward with your gun. Dirty Brit turd! Filthy Brit bastard!"

Carroll almost didn't hear the angry shouts. He had only one thought—follow the continuing radar blips. Find Caitlin.

Caitlin covered her head with both arms. She was trying desperately to squirm and struggle away from the IRA men. The air in the tenement room was heavy, impossible for her to breathe.

"You filthy whore, you! Whore! You filthy swine!" the head man screeched at the top of his voice, inches from Caitlin's face. A contact radio was crackling nearby, blaring the latest street reports into the IRA hideout.

"It's a trap. Infuckingsane. She's carryin' some kind of signal, Dermot! Police cars, damn Brit soldiers, are swarming the street out there. Soldiers're everywhere!"

It was the most horrifying, helpless moment Caitlin could ever have imagined. She knew what they were going to do to her. She knew instinctively she was going to be shot, murdered in seconds. She wondered when that moment of resigned calm would come, that transcendental moment you were supposed to experience when you understood you were going to die.

The IRA group leader continued to scream; his black masked face was terribly close to hers. "You bloody knew! You dirty bitch."

"No, I didn't know. Please. I don't understand."

The Irish terrorist suddenly lunged forward, propelling himself out of the blinding white floodlights. He ripped off his mask. She saw a dirty, reddish blond beard, black holes for eyes. She saw the gaping mouth of a Russian SKS assault rifle . . .

222

Tears flooded her eyes. She tried to tell the terrorist not to fire, to stop, please stop. Her senses were overwhelmed with horrifying impressions. She wondered if this was the way it was going to be, one burst of crazy clarity and then death, that last solitary moment.

There were shrill police sirens and ambulances and gunfire outside; the air was pierced with the maddening noises. Through her tears she watched the door of the apartment burst open. Somebody she'd never seen before stood poised with a drawn pistol—

A deafening volley of automatic gunfire aimed at Caitlin's face. *Oh, no! Oh, God, no—*

Caitlin tried to twist and turn away. That urgent, paramount thought stuck in her mind: *Get away now! Get away! Get away! Get away!*

Only she couldn't seem to move.

Caitlin Dillon simply fell.

"Get out of my way! *Get out of the way, you bastards!*"

Carroll screamed wildly at the three Belfast men standing squarely in his path. The Irish hoods were stubbornly posted between him and the tenement house stairway. They were viciously waving Gaelic football bats in the dimly lit hallway.

"Why don'tcha make us move, mate? Come on now. Make us move. See if you can?"

The tracking beeper was singing desperately, actually vibrating in his jacket pocket. Caitlin had to be upstairs. She was somewhere in this building.

Police sirens and emergency army sirens were shrieking everywhere. Steady sniper gunfire was still raining and ricocheting down on Falls Road. *Move! Now! Move!*

Carroll leapt between the three surprised Irish youths. They wisely sidestepped the charging, bull-shouldered American. Carroll crashed two and three steps at a time, up a twisty flight of dusty, darkened stairs. *Please, God, no!*

He was fighting against furious rage and an even worse fear building inside him. He kept the machine gun clipped off automatic fire. There were too many civilians swarming inside the tenement.

Apartment doors kept opening, then slamming shut. There were dangerously hostile looks and abusive screams in every direction as he charged upward.

As Carroll finally reached the top landing, the fourth floor of the dismal building, he saw the dingy yellow door to an apartment thrown open.

His brain was going to explode. Suddenly he knew what he was going to find there. He just knew.

He could already see inside the grubby doorway. Then he could see Caitlin lying there, still in her coat. Her gaily striped muffler was off casually to one side. She lay against a fallen wooden chair.

The IRA henchmen were gone, up to the roof, up over other roofs, gone, escaped somewhere.

"Oh, God, no." Carroll choked back a horrible sob, a desperate, hopeless prayer. He experienced that awful, hollow bitterness of death all over again. He felt a terrible hurt, an infinite pain.

Very slowly, then, Caitlin rolled over. She rolled just a few inches and struggled to sit up. Her face was a blank . . . but she was alive.

Carroll ran to her and cradled her gently like an injured child against his broad chest.

Then she suddenly drew away from him; she stared at something across the room that obviously terrified her. Carroll followed the line of her eyes to an inert shape that lay on the other side of the barren room. The body seemed to be that of a young man, but you couldn't tell. Half his head had been blown away. The darkish hair was matted with blood. The figure was dressed in the dark blue uniform of a Belfast policeman.

"Who is he?" Carroll asked.

Caitlin weakly shook her head. "I don't know. I only know that if he hadn't come when he did, I'd be dead. He came through that doorway and started shooting at them."

Carroll couldn't take his eyes away from the murdered Irish policeman. A hero, Carroll thought. A hero with no name or face anymore. Police work in all of its glory.

Caitlin was sobbing quietly.

"Shhh, now, shhh," Carroll whispered.

Caitlin couldn't control herself anymore. She sobbed into Arch Carroll's chest. She held him with all of her remaining strength.

They were still enfolded that way, holding each other tightly, when the teams of British Special Branch men and Irish police arrived. Once again, Green Band had disappeared.

# Chapter 21

BY THE EVENING of December 12, the letters, all stuffed inside nine-by-twelve manila envelopes, had finally arrived. More than three thousand bulky letters had been mailed to every region across the United States.

The letters had come to the strangest and most unlikely places: Sedona, Arizona; Dohren, Alabama; Totowa, New Jersey; Buena Vista, California; Iowa City, Iowa; Stowe, Vermont; Cambridge, Massachusetts; Boulder, Colorado.

Kenny Sherwood in Eire, Pennsylvania, turned out to be one of the chosen few.

Sherwood stayed home from work that day because if he went to the mill, he'd just say something dumb and either get his ass royally chewed out or be fired. For nine years he'd been a machine operator with Hammond Tool and Die.

He made almost twenty-four thousand now, thirty-five hundred of which went for shrink sessions with a psychologist in

Pittsburgh—little goateed fellow who treated him for his recurrent war dreams.

There was a neatly typed cover letter inside the envelope; it looked government official, a little scary, even.

Dear Mr. Sherwood:

During the years 1968 to 1972, you served your country proudly as a specialist in the U.S. Army. You were a POW from January 1970 to June of 1972. You received two Purple Hearts in Vietnam.

Please consider the enclosed a token of our appreciation for your services, a chance for your country to serve you.

Kenny Sherwood cautiously slid a peculiar piece of parchment out of the envelope. Now what the hell was this?

There was some kind of chained woman holding a globe of the world at the top of the paper. Farther down, the certificate clearly read "General Motors common stock."

The legend went on: "This certifies Kenneth H. Sherwood is the owner of five thousand shares." It was tied with a shiny green ribbon, a green band.

# PART TWO

## BLACK MARKET

# Chapter 22

COLONEL DAVID HUDSON woke with a headache in his room in the Washington-Jefferson Hotel. It was snowing lightly outside, the satiny whiteness evenly blanketing West Fifty-first Street.

Hudson pinched his wristwatch off the wobbling night-stand. It was just past two. He sat up and yielded to an uncharacteristic moment of panic. His throat was dry, his hands clammy. His whole body felt feverish.

It wasn't Green Band troubling him this time.

Green Band was hurtling along without an apparent hitch. Even at its psychological core, Green Band was moving beautifully, creating uncertainty in all the places where Hudson wanted to create it.

It wasn't the time he'd spent in a North Vietnamese prison

camp, either. The memories of the shrieking, taunting Lizard Man had stayed out of his dreams that night, at least.

None of these things bothered David Hudson right now. It was something else . . . something completely unexpected and unplanned.

It was Billie Bogan . . .

Like the poet, Louise.

He was angry with himself, disappointed that he'd let the Englishwoman affect him. It was unlike him; it was so undisciplined and out of character for Hudson to permit such a distraction before his mission was complete. Yet somehow he felt he could handle it, that he could keep everything in perspective . . .

Or was he fooling himself? Or was she going to ruin everything? The one serious slipup, the one fatal flaw? Would he allow himself to blow Green Band because of Billie Bogan? This woman he barely knew, this expensive escort.

He needed to see her at least once more, he decided. Now, if he could. The most vivid images of Billie suddenly drifted past his eyes in the darkened West Side room. Hudson was aroused. He threw on an old mufti shirt and trousers and went down to the Washington-Jefferson lobby, where he prowled around nervously, watched by a suspicious clerk at the desk. Finally he called Vintage Service, not wanting to use the phone in his room again.

"I'd like to see Billie. Would that be possible? This is David. Number three twenty-three."

There was a pause as he was put on hold—three or four minutes, which seemed even longer.

"Billie's not on her beeper, love. She doesn't seem to be available right now. You could meet one of our other escorts.

They're all very beautiful. Former and part-time models and actresses, David."

David Hudson hung up. He felt disappointed, unsatisfied, and empty in a cold, gnawing way . . . Maybe he *couldn't* handle this right now. Maybe he shouldn't ever try to see Billie Bogan again.

The idea of blowing Green Band over some English whore—it almost made him laugh. It would indeed be ludicrously funny if it all ended like that. But Hudson knew that was quite impossible. The final Green Band plan was designed to be flawless. It was so good, it could work without him from here on.

Deception, Hudson remembered. The very beginnings of Green Band. Deception and illusion that had started in Vietnam.

*La Hoc Noh Prison, North Vietnam*

Captain David Hudson's tortured one-hundred-and-fifteen-pound frame slumped forward like that of a barroom drunk. The fragile shell of his body threatened to shatter into pieces, to finally collapse in exhaustion or perhaps death. Hudson's mind screamed for him to give up this useless fight.

What remained of his body was racked by excruciating pain, intense suffering that would have been unthinkable before the last eleven months in North Vietnamese prison camps. He was trying unsuccessfully to put his mind somewhere else now. He ached to be outside the seething bamboo hut, somewhere safe and relatively sane in his past, even as far back as his Kansas boyhood.

He'd been trained to resist interrogation and enemy

233

brainwashing. "Sisyphus" the program was called at Fort Bragg, North Carolina.

He remembered that now. Sisyphus had supposedly prepared him for enemy interrogation—or so the army instructors had told him.

You must put your mind in another place altogether.

It had sounded so simple, so coldly logical. Now it seemed highly unlikely and absurd, infuriating in its stupidity and typical American arrogance. Sisyphus had been yet another cruel fraud invented by the United States Army . . .

The Lizard Man, the obdurate North Vietnamese commandant of La Hoc Noh, raised a white stone game marker and decisively put one of Hudson's black stones in check.

There was a hard *clack* of the playing piece against the highly polished teak board.

The North Vietnamese prison guards, all dressed in muddy black pajamas, tipped homemade rice wine from long-necked green bottles. They snorted out ridiculing laughter at this obvious mismatch of competitors.

The camp commandant was frightening, swift, sure of his game moves. He was on a different skill level, Hudson understood that.

According to the strict rules of Go, the game should have been played with a sizable handicap called *okigo*. Should have been . . . But strict adherence to rules meant nothing here.

"Yow play!" the Lizard Man once again screeched. "Yow play now!"

He wanted his victory now—the cruel bloodletting, the slow death for the loser in the festering jungle swamps just beyond the prison camp.

The guards were physical extensions of their leader's

personality. They, too, became impatient now, grumbling and growling for faster action, like spectators at a cockfight who weren't getting the fix of swift, bloody action they needed.

*Clack!*

David Hudson finally made a ridiculous, arbitrary move on the game board. He smiled crookedly at the commandant, as if he'd suddenly turned the game in his favor. "*You* play!" Hudson snapped. He knew the smile on his face was hopelessly spacey, but he savored the small moment of triumph.

The Lizard Man was momentarily confused, clearly so. Then he howled shrill, birdlike laughter.

The Vietnamese soldiers howled high-pitched laughter as well. They inched even closer to the two players as the commandant made a surprisingly conservative move with one of his white stones.

Disappointment immediately etched itself across the soldiers' faces. Here was uncertainty for the first time. David Hudson was amazed at the commandant's sudden hesitation.

"Yow!" Lizard Man screamed. "Fast play! Yow play riii now!"

"Fuck you, asshole . . . Watch this one."

A faint smile, hollow and incomprehensible, slipped across David Hudson's blistered white lips. Once again he made a bizarre and seemingly pointless and foolish game move.

"You play!" he said in a barely audible whisper. "You play *fast*, too."

The Lizard Man squinted and studied the exquisite, highly reflective teak board more closely. He gazed into Hudson's bloodshot eyes, then looked down again at the Go board.

The North Vietnamese guards crushed in closer.

This was getting better, much more dramatic, finally. A real game was starting to develop.

The soldiers began to whisper conspiratorially among themselves. They were like the professional gamblers, the unsavory flotsam always crowded into the fan-tan parlors of Saigon.

Something interesting and very curious was happening in the game now. Even the wily camp commandant was confused, troubled for the moment by his American opponent, by his seemingly unfathomable moves.

For the first time, one of the prison guards offered a side bet on the American soldier. The commandant threw the soldier a threatening glance.

Suddenly, then, so smoothly and so coolly, as if he were performing an ordinary movement such as lighting a cigarette, Captain David Hudson removed the revolver from one of the Vietnamese soldiers' loosely dangling holsters.

Hudson swiveled back to face the hated Lizard Man.

Once again, the faint half-crazed smile crossed David Hudson's blistered lips. "Fucker. Miserable shit fucker."

A heartbeat later, the revolver thundered.

It was like an army field cannon in the tiny bamboo room. White smoke blossomed everywhere around the game table.

The commandant's small head flew back. Bone cracked hard against the wooden wall's main support post. The commandant's military hat sailed away, saucer style, across the smoking hut.

A dark hole gushed in the Vietnamese officer's forehead. The Lizard Man's mouth dropped open, to show broken, ugly yellow teeth. A lathering, pale white tongue flopped out.

David Hudson reflexively fired the service revolver a second time. And a third time. He felt like a confused child—playing with a toy gun. *Bang, bang, bang.*

He thrust the point of the revolver directly into the frozen wide eyes of a guard. The man's face shattered like delicate pottery. Skull, flesh, bone, flew apart.

He shot another guard in the throat.

The two remaining guards had dropped their near empty liquor bottles; they were struggling frantically to get out their holstered revolvers.

The next three deafening gunshots tore through a chest, pierced the other's stomach, then his heart. The foul-smelling, boiling jungle hut was suddenly a bloody, smoking abattoir.

Shakily, David Hudson ran outside the command hut. He was limping badly, as if his legs belonged to someone else. He stumbled, scrambled forward, on the unfamiliar, unsteady supports. His legs were like wooden stilts.

Every object he saw now seemed part of a blurred, impossible dream. Everywhere he looked, there was harsh unreality. A late afternoon sun flared orange and bright red over the dense wall of jungle green. Screeching monkeys skittered away. Insects buzzed angrily between the trees.

The humidity, stifling, choking, filled his lungs. He thought he would surely drown in the moist weight of this awful air.

Machine-gun fire suddenly erupted from a bamboo guard post overhead, a control post that subtly blended into the dark green of the jungle.

David Hudson awkwardly weaved back and forth across the exposed exercise yard. Prisoners cheered from their locked cells, their bamboo animal cages.

He ducked into the thick jungle that kept threatening to swallow up the prison camp and served as a natural barrier against escape for all the prisoners. David Hudson lunged forward. He tripped ahead, anyway.

He had no choice now.

Nowhere else to go but into the terrifying jungle.

Death in the jungle.

He was breathless, crashing clumsily against trees and through thick, tangled jungle brush. He kept running, faster than he thought possible. Dizziness grabbed and clawed at him. Whirling bright, then rolling colors came. Shivering cold flashes. Diarrhea. Vomit that wouldn't stop flowing. He kept running, zigzagging forward. As the jungle foliage got thicker, the trail became darker—almost complete blackness less than three hundred yards from the Vietnamese camp.

He ran forward, anyway. A half mile, a mile—he had no idea of time or space now.

A cold, paralyzing thought struck him. They weren't even chasing him . . . They weren't even giving chase.

Hudson continued running—falling and picking himself up.

Then it was so dark that it seemed as if there were suddenly nothing left in the world. Hudson kept running all the same. Falling, picking himself up. Falling, picking up. Falling, falling, falling . . .

A song from the Doors played in his head: "Horse Latitudes" . . . Then nothing at all . . .

Hudson woke with a nightmarish jolt. A scream never quite made it out of his tight, dry larynx.

Long grass was stuck to one side of his face. Sticky, gummy tears had formed in his half-closed eyes. Fat black flies had attached themselves to his lips and nostrils. Hundreds of black flies were plastered all over his body.

Trying to right himself, he nearly laughed. It was exactly as he'd always believed this putrid affair called life to be: resolutely unfair, pointless in the end, and in the beginning, and in the middle, too. Anyone with any reason could see the absurd

238

eternal pattern. David Hudson fell away into the unrelenting darkness once again. "Horse Latitudes" played again. Why that fucking song now?

Strangely for him, the incessant fighting, the mind-numbing combat, the suffering and death in Vietnam, had worked for a time against the bitter truth of his life. It had distracted him from his natural cynicism, the overwhelming pessimism, his natural self-destructiveness.

Just before his capture, he'd been secretly dreading going back to the States, trying mentally to fit himself into civilian life somehow, even into the droning subexistence of the peacetime army . . . He knew a lot of others who felt as he did. A lot of his men felt that way . . .

He woke again. Wildly confused. Unnaturally alert. He had to concentrate everything, every trace of energy he had now. He wrestled with himself to stay awake, to hold on to a thin, sane lifeline. Tormenting waves, disconnected images and thoughts, kept coming. Ghosts just beyond his full comprehension. Raging rivers of shadowy, half-formed images, words, hellish fantasy shapes. Almost a psychedelic experience. As if he'd been smoking the strongest Thai sticks. Shooting scag . . . There was no sense of real time or spatial relationships out here. He was on sensory deprivation overload. He had this shifting, disturbing sense of place.

He began to gag. His entire body squeezed and relaxed, squeezed and painfully released.

This was so horrible, too horrible, too much for anyone to take much longer. What did it feel like when you cracked wide open? . . . The severe gagging stopped as soon as he put it out of his mind.

David Hudson began to scream. He was swimming toward

some kind of release. Eternity was rushing forward—leaping at him in the form of a sea of leeches; screeching, clawing monkeys; indistinct, shadowy jungle insects; and reptiles. He screamed for hours and hours. The hallucinations were so powerful and real, they became his only reality.

They were there! The prison guards! On him! Everywhere!

They'd finally come to take him back. Busy hands were scrabbling, poking, reaching all over his body . . . Hot hands were probing, poking him continually. Blood roared in the funnels of Hudson's ears. The vicious leeches were crawling all over him, too. Sharp little leech strings. Strong hands were suddenly lifting him.

Then whispering, almost choral voices. There were no distinct, recognizable words.

"Leave me alone! Leave me alone!" David Hudson was pinioned down and helpless. *"Please leave me alone!"*

Something very large and black, a huge flapping bird grabbed on to his face. It smelled like burning rubber, but worse than that, it began to crawl all over his face. *"Get it off me! Get it off me! Please get it off me!"*

Then a shaft of light—gleaming, beautiful light shone in his deep dark tunnel of terror.

A scream came that seemed very far away . . . It was his.

Impossible.

Army corpsmen were staring down.

Ours.

*Our corpsmen!*


"Breathe deeply, Captain Hudson. Just breathe now. Just breathe. Breathe. There, that's good. That's very good . . . That's excellent, Captain Hudson.

"It's pure oxygen, Captain. Oxygen! Breathe. Breathe. Breathe deeply."

White cloth straps were holding him tightly, painfully so. Blue and red plastic tubes ran in and out of his nose. More tubes were connected to his arms and legs. Colored wires and rubber plugs were attached to his chest and from there to an icy blue machine.

"Captain Hudson. Captain Hudson, can you hear me? Can you understand me? You're in the Womack Hospital at Fort Bragg, Captain. You're going to be all right. Captain, can you understand me? You're in the Womack Hospital."

*"Oh, please help me."*

He was sobbing uncontrollably for the first time since he'd been a little boy. What was happening? Oh, please, what was this? What was real and what wasn't?

"Captain, you're in the Fort Bragg Center. You're in the JFK Special Warfare Center . . . Captain Hudson? . . . Captain? . . . Just breathe the oxygen! Captain, that's an order. Breathe in . . . breathe out . . . that's very good. Very, very good. *That's excellent*, Captain."

Lying on his back, staring silently up at vague forms and swimming shapes, David Hudson thought that maybe he knew this man.

Familiar voice? Familiar drooping walrus mustache. Did he know him? Was the man actually there? Hudson reached out to touch, but the cloth straps restrained him.

"Captain Hudson, you're in Fort Bragg. This was a stress and tolerance test. Do you remember now?

"Captain Hudson, this has been a drug-induced test. You haven't left this hospital room. You were flashing back to Vietnam."

None of this happened?

No—there had been a Vietcong prison camp! Hallucinations?

There had been a Lizard Man!

Oh, please, make this all stop now.

"Captain Hudson, you revealed nothing about your mission. You passed your tolerance test. Flying colors, pal. You were really great. Congratulations."

Mission?

Test?

Sure thing. Just a little pop quiz. Okay.

"You're beginning to understand illusion, Captain. You refused to be interrogated under drugs . . . You're learning to be illusion's master. You're learning the fine art of deception, Captain Hudson. The art of our deadliest enemies . . ."

"Horse Latitudes" was playing somewhere in the hospital . . . in the Special Forces Center. Deception.

"Breathe that good air, Captain Hudson. Just breathe in easily. Pure, pure oxygen. You passed, Captain. You're the best so far. You're the best we've tested." Stress and tolerance tests.

The Womack Hospital at Fort Bragg.

Deception.

He was learning to be illusion's master.

Deception.

You passed, Captain Hudson. Flying colors, pal.

Of course—I'm the best you have!

I've always been the best—at everything.

That's why I'm here, isn't it?

That's why I was chosen for this training.

Hallucination.

"Breathe that pure oxygen, Captain Hudson."

Deception.

242

# Chapter 23

*Riverdale, New York City*

ARCH CARROLL WAS only barely awake, barely functioning. Familiar home surroundings coalesced:

Books on the mantel—Carroll loved nonfiction and also mysteries: *The Brethren, Fatal Vision, The Pope of Greenwich Village, The Fate of the Earth.*

An oil painting of his father, done by Mary Katherine, hung on one wall.

And there were children. Lots and lots of small children.

They were eyeing him suspiciously, waiting for him to speak his mind, to say something characteristically flip and amazing.

Carroll slowly sipped fresh-brewed coffee from a cracked *Return of the Jedi* mug. "Sunrise Semester" flickered on the portable TV with the sound off. The horizontal line lazily flipped out of sync with the rest of the room.

243

The Carroll clan was together for a rare family conference. The menu comprised coffee, cocoa, and Arch Carroll's world-famous pop-up toaster waffles. It wasn't quite 6:00 A.M. on the morning of December 14. Green Band felt dead and buried in his mind.

"Mmff . . . mmff . . . Lizzie mmff . . . Lizzie was a son of a bitch, Dad. While you were gone away."

Mickey Kevin reported this important news as he chewed gooey, heavily syruped wads of waffle. His mouth flapped open in a rubbery, half-smiling circle.

"I think I told you about that kind of gutter talk."

"Mmff, mmff. *You* use gutter talk."

"Yeah, maybe *my* dad didn't kick my rear end enough. I won't make that same mistake, okay?"

"Besides, I wasn't a son of a bitch. He was." Lizzie suddenly glared up from the soggy remains on her plate.

"Lizard! You're not too big to get an Ivory soap sandwich, either. Big bar, right fresh out of the wrapper."

The most angelic smile lit up Lizzie's face. "An Ivory soap sandwich, Daddy? . . . Better than Eggo, still-a-little-frozen waffles!" She leveled her father with a deadpan, brutal evaluation of his not entirely home-cooked breakfast offerings.

They all began to laugh, then. Clancy and Mary started to giggle, nearly falling off their chairs. Mickey Kevin did topple off, like a carnival Kewpie doll. Carroll finally gave up and broke into a sleepy smile. He winked over at Mary K., who was letting him run the familiar four-ring circus this morning.

He had been trying to tell them about his almost tragic trip to Europe. He'd been trying to be a reasonably good dad for the four of them . . . He fuzzily remembered how his own

244

father had done the same sort of thing; telling sanitized stories about the 91st Precinct, right in that very same breakfast nook on Sunday mornings.

Finally, after putting it off at least thirty minutes, Arch Carroll came to the really difficult part of his story—the punch line, so to speak—the core of his tale of adventure and foreign intrigue in England and Ireland . . .

He was going to try to make this all sound very casual now . . . No big deal, right? So begin.

"Over in Europe, I was working with someone . . . They had these special teams of police and financial people. Our best people. We worked in London, then in Belfast, together. A lady was nearly killed there, in fact. Over in Ireland. Her name's Caitlin. Caitlin Dillon."

Silence. The big chill comes to the Carroll house.

Keep going. Don't stop now.

"Sometime I'd like you guys to meet her. She's originally, uh, she's from out in Ohio. She's pretty funny, actually. Very nice. For a girl. Ha ha."

Absolute, stone-cold silence . . .

Finally, a very tiny muffled reply from Lizzie. "No, thank you."

Carroll's eyes slowly, ever so slowly, passed from face to small, stony face.

Mickey, who looked all soft and vulnerable in his Yankee pin-striped pj's with slipper socks, was amazingly close to tears. Clancy, in an oversized robe that made him look like ET in the movie's beer-drinking scene, was silent and more stoic. His small body was rigid with control.

They were angry and unbelievably hurt—all at the same time. They knew *exactly* what was happening here.

"Hey, come on, lighten up, okay?" Carroll tried to make it seem a little funny. Bill Murray on "Saturday Night Live," which he did pretty well, despite the lack of any facial resemblance.

"I *talked* to a woman who I *happen* to work with. Just *talked*. Hello, blah, blah, blah, good-bye."

They wouldn't say a word to him. They stared at him as if he had just said he was going to leave them. They made him feel so horribly bad.

Come on, it's been three goddamn years.

I'm closing up inside. I'm actually dying.

"Come on, kids." Mary Katherine finally spoke up from her purposely low-key spot at the kitchen table. "Be a little fair, huh. Doesn't your father get to have some friends, too?"

Silence.

No, he doesn't.

Not women friends.

Lizzie finally started to cry. She tried to muffle her sobs, choking back the breathless gasps with both little hands.

Then they were all crying, except Mickey Kevin, who kept staring murderously at his father.

It was Carroll's worst moment with them since the night Nora had died on some high-and-mighty, antiseptic white floor in New York Hospital. His chest was beginning to heave now, too; he felt as if he were being cruelly, brutally, ripped in half.

They weren't ready for someone else—maybe he wasn't ready, either.

For the next several minutes, nothing he could say could make it any better. Nothing could make any of the kids laugh. Nothing could make them loosen up at all. They all hated

Caitlin. They weren't going to give her a chance. Period. End of nondiscussion.

They were fiercely determined to hate anyone who tried to take the place of their dead mother.

# Chapter 24

*Manhattan*

TWO HOURS LATER, on duty, Carroll's head was throbbing with dull pain. He felt he needed a stiff shot of Murphy's Irish whiskey. He also felt like going back to the role of Crusader Rabbit, running away into the convenient, strangely comfortable fantasy of the bag man. For the first time, maybe, he thought he was beginning to understand the past three years of his life.

Later, at around nine o'clock, he would vaguely remember weaving a mostly aimless path inside number 13 Wall Street. The fluorescent lights were too bright; the glaring overhead lamps were harsh, tearing at his eyes.

It was all wrong, the place felt wrong. There was too much gloom and doom, palpable frustration evident everywhere. The police investigators and Wall Street researchers bent over mountainous documents or hunched in paralysis in front of computer screens were like people who had been trapped indoors too long, men and women who hadn't seen the light of day for weeks. Even his own people, the usually unflappable Caruso included, had the quirky, tense mannerisms of heavy smokers suddenly deprived.

Around nine-thirty Arch Carroll set to work again inside his monastic office.

The broken windowpane hadn't been replaced, and the sheet of brown paper he'd stuck in the space hung limply now, like a beat-up old blind in an abandoned tenement. He kept the ceiling lights purposely bright, glaringly unpleasant. The door was shut tight so the radiator heat would build up.

An illusion of warmth, he thought.

Carroll was dressed appropriately for the overheated room: a Boston Celtics T-shirt that had the look of something left over from a banquet of moths, Levi's jeans, Crusader Rabbit's very own work boots. He was going to be comfortable, at least.

He also had a bottle of Murphy's Irish whiskey on the desk. What would Walter Trentkamp say? Oh, to hell with Walter and his imposing virtues, his old-world cop mores.

For a few minutes, slowly sipping the Irish, Arch Carroll thought about his job, jobs in general, the overwhelming job of life.

This particular job had been an important part of *his* life for almost nine years now. He hadn't exactly planned it like that, but life tended to go its own idiosyncratic way. After the army tour, Carroll had finished law at Michigan State. He'd also married Nora. Right about the same time, both his father and

Walter Trentkamp had come along to convince him to do some legal work for the DIA. So Carroll had become an agent as the result of a combination of financial pressures, his long policeman heritage, and the coaxing of Trentkamp and his father.

It was weird, completely unfathomable, the ways of life. Society chose to overplay Wall Street salesmen, various marketing experts, obfuscating corporation lawyers, investment bankers. At the same time, society grossly underpaid the teachers of its children, its police, even its political leaders. Some kind of crazy society.

Well, they seriously underpaid him to work at protecting them from harm's way. But he was going to protect them, anyway—as well as he possibly could.

The nagging question was whether his best was going to be good enough. He'd had six good men, plus himself, on the streets since the night of December 4. So far they'd come up with almost nothing. How the hell could that be possible?

He wandered around the cramped room for a while, like a man without any particular sense of direction. Then he went to his desk and sat down, waiting for the day's first suspects to appear.

Green Band—why did he have the feeling just then that there was something important at the top of his mind, an obvious insight that had evaded him until now? It was infuriating and elusive.

Did it have something to do with Green Band's inside information? A spy at 13 Wall?

*From a transcript taken in room 312; number 13 Wall; Monday, December 14. Present: Arch Carroll; Anthony Ferrano; Michael Caruso.*

CARROLL: Hello, Mr. Ferrano, I'm Mr. Carroll, Antiterrorist Division, State Department. This is my associate, Mr. Caruso. Mr. Ferrano, to get right to the point, not to waste any of your time, or mine, I need some information . . .

FERRANO: Figured that out already.

CARROLL: Uh-huh. Well, I read your earlier transcript. I just read over the conversation you had with Sergeant Caruso. I'm a little surprised you haven't heard *anything* about the bombing on Wall Street.

FERRANO: Why's that? Why should I have?

CARROLL: Well, for one thing, you being a heavy gun and explosives dealer, Mr. Ferrano. Doesn't it strike you as odd, uh, peculiar, you wouldn't have heard something? There must be rumors floating around on the street. I'm sorry, would you like a sip of whiskey?

FERRANO: I want whiskey, I got money in my pocket. Listen, I told you, I told somebody, him, I don't deal guns. I don't know what you're talking that shit for, I own Playland Arcade Games, Inc., on Tenth Avenue and Forty-ninth Street. You got that straight now?

CARROLL: Okay, that's *bullshit*. Who do you think you're talking to? Some punk off the street? Just some street *punk* here?

FERRANO: Hey, all right, fuck you. I want my lawyer in here now! . . . Hey, you understand English, pal? Lawyer! Now! . . . Hey! Hey! . . . Ohhh . . . oh, *shit!*

(Loud scuffling, fighting sounds. Furniture crashing; man groaning.)

CARROLL (breathing heavily): Mr. Ferrano, I think . . . I feel it's important you understand something. Listen carefully to what I'm saying. Watch my lips . . . Ferrano, you've just entered the Twilight Zone. You *don't* have the right to remain silent in the Twilight Zone. All of your constitutional rights have been temporarily canceled. You have no lawyer. All right? We set to continue our discussion, fuckhead?

FERRANO: Shit, man. My tooth's broken. Gimme a break for . . . Awhh, shit, man.

CARROLL: I'm trying to give you every break in the world. Don't you understand anything yet? What this is here? What's happening? . . . Somebody stole money from the man. Some very important people are severely pissed off. Big, big people. Why don't you imagine that this is Vietnam and you're the Vietcong? Would that help you?

FERRANO: Wait a minute! I didn't do anything!

CARROLL: No? You sell pump-action shotguns, revolvers, to fourteen- and fifteen-year-old kids. Black, P.R., Chinese kids in gangs. I'm not gonna say any more than that . . . Your lawyer is a Mr. Joseph Rao of 24 Park Avenue. Mr. Rao doesn't want any part of this . . . I think you better tell me everything you've heard on the street.

FERRANO: Look. I'll tell you what I know. I can't tell you what I don't know.

CARROLL: That I can buy.

FERRANO: All right, I *heard* there was some heavy artillery available. In the city. This was about, beginning, I guess, maybe middle of November. Yeah, five weeks ago.

CARROLL: How heavy are we talking about?

FERRANO: Like M-60s. Like M-79 rocket launchers. Soviet RPD light machine guns. SKS automatics. That kinda stuff. *Heavy!* I mean, what the fuck they gonna do with that kind of munitions? That's basic ground-assault equipment. Like in 'Nam. What you'd use, take over a country. That's all I heard . . . I'm telling the truth, Carroll . . . Hey, that's all *anybody* knows on the street ... Awhh, c'mon, don'tcha believe me? ... Hey! Seriously!

CARROLL: Tell me what you know about François Monserrat ...

FERRANO: He ain't Italian.

CARROLL: Mr. Ferrano, thank you so much for your help. Now get out of my office, please. Mr. Caruso will show you to the nearest rathole.

*From a transcript taken in room 312; number 13 Wall. Present: Arch Carroll; Muhammed Saalam.*

CARROLL: Hello there, Mr. Saalam. Haven't seen you since you had Percy Ellis killed on 103rd Street. Very nice djellaba. Sip of Irish whiskey?

SAALAM: Liquor is against my religious belief.

CARROLL: This is Irish whiskey. It's blessed. Well, we'll get right down to official police business, then. Tell me, uh, are you a hunter, Mr. Saalam?

SAALAM (laughs): No, not really. A hunter? ... Actually, if you stop to think about it, I'm a *huntee*. Ever since I fought for you whites in Southeast Asia. My name is Sah-*lahm*, by the way.

CARROLL: Sah-*lahm*. I'm sorry ... No, you see, I thought you must be a hunter. Something like that. You see, we found all of these hunting guns, these hunting bombs, in your apartment up in Yonkers, M-23 squirrel-hunting guns. Opossum-hunting sniper rifles, the ones with star nightscopes. Chipmunk-hunting fragmentation grenades. B-40 duck-hunting rockets.

SAALAM: You bust into my place?

CARROLL: Had to. What do you know about a Mr. François Monserrat?

SAALAM: You had a warrant from a judge?

CARROLL: Well, we couldn't get an official warrant. We did talk to a judge off the record. He said don't get caught. We took it from there.

SAALAM: No search warrant or nothing?

CARROLL: You know, this is really shocking. Didn't *anybody* read that *Time* magazine story on me? Little squared-off red box thing? Doesn't anybody understand who I am? I'm a terrorist! Just like you guys . . . I don't play by international Red Cross of Switzerland agreements. Mr. Saalam, you sold some M-23 squirrel-hunting guns, also some quail-hunting sniper rifles to a couple of fellas. About six weeks ago. Who . . . are . . . they? . . .

(Long pause.) Uh-oh. Uh-oh . . . Mr. Saalam, please let me explain something else to you. Explain this as clearly as I can . . . You're a bright, U.S. college-educated terrorist. You went to Howard University for a year; you did a little time in Attica. You're one of the Mark Rudd-Eldridge Cleaver-Kathy Boudin school . . . Me, on the other hand, I'm a terrorist of the PLO-Red Brigade-Blow-away-anything-that-moves school . . . Now then. You sold a full case of stolen M-23s on or about November 1. That's a fact we both know about. Now say—Yes, I did, or I'll break your right hand. Just say Yes, I did . . .

SAALAM: Yeah, I did.

CARROLL: Good. Thank you for your forthrightness. Now, *who* did you sell the M-23s to? Wait. Before you answer. Remember that I'm the PLO. Don't say anything you'd be afraid to say to a PLO investigator in Beirut.

SAALAM: I don't know who they are.

CARROLL: Oh, *Jesus* Christ.

SAALAM: No, wait a minute. *They* knew who I was. They knew everything about me. I never saw nobody, I swear it. I felt like they had set me up.

CARROLL: I love former-inmate sincerity. Unfortunately, I happen to believe you . . . Because that's what your current roommate, Mr. Rashad, said, too. Please get the hell out of here now . . . Oh, by the way, Mr. Saalam. We had to rent your apartment up in Yonkers. We rented it to a very nice welfare lady, with these three little kids.

SAALAM: You did what?

CARROLL: We rented the apartment you were selling guns out of. We rented it to a nice lady with a batch of kids. Skoal, brother.


"It's all so incredibly methodical. That's what is so mystifying. They keep evading all contact with this huge international police dragnet. *How?*"

Caitlin Dillon lit up a cigarette and slowly drew in millions of carcinogens.

She and eighty-three-year-old Anton Birnbaum, both red-eyed and exhausted, sat together on stiff leather Harvard chairs in Birnbaum's Wall Street office. Caitlin was a good six inches taller than the birdlike, deceptively frail financier. Earlier in her career, when she had worked for Birnbaum, he wouldn't walk anywhere on Wall Street with her for that very reason. "Vanity is a living legend," she'd kidded him once she found out the truth.

Anton Birnbaum rubbed the small of his back as he talked. "Something so very methodical, so carefully orchestrated . . .

something absolutely systematic is happening throughout Western Europe right now."

Caitlin watched Birnbaum's face with its corrugated lines, which shifted and moved as he spoke. She waited patiently for more to come. It usually did with Anton, who thought much faster than he could now speak.

"There is a book . . . *The Real War*, it's called. The book's central thesis is that Germany and Japan have found an eminently reasonable road to further world conquest. Through commerce. That's the real war. As a country, we're losing that war spectacularly, don't you think, Caitlin?"

The former chairman of the venerable investment house, Levitt Birnbaum, was something of a prig, Caitlin knew. He could be savagely impatient with people he didn't like or respect, but he was also undeniably brilliant. Anton Birnbaum had been adviser to presidents, to kings, to multinational corporations such as Fiat, Procter & Gamble, Ford Motor. He had controlled the fate of untold billions of dollars. Anton Birnbaum had also been one of Caitlin's staunchest backers ever since she'd first left the Wharton School. Only as she'd come intimately to know Birnbaum had she begun to understand why.

Caitlin Dillon was a challenging mystery that Birnbaum still hadn't completely solved. She was a natural businessperson, perhaps the most gifted Anton Birnbaum had met. She had the intelligence, the necessary discipline, and the kinds of instincts Birnbaum rarely saw anymore. Yet she seemed to have little interest in actually making money.

She was a confounded mystery in other ways as well. She had been brought up in a small Ohio town, yet she exhibited the most cosmopolitan tastes and opinions. She spoke

German and French fluently. She kept surprising Birnbaum with new talents whenever they spent time together.

Of course, her father had been teaching her about the stock market since she had expressed an interest in high school. But there was more to it than early coaching. Caitlin Dillon obviously wanted to be a force on Wall Street. Anton Birnbaum was certain that she wanted to be a legend one day herself. He steadfastly refused ever to say it out loud, even to hint it to his male peers, that the financier's protégée was a woman.

"What do you think is happening in Western Europe? We're having an impossible time piecing it together, Anton. Some very important data are missing. The absolutely essential thread of logic that might explain who they are." Caitlin stood up and wandered around the old man's office as she talked.

She stopped with her back to the window and looked at the framed photographs on the walls. There was Anton, snapped in the company of the very powerful and famous. Statesmen, controversial industrialists, people from the entertainment industry . . . there were photos of Konrad Adenauer, Harold MacMillan, and Anwar Sadat. Also Henry Ford and J. Paul Getty. John Kennedy, Richard Nixon, and Ronald Reagan.

Anton Birnbaum scratched the bridge of his blotched and mottled nose as he contemplated his choice of words. He was reminded once again that Caitlin was one of the few people on Wall Street he could really talk to. Complex explanations of his theories and insights were unnecessary when speaking with her.

"The Europeans simply don't trust us. Which is precisely why they don't talk to us anymore. They believe we have different attitudes, different priorities toward the Middle East, also toward the Soviet bloc. They're certain we're too casual about the dangers of a nuclear war. They don't feel we understand Marxist-Leninist ideology."

Birnbaum stared directly into Caitlin's deep brown eyes. His own eyes were watering hopelessly behind thick glasses. He reminded Caitlin of Mole in *The Wind in the Willows*.

"I sound like an alarmist, no? But I feel the intrinsic truth of what I'm saying. Almost prima facie, I feel it. There will be a crash now. I believe there will be a serious crash, possibly another Black Friday. Very, very soon."

Caitlin sat down on the stiff leather chair.

Another Black Friday, her mind raced. A stock market crash! Her own worst fears had been confirmed by the man she most respected on the Street. Her father's jeremiads twenty years before had finally come home to roost.

Complete collapse; the entire economic system falling. Impossible ideas were formulating in her brain.

She stared at Birnbaum and saw that he was watching her with an expression of vague sorrow. The light from an antique brass lamp turned the lines on his face into deep dark bands.

Complete collapse . . . The phrase continued to ring. It meant the end of an entire way of life.

And after the failure of an economic system, who would survive? Who would finally crawl out of the rubble and be able to go on? If she had the answer to that, maybe she'd also have the answer to the mystery of Green Band.

Anton Birnbaum spoke again. "As I said, I think we could be in the middle of a war. The money war. The great Third World War we have so long feared—it may already be upon us."

# Chapter 25

*Manhattan*

"GODDAMN IT! LOOK at this! Look at this now!" The speaker was Walter Trentkamp, and his voice was harsh with disbelief. "Gentlemen, it's happening everywhere!"

Philip Berger, Trentkamp, and General Frederick House were gathered around the computer terminals when Caitlin and Carroll arrived. Several display screens were working simultaneously, rapidly flashing words as well as color graphics.

Berger glanced up as Caitlin Dillon and Carroll hurried across the crisis room.

"Emergency reports have been coming in for about fifteen, twenty minutes," he said to the others. "Since three-thirty our time. They've definitely got something hopping. Something's happening *all over the world* this time."

*Paris, France*

At one o'clock Paris time, on December 14, La Compagnie des Agents was suddenly closed by official order of the president of France.

All stock trading was immediately halted on the Bourse.

Bourse officials reluctantly admitted that the market's CAC Index had fallen more than *three* percent in a single morning.

The afternoon newspapers in Paris carried the most shocking headlines in four decades:

MARKET CLOSE TO PANIC!
BOURSE CRASH!
PARIS MARKET IN SHAMBLES FINANCIAL DISASTER!

For once, however, the tabloids were actually being written with some understatement.

Emergency government meetings were immediately called in the Palais de Élysées, rue de Faubourg-St-Honoré. But no one knew what to do next about the unparalleled financial panic in Europe.


*Frankfurt, West Germany*

The Frankfurt Stock Exchange was in complete chaos, meanwhile, but still managed to stay open for the entire session.

The Commerzbank Index had fallen under a thousand for the first time since 1982. The largest losers for the immensely tragic day included Westdeutsche Landesbank, Bayer, Volkswagen, and Philip Holzmann.

Yet none of the economists in West Germany understood why prices were dropping or how far they might plummet in the very near future.

## Toronto, Canada

The Toronto Stock Exchange was one of the very worst hit. The exchange's composite index of three hundred stocks fell 155 points to under 2000.

Trading volumes set new records, until the major Canadian exchange was officially closed at 1:00 P.M.

## Tokyo, Japan

The Nikkei–Dow Jones Index was extremely shaky all day, finally closing at 9200. This was a full 12.5 percent decline in a single day.

Hardest hit were all companies trading heavily with the Middle East. These included Mitsui Petrochemical, Sumitomo Chemical, and Oki Electric. Almost on cue, Japanese student riots broke out in major cities all over the islands.

## Johannesburg, South Africa

Heavy European and American deposits made the Johannesburg Stock Exchange the only apparent winner. Bullion was suddenly trading at one thousand dollars an ounce. The rand instantly appreciated to one dollar and fifty cents.

Hundreds of millions of dollars were made in South Africa. Suspicions rose, but still no satisfactory answers came.

*London, England*

London dramatically shut down at noon, four and a half hours shy of regular closing.

The *Financial Times* Index of seven hundred and fifty companies had fallen nearly 90 points; it was down almost 200 since the initial Green Band bombing in New York.

The scene on Threadneedle, near the Bank of London, was nearly without hope and as bleak as bombed-out Wall Street in New York.

*Manhattan*

With its forty-button telephone-computer consoles, the crisis room at 13 Wall Street was beginning to resemble the starship *Enterprise* more than the traditional Chippendale feel and look of the Street. Nonetheless, the thirty or so police, army, and financial experts in the room had absolutely no idea what they were supposed to accomplish next.

The Western economic system seemed to be crashing to a disastrous halt, right before their eyes. No one knew why.

There was only maddening silence from Green Band.

*

Major General Radomir Raskov peered nervously over half-moon reading spectacles. He studied the august group seated at the long, highly polished mahogany conference table inside the Moscow KGB offices—specifically, the offices of the Directorate.

The Politburo officials who had been at Zavidavo were also at the emergency meeting. They were joined now by Mikhail Slepovik, director of Soviet security, and a very cultured gentleman, Popo Tvardevsky, undersecretary of the Communist party, some said the future premier.

Premier Yuri Belov slapped shut the thin black folder set before him. He looked at the others and scowled menacingly. "I find it utterly, *utterly* incomprehensible that we have no more knowledge than this. During this crisis! During this world-threatening emergency situation!"

Premier Belov's gray eyes were piercing, forbidding to encounter for more than a brief glance. "Not five months ago, I sat in this very room and I *listened* to a plan, the 'Red Tuesday Plan.' In this highly detailed proposal, it was *clearly and emphatically* stated that it was in the best interests of the Soviet Union to sabotage and disable Wall Street, in effect, the entire Western economic system.

"This plan, as you may all recall, was thoroughly analyzed and finally approved by the parties here in this room. It was an immaculate plan and a daring one, and there was every possibility it would succeed."

Premier Belov paused. His jaw twitched. "*Now, that very thing has happened!* And you expect me to believe that we have no complicity, no knowledge whatsoever, of any of the causes?" Belov slammed his heavy palm on the gleaming wooden table.

His next words were spoken in a gravelly voice, almost a whisper. Several of his listeners had to lean forward to hear every word.

"The entire world is hurtling toward chaos, perhaps even its economic destruction . . . Now someone please tell me—what is Green Band? What is Green Band's precise relationship to the 'Red Tuesday Plan'? For there is *some* relationship . . . Who is running Green Band? . . . And *why?*"

# Chapter 26

*Manhattan*

THE INFERNAL NOISE Arch Carroll heard inside his head was the sound of financial markets collapsing all over the world. It was a brutal and grinding thought.

He and Caitlin were sitting on an old floral couch in Carroll's Manhattan apartment, facing down over the Seventy-ninth Street Boat Basin. A Beethoven concerto played soothingly on the tape deck. River winds occasionally buffeted the dark living room windows.

Once again they were waiting for Green Band. There was nothing to do but wait for morning.

"I think I have to turn in." Caitlin was already half asleep. She kissed Carroll's forehead. "I'll get a few hours, anyway."

Carroll looked at his wristwatch. His eyes felt unbelievably heavy. "What a party pooper. No sense of adventure. It's only two-thirty."

"People from Ohio go to bed at nine-thirty, ten o'clock. The Lima Holiday Inn restaurant is filled at five-thirty. Closed down by eight," said Caitlin.

"Yeah, but you're a sophisticated New Yorker now. We party until two or three on weekdays here."

Caitlin kissed Carroll again, and the idle talking stopped. He was amazed at how comfortable he was with her. Watching someone you thought you cared about almost being killed seemed to accelerate the courting process.

"Is anything the matter? You look, I don't know, a little sad. Tell me . . ."

"It's probably my dumb Irish-Catholic conscience. Guilt about not doing my duty properly. Taking myself too seriously, as usual."

"Are you telling the truth? About being all right? Sometimes I can't tell with you." She nestled gently against Carroll's shoulder. She was no longer untouchable.

"I'm not quite ready for bed yet. That's all. I'm overtired, I guess. I'll be in soon. You go ahead."

Caitlin leaned in closer and kissed Carroll very softly again. She always smelled so wholesome and nice, he thought. She had the softest lips he could imagine kissing.

"Do you want me to stay with you?" she whispered.

Carroll shook his head decidedly.

Caitlin finally left the living room, sleepily cocooned in a blanket.

Carroll immediately got up from the couch. He started to pace back and forth, past the darkly reflective windows. His body felt all wrong: wired, incandescent.

He went to his desk and began to shuffle through the dusty, littered drawers. Then he looked inside an antique blanket

266

chest he'd bought years back in central Pennsylvania. His mind was wandering into very odd places, weird time zones . . .

He wondered if Caitlin liked kids much . . .

He thought for a few minutes about the possibility of getting hurt by Caitlin. How she just might move on after Green Band was finally over. Her romantic interlude with a real-life policeman.

He then considered what he felt to be a somewhat lesser possibility: that he might somehow hurt her. She'd already told him things about her two previous love affairs. One guy had been a highly successful New York investment lawyer, who was so busy making his second or third million, he hadn't bothered to notice that Caitlin wasn't just an extraordinarily pretty face, an asset in certain demanding social situations . . . Her second lover had been a professional tennis player, "with an ego as big as Forest Hills Stadium," as Caitlin had described him. Number two had expected her to be his housemate, his sexy Playboy bunny, and his mom. Caitlin had finally said no to all three roles.

Jesus, he was so incredibly wired. So uptight tonight.

Finally he did it, though. The absolute worst thing he could have done under the particular set of circumstances.

On the anniversary.

Nora's death three years before.

December 14.

First, he gathered up a handful of old photographs. He found most of the photos on a cluttered bottom shelf inside a glass-enclosed book cabinet. Next, he pulled a tattered wicker chair up close to one of the tall windows facing the lights of Riverside Drive and the river.

Carroll stared down at the West Side Highway, the

peacefully quiet boat basin. He was letting the present go all fuzzy and blurred.

Then he stood up again.

He took three particular record albums off the uneven stacks on the stereo. One album was *52nd Street*, Billy Joel self-consciously holding a trumpet on the cover. The second album was mainstream country and western, *I Believe in You* by somebody called Don Williams. The third was Barbra Streisand and Barry Gibb *Guilty*.

Carroll switched on the stereo, and the big floor speakers immediately hummed. He felt the power surge through the soles of his bare feet. He turned the volume way down.

He'd never been a big Streisand fan, but there were two particular songs he wanted to hear on this album: "Woman in Love" and "Promises." Out in the world, a moving van rumbled along Riverside Drive.

He still kept an old framed picture of Nora, hidden away facedown in the bottom of the bookcase. He slid it out now and carefully propped it on the arm of the couch.

For a long, pensive moment, he stared at Nora in her hospital-issue wheelchair. Anniversary of her death. Pain still sharp and fresh as yesterday, it seemed. He could remember *exactly* when the snapshot had been taken. After they'd operated. After the surgeons had failed to remove her malignant tumor.

In the photo, Nora was wearing a simple yellow-flowered sundress, a knitted blue cardigan sweater. She had on a pair of crazy high-topped sneakers that became her trademark as an invalid.

She was smiling radiantly in the picture. Not once to his knowledge had she completely broken down during the illness; not once had she felt sorry for herself. She'd been thirty-one years old when they'd found the tumor. She'd had to watch her blond hair fall out from the chemotherapy treatments. Then she'd had to adapt to life in the inflexible iron clutches of her wheelchair. Nora had somehow accepted that she wasn't going to see her children grow up or anything else the two of them had laughed and dreamed about and always taken for granted.

Why couldn't he finally accept her death?

Why couldn't he ever accept the way life was apparently supposed to be?

Arch Carroll stopped and listened more closely to Barbra Streisand singing.

The song "Promises" made him remember the stretch when he'd visited Nora every night, night after night, at New York Hospital. After the hospital visits, he would eat at Galahanty's Bar up the hill on First Avenue. A very tired burger, soggy home fries, draft beer that tasted the way swamp grass smelled. Probably the beginning of his drinking problems.

The two Streisand songs had been local favorites on Galahanty's jukebox. They always made him think of Nora—all alone back at that scary, skyscraper hospital.

Sitting in the bar, he'd always wanted to go back—at ten, eleven o'clock—to talk with her just a little bit more; to sleep with her; to hold her tight against the gathering night inside her hospital room. To squeeze every possible goddamn moment out of the time they had left together . . .

The worst, the very truest line for him in "Promises" finally came . . .

Tears rolled slowly down his cheeks. The pain inside was like a rock-solid column that extended from the center of his chest all the way up to his forehead. The sadness and inconsolable grief were for Nora, though, not for himself—the unfairness of what had happened to her.

He began to hold himself fiercely tight, squeezing hard with both arms. He was remembering more than he wanted to about the time around Nora's death. He was going to blow apart one of these times. Real tough cop, right?

When would this cold, hollow feeling please stop? The past three years had been unbearable. When would it please fucking stop?

He always had this same insane urge—to break glass.

Just to punch glass.

Blindly, irrationally punch glass.

Caitlin, meanwhile, stood immobile, perfectly silent, in the darkened hallway. She couldn't catch her breath, couldn't even swallow right then. She had wandered back from the bedroom when she'd heard noises. Faint strains of music . . .

So sad to watch Carroll like this, with the old photographs.

Finally she walked back to the bedroom and huddled deep down into the body-warm covers and sheets.

Lying there alone, she bit down hard on her lip. She understood and felt so much more about Carroll now. Maybe she understood more than she wanted to.

She stared at shadows walking the bedroom ceiling; she thought about her own life since she'd come to New York. Somehow she'd known she would never completely fit in Lima, Ohio. There were so many other experiences she needed to try. There was her long-standing need to involve herself in the financial arena. Maybe to vindicate her father, maybe just to make him proud again. She'd become a success; everybody acknowledged that.

Only recently, for the first time in many years, she wasn't

sure if success was what she wanted now, if she'd even done the right thing leaving the Midwest. Right at the moment, she was not completely sure about anything.

Except maybe one thing: she was in love with Carroll. She was falling deeply in love.

She wanted to hold him right now, only she was afraid. Caitlin closed her eyes and felt a great sense of solitude assail her. Would she always be a trespasser in Carroll's life?

She didn't know exactly how long she'd been alone. The bed felt so empty without Carroll.

The telephone on the nightstand began to ring.

It was three-thirty in the morning.

Carroll didn't pick up in the living room. Where was he?

She waited, four, five rings, and he still didn't pick up. Finally she grabbed the receiver.

A high-pitched and very excited voice was on the line. A man was talking before she had a chance to say a word.

"Arch, sorry to wake you. This is Walter Trentkamp. I'm down at number Thirteen right now. The stock exchange in Sydney just opened. There's a massive panic! You'd better come now. *It's all going to crash!*"

# Chapter 27

*Manhattan*

AT 3:40 A.M., while Caitlin and Carroll were hurrying downtown, a restless David Hudson was riding aboard the strangely crowded Eighth Avenue subway.

The rattling, gray metal cars were filled with staggering, vacant-eyed drunks. There were clusters of Forty-second Street prostitutes. Here and there a late night Irish bartender or transit worker sat in wary silence.

In order to avoid the unpleasant sweet-sour liquor smells, Hudson had stationed himself in the open bridge between two of the jouncing cars. Sometimes when he couldn't sleep, he would ride the mesmerizing subways for hours like this— nothing on his mind but the passing stations and the speed. It was a little like walking a night patrol in Vietnam.

He'd worked late at the Vets garage. It was down to the

agonizing final details now, always the last details to get exactly right.

It all happened so quickly, so unexpectedly, on the train . . .

As the subway relentlessly raced north, the heavy metal door between the cars suddenly opened. Two black men in their middle twenties squeezed into the swaying space between the cars.

"Mind movin' on, my man!" One of the two sniffled and showed a row of dull gold caps.

Hudson said nothing. The train was just braking into the Fifty-ninth Street station, a maze of connecting, blue-tinted platforms that were flashing by.

"I said—*move on*, my man!"

Colonel David Hudson's feet shifted slightly on the throbbing steel plates. He automatically slipped into the combat stance. The train bucked and squealed loudly to a stop, and the one with the gold caps started to move.

The rest was like a familiar dream for Hudson. His clenched fist shot forward, followed immediately by a martial-arts kick.

The lightning blows were lethal. One accurately smashed into the group leader's temple; the second crunched his jaw. He reeled backward and fell from the train.

The second man pulled a knife. Hudson struck before the man could use it. Blood exploded over the attacker's right eyebrow.

"You! *Hey, you! Stop right there!*"

David Hudson heard shouts as the subway doors slid open. Two transit authority police in black leather jackets, a man and a woman, were running his way. They were coming fast, a dark blur hurtling down the crowded platform.

The police officers had their nightsticks out. The heavy wooden Billy clubs were flying, pumping up and down as they ran.

Colonel David Hudson burst from the gaping train doors before they could reach him.

"You! Stop! Stop!" The transit cops screamed their sharp commands from the rear.

David Hudson felt incomprehensible terror as he pushed and stumbled along the jammed subway platform. The Lizard Man was flashing back. The lessons of the Lizard Man . . .

For it to all end like this was so absurd. So impossible to foresee. He had a "sample" bond inside his jacket, and they'd search him for certain.

How could Green Band end *here?* In a mundane New York City subway station?

David Hudson could see the careful planning, the detailed pieces of Green Band, swept into disarray by nothing more significant than a stroke of bad luck. He ran alongside colorful advertising billboards. Long-running plays, Perdue chickens, current movie hits, went swirling past in a Technicolor blur.

The stone floor was slick with rainwater that had drained down from the street. The smell of urine was overpowering in the endless, fetid tunnel.

For it all to end like this was unthinkable.

"Stop! Stop, you!"

Not a single person dared to help the trailing police team. Hudson looked too determined, too potentially dangerous, to grapple with. He was a flying, one-armed madman!

His legs were pumping furiously high, and his face was fearsome in its intense concentration. He sideswiped a weaving drunk and didn't feel the insubstantial body bounce off.

It was too absurd for the mission to end here! *Wasn't* it too absurd?

An explosion suddenly echoed through the long stone tunnel behind him. People all over the station began to scream. A teenaged Puerto Rican girl crouched low, her palms flat against the wet concrete. An elderly man held down his feathered fedora with both hands.

The cops had actually fired warning shots.

They were shooting inside the late night subway station.

Dark stone stairs were off to his right! Stairs to what though? Hudson could see the street looming above, a patch of purplish gray sky. He ran three steps at a time.

*Up*, he screamed at himself. *Outside!* Out of this careless, stupid trap he'd stumbled into.

Hudson sprinted blindly down West Sixtieth Street. He ran across the empty street against the red light, trailing rags of his own breath. He continued down Sixtieth Street, past Columbus, slipping into a maze of high-rise beige and gray apartment buildings. His heart pounding, he finally stopped in a darkened doorway.

Seconds later the two cops spun around the same corner of the gray brick building. He hadn't lost them, after all.

Hudson slid his gun from his coat and trained it on the male. His finger curled round the trigger . . . Heart shots would be necessary here. He watched as they searched among the buildings' shadows.

"Where the hell did he go?" the cop asked, breathing hard, wheezing like a much older man.

Colonel Hudson continued to watch from the building's doorway . . . They only had to start walking toward him, and they were dead. Both of them . . .

"You wanna call this off?" the patrolman asked. "I don't see him."

The female cop shrugged as she pulled off her duty cap.

David Hudson held his breath. Don't come any closer, he thought. Not another step closer.

Please, don't.

"Yeah. He's probably miles away. That creep could *run*," the patrolwoman said in a shrill voice.

Hudson listened to their footsteps slowly fading. Cruel pain exploded inside his chest. He finally had to sit down on the curb.

If he'd had to shoot those two cops . . .

He stuck the gun inside his jacket. No need for that now. He didn't need any kind of disaster.

Everything was going to come soon. The high-and-mighty United States was going to come crashing down to reality. Colonel David Hudson thought it was a fate well deserved.

# Chapter 28

"WHAT'S HAPPENING, ARCH, *I think*, is a disorderly, almost a riotous market condition. Everybody desperately wants to sell. Except there's a corresponding lack of buyers," Caitlin said.

"What *exactly* does that mean?" Carroll asked. "What happens now?"

"It means the bottom-line price of stocks and bonds has to plummet dramatically . . . The crash that's apparently coming could last a few hours, days, or drag on for years."

"Years?"

"Back in sixty-three, on the day Kennedy was assassinated, the market collapsed and was shut down early. The next day it recovered. But it wasn't until after the Second World War that the market recovered from the crash of 1929. There's *never* been a situation to match this one against, though. This panic is happening all over the world. All at the same time."

Carroll and Caitlin Dillon were hurrying across the

immense marble lobby of the World Trade Center. It was here, on the ground floor and mezzanine, that the fiduciary nerve center of the banks and trust companies had been established after the bombing on Wall Street.

The escalator stairs to the mezzanine were frozen to a stop. An impromptu sign over a red arrow read FINANCIAL SECTION and pointed straight up.

Carroll and Caitlin started to jog up the motionless metal stairs. It was just past 4:00 A.M.

"This looks a little more organized than number Thirteen. Not much, though," Carroll observed.

Red and blue intercom wires were strung up everywhere, hanging like Christmas decorations over the escalators and fire exit stairways. Open radio channels connecting uptown offices with the financial center squawked and chattered endlessly. Even at that time in the morning, the hum and buzz of electronic noise was unrelenting.

From a row of high-vaulted windows, Carroll and Caitlin could see a black Bell army helicopter landing. Limos and official cars were discharging somber-looking men carrying briefcases.

"What's causing the worldwide panic?" Carroll wanted to know as he and Caitlin entered a cavernous marble hallway with no visible exit.

Caitlin rubbed her arms warm as she walked. The glass doors to the outside were opening constantly, and the building was as cold as a meat freezer.

"None of the usual safeguards in the systems are working Not enough fail-safe devices were ever built in for a situation like this. Academic economists have been warning the New York Stock Exchange for years. Every MBA candidate in the country knows that something like this could conceivably happen."

Carroll pushed open heavy pine doors into a huge, frantic conference room, almost a miniature stock exchange. Brakers on complex NYNEX telephone consoles, analysts with IBM desktop computers, were talking all at once.

The room was jammed with frenetic shadowy figures many of whom were shouting into phone receivers they managed to cradle, in a practiced defiance of gravity, between jaw and shoulder. It was bedlam. It reminded Carroll of, give or take some modern accoutrements, a print he'd once seen of a Massachusetts insane asylum in the late 1800s.

Unconditional orders were being issued to sell, at the very best price possible. Jobs and business relationships were being routinely threatened over the long-distance telephones.

Jay Fairchild, tall, jowly, bald as an infant, lumbered out of a clique of gray suits to meet Caitlin and Carroll. Fairchild was the undersecretary of the Treasury, a man who'd come to rely regularly on Caitlin's judgments, her usually astute, almost uncanny hunches about the market.

"Jay, what the hell has happened tonight?"

Fairchild's eyes had all the animation of glass beads. There was a standing joke that all undersecretaries were illegitimate children of past congressmen and presidents. They definitely had a rare, collective ability to look completely out of place.

"Just about *every* nightmare scenario you or I could ever have imagined has come true tonight," Fairchild said. His voice held a tiny, whistling sibilance. "At the end of the day yesterday, out in Chicago, metal skyrocketed. A ton of futures, coffee, and sugar flopped badly. Bank of America and First National began calling in their loans."

Caitlin couldn't hold back her anger at that news. "Those unbelievable shits! Morons! The commodity people out of Chicago won't listen to anybody, Arch. There have been all sorts of speculative excesses on the options market long before this. For years and years. That's one more reason we were ripe for this panic."

"None of that is the *real* problem right now, though," Jay Fairchild said. "The crash is being precipitated by the god-damn banks! . . . The banks are almost completely responsible. Let's wander back to the lobby. You'll see what I mean. It's worse than it looks up here."

FBI agents and hard-nosed-looking New York City police officers were conscientiously screening the credentials of everyone trying to get into the conference room on the ground floor. Carroll knew the FBI men. They had no problem getting in.

Once inside, the thundering noise and activity were easily double what Carroll and Caitlin had witnessed and heard upstairs. It was still only 4:30 A.M., but a nightmarish fear had taken firm hold—you could see it on every face inside the overcrowded room.

The business investigators who squeezed into the conference room included some of the more sophisticated new breed of bankers. In the not-so-distant past, most banks had wanted to be viewed as impregnable places for their depositors' money, secure fortresses of capital. So bankers tended to be characterized by physical and emotional restraint, by almost compulsive neatness, by conservatism in their behavior and their thinking.

That was hardly the case with the men and women packed into this room. These were glossy, well-tailored globe-trotters, most of them as comfortable in Geneva, in Paris, or in Beirut as they were in New York. The spiritual leader of this cosmopolitan group was Walter Wriston, the now retired head of Citicorp. In Caitlin's opinion, Wriston had been little more than a glorified traveling salesman, but some thought him a genius.

"There's another factor contributing to the current disaster," Jay Fairchild said. "The very real possibility of a worldwide crash, rather than an isolated one in the United States. This time, the whole bloody world really could go down. It's been that volatile a situation, potentially, for at least the last four years."

Everyone they passed in the formal conference room appeared hopelessly grave and, once again, battle weary to Carroll. The scene was something like a general alarm on a warship.

Caitlin said, "Seven days of brokerage transactions are now unresolved. The bankers are competing, they're actually competing to see who can take the most clear-cut, amoral advantage of the chaos!" Her face was flushed, and there was an anger in her voice that Carroll hadn't heard before.

Carroll didn't technically understand some of what was being said, but he grasped enough. When you misappropriate people's money, a lot of small investors' money given to you on trust, he figured you were a common criminal.

Call him naive and old-fashioned, but that was how he felt.

"It sounds to me like *nobody's* protecting the ordinary investor right now."

Jay Fairchild nodded. "Nobody is. The big banks are all busy maneuvering for the oil billions. They couldn't give a damn about the poor bastard out there with a hundred shares of Polaroid or A T and T."

"Arch, Arab oil money is the name of the game. Arab money is almost always conservatively managed. Since last Friday they've been trying to move out of the U.S. Treasury bills. Into gold. Into other precious metals. The banks are all shamelessly scrambling for the huge Arab fees. They're like rats on a sinking ship, bailing out of the dollar—rushed into sterling, the yen, the Swiss franc, all the more stable currencies . . . Chase, Manufacturers, Bank of America, they're making small fortunes right now." Caitlin's lips were tight as she spoke.

"Do the two of you really know what you're talking about?" Carroll finally asked in desperation.

Caitlin and Jay Fairchild looked at each other. They answered almost simultaneously:

"Right now, no."

"*Nobody* knows *exactly* what this is about. But what we've just told you is generally true."

The three of them stood by helplessly watching the potential stock market crash gain a frightening momentum of its own.

Reports from London, Paris, Bonn, and Geneva came rushing in. The news was as depressing as that of a natural calamity.

Men in white shirtsleeves and loosened neckties took turns calling out the more substantial telex quotes for the benefit of beleaguered clerks who reported them into a massive central computer.

| Phibro-Salomon | bought at | 121/2 | down 22 |
| General Electric | bought at | 35 | down 31 |
| IBM | bought at | 801/2 | down 40 |

By eleven-thirty on the morning of December 15, most U.S. banks, including every savings and loan, had been closed. The Chicago, Philadelphia, Boston, Pacific, and midwest exchanges had all been officially shut down. The emotional panic for investors was in full force; it was virtually unstoppable in every city, every small town, across the United States.

At noon an elderly man made his way toward the hub of action at the front of the World Trade Center crisis room. Many of the young brokers and bankers didn't recognize Anton Birnbaum. Those who did regarded him with sharp, uneasy glances. It wasn't every day that one encountered a Wall Street legend.

Birnbaum actually looked more like an ancient New York City pawnbroker than one of the world's acknowledged financial geniuses, a man with an unblemished reputation during all of his years in business.

President Justin Kearney had arrived by helicopter from Washington less than thirty minutes before. He was conferring with Philip Berger from the CIA. Both recognized Anton Birnbaum as the old man approached. The president greeted the financier warmly, speaking with great deference and sincere respect.

"It's awfully good to see you again, Anton. Especially right now." The president spoke formally, as he would to a visiting foreign dignitary. Lately his manner had been more than a little uncertain. For more than a week both the American and the foreign press had been lashing his administration for its failure to deal with the economic crisis. It had had the same effect on Kearney as a shameful public flogging.

Kearney and Anton Birnbaum eventually disappeared into

a small private office, the door of which was guarded by beefy protectors from the Secret Service.

"It's good to be seen out in the world, Mr. President. I don't get out so much anymore. Mr. President, if I might be allowed to speak first, I have an idea, a plan you might wish to consider . . .

"I have just gotten off the phone with two gentlemen you've possibly never heard of. It's worth repeating both conversations. One man is from Milwaukee, a Mr. Clyde Miller. The other man resides in Nashville, Tennessee—Mr. Louis Lavine."

Anton Birnbaum said this in a slow, very deliberate style that made each word seem vitally important.

"Mr. Miller is the chief executive officer of a large Milwaukee brewing company. Mr. Lavine is currently treasurer for the state of Tennessee . . . I have just convinced Mr. Miller to buy five hundred thousand shares of General Motors stock, which is right now at forty-seven. He will buy the stock, and keep buying it until the price goes back to sixty-seven. He is prepared to invest up to two hundred million dollars.

"I've asked Mr. Lavine to buy NCR stock, which is now at nineteen, and continue to buy it until the price moves up to thirty. He's prepared to commit up to seventy-five million dollars for the purchase." Birnbaum then went on to explain to the president why the plan he'd conceived could actually work.

"I only hope that the courage of these two gentlemen will actually turn the direction of this catastrophe. I pray it will restore some necessary optimism. Mr. President, I have a belief that it will . . . Once the market sniffs a demand for these two bellwether issues, smart money will undoubtedly start

284

moving. The risks arbitrageurs, who can spot an uptrend in an avalanche and who command billions in ready cash, will begin testing the waters.

"I have advised a select few of my associates, who have responsibility for mutual and pension funds around the country, that a dramatic break in the crisis situation is now imminent. I have strongly suggested that they look for opportunities to begin bargain hunting before they lose out on a very fast and favorable profit spiral. A spiral back close to where the market began this morning."

The news of Anton Birnbaum's recovery plan traveled with appropriate dispatch through the main conference room. Emotional arguments over whether the daring strategy was right, or disastrous, raged immediately.

"Clyde Miller has just bankrupted his own corporation." One of the harsher detractors laughed with derision at the news.

Two other middle-aged bankers argued their way into a fist-fight. Creaking haymakers were thrown and somehow managed to connect with some authority. A loop of bankers and stock analysts surrounded the breathless, wheezing pugilists, and at least a couple of side bets were laid. The fight ended with both bankers leaning against each other as if each were trying to shore up the other's dignity. In a small way they symbolized the shambles of the system that had worked in spite of itself for so long.

As the winter morning passed into steely-gray afternoon, however, it was obvious that the dramatic Birnbaum plan was either too late or too little. There was no significant change in attitude, and therefore the plan was unable to stop the momentum of the declining market.

The largest single-day losses ever had already been recorded on the world's stock markets.

On October 29, 1929, losses had been fourteen billion dollars.

On December 15, the single day's recorded losses around the world exceeded two hundred billion dollars.

# Chapter 29

AT SEVEN THAT night, Carroll and Caitlin Dillon watched a chilling news report with more than a hundred of the principals who were actually making the headlines inside the World Trade Center. TV camera teams, top free-lance national magazine and newspaper photographers, and network radio reporters carrying lightweight tape recorders on their shoulders were swarming all over the man on the street in New York City.

A TV news interviewer stopped a man entering St. Patrick's Cathedral on Fifth Avenue. "How do you personally react to today's financial tragedy?" he asked. "What they're now calling a Black Market?"

"It makes me very frightened. Very sad. Nothing in this society of ours seems secure anymore. I had a few dollars. Safe. In IBM, in A T and T, the blue-chips only. Now I have virtually nothing. I'm seventy-three years old. What am I going to do?"

A TV interview crew from "Eyewitness News" was set up to

intercept pedestrians near Lincoln Center on Columbus Avenue.

"Excuse me, sir," called the reporter to one man. "What's your response to the latest reports, the critical situations on Wall Street?"

"My response! I'll tell you what. There's nothing you can believe anymore. After Watergate, you couldn't believe in the president of the United States. After Vietnam, you couldn't believe in our military's moral stance. You can't believe in church leaders anymore. Now? Now you can't even believe in the almighty dollar . . ."

TV news teams roamed Forty-second Street near Grand Central Station. One interviewer even thrust his mike at a cop.

"You're a police officer. You've undoubtedly seen this city in other times of great stress . . .blackouts, racial riots . . . How do you compare this situation right now?"

"This is about the hairiest I've seen it in New York. Not violent. Not yet, anyways. It's just, people are like, they're like walking zombies. Everybody I talk to, totally blitzed. It's like somebody changed all the rules."

TV camera crews were a constant fixture all over Wall Street and the World Trade Center area. TV newsman Curt Jackson had actually been living in a construction-company trailer on Wall Street since the Friday-night bombing. He promised his audience he wouldn't leave until the crime, the Green Band mystery, was solved.

"You're a native New Yorker, sir?" Curt Jackson asked a gentleman in his familiar, authoritative voice.

"That's right. I'm a New Yorker, thirty-eight years."

"What comment do you want to make about the terrible panic, the tragedy in the market today?"

"A comment for you? Well . . . you see this gold chain I wear? You see this beautiful gold watch I wear? That's where I keep my emergency money . . . always ready to travel. Always right here with me at all times . . . Any more trouble like this, it's adios, New York City. You oughta buy a gold watch for yourself. Just in case we don't do so good tomorrow."

Around ten-thirty, Caitlin and Carroll ran into Walter Trentkamp. They had been walking the long, broad hallways inside the World Trade Center, still waiting for definitive news from around the world. They were holding hands when they came upon the avuncular FBI head.

Walter didn't say anything, but his gray-green eyes fairly sparkled with delight. "You see," he said to Caitlin and Carroll, "something decent can come out of anything. Damn, this is the first good thing I've seen or heard in a week." With that, and a special wink toward Caitlin, Trentkamp continued on his way down the corridor.

Suddenly he turned and called out to Carroll. "Hey, I thought I told you to keep me posted on what was going on!"

Then he disappeared around the corner.

Late that night, Caitlin swallowed sips of warm diet soda and sat entranced before a forty-inch television screen just off the main crisis room. The monitor's reception was crisp and terrific. The antennae for all the major national networks were on the roof.

"This is it," she whispered to Carroll. "The exchange in Hong Kong will be the first important one to open around the world. Sydney and Tokyo are both staying closed until noon, we hear. Yesterday, the Hang Seng Index fell eighty points. This will really tell the story."

Caitlin and Carroll were sitting with a tightly clustered nest of Wall Street bankers, frayed men and women who were like spectators burned out by watching some unlikely event. A closed-circuit TV broadcast was being beamed by satellite from Asia to New York. The blackest gallows humor had gained control of the waiting room—as it often does in the worst disasters and emergencies.

On the flickering color TV screen, they all watched cameramen and news reporters—live—recording history from behind Hong Kong police lines. Farther down the crowded, rowdy street, tens of thousands of Hong Kong residents were chanting loudly, waving hand-printed political placards. Meanwhile, single lines of dark-suited stockbrokers were beginning to march solemnly into the exchange itself.

"The brokers look like pallbearers," Carroll whispered to Caitlin. He stroked her arm lightly.

"It isn't exactly a cheery sight, is it? It certainly *does* look like a state funeral."

"Yeah. And whose funeral?" Carroll asked.

A foreign correspondent for one of the major American networks eventually stepped up to a TV camera planted on the mobbed cacophonous Hong Kong street. The newsman wore a rumpled seersucker suit and spoke with an affected, clipped British accent.

"Never before have we seen such a graphic demonstration of the polarization between Third World and Western hopes and dreams. Here in Hong Kong, I believe we are seeing a minidrama of the imminent future of the world. It is now the day after stock prices have tumbled precipitously everywhere . . . The bond market is in shambles; the French and Arabs are liquidating their holdings at the rate of billions a day ... And in Hong Kong this morning, many people are deeply concerned, even sad-faced ... But *the majority*, surprisingly large numbers, mostly university and street-gang youths, but also the unemployed—are shouting anti-U.S. slogans, even praying for a shattering stock market crash. These people are clearly rooting for a full-scale world economic crash. They're expecting the worst, and they're gleeful about the expected disastrous outcome ... The long-awaited fall of the West."

Suddenly, everything changed!

Unbelievably.

Beautifully, and all around the world.

Almost as if it had been prearranged, too.

Not forty minutes after the Hong Kong Exchange opened, stock prices on the Hang Seng began to stabilize; then stock prices actually started to rise—to surge powerfully upward on the index.

To the keen disappointment of many of the jeering university students and workers mobbing the streets outside, a dizzying spiral of nearly 75 points followed in the next hour alone.

The exchange in Sydney opened in very much the same manner. Grim and exhausted brokers at first, highly organized labor and student rallies against capitalism, against the United States in particular—then a burst of excited buying. A dramatic spiral up.

The same scenario followed at the late-opening exchange in Tokyo.

In Malaysia an hour later.

*Everywhere.*

Carefully orchestrated recovery.

The manipulator's manipulation—but to what end?

At 8:30 A.M. New York time, looking as if he'd recently been liberated from the dustiest carrel in the New York Public Library, Anton Birnbaum peered inside the World Trade Center emergency meeting area. This time, however, a boisterous entourage surged forward and escorted the financier to the front of the pandemoniacal room.

President Justin Kearney appeared relaxed, almost jovial, as he met the aging financial mastermind. Vice President Thomas Elliot was standing beside him, still looking controlled and restrained. The vice president was the coolest of the Washington leaders. Birnbaum himself seemed astonished by the general hubbub, the strange celebration, so early in the morning. He was equally astonished by the way the market, like some whimsical thing subject not to the rules of money, but to the patterns of the wind, had come back so strongly.

"Mr. Birnbaum. Good morning."

"Yes. Good morning, Mr. President, Mr. Vice President. And I hear it is a pretty good morning."

"By God, you did it."

"By God. Or in spite of Him, Mr. President."

"This is amazing. It's quite moving. See? . . . Real tears." Caitlin was hanging lightly on to Carroll's arm. She dabbed her eyes and was not alone in the gesture.

They were at the heart of the frenzied celebration. Off to one side of the room, President Kearney was emotionally clutching his chief of staff. The secretaries of Treasury, State, and Defense were positively boyish with their loud whoops, their hand clapping. The gray-suited chairman of the Federal

Reserve had danced briefly with the cantankerous chairman of the Joint Chiefs of Staff.

"I don't believe I've ever seen bankers so joyous before," Caitlin said.

"They still dance like bankers, though." Carroll smiled at the odd but genuine scene of relief. "No threats to Michael Jackson here."

He couldn't help feeling elation in the midst of this crazy, almost riotous room. It wasn't as if they'd actually found Green Band, but it was something, a sliver of merriment at the heart of all the recent grimness and frustration.

Caitlin nuzzled the side of his face with her mouth. "I'm already getting worried again. I only hope . . ."

"What do you hope?" Carroll held Caitlin's arm. He felt unbelievably close to her. They had already shared more charged moments than some people did in a lifetime.

"I hope that it continues like this, and doesn't come crashing down."

Carroll was silent, studying the oddly uplifting scene before him. Somebody had found a phonograph, and the sound of Scottish bagpipers could be heard over the general din. Somebody extremely resourceful was dragging in a couple of cases of champagne. There was something just a little forced in the sudden celebration—but what the hell? These were people who'd been about to fall off the edge of their world, and slippery though it might be, they'd found some kind of temporary footing.

Still . . .

Still . . .

Even as Carroll sipped his champagne, something kept him from getting too hopeful. This is all premature, and therefore dangerous, he was thinking as the party heightened in intensity. The policeman inside him never stopped working, never stopped probing, never stopped figuring out all the possible angles. Damn it, police work *was* in his blood.

Where is Green Band? Is Green Band watching right now?

What are they thinking? What kind of party are they having today? *Who's telling them everything we do before we even do it?*

# Chapter 30

THERE WAS NO more time to waste. Clearly, there was no time at all. Every passing hour was vitally important. Anton Birnbaum's hyperactive mind was clicking automatically like a computer.

Birnbaum had begun to make urgent phone calls from his eleven-room apartment on Riverside Drive, near Columbia University. He had definite hunches now—strong suspicions after talking to Caitlin Dillon and her policeman friend Carroll.

At junctures in his life, Birnbaum had been thought of as the consummate international businessman, at times as the world's preeminent economist. Certainly he was an intense student of life, intrigued by the vicissitudes of human behavior. His curiosity was boundless, even at his age.

Never a day passed that Birnbaum didn't read for at least six or seven hours. Because of that lifelong habit, the financier knew he was still several steps faster than the other people in his business, especially the lazy boys on Wall Street.

What was the operative connection between Green Band, the bombing of December 4, and the dangerous economic events of the past two days?

Why had nothing conclusive been discovered about Green Band yet?

Why were the Green Band provocateurs consistently two steps ahead of those conducting the investigation? How could that be happening again and again?

Like nature, Anton Birnbaum abhorred a vacuum, and that was precisely what Green Band had masterfully created: a huge empty space in which logical questions had no apparent answers.

Months back he had heard rumors of a Russian-sponsored plot to dramatically disrupt the stock market . . . His closest and most reliable contacts at the CIA had been worried about the activities of the wretched François Monserrat. Was Monserrat somehow connected with the Green Band plot? And what about certain members of the government here in America? The CIA's Philip Berger? He was a character Birnbaum had never found it in himself to trust . . . Or Vice President Thomas Elliot? He was a chilly one as well, and he played everything close to the vest.

Too many possibilities. Almost as if *that* were part of the plan.

As the tiny ancient man made his inquisitional phone calls that morning—to Switzerland, England, France, South Africa, to both West Germany and East Germany—he felt like someone who had an important name on the tip of his tongue but just couldn't remember it.

Anton Birnbaum wrote down the most suspicious names.
Philip Berger

Thomas More Elliot

François Monserrat

And perhaps the connecting link: Red Tuesday.

The clue was there—the beginning of the answer they were searching for. He was certain of that.

If he could just find the one clue . . . If he could just figure out the motive for the events thus far. It was here, somewhere.

Anton Birnbaum worked at his desk, sketchily making notes, making highly confidential calls. He worked feverishly, like a man who felt his time running out.

Carroll had decided to start at square one again, to thoroughly check and recheck every lead, every hunch he'd ever had about Green Band. The task would take countless hours, he knew. It would require an intense search through the computers, even allowing for the fact that he had high-speed data at his disposal. Ah, police work.

He asked for clearance from the CIA and the FBI to make a search of their computer files. Neither organization gave him too much trouble, although Phil Berger imposed certain limitations on his access, for the usual reasons of national security.

Nearly eleven hours later Carroll stood before the dozen or so computer screens inside the crisis room at 13 Wall Street. He stared at the screens, and his eyes ached from the dull green glow.

He glanced at Caitlin, who sat with her slender fingers raised over a computer keyboard, ready to type out a password for further access to the FBI's files. There was no skill she didn't seem to have.

When the display screen answered, she rapidly typed again, this time requesting a readout of active and nonactive Vietnam veterans who, for whatever reason, had been under police sur-veillance during the past two years—a time frame she and Carroll had agreed on.

She added the subcategories: Explosives Experts; New York and Vicinity; Possible Subversive Leanings.

There was a long pause, a spooky electronic pause, and then the machine began its requested readout of Vietnam veterans.

Carroll had been down this particular route of investiga-tion, only not with this equipment and Caitlin's help. American terrorist-related groups were out there, but none was consid-ered very powerful or well organized. Phil Berger of the CIA had been investigating American paramilitary groups himself. He had waved Carroll off that trail once before.

"Can you print out a list of the real hard cases?" Carroll asked Caitlin.

"This is a computer. It can do anything if you ask it nicely."

The printer obligingly kicked back into life. Paper slid through it as the dot matrix clacked back and forward. A total count showed no more than ninety names of current soldiers and veterans with extensive explosives experience in Vietnam—men whom the FBI considered important enough to keep track of. Carroll ripped the paper from the printer and took it to a desk.

Adamski, Stanley. Corporal. Three years VA hospital, Prescott, Ariz. Member of left wing-oriented veterans group called the Rams, ostensibly a bikers club.

Carroll wondered how much of this was standard FBI para-noia.

The list was filled with dizzying cross-references, he soon

298

discovered. One name was connected to another, creating a mazelike effect. He could spend months working on all the permutations.

Keresty, John. Sergeant. Munitions expert. Discharged VA hospital, Scranton, Pa. 1974. Occupation: custodian, plastics corp. Member of the American Socialist party. Ridgewood, N.J. SEE: Rhinehart, Jay T.; Jones, James; Winston files.

The lists went on and on.

Carroll massaged his eyelids. He went for two coffees, then returned to the desk and even more sprawling computer sheets.

He said, "Any one of these men, or two or three of them could have helped blow up the financial district."

Caitlin gazed over his shoulder at the printout. "So where do we start?"

Carroll shook his head. He was filled with doubts again. They would have to investigate, maybe even visit, every name on the lists. They didn't have time.

Scully, Richard P. Sergeant. Plastique expert. Hospitalized Manhattan, 1974, for alcoholism. Extreme right wing sympathizer. Occupation: cabdriver. New York City.
Downey, Marc. Military assassin. Hospitalized 1971–73. Occupation: bartender. Worcester, Mass.

Carroll gazed at the burgeoning list again. An army officer, maybe? A disaffected officer with a grudge or a cause? Somebody exceptionally smart, nursing a grievance, year after year.

He laid his hands on the warm computer console. He wished he could coax all the secrets out of it, all the electronic links of which it was capable. He stared at the lengthy printout again. "An officer," he said. "Try that."

Caitlin went back to the keyboard to request more information. He watched her fingers move expertly over the keys. She was requesting information on known or suspected subversives who had been officers in Vietnam. Under the general rubric of "subversive" were included all kinds of people.

The screen began to issue more names. Colonels. Captains. Majors. Some were listed in these official records as schizophrenics. Others were supposedly burned out on drugs. Others had become evangelists, panhandlers, small-time bank and liquor store robbers. Carroll received a printout of these names as well. There were twenty-nine of the hard-core category in and around New York City.

The screen flickered again.

Names of the various officers on the FBI list now shimmered forth. Carroll once again ran his eyes over them.

Bradshaw, Michael. Captain. Discharged VA hospital, Dallas, Tex., 1971. Occupation: real estate salesman, Hempstead, Long Island. Post traumatic stress disorder victim.
Babbershill, Terrance. Major. Discharged dishonorably, 1969. Known Vietcong sympathizer. Occupation: English-language tutor for various Vietnamese families. Brooklyn, N.Y.

Carroll tried to focus. His eyes were beginning to water. He needed to feel the fresh cold night air on his face. But he continued to run his eyes up and down the screen.

Rydeholm, Ralph. Colonel.
O'Donnell, Joseph. Colonel.

Schweitzer, Peter. Lieutenant colonel.

Shaw, Robert. Captain.

Craig, Kyle. Colonel.

Boudreau, Dan. Captain.

Kaplan, Lin. Captain.

Weinshanker, Greg. Captain.

Dwyer, James. Colonel.

Beauregard, Bo. Captain.

Arnold, Tim. Captain.

Morrissey, Jack. Colonel.

Too many names, Carroll thought. Too many casualties in a war of total waste.

"Can you get me cross-references, Caitlin? Associations and connections between any of these men? The officers. The real hard-asses out of Vietnam?"

"I'll try."

Caitlin tapped a few keys. Nothing happened this time. She stared at the screen thoughtfully, then tapped another brief message.

Nothing happened.

She tapped out another message. Still nothing happened.

"Is something wrong?" Carroll asked.

"This is the best I can get, Arch. Damn it."

The unfortunate message that shone in front of them read "Further data: see files."

"See files?" he asked. "These *are* the files."

"They apparently have more information in FBI files that aren't on the computer, Arch. They're down in Washington. Why is that?"

*

At ten o'clock on the evening of December 16, Sergeant Harry Stemkowsky was thinking that he was actually solvent. He was financially comfortable, probably for the first time in his entire adult life.

He'd just bought a new Ford Bronco, also a luxurious beaver coat at Alexander's for Mary. Life was suddenly getting decent for them, for the first time in all their years together.

But Harry Stemkowsky couldn't bring himself to believe in any of it comfortably. This was all like Santa Claus and trips to Disney World—that kind of transient shit.

Who could identify with a sudden net worth of $1,152,000?

Stemkowsky felt a little like one of those Looney Tunes who won the New York State Lottery, then nervously kept their little jobs as janitors or U.S. postal employees. It was a matter of too much too fast. He kept getting the uneasy feeling that somebody was going to take it all away again.

At twenty past ten that evening, Stemkowsky carefully nosed his Vets cab out of the street noise and blazing yellow lights of midtown Manhattan. He'd finished his regular ten-hour shift, all according to Colonel Hudson's prescribed step-by-step plan for their ultimate success. The Checker cab bumped and rattled onto the Fifty-seventh Street entrance to the bridge.

A few minutes later the cab turned onto a busy avenue in Jackson Heights, then edged onto Eighty-fifth, where Stemkowsky lived with his wife, Mary. He absently licked his lips as he drove down the street. He could just about taste the stew Mary had said she was fixing when he'd left in the morning. The sudden expectation of beef, shallots, and those little light-puffed potatoes she usually made was mouthwatering.

Maybe he and Mary should retire to the south of France after this was over, he began to think. They'd be filthy rich

302

enough for sure. They could eat four-star French food until they got absolutely sick of it. Maybe move on to Italy. Maybe Greece after that. Greece was supposed to be cheap. Hey—who cared if it was cheap or not?

Harry Stemkowsky began to accelerate down the last flat stretch toward home.

"*Jesus Christ, buddy!*" he shouted suddenly, and pounded his brakes.

A tall bald-headed man, with an incredibly pained look, had run right out in front of the cab. He was frantically waving both arms over his head; he was screaming something Stemkowsky couldn't make out with the windows up.

Harry Stemkowsky recognized the look from Vietnam, though, from dreaded cleanup patrols into villages after devastating Phantom air strafes. His heart had already dropped through the floorboards of the cab. Something horrible and unexpected had happened here—something awful had happened in Stemkowsky's own neighborhood.

The terrified man was up against the cab window now, still screaming at the top of his voice. "Help me, please! Help! Please help!"

Stemkowsky finally got the window rolled down. He had his radio mike in hand, ready to call for whatever emergency help was needed. "What the hell happened? What happened, mister?"

Suddenly a small black Beretta was shoved hard, crunching like a nightstick, against Harry Stemkowsky's temple. "*This* is the matter! Don't move. Put back that mike." A second man appeared now, quickly emerging out of the smoky side-street darkness. He yanked open the creaking passenger-side door.

"Just turn the cab right around, Sergeant Stemkowsky. We're not going home quite yet."

303

An indefinite time later—hours? maybe days? There was no possible way to accurately gauge because all time had collapsed under him—Harry Stemkowsky felt hands angrily ripping under his armpits, lifting him rudely. The hands propped him hard onto a creaking wooden chair again. They'd injected him twice with drugs, probably Pentothal.

A man's face, a blur of soft pink, seemed to float down and step close to Stemkowsky's face. Harry Stemkowsky was aware of minty breath and musky cologne. Then his mind went into complete shock. He couldn't believe who this was.

*This face*—he'd seen it before, recently always distilled by a network TV screen or a newspaper . . .

No, he was confused. The drug had fucked his brain over—

What was going on here? This person couldn't be—

The face smiled horribly and said, "Yes, I'm François Monserrat. You know me under another name. This is an extraordinary shock, I know."

Harry Stemkowsky shut his eyes. This was all a bad dream. It would go away.

He opened his eyes and shook his head, which ached unbelievably. His eyeballs felt indescribably heavy. He simply could not believe it. So incredibly near the top. The ultimate traitor . . .

When Stemkowsky finally spoke, he was almost incoherent; incomprehensible words squirmed through his gummy, swollen lips. His tongue felt at least twice its normal size.

"Ga fuh-fuh-fuck yrrself. Fuh-fuck yrrself."

"Oh, please. Your time for being morally indignant is long past . . . All right, then . . . look at what we have here. Look at this."

Monserrat's hands were holding out a brown paper shopping bag. From it, he took out a familiar blue cooking pot.

Harry Stemkowsky screamed! He fought insanely against his bonds, forcing them to rip into his skin. Up close to his eyes, a fork dipped slowly into the depths of the pot. The fork speared a dripping chunk of beef bourguignonne that oozed brown gravy.

Stemkowsky screamed. He screamed again and again.

"It seems you guessed my little secret. You should also know by now how deadly serious this interrogation is. How important this is to me." Monserrat turned to his lieutenants.

"Bring in the unfortunate cook."

Harry Stemkowsky recognized Mary, but only slightly. She was such a pitiful caricature of her former self. Her face was badly bruised, purplish, and raw. Her bloated mouth opened crookedly as she saw Harry. Some of her front teeth were missing; her swollen gums were pulpy and bloody.

"Puh-puh-pleez?" Stemkowsky struggled; he lifted the chair legs right off the floor with his tremendous arm strength. "*She don know.*"

"I know that. Mary doesn't know how you came to possess stolen stock market bonds in Beirut, then in Tel Aviv. *You* know, though."

"Pleeze. Don-don-don hur' her . . ."

"I don't want to hurt her. So you tell me what you know, Sergeant. Everything that you know. You tell me right now. How did you get the stolen stock market bonds?"

Once again, that horrible smile from Monserrat.

It took another excessively cruel and gruesome fifteen minutes to get the information, to find out *some*, not all, of what Sergeant Harry Stemkowsky knew . . .

Information about the stolen bonds and Wall Street securities;

305

about the bombing on December 4. Not where Colonel Hudson was right now. Not even precisely who the Vets leader was. But a start, a beginning, at least. And a beginning was better than what Monserrat had been accustomed to recently.

François Monserrat stared down at a crippled Harry Stemkowsky and his wife. From Stemkowsky's perspective the terrorist leader seemed to be looking right through them, as if they were both totally insubstantial. The look on Monserrat's face was almost inhuman, frightening, sickening.

"You see now? None of your pain and none of poor Mary's suffering were necessary. It could have been five minutes of talking together, at most. Now, how's this for just rewards?"

A compact black Beretta appeared, paused so that the Stemkowskys could see what was coming, then fired twice.

The very last thing U.S. Army Sergeant Harry Stemkowsky ever thought was that he and Mary never got to enjoy their money. Over a million dollars, which he'd earned. It wasn't fair. Life wasn't ever fair, was it?

That night Arch Carroll went to his home in Riverdale. As he trudged up from the floodlit clapboard garage, the ground around him seemed to be spinning.

He climbed the creaky porch steps. Twinges of guilt struck painfully hard. He'd been neglecting the kids for too long this time.

Only the night-light was on downstairs. There was the soft electric buzz of kitchen appliances. Carroll took off his shoes and tiptoed upstairs.

He stopped and peeked inside the front bedroom where Elizabeth, AKA Lizzie, bunked with Mickey Kevin. Their tiny baby figures were delicately sprawled across twin beds.

He remembered buying the beds years before, at Klein's on Fourteenth Street. Just look at the little creepolas. Not a problem, not a care in the world. Life as it ought to be.

An ancient Buster Brown clock from Carroll's own childhood glowed and clicked softly on the far wall. It was next to posters of Def Leppard and the Police. Strange world for a little kid to grow up in.

Strange world for the big kids, too.

"Hi, you guys," he whispered too low to be heard. "Your old dad's home from the salt mines."

"Everybody's just fine, Archer," Mary K. said.

"You scared the living shit out of me, Mary. I never heard you come in."

"They understand all the problems you're having. We've been watching the news."

Mary K. gave her big brother a hug. She'd been seventeen the year both their parents had died in Florida. Carroll had brought her up after that. He and Nora had always been around to talk to her about her boyfriends—about Mary Katherine wanting to be a serious painter, even if she couldn't make any decent money at it. They'd been there when she needed them, and now it was the other way around.

"Maybe they understand okay about my work. How about the other things? Caitlin?" Carroll's head turned slowly toward his sister.

Mary K. took his arm and draped it over her shoulder. She was such a softie, such a sweet, gentle, and good lady. It was time she found someone as terrific as she was, Carroll often thought. Probably she wasn't helping her cause, living with him and the kids.

"They trust your parental judgment. Within reasonable bounds, of course."

307

"That's news."

"Oh, you're the Word and the Light to them, and you know it. If you say they'll like Caitlin, they instinctively believe it—because you said it, Arch."

"Well, they didn't show it the other morning. I *think* they'll like her. She's a terrific person."

"I'm sure she is. You have good instincts about people. You always knew which of my beaux was worth a second look. You're a sucker for people who are full of life, full of love for other people. That's what Caitlin's like, isn't she?"

Arch Carroll looked down at his baby sister and shook his head gently. He grinned. Mary K. was so smart. She had an artist's sensibility, but she was so practical. A curious combination, and irresistible in his opinion.

Carroll stretched his arms. The wound, that souvenir of a morning in France, still ached. "One day soon I'm going to take a week off. I swear it. I've got to get back in touch with the kids."

"What about your friend, Caitlin? Could *she* take a week off, too?"

Carroll said nothing. He wasn't sure if that was such a good idea. He went off to bed, where he lay exhausted but unable to fall over the edge into sleep. The computer screens at 13 Wall were still running through his mind, perplexing images. If there was any one avenue he could follow in the trail of Green Band, it would lead inevitably to Washington and deeper into the restricted files of the FBI.

Arch Carroll snored quietly, slept dreamlessly, and when his bedside alarm went off, it was just before dawn and still dark.

# Chapter 31

*Washington, D.C.*

WASHINGTON, CARROLL HAD always thought, was the ultimate Hitchcock movie location: so elegant, so quietly lovely and distinguished, yet paranoiac in all of its twisting, changing forms.

At 9:00 A.M. he squirmed out of a faded blue cab with a badly dented fender. His face was immediately slapped with raw cold and drizzle on Washington's Tenth Street. He hiked up his jacket collar. He squinted through the thick, soupy morning haze that obscured the concrete box that was the J. Edgar Hoover Building.

Once inside, he found the procedure at the escort desk mechanical and unnecessarily slow. It irritated him. The Bureau's famous procedures, the inefficiency they created, played like a mocking skit appropriate for "Saturday Night Live."

After several minutes of serious and pompous phone checks, he was granted a coded blue tag with the FBI's official insignia. He slid the plastic card into a metal entry gate and passed inside the hallowed halls.

An attractive woman agent, a researcher for FBI Data Analysis, was sitting outside the elevator on the fifth floor. She wore a man-tailored suit; her chestnut hair was wound back in a tight, formal chignon.

"Hello, I'm Arch Carroll."

"I'm Samantha Hawes. People *don't* call me Sam. Nice to meet you. Why don't you come this way, please."

She started to walk away, pleasant but efficient. "I've already collected as much material as I can for you to look at. When you told me what you were fishing for, I put in some hours of overtime. My material comes from the Pentagon and from our own classified files. Everything I could collect this quickly on your lists of names. It wasn't easy, I must say. Some of it I transcribed from material already on computer file. The rest—as you can smell—is contained in some really musty documents."

Samantha Hawes escorted Carroll to a library-style carrel beside a silent row of gray metal copiers. The desk was completely covered with thick stacks of reports. Carroll nearly groaned as he gazed at the mountainous stacks. Each report looked like every other. How was he supposed to find something unusual in this yawning heap of history?

He walked around the table, sizing up his task. Hidden among all the folders were connections between men—the tracks, the spoor they laid down; the events they lived through during and after Vietnam. Somewhere, surely, tracks would have crisscrossed, correspondences would have been made, relationships established.

"I have more. Do you want to see them now? Or is this enough to hold you for a while?" Samantha Hawes asked.

"Oh, I think this will do me pretty well. I didn't know we collected this much dirt on everybody down here."

Agent Hawes grinned. "You should see your file."

"Did you?"

"I'll be back over there, working in the stacks. You just holler if you need any more light reading, Mr. Carroll."

The FBI agent started to turn away, then, suddenly, she turned back. Samantha Hawes *seemed* to be a very contemporary woman, very pretty, very confident, and genteel southern, from her looks, anyway. Carroll couldn't help thinking that in days of old she would already have been a young mother of two or three, tucked away in Alexandria.

"There *is* something else." She looked concerned. "I don't know exactly what this all means. Maybe it's just me. But when I went through these files yesterday evening . . . I had the distinct feeling that some of them had been tampered with."

A small, very unpleasant warning bell rang in Arch Carroll's head. "Who would tamper with them?"

Samantha Hawes shook her head. "Any number of people have access to them."

"What do you mean when you say they've been tampered with."

"I mean that I think documents are missing from certain files."

Carroll reached out and grasped her wrist lightly. The information excited him. It meant that certain files, in some ways, were important to someone. Someone else had looked at them. Someone had possibly pilfered some of the documents.

Why? Which files?

He saw a strange look cross her face, as if she were asking herself about the precise nature of this unorthodox man who'd been admitted to FBI headquarters.

"Can you remember which files?"

"Of course I can." She moved toward the worktable and began sifting. She picked out five thick files, dropping them in front of Carroll. "This one . . . and this . . . this one . . . this one."

He gazed quickly at the names on the files.

Scully, Richard
Demunn, Michael
Freedman, Harold Lee
Melindez, Paul
Hudson, David

Why these five?" he asked.

"They served together in Vietnam, according to their documents. That's one good reason."

Carroll sat down. He still expected to come away from Washington empty-handed. He expected that the faint sense of anticipation he now felt would turn out to be nothing more than a false alarm. Five men on the FBI computer list of "subversives"—a term he knew was next to meaningless, at least the way the FBI used it.

He checked his own printouts, and his heart began to beat rapidly.

Scully and Demunn had been explosives experts.

And David Hudson had been a colonel, who, according to the brief note on the printout, had been active in the organization of veterans groups and veterans rights after Vietnam.

*Five men who had served together in the war.*

*Five men who were on his list and the FBI's.*

He slipped off his jacket and then the tie he'd worn especially for his big trip to Washington. He began to read about Colonel David Hudson.

# Chapter 32

*Washington, D.C.*

WHEN HE HAD finished reading, Arch Carroll softly shook his head.

U.S. Army Colonel David Hudson's thick 211 file, his entire life in the military, was spread out on the desk before him.

*Colonel David Hudson was the final enigma.*

David Hudson's military career had begun with high promise at West Point, where he'd been an honor graduate in 1966. He'd been a four-year member, and finally captain, of the tennis team. He was also a popular cadet, according to the available reports—a modern-day version of the all-American boy.

It got even better. David Hudson had subsequently volunteered for Special Forces "Q" courses, followed by special Ranger training. On a first impression, at least, the army couldn't have asked for a more diligent or professional young soldier.

Colonel David Hudson: all-American boy.

Every succeeding report Carroll read was highlighted and underscored with phrases like "one of our very best"; "the kind of young officer who should make us all proud"; "a model soldier in every way"; "unbridled, absolutely infectious enthusiasm"; "definitely one of our future leaders"; "the kind of material we can build the modern Army around."

In Vietnam Hudson had been awarded the Medal of Honor and the Distinguished Service Cross during his first tour. He had been captured and transported into North Vietnam for interrogation. He'd spent seven months as a POW. Apparently he'd almost died in the prison camp . . . He had then volunteered for a second tour and performed with "conspicuous gallantry and intrepidity" on several occasions.

Then, three months before the evacuation of Saigon, he'd been savagely wounded by a Vietcong grenade blast and subsequently lost his left arm. Hudson had reacted with characteristic bravura.

A hospital report read: "Colonel David Hudson has been a godsend, helping other patients, never seeming to feel sorry for himself . . . In every way, a thoroughly idealistic young man."

Following Vietnam, though, quite suddenly after his return to the United States, Colonel David Hudson's career, his entire life, became disturbingly unhinged. According to the files, the change was bewildering to his friends and family.

"It was almost as if a different man had returned from the war." His father was interviewed and quoted several times. "The fire, that wonderful, contagious enthusiasm, was burned out of David's eyes. His eyes were those of a very old man."

Colonel David Hudson: enigma, almost phantom, after coming home from the Vietnam War.

Hudson was stationed first at Fort Sam Houston in Texas, then at Fort Sill in Oklahoma. At Fort Polk in Louisiana, Hudson was quietly disciplined for "activities detrimental to the Army." Another report indicated that he was transferred twice within three months, for what seemed on the surface to be petty insubordinations . . . His marriage to Betsy Hinson, his hometown sweetheart, ended abruptly in 1973. Betsy Hinson said, "I don't even know David anymore. He's not the same man I married. David's become a stranger to everyone who knows him."

Hudson, in the postwar years, had become almost obsessive about his participation in a handful of Vietnam veterans organizations. As an organizer and spokesman at rallies around the country, Hudson had met and been photographed with liberal motion picture stars, with sympathetic big-business leaders, with recognizable national politicians.

At one point during the morning, Arch Carroll meticulously laid out Xerox copies of every available photo of David Hudson.

He rearranged the pictures until he liked the pattern of his collage. One photo was stained with coffee or cola. The stain looked recent. Samantha Hawes? Someone else? Or was he just getting squirrely?

In the photographs, Colonel David Hudson looked like the classic, idealized military man of past decades. With his Jimmy Stewart wholesomeness, he looked the way American soldiers had been pictured in the years before Vietnam. He had short blond hair in almost all the war photographs, a tightly set, somewhat heroic jaw, a pinched, slightly uncomfortable smile that was disarming. Colonel David Hudson was clearly very sure of himself and what he was doing. He was obviously proud, fiercely proud, to be an American soldier.

Carroll got up from the mess of official papers and wandered around the research room. Okay—what did he have here?

A leader, a natural soldier, who somewhere along the way had fucked up royally. Or maybe Hudson had been royally fucked?

There were probably hundreds, maybe even thousands, of men like David Hudson across the country. Some of them went berserk and had to be removed to the "screaming floors" in VA hospitals. Others sat quietly in dingy, lonely rooms and ticked slowly like time bombs.

Colonel David Hudson? . . . Was he Green Band?

Samantha Hawes reappeared with a pot of coffee, deli sandwiches, and assorted salads on a tray. "Getting into it, I see."

"Yes, it's something all right. Odd, and absolutely mesmerizing. Hard to figure, though."

Carroll rubbed the palms of his hands in circles over his red-rimmed eyes. "Thanks for the food, especially the coffee. The whole file is extraordinary. Colonel Hudson, especially. He's a very complex, very strange man. He's too perfect. The perfect soldier. Then what? What happened to him after he returned to the States?"

Samantha Hawes sat down beside Carroll. She took a healthy bite of an overstuffed sandwich. "As I said, there are some peculiar gaps in his military records. In all of their records. Believe me, I look at enough of them to know."

"What sort of peculiar gaps? What should be in there that isn't?"

"Well, there were no written reports on his special training at Fort Bragg, for example. There was nothing on his 'Q' or his Ranger training. There was almost nothing on his time as a POW. Those should all be in there. Marked highly confidential if need be, but definitely there in the file."

"What else is missing? Would there be photostated copies or originals anywhere else?"

"There should definitely be more psychological profiles. More reports after he lost his arm in Vietnam. There's very little on that. He was tortured by the Vietcong. He apparently still has flashbacks. All the backup data on his POW experience is conveniently missing. I've never seen a two eleven file without a complete psych workup, either."

Carroll selected a second roast beef sandwich half. "Maybe Hudson took them out himself?"

"I don't know how he could get in here, but it makes as much sense as anything else I read yesterday."

"Like? Please keep going, Samantha."

"Like the way they made him a cipher right after Vietnam. He had very high-level intelligence clearance in Southeast Asia. He was a heavy commander in Vietnam. Why would they give him such a nothing post back in the States? The arm? Then why not write it up that way?"

"Maybe that's why he ultimately quit the service," Carroll suggested. "The second-rate assignments once he got back home."

"Maybe. But why did they do it to him in the first place? . . .

318

They were grooming David Hudson before he came home. Believe me, they had serious plans for him. You can see tracks to glory all over those files. In the early years, anyway. Hudson was a real star."

Carroll jotted down a few notes. "What would a more predictable assignment have been? Once he was back in the States? If he was still on the fast track?"

"At the very least he should have gotten the Pentagon. According to his records, he was on an extremely fast track. Until the disciplinary problems, anyway. He got bush-league assignments before he did anything to deserve them."

"It doesn't make sense. Maybe they'll know something at the Pentagon. That's my next stop."

Samantha Hawes extended her hand. "My sincere condolences. The Pentagon makes this austere place seem like a hippie commune."

"I've heard they're a party group." Carroll smiled back at Agent Hawes. She was smart, and he liked her.

"Listen," she said. "There is something else you should know. One other person definitely went through the two eleven files in the past two weeks. On the fifth of December, actually."

Carroll stopped packing up and stared at Samantha Hawes. "Who?" he asked.

"On that day, certain two eleven files were ordered over to the White House. Vice President Elliot wanted to see them. He kept the files for more than six hours. Listen, Carroll. You come back here if you need any more help. Officially or otherwise . . . Promise?"

"I promise," Carroll said, and absolutely meant it.

*Riverdale, New York City*

The young Carroll boy had his marching orders, really strict orders, too.

Six-year-old Mickey Kevin Carroll had been allowed to walk the three blocks home from CYO basketball practice since the second month of the school year. He had very precise orders for the walk, which his Aunt Mary K. made him write out in his composition notepad:

- Look both ways at Churchill Avenue.
- Look both ways at Grand Street.
- Don't talk to strangers for any reason at all.
- Don't stop at the Fieldstone store before supper.
- If you do, it's instant death by torture.

Mickey Kevin was pondering the confusing mechanics of the basketball lay-up as he covered the long double block between Riverdale Avenue and Churchill Avenue. Brother Alexander Joseph had made it look kind of easy. Except when Mickey tried it himself, there were just too many things to remember, all practically at once. Somehow your leg and your arm had to come up; then you had to throw the ball perfectly into the high, high hoop. All at the same time.

As he rehearsed the confusing sport's primary action, Mickey Kevin gradually became aware of footsteps growing louder behind him.

He turned and saw a man. The man was walking his way. Walking pretty fast.

Mickey Kevin's body tightened. TV movies and stuff like that made you scared when you were alone. Somebody was always out to get the little kid or the baby-sitter all alone at home. It was a pretty creepy world. Some of the people out there were unbelievably creepy.

The man walking behind him looked pretty normal, Mickey guessed, but he decided to hurry it up a little anyway. Without looking too obvious, he started to take longer steps, faster steps. He walked the way he always did when he was trying to keep up with his dad.

There weren't any cars or anything at the corner of Grand Street. Mickey stopped according to the rules, anyway. He looked both ways.

He looked back then—and the man was really close. Really, really close.

Mickey Kevin *ran* across Grand Street, and Aunt Mary K. would have killed him on the spot. His heart was pounding now. Really thumping out loud. Right down into his shoes, he could fell his heartbeat.

Then Mickey Kevin did the really, really dumb thing. He knew it the second he did it. The instant!

He cut through the empty lot at the Riverdale Day School.

There were all of these tricky bushes and stuff back there. Everybody left empty beer cans and broken wine and liquor bottles. Mary K. had forgotten to put that on the list: Don't cut through the Riverdale Day School lot. It was too obvious for words.

Mickey pushed the prickly bushes out of his way, and he thought he heard the man coming through the lot behind him. Crashing through the lot. He wasn't completely sure. He'd have to stop walking to listen so he could tell. He decided to just keep running, to run like hell.

Full speed ahead now. As fast as he could, with all the

dark, thorny bushes, the hidden rocks and roots trying to trip him.

Mickey Kevin stumbled forward, his feet seeming to catch in dirt holes. He glided over slippery leaves. He nicked a rock and almost went over headfirst. He was panting now, his breath was too loud in his own ears, his footsteps were echoing like gunshots.

The back of his house suddenly appeared: the glowing amber porch lights, the familiar gray outline against the darker blackness of the night.

He had never been so glad to see home.

Fingers touched the side of his cheek, and Mickey yelled out, "Hey!"

*A stupid tree branch!*

He almost had a heart attack. Mickey ran across the last icy patch of back lawn. He ran like a midget halfback bound for seven. Halfway there, his metal lunch box popped open. It just about exploded—an orange, rolled-up papers, and a thermos tumbled out.

Mickey Kevin dropped the lunch box. He crashed up the back steps and put his hand on the cold metal storm door.

And then . . .

Mickey Kevin turned. He had to look back.

His chest was pounding nonstop now. *Ka-chunk, ka-chunk*, like a huge machine was inside there. Making ice or something equally noisy. He had to look back.

Oh, brother! *Oh boy, oh boy!*

Nobody was behind him.

Nobody!

It was completely quiet in the backyard. Nothing moved.

His lunch box lay in the middle of the snow. It glowed a little in the dark.

Mickey squinted real hard. He was feeling pretty stupid now. He'd made it all up; he was almost sure of it . . . But he still wasn't going to go back and pick up his lunch box. Maybe in the morning. Maybe in the spring sometime.

What a little baby! Afraid of the dark! He finally went in the house.

Mary K. was in the kitchen dicing vegetables with a big knife on the butcher block. The TV was turned on to "The Mary Tyler Moore Show."

"How was practice, Mickey Mouse? You look beat up. Wash, huh? Dinner's almost ready. I said—how was your basketball practice, fella?"

"Oh, uh . . . I don't know how to do a stupid lay-up. It was okay."

Then Mickey Kevin smoothly disappeared, slid like a shadow into the downstairs bathroom. He didn't wash his hands and face, though, and he didn't turn on the overhead light.

Very slowly, he lifted a handful of lace curtain. He stared out into the dark, very creepola backyard, squinting his eyes tightly again.

He still couldn't see anybody.

The stupid cat, their stupid cat Mortimer, was playing with his lunch box. There was nobody else. Nobody had really chased him, he was suddenly sure.

But Mickey Kevin couldn't see the real-life bogeyman watching the Carroll house from the darkened back lot. He couldn't see the fearsome Sten machine pistol or the man holding it, fingering it so expertly.

*Washington, D.C.*

It was just after five o'clock when Colonel Duriel Williamson strode into a windowless office hidden away inside the twenty-nine-acre concrete complex known as the Pentagon.

Arch Carroll was already waiting in the Spartan, bureaucratic green room. So was Captain Pete Hawkins, who had formally escorted Carroll from the visitor's pickup desk back through the dizzying grid of tightly interlocking Pentagon corridors.

Colonel Williamson was an imposing black man. He was in the full-dress uniform of the U.S. Special Forces—including a blood-red beret, cocked jauntily. His hair, a bristly salt and pepper, was regulation length and looked appropriately stern. His voice was starched but showed heavy hints of irony.

Everything about Duriel Williamson said "No bullshit permitted here. State your business, mister."

Captain Hawkins made the introductions in a polite if strictly formal military fashion. Hawkins was clearly a career bureaucrat, a survivor.

"Mr. Archer Carroll from the Defense Intelligence Agency, on special assignment by order of the president . . . Colonel Duriel Williamson from Special Forces. Colonel Williamson is stationed at Fort Bragg, North Carolina. Colonel Williamson was David Hudson's immediate superior during both phases of his Special Forces training. Colonel, Mr. Carroll is here to ask you some questions."

The Special Forces officer smiled amicably. "Glad to meet you, Mr. Carroll. May I sit down?"

"Please, Colonel," Carroll said. Both men sat down, followed by Captain Hawkins, who would remain in the room for the interview, a matter of protocol.

"What is it you need to know about David?"

"The two of you were on a first-name basis?"

"Yes, I knew David Hudson fairly well. I should amend that, to be as accurate as possible. I spent some time with David Hudson. Not at or because of the Special Forces school. This was after the war. I bumped into him a few times. At different veterans affairs, mostly. We were both active. We had a couple of beers together a couple of times."

"Tell me about it, Colonel. What was Hudson like? What was he like to have a beer with?"

Carroll controlled his eagerness to ask more probing questions. His mind was still clouded from the long morning at the FBI, but he knew better than to pressure a Special Forces colonel.

"David Hudson was stiff at first. Though he tried like the devil not to be. Then he was just fine. He knew a lot about a lot of things. He was a thoughtful man, extremely bright."

"Colonel Hudson's army career seemed to disintegrate after Vietnam. Do you know why?"

Duriel Williamson shrugged. "That's something that's always troubled me. All I can say is that David Hudson was a very outspoken man."

"Meaning, Colonel?" Carroll continued to probe carefully.

"Meaning he was capable of making important enemies inside the army . . . He was also extremely disappointed. Bitter, I guess is the better word."

Bitter, Carroll thought. Exactly how bitter? He studied the colonel in silence.

"The treatment our men got after Vietnam made David Hudson a very angry person. I think it disillusioned him more than most of us. He considered it a natural disgrace. He blamed

President Nixon at first. He wrote personal letters to the president, also to the chief of staff."

"Just letters? Was that the extent of his protests for the veterans?" I need somebody, Carroll thought, with the kind of bitterness that would go well beyond letters. Hell, anybody could sit down and write a crank letter.

"Actually, no. He was involved in several of the more vocal protests."

"Colonel, any answers you can elaborate on would be helpful. I've got all night to listen."

"He called attention to Washington's long string of broken promises to our veterans. All the betrayals. 'The disposable GI' was a phrase he liked to use . . . Let me tell you, Mr. Carroll, that kind of high-profile activity can earn you a fast assignment to Timbuktu, or to some Podunk reserve unit. That would put him in the Pentagon computers, too. Hudson was very active with radical veterans."

"What about his training at the Special Forces school? At Fort Bragg?" Carroll then asked. "Colonel, please try to be thorough."

"Some of this was quite a while ago. It didn't seem so important at the time. I'll try."

For almost an hour Colonel Williamson painstakingly described a brilliant young army officer, with boundless energy, with small-town American enthusiasm and talent— a model soldier. Many of the epithets Carroll had read earlier in the 211 files, he heard again from Colonel Williamson.

"What I remember most, though," Williamson said, "what stands out to this day about Hudson, is the time at Fort Bragg. We were instructed to push and drive him. Push him to his physical and emotional limits. We redlined David Hudson at Bragg."

"More than other officers who were assigned to the Bragg program?"

"Oh, absolutely. Absolutely. Without any doubt we pushed him more. No punches were pulled. His POW experience was used to pump up his hatred for 'our enemies.' Hudson was programmed to seek revenge, to hate. In my opinion, he was a walking time bomb."

"Who instructed you to do that, Colonel? Who told you to push Colonel Hudson? Somebody obviously must have singled him out for special attention."

Colonel Hudson paused. His dark eyes didn't leave Carroll's face, but there was a perceptible change in him. Carroll couldn't quite read the change at first.

"I suppose you're right. At this point, uh, after all these years . . . I'm not sure I can tell you who, though . . . Isn't that funny? I remember we were unusually tough on him. Also that Hudson was pretty much up to it. He definitely had character to spare. Great stamina. The heart of a teenager."

"But his training wasn't typical, not the regular course? His was different somehow?"

"Yes. David Hudson's training at Fort Bragg was beyond the established norm, which was demanding in itself."

"Give me some idea, Colonel. Put me at the training camp. Can you make it come alive for me? What was the actual training like?"

"All right. I don't think you can imagine it, unless you actually went through it . . . Up at two-thirty in the morning. Physical abuse. Drug-induced nightmares. Interrogation by the best in the army. Pushed like a dirt-farm tractor until you dropped at eight. Up again at two-thirty—I mean pushed, drained. Each day was one hundred percent harder than the last. Physically and emotionally, and psychologically . . . The men chosen to go to Bragg were all considered top rank. Hudson had West Point *and* extensive combat behind him. He'd been a successful commander in 'Nam . . . Uh, Colonel Hudson was also a military assassin in Vietnam. He was very heavy. With a good rep."

Carroll, hearing the word *assassin*, felt that he had taken still another step into the endless Green Band maze. The farther he moved, the more confusing it became. The all-American soldier had an even darker side: assassin. He brought Hudson's clean-cut image in the photographs back to mind: the sunshine face of determination, the crew cut, the honesty in the eyes.

"Meaning what, Colonel? What does a good rep mean in that context? As a military assassin."

"It means he wasn't a thrill killer—which most of the top hitters were . . . A very real problem is what to do with some of those guys once they leave the army. If the generals had decided to take out Ho Chi Minh, someone very big, very delicate, Hudson most likely would have been considered. I'm telling you, he was one of the fair-haired boys."

"You seem a little awed by Hudson yourself."

Williamson smiled absently; he finally chuckled softly into his chest full of medals. "I don't know about awe. Awe isn't the right word. Definitely respect, though."

"Why?"

"He was one of the best soldiers I've ever trained. He had physical endurance and all the technical skills. He had strength and tremendous smarts. A martial-arts background. He also had something else. Dignity."

"So what went wrong? What happened to Hudson after the war? Why did he finally leave the army in 1976?"

Colonel Williamson rubbed his hard-boned, clean-shaven jaw. "As I said, the one potential problem was his attitude. He could be extremely judgmental ... He also thought he had answers to some controversial army problems. Some career officers might not have appreciated Hudson's judgment of them and their actions. The other thing was the loss of his arm. David Hudson had big, big plans for himself. How many one-armed generals are you aware of?"

Arch Carroll thought before he spoke again. For all the apparent cooperation, he had a sneaking feeling that Colonel Williamson was still holding something back. It was the army way, he remembered from extensive past dealings with the Pentagon. Everything had to be a huge "need to know' secret, shared only inside the sacred fraternity of army blood brothers, shared only with the other warriors.

"Colonel Williamson, I've got to ask the next few questions with the authority of the commander in chief. That means I need complete answers."

"That's what you've been getting, Mr. Carroll."

"Colonel Williamson, did you know the official purpose of David Hudson's Special Forces training at Fort Bragg? Why was he at the JFK school? If that information was in any of your orders, if you heard it anywhere on the base I need to know it."

Colonel Duriel Williamson stared back hard at Arch Carroll, then at Captain Hawkins. When he spoke, his voice was softer, deeper than it had been. "Nothing was ever written down in any of the orders . . . As I said, I don't remember who actually issued our daily orders. I do know *why* he was supposed to be there, though . . ."

"Go on. Please, Colonel Williamson."

"It was something we were told at the very first briefing on David Hudson. Verbally told. The first briefing sounded like total CIA bullshit, by the way. Until we actually met Hudson . . . You see . . . they told us Colonel David Hudson had been specially chosen to be our version of the Third World superterrorist. David Hudson was selected and trained to be our version of the terrorist Juan Carlos."

Arch Carroll became very tense now. He leaned forward on his chair. "That's why he was at the Bragg school? Why he was pushed ahead, beyond all the others?"

"That's what we helped teach him to be . . . And Mr. Carroll, Hudson was frightening. He is *still* frightening, I'm sure. From potentially planning a terrorist raid to even a cold-blooded mass murder, if it was necessary, David Hudson was on a level with Carlos. He's on a level with that madman Monserrat! . . . The United States Army trained Hudson to be the best in the world . . . and in my opinion, he was. Maybe that's why they couldn't keep him content in the peacetime army."

Carroll didn't speak—because right at that moment he couldn't. The realization that the United States Army had secretly trained its own Carlos, and that he had now quite possibly turned, was unbelievable. Colonel Williamson's words rang in his ears: *From potentially planning a terrorist raid to even a cold-blooded mass murder, if it was necessary.*

"Colonel Williamson, in your opinion, could David Hudson have been involved with Green Band? Could he have technically masterminded an operation like that?"

"I don't doubt it, Mr. Carroll. He has all the technical skills."

Williamson sighed. "One more fact about Colonel David Hudson, though. When I knew him, at least, and I think I knew the man fairly well, he loved the United States very much. He loved America. Make no mistake, David Hudson was a patriot."

When Arch Carroll drove out of the vast, nearly empty Pentagon parking area at a little past ten that night, his mind was rapidly turning over all kinds of possibilities. Finally, something had connected. Something made sense in Green Band.

As he drove, weary and stone-faced, to the Washington Hotel, he tried to review the long day. His eyes were red and they burned. But he felt legitimately close to something for the first time since Green Band had begun.

Colonel David Hudson was trained to be our version of Carlos . . . our version of Monserrat.

David Hudson was a patriot.

Was David Hudson also a traitor? Perhaps the most significant traitor since Benedict Arnold?

A blue sedan unobtrusively followed Arch Carroll as he drove through the suburban fringes of Washington. Both cars slipped and curled around icy George Washington Parkway. When Carroll turned onto Constitution Avenue at a sedate thirty-five miles an hour, so did the blue sedan.

A team of eight professionals then alternated through the night both in and outside Georgetown's Washington Hotel. They watched to see if Arch Carroll went out, if he met anyone else at the hotel, if he tried to reach Colonel Duriel Williamson or Samantha Hawes.

Carroll's room and telephone were expertly bugged. There was a single incoming call, which was recorded by the surveillance team.

"Hello. This is Carroll speaking."

"Archer, it's Walter. I just spoke with Mike Caruso. He said you were in Washington."

"It's as weird as ever down here, Walter. Maybe even a little weirder right now."

"Mike told me about your latest theory. I think it's a good one. One thing bothers me a lot. I wonder why Phil Berger warned you off the track of Viet veterans earlier?"

"I wondered about that, too. Maybe he thought he had it covered. At any rate, I'm definitely touching exposed nerves down here."

"Well, be careful about that. Philip Berger and the CIA aren't easy to fool, or to underestimate, either. And Archer—"

"Yeah, I know, I'll try to keep you involved."

"If you don't, you could wind up all alone on this. And I mean *all alone*. I'm serious, Archer. Be careful as hell in Washington."

Carroll made one call home to Riverdale and a second to Caitlin Dillon in Manhattan. He made a late call to Samantha Hawes at her home in Arlington. Then he slept.

The surveillance team was wide-awake.

# Chapter 33

IT WAS PAST one-thirty in the morning and the White House was quiet, deceptively still, along the second floor. The president was feeling completely debilitated and old, decades older than his forty-two years. The sheen of sweat covering his neck was cold, and it made him feel ill.

As he walked the corridors of power, the president of the United States held a confidential document under his arm. The sheaf of papers seemed to burn through his suit and shirt.

Nearly every president, as well as a few chosen first-time senators and key congressmen, had learned an important American history lesson when they arrived in the capital. Justin Kearney had learned his within the first month of his presidency. The history lesson was that within the broadcast scope of American power and its immense wealth, the politician was little more than an appendage to the system. A concession to form, a necessary inconvenience in many ways.

The politicians, all elected officials—even the president—were grudgingly tolerated, but each was expendable.

The presidents before Justin Kearney—Reagan, Carter, Ford, Nixon, Johnson, Kennedy—had all learned the invaluable lesson in one way or another. Even the seemingly powerful and secure Secretary of State Kissinger had eventually learned his lesson . . .

There was a higher order working inside, working above and beyond the United States government. There had been a higher order for decades. It made all the sense in the world; it made sense of almost everything that had happened over the past forty years: the Kennedys, Vietnam, Watergate, the "Star Wars" plan.

They were waiting for President Kearney in the dramatic and imposing National Security Council briefing room. Twelve of them had been there for some time, working right through the night.

They appeared to be an ordinary committee, all in white shirts and loosened ties. They stood en masse as the president of the United States entered. They rose out of respect for the office, for the lofty traditions, for what they themselves had rigorously maintained about the office.

The forty-first president of the United States took his seat at the head of the highly polished oak wood table. Pens and lined yellow writing pads had been set neatly at his place.

"Did you read the position papers through, Mr. President?" one of the twelve committeemen quietly asked.

"Yes, I read them in my office just now," the president answered solemnly. His strong, handsome face was pale.

The president then laid the confidential papers he'd been

carrying on the table. The booklet was approximately one hundred and sixty typewritten pages. It had never been copied and never would be. It looked somewhat like an investment-offering book or perhaps a condominium plan. On the dark blue cover something had been printed in regal-looking gold letters.

*Green Band. Extremely Confidential and Classified.*

The title page was dated May 16.

Nearly seven months before the actual bombing attack on Wall Street.

# PART THREE

## ARCH CARROLL

# Chapter 34

FRIDAY IN WASHINGTON, D.C., dawned with rain clouds rolling across a colorless horizon. A spitting wind blew wintry gusts in from Maryland. The temperature was dropping hourly. From 7:00 A.M. on, Arch Carroll waited impatiently on the front seat of a rented sedan parked in the nearby suburb of McLean.

The dark car blended in neatly with a wall of even darker fir trees overhanging Fort Myers Road.

Detective work, Carroll thought as he stared off into nothingness. First you wait. Always you wait.

Carroll passed the time eating breakfast out of a box from Dunkin' Donuts. The actual doughnuts weren't nearly as hot as the box itself. They also had no taste that he could discern. The coffee he sipped was room temperature, a little less satisfying than the doughnuts.

Carroll read some Tracy Kidder, *The Soul of a New Machine*, and that was quite good, at least. Several times he found himself thinking about Colonel David Hudson. The classic all-American Boy? West Point honor student . . .

Then Vietnam assassin? America's Juan Carlos? America's jackal? America's François Monserrat?

He wanted to meet David Hudson now. He wanted to encounter him one on one, face to face. Maybe inside the cramped interrogation room at number 13 Wall, Carroll's own turf. Tell me, Colonel Hudson, what do you know about the Green Band firebombing? What about the stolen Wall Street securities? Tell me why you left the army, Colonel Hudson.

He wondered how far he'd get with somebody like Colonel David Hudson, a U.S. saboteur trained to resist interrogation. It would be a battle, and one Carroll was sure he'd lose.

About seven-thirty a second-floor light blinked on inside the white colonial across the roadway. A second light followed moments later. Bedroom and bathroom, probably. Showtime at General Thompson's was about to begin.

Moments later a light went on downstairs. Kitchen? Then the porch light blinked out.

Just past eight, which Carroll thought a respectable hour, he trudged up the flagstone front walk and rang the bell, which made a chimey sound like old department-store bells.

A tall, distinguished man of about sixty appeared in the pristine white doorway. He wore plaid trousers, house slippers, a powder blue cardigan sweater. His head, shaped like a torpedo, was topped with white-gray stubble.

General Lucas Thompson, former commander in chief of the United States Evacuation Forces in Vietnam, had a craggy, commanding presence. He still appeared capable of taking on the most difficult combat duty demands. There was something hard and alert in his gray eyes, as if small electric light bulbs were burning there.

"General Thompson, I'm Arch Carroll, with the DIA. Sorry to bother you so early in the morning. I'm here about the Green Band investigation."

General Thompson looked appropriately suspicious. "What about it, sir? I'm up, but as you say, it's still quite early in the morning."

"I would have called last night, to say I was coming, General. It was late when I left the Pentagon. I thought that might have been a worse breach of etiquette than just coming out here this morning."

The suspicious look faded on General Thompson's face. It was as if the mention of the word *Pentagon* had reassured him; a look of pleasant recognition spread across his features.

"Of course. Arch Carroll. I've read about you."

"General Thompson, I have just a few questions. It's about your command in Southeast Asia. It shouldn't take more than, say, twenty minutes."

"That means an hour," Lucas Thompson said with a sniffling laugh. "Come in. I have the time. Time is plentiful these days, Mr. Carroll." He spoke in the tone of a retired soldier about to write his memoirs: vaguely frustrated, a little bored, and lacking a sense of purpose.

General Thompson led the way through a formal dining room, into an even more imposing library chamber. There was a white-birch fireplace screened by a brass curtain with heavy brass andirons. Tall oak bookshelves stood erect on every wall; a double bay window looked out onto a backyard with a covered pool and yellow-and-lime-striped cabana.

General Thompson sat on a comfortable wing chair. "Out of

sight in Washington, pretty much out of mind. Since my retirement, I've had very few official visitors down here. Other than my two granddaughters, who fortunately live up the lane and who adore their grandmother's baked goods and double fudge."

General Thompson shook his head and smiled warmly.

Carroll had heard that in Vietnam Thompson had been an extremely rigid disciplinarian. Now, in his retirement, Lucas Thompson seemed like just another grandfather, waiting patiently for the next smiling Kodak snapshot to be taken.

"I'm searching—groping, is the word I think I want—for some useful information about a Colonel David Hudson. Hudson was on your command team in Saigon, right?"

General Lucas Thompson nodded in the manner of a practiced good listener. "Yes, Colonel Hudson served on my team for about fifteen months. If my recollection is holding up better than the rest of me."

"Your recollection and my records match exactly," Carroll said. "What can you tell me about Hudson?"

"Well, I'm not sure where you want me to start. It's fairly complex. David Hudson was an extremely disciplined and effective soldier. Also a very charismatic leader, once he got his command over there . . . When I first met him, he was ramrodding a demolition team, I believe. He'd also been trained to sanction—that is, terminate—human targets. He sanctioned trash, Carroll. War profiteers, a couple of high-level infiltrators. Traitors."

"Why was he chosen to be a military assassin?"

"Oh, I think I have the answer for that one. He was chosen because he didn't like to kill. Because he *wasn't* a psycho. I think Hudson's philosophy was that once you undertook to fight in a just war, you fought. You balls-out fought with everything you had. I happen to believe in that philosophy myself."

During the next thirty minutes General Lucas Thompson elaborated on his association with David Hudson. It was a laudatory review overall—high marks for conduct, combat-team leadership, especially high marks for courage.

Arch Carroll kept getting the very uncomfortable feeling that he was chasing after a goddamned American war hero. Once again, it didn't make any sense. General Thompson was now beginning to repeat himself slightly. He seemed to be slipping into a genial storytelling mode. It was a little sad. In a way, it reminded Carroll of his own father, retiring from the New York Police Department to Sarasota. Dead of heart failure, or maybe it was boredom, within nine months.

Except that Carroll didn't believe General Lucas Thompson's act for a minute.

Carroll had checked carefully—and General Thompson had been receiving official visitors in McLean; high-ranking VIPs from the Pentagon, even regular visitors from the White House. General Lucas Thompson was *still* an influential adviser to the National Security Council.

"There are a couple of things that continue to bother me, General."

"Shoot away, then."

"Just for openers: Why can't anyone tell me where Colonel Hudson is now? . . . Second point: Why can't anyone explain the mysterious circumstances under which he left the army in the mid-seventies? Third point: General Thompson, why did somebody rifle through his war records at the Pentagon and the FBI before I could see them?"

"Mr. Carroll, judging from the tone of your voice, I think maybe you're getting a little out of order," General Thompson said in a voice that remained low, perfectly in control.

"Yeah, well, I do that sometimes. Fourth point: The last thing that bothers me—really frosts me: Why was I followed from the Pentagon last night, General? . . . Why was I followed out here to McLean? On whose orders? What the hell is going on in Washington?"

General Lucas Thompson's shiny, clean-shaven cheeks and crinkle-cut neck blossomed a bright red. "Mr. Carroll, I think you'd better leave right now. I believe that would be best for all concerned."

"You know, I think you're probably right. I think I'd be wasting my time here . . . General Thompson, I think you know a whole lot more about Colonel Hudson. That's what I think."

General Thompson smiled, just a faint condescending twist of his upper lip. "That's the unappreciated beauty of our country, Mr. Carroll. It's free. You can think whatever you like . . . I'll show you to the door."

# Chapter 35

*Manhattan*

ON THE MORNING of December 18, in New York, Colonel David Hudson was feeling more self-conscious about his affliction than he had in many years. Nervously clutching Billie Bogan with his good arm, he steered her in a protective manner through the onrushing tide of people on Fifth Avenue. He didn't want to think about the resumption of Green Band, not for a few more hours, anyway.

David Hudson's self-consciousness was particularly unnecessary that morning. The two of them, paired together, were undeniably striking. They looked as if they'd been painted with thick, very bold strokes—while everyone else had been lightly drawn by pencil or pen.

Billie Bogan watched David from the corner of her eye—so very serious, charting their appointed path through the crowd. She felt an odd but growing fascination. That he was obviously taken with her made the attraction she felt much more irresistible. She allowed herself to be pulled along . . .

Toward whatever was looming ahead.

Where were they headed, anyway?

"Are you a Christmas lover?" Billie asked as they moved through the cold winter day around them.

"Oh, it depends on the Christmas. This Christmas, I have a strange passion for the season . . . I want to drink in the sights: the evergreen trees and the holiday wreaths, the glimmering store windows, Santa Clauses, churches, choral music."

"You do seem to go all the way on things," she teased Hudson.

"Or not at all. Just look at this insanity! This wonderful monstrosity!" He suddenly whooped and grinned broadly. It was quite unlike his usual self, at least the part she'd seen.

They'd finally come up close to the glittering extravagantly decorated Rockefeller Center tree. A crowd, college-age lovers mostly, was clustered overlooking the skating rink and attached restaurant. A boys choir, innocent in cassocks and surplices, sang the loveliest carols down below.

Colonel David Hudson's brain had finally slowed; he was relaxed and comfortable now. An exceedingly rare treat, one to be savored. He occasionally felt a stab of guilt about his mission, but he knew the release of tension could be valuable, too.

"Do you miss your family, your home? Being away from England during the holidays?" he asked.

In spite of the crowd, they felt as if they were all alone.

"I miss certain incidents from the past . . . Some charming things about my sister, my mother. I don't miss home too much, no. Life in the Midlands. All the young people, all the bright ones, want to get away from Birmingham. If you remain, you work for British Steel, or perhaps the exhibition center. Once you marry, you stay home with your brood. Watch the new morning BBC. You get fat, your thinking petrifies. After a few years, no one can imagine that any of the women were ever pretty slips of young girls. Almost no one over forty looks like they were ever young."

"So you escaped? London? Paris?"

"I went to London when I turned eighteen. I was very crude, unpolished, in the way that I looked, the way I thought about the world. I wanted to be an actress, a fashion model, anything that would keep me from ever going back to Birmingham. Ever."

Billie smiled, and she was so charming and self-effacing. "I made a few minor misjudgments in London," she said with a mocking laugh.

"And then?"

"After, I guess it was five years there, I decided to come to New York, or Paris. That's me up to the present. I'm hopeful I can do well as a model. I'm putting together a book for press advertising—magazines and newspapers. I know I'm attractive—physically attractive, at least."

She had delivered most of the autobiographical speech very shyly, with her eyes downcast, glancing anywhere but into David Hudson's eyes. Color had crept up from her neck, finally covering her face.

"I've made a few tiny misjudgments myself. Just a few." Hudson laughed. So many stored-up emotions were being released. It had been so long since he'd allowed himself this.

Billie began to laugh again. "Oh, to hell with the past," she said. Her eyes were a little sad, however, ironic, slightly pinched at the corners. They both ran out of words at exactly the same time. The moment seemed especially poignant to them.

Billie turned to face Hudson again. She spoke very softly, feathers of her warm breath touching his ear.

"Please kiss me, David. That might not sound like anything so very dramatic . . . Except that I don't think I've said it to anyone, and meant it, since I was about sixteen or seventeen years old."

David Hudson and Billie Bogan kissed in the deep shadows of the grand Christmas tree. Holiday music played sweetly around them: "Adeste Fidelis," "Silent Night," "Joy to the World."

For that moment, Colonel David Hudson conveniently forgot his other plans for the world.

Something that was badly needed.

Revenge for a very special few.

Justice for mankind.

# Chapter 36

CAITLIN DILLON HURRIEDLY entered the crowded formal conference room in 13 Wall Street. She passed repairmen plastering over cracks in cement. Three cleaning women hauled buckets at the end of the hallway. Caitlin was thinking right then how much she missed Carroll, who was expected back from Washington at any moment. He'd called, but his voice had sounded strained, almost as if he'd been afraid to tell her anything over the telephone.

She stepped into the meeting room, passing through a phalanx of policemen and army personnel. The word had already spread up and down the hallways—there had been some sort of significant break in the Green Band investigation. Finally, a break.

Walter Trentkamp stood in dramatic silence before the restless audience. He was tense. Streaks of light sweat highlighted his face, and the collar of his shirt was damp. Caitlin hadn't seen the FBI chief this anxious before.

Trentkamp cleared his throat. The scene reminded Caitlin of high-level press conferences held in Washington, emergency meetings called on short notice.

"You have no doubt heard the rumor that a significant development has occurred in the Green Band investigation . . . It was uncovered through the tireless effort of Captain Francis Nicolo and Sergeant Rizzo in NYPD Ballistics."

Nicolo—"Waxy Frank"—appeared in the crowd alongside Joe Rizzo. Both men were beaming, taking an imperceptible bow.

"These men have been working tirelessly since the bombing on December fourth. Finally, their labors have paid a big dividend."

There were a couple of appreciative mumbles in the room and a halfhearted attempt at applause. Nicolo and Rizzo shuffled their feet like schoolboys at an honors presentation.

"Sergeant?" Trentkamp said. "Come up here, please."

Rizzo stepped forward awkwardly and hoisted a chart onto a metal stand. On the chart a police artist had sketched the major buildings of the financial district in black and white. The structures that had been bombed were colored traffic-signal red. Each of the bombed-out buildings also had a bold violet ring drawn around it. Caitlin noticed that the purple rings were at widely different levels on the fourteen buildings.

Rizzo began, "The buildings marked with red were all hit around six-thirty on December fourth. The bombs were definitely detonated by remote signals. The signal might have been operated from as far away as eight or ten miles."

Rizzo paused, blew his nose in a big white handkerchief, then went on: "The violet rings on the buildings were drawn to indicate where the explosions actually took place. The plastique packages were actually placed here, here, here, et cetera.

"As you can see, the plastique was planted on different floors in all fourteen buildings. The second floor at Twenty-two Broad. Fifteenth floor at Manufacturers Hanover. And so on. You can all see that plainly." Rizzo looked around at the faces in the room as if he were challenging someone to disagree.

"There's no special pattern to this. At least, that's what we thought up to now. Last night, though, we found a connection we'd missed . . .

"Look here! Each of the circled floors actually contains one of that building's messenger rooms. Either a drop-off or a package-mail station. What threw us off this approach was the fact that messenger drop-off stations and the mailroom in these buildings aren't always the same. Not even on the same floor. Some of the Wall Street buildings have drop-off stations on every floor. You all see what I'm driving at?"

Sergeant Joe Rizzo paused for effect, then said, "Gentlemen, the actual bombs were all hand-delivered. Probably by a regular commercial messenger who would go unnoticed."

Rizzo once again looked around the suddenly quiet room. "There are more than two hundred messenger services in and around Wall Street. Jimmy Split, Speedo, Fireball, Bullet, to name a few. You've probably seen most of them yourselves. We're going to contact every single one of those services. Chances are at least one of them was contacted by our friends, Green Band. Perhaps several were used to deliver the plastique on December fourth!"

Rizzo paused again. "What this means is that some goof-ball messenger is going to help break this thing open! Tonight we hit the streets. Tonight we run this thing down!"

Caitlin felt the tremendous surge of energy that coursed through the room as the men began to disperse. They had suddenly come alive, after days of pounding on walls, days of pursuing an investigation that had been going absolutely nowhere. She was almost swept aside as eager policemen and detectives crushed toward the door.

A Wall Street messenger service.

A slight shiver traveled through her.

Messenger service? . . .

Caitlin turned and left the meeting room; she started back to her own office. She had just remembered something.

She started to run down the corridor.

Carroll was certain he was being followed. A dark car had tracked his cab from Kennedy Airport all the way into the financial district.

When he stepped out of the taxi at 13 Wall Street, the tracking car went skirting past. He couldn't see the faces inside, only shapes, two or three men huddled together. Why were they following him? Who had sent them? Who was tracking the tracker?

He disappeared into number 13 and went quickly to Caitlin's office. He was filled with the strongest need to see her, to talk to somebody he could trust.

She rose from her desk, where she'd been studying a printout of the names of U.S. veterans the computer had supplied before. She hugged him, and Carroll didn't want to let her go. They pressed tightly into each other's bodies. They kissed with an urgency neither of them had acknowledged before.

Caitlin finally disentangled herself. "How was Washington?" She was smiling, relieved to see him.

"Interesting. More than just interesting," Carroll said.

He told her about the FBI's file on David Hudson, about his visit with General Lucas Thompson.

Caitlin brought him up to date on the developments explained by Sergeant Rizzo. She indicated the computer printout she'd been studying when he had arrived. "Maybe this is coincidence, Arch. Maybe it doesn't mean a thing. But on this FBI list of veterans there's an explosives expert whose occupation is cabdriver and messenger. The home address is New York City."

"Which name?" Carroll asked. He was already scanning the lengthy list.

"A man called Michael Demunn . . . who just happened to serve under Colonel David Hudson in Vietnam."

"Does it say which messenger service?" He looked up from the printout.

Caitlin shook her head. "It shouldn't be too difficult to find out. Let's see."

Carroll waited while Caitlin made a couple of quick telephone calls. He slid his investigation pad out of his coat and impatiently flipped through those familiar pages that had chronicled Green Band's false starts and stops from the beginning.

There were several different organizational headings now:

Interviews. Physical Evidence. Suspects. Miscellaneous.
David Hudson . . . the mastermind?
West Point. 1966. Special Forces. Rangers.
Golden boy? The all-American boy?
Fort Bragg. JFK Special Warfare Center and School. Severe stress testing. Experimentation with drugs. Preparing Hudson

for what? Special terrorist training. By whose orders? Where did that particular chain of command end?

Carroll finally shut the pad in frustration. He absently studied Caitlin, the delicate curve of her spine as she stood with her back to him. The way she was poised on one foot—with the phone cord twisted around her waist.

What do I know that I don't know I know? Carroll's thoughts went back to Green Band.

Washington, D.C.? General Lucas Thompson? A genial white-haired liar. Somebody following me now.

For what reason? On whose orders?

He watched Caitlin put down the receiver.

"Vets Cabs and Messengers," she said with a sudden grin. "They have a garage in the West Village."

Carroll stood up. "Call Philip Berger. Then could you call Walter Trentkamp? Tell them to get their men organized, to meet me at—"

"There's more, Arch," Caitlin interrupted.

She paused for just a beat. "David Hudson works there, too. He's been there for over a year. I think we've finally found Colonel Hudson. We've found Green Band."

# Chapter 37

JUST PAST MIDNIGHT on December 19, Colonel David Hudson emotionally addressed the assembly of twenty-four Vets gathered inside the Jane Street garage.

"This has been a long and particularly hard mission for all of you," he said. "I know that. But at each important stage you've done everything that has been asked of you . . . I feel very humble standing here before you."

Hudson paused and looked at the upturned faces. "As we approach the final stages of Green Band, I want to stress one thing. I don't want anyone to take needless risks. Is that understood? Take no chances. Our ultimate goal from here on is zero KIA."

Again Hudson paused. When he finally spoke, there was an uncharacteristic edge of emotion in his voice. "This will be our last mission together. Thank you once again. I salute you all."

\*

From that moment, Green Band was designed to be a thoroughly disciplined army-style field maneuver. Every possible detail had been scrutinized again and again.

The grease-stained garage doors at Vets Cabs and Messengers rolled open with a heavy metallic roar. Diffused amber headlights pierced the darkness.

Vets 5, Harold Freedman, ran outside the Vets building. He looked east and west on Jane Street, then began to bark orders like the army drill sergeant he'd once been.

It was just past 12:30 P.M.

If anyone in the West Village neighborhood saw the three army transport trucks emerge from the garage, they paid little attention, in the tried-and-true tradition of New Yorkers.

The trucks finally hurtled down West Street.

Colonel David Hudson crouched attentively on the passenger seat of the lead troop truck. He was in constant walkie-talkie contact with the two other troop transports . . . This was a disciplined field maneuver in every respect.

They were carefully moving into full combat again. None of them had realized how much they missed it. Even Hudson himself had forgotten the intense clarity that came before a major battle. There was nothing else like this in life, nothing like full combat.

"Contact. This is Vets One. You are to follow us straight down West Street to the Holland Tunnel entrance. We'll be maintaining *strict* military speed limits in the city. So sit back. Just relax for the ride. Over."

Two hours passed before the lead transport truck pulled to a shuddering stop at a military guardpost less than sixty yards off Route 35 in New Jersey. Over the wooden sentry box the sign read FORT MONMOUTH, UNITED STATES ARMY POST.

The private on duty had been very close to falling asleep. His eyes were glazed behind horn-rimmed glasses and his movements comically stiff as he approached the lead truck.

"Identification, sir." The private cleared his throat. He spoke in a high-pitched whine and didn't look much more than eighteen years old to Hudson. Shades of Vietnam, of brutal wars fought by innocent boys for thousands and thousands of years.

David Hudson silently handed across two plastic ID cards. The cards identified him as Colonel Roger McAfee of the Sixty-eighth Street Armory, Manhattan. The inspection that followed was pro forma. The regular guard-duty speech was given by the sentry.

"You may proceed, sir. Please obey all posted parking and traffic regulations while you are at Fort Monmouth. Are those transports behind you with you, sir?"

"Yes, we're going on bivouac. We're here to pick up supplies. Small arms and ammunition for our weekend in the country. Two helicopters have been requisitioned. They'll have the details inside. I'm to see Captain Harney."

"You can all proceed, then, sir."

The youthful sentry stepped aside. He crisply waved on the small army reserve convoy.

"Contact. This is Vets One." As soon as they passed the gate, Colonel Hudson spoke into the PRC transmitter. "We're now less than twelve hours until the termination of operation Green Band. Everyone is to use extreme, *repeat*, extreme caution. We're almost home, gentlemen. We're almost home at last. Over and out."

Inconspicuous and drab, the Vets garage on Jane Street wasn't the kind of place to draw attention. It sat in the middle of a

357

West Village block, its large metal doors rusted and grease-stained and bleak.

At both ends of the block, the desolate street had silently been cordoned off. NYPD patrol cars were positioned everywhere around the garage. Carroll counted seventeen of them.

Beneath the darkened edifice of a Shell gas station, he could see unmarked FBI cars and as many as thirty heavily armed agents. Each of them watched the front of the garage with the kind of intensity that represented professionalism in the Bureau.

The police and the FBI agents carried M-16 automatic assault rifles, twelve-gauge shotguns, and .357 Magnums. It was as frightening an arsenal and attack force as Carroll had ever seen.

He leaned against his own car, studying the metal doors, the crooked, bleached sign that read VETS CABS AND MESSENGERS. He tapped his fingers nervously on the car hood.

Something was wrong here. Something was definitely wrong.

Arch Carroll peered hard in the direction of the Shell station. The FBI guys stood perfectly still, waiting for the signal that would bring them rushing into action.

At Carroll's side was Walter Trentkamp. He had kept Walter informed. Now Trentkamp was inside the dangerous maze with him.

Carroll took out his Browning. He turned the heavy weapon over in the palm of his hand and thought it was strange how some voice in his head was telling him to be careful. Careful, he thought. He hadn't been careful before—so why start now? He thought he knew why.

"Archer." Walter nudged him. A black limousine was threading its way down the grim, quiet street.

Police Commissioner Michael Kane solemnly climbed out. The commissioner, whose street experience was limited and who was more politician than cop, had a gleaming bullhorn in one hand. He held it as if he'd never touched such a thing before.

"Oh, Jesus Christ, no," Carroll muttered.

Commissioner Kane's voice echoed down the deserted West Village street. "Attention . . . this is Commissioner of Police Kane . . . You have one minute to emerge from the Vets garage. You have sixty seconds before we open fire."

Carroll's eyes roamed over the red brick garage. He was tense, his neck and forehead damp. He slowly raised his pistol to the firing position.

The Vets garage remained quiet.

Something definitely wasn't right about this.

"Twenty-five seconds . . . come out of the garage . . ."

Walter Trentkamp leaned close. One of the things Carroll appreciated was that Walter was still basically a street cop. He still needed to be in on the action himself. "Suppose this is all bullshit? Suppose we've got the wrong men, the wrong messenger service? Something's not right here, Arch."

Carroll still said nothing. He was watching and thinking.

"Twenty seconds . . ."

"C'mon, Walter . . . come with me."

Carroll suddenly stepped forward. Walter Trentkamp, somewhat reluctantly, followed him toward the garage doors. The police commissioner had stopped counting down. Then FBI agents and city cops were everywhere, pushing through the jagged edges of the broken doors and into the darkened building itself. Somebody turned on a light, revealing a somewhat ordinary, gloomy, and cavernous garage.

Carroll, Browning in hand, froze. He could smell oil and grease, all the harsh odors left behind by sick and aging automobiles. Slick puddles of oil covered the concrete floor. There were mechanics' tools lying around.

And nothing else.

There were no vehicles of any kind.

There were no people, no Vietnam veterans. Colonel David Hudson was nowhere to be seen.

Carroll and Trentkamp wandered around the garage, their guns still drawn. They entered each small side room in a careful police crouch. They finally climbed the narrow, twisting stairs to the top floor.

And then they saw it.

It was taped to the grease-stained wall mocking them, mocking them all.

A green ribbon had been tied in a perfect bow, and it hung on a barren wall. They couldn't miss it. Green Band had disappeared from the garage on Jane Street—still one frustrating jump ahead of them.


Caitlin Dillon carried a leather portfolio, overflowing with her notes, down the darkened hallway of an Upper West Side apartment building. The door to 12B was halfway open.

Anton Birnbaum was standing there, waiting. Caitlin wondered why he had called her so late at night.

They went to his library, a room crammed to its high ceiling with old books and periodicals.

"Thank you for coming right away," he said. He seemed incredibly relieved to see her. "Coffee? Tea? I've been living on the unhealthy stuff lately." He gestured to a tarnished espresso pot near the glowing fireplace.

Caitlin declined. She sat down on an antique sofa and lit a Du Maurier as the old financier poured himself a demitasse from the pot.

His hands were trembling slightly. This whole room, in its papery disarray, indicated that Anton Birnbaum had been feverishly burning the midnight oil.

"Let me go all the way back to Dallas, Caitlin. The tragic assassination of President John Kennedy . . . The assassination was probably orchestrated, as we all know." Caitlin crushed out her cigarette. Anton Birnbaum was very agitated now.

"Next comes Watergate, 1972. I think, I firmly believe, that Watergate was permitted to escalate. Its flames were purposely fanned . . . in order to remove Richard M. Nixon from office. That, my dear, is history. American history." Birnbaum's cup rattled gently in the saucer. "Both these events were clearly orchestrated. Both events were devised by a cabal cleverly working both inside and outside the United States government. This elitist group is a remnant, a cell of the old OSS, our own World War Two intelligence network. I have heard them called the Wise Men. I've also heard them called the Committee of Twelve. They exist. Permit me to continue before you comment.

"In 1945, the men who ran the OSS realized that the cloak of responsibility they had assumed in wartime was coming to an end. They were suddenly faced with giving their enormous power back to the same politicians who had almost managed to obliterate the human race a few years before . . . They had no desire to do so, Caitlin. None at all. In many ways, one can almost justify their actions."

Birnbaum sipped his coffee. He made a sour face. "A high-ranking clique of these OSS men surrendered only some of their wartime powers to President Truman. They remained working behind the scenes in Washington. They began to maneuver a long series of political puppets. These men, and their protégés, the current Committee of Twelve, have gone so far as to select the presidential candidates for political parties. For both parties, Caitlin, in the same election."

Caitlin stared at the old man. The Wise Men? The Committee of Twelve? A secret cabal with unlimited powers? She already knew a great deal about real and imagined government conspiracies. They had always seemed woven firmly into the tapestry of American history. Unconfirmable rumors; uncomfortable realities. Uncomfortable whispers in high places. "Who are these men, Anton?"

"My dear, they are not exactly faces familiar from *Newsweek* or *Time* magazine. But that's beside the point right now. What I am trying to tell you is that I have no doubt this group is somehow involved in the Green Band incident. Somehow they encouraged or caused the December fourth attack on Wall Street. They're behind whatever is happening right now."

Caitlin didn't have the appropriate words to respond to what Birnbaum was saying. With any other person she might have dismissed this whole thing; but Birnbaum, she knew, wouldn't have told her any of this if he wasn't certain himself. Anton Birnbaum double- and triple-checked all of his information, no matter the source.

The financier stared at Caitlin, and there was a weary glaze over his eyes. She looked slightly European smoking Du Mauriers, not completely like herself, he thought. He started again.

"This veterans group—"

"You've heard of them already?" Caitlin was surprised, alarmed.

Birnbaum smiled. "My dear, information has always been the wellspring of my success. Of course I have heard of the veterans group. I have my sources inside number Thirteen. But what I don't know yet is whether the Committee of Twelve manipulated these poor misfits or whether the veterans are actually paid operatives . . . I do believe I know why the dangerous mission was undertaken . . . I think it can be traced directly to a dangerous Soviet-run provocateur called François Monserrat. A cold-blooded mass murderer. A killing machine that has to be destroyed."

"But what is Monserrat's connection with the Committee of Twelve? What's going to happen now? Can you tell me that?"

Anton Birnbaum smiled, but the smile was strangely tight. "I believe that I can, my dear. Are you sure you don't want some coffee or tea? I think you should have something warm against the cold."

# Chapter 38

*Queen's, New York City*

SUNDAY MORNING, COLONEL David Hudson patrolled the dimly lit corridors of the sprawling Queens VA hospital. The home of the brave, he thought bitterly.

The Queens VA extended-care section was situated at Linden Boulevard and 179th Street. It was a dismal red brick complex that purposely called no attention to itself. Eleven years before, David Hudson had been an outpatient there, one of tens of thousands who had been subjected to VA hospitals after the Vietnam War.

He felt a hollowness as he plunged deeper and deeper into the hospital complex. There were buzzing voices, but no people he could see. Ghosts, he thought. Voices of pain and madness.

He turned a corner—and he suddenly encountered a gruesome row of veterans. They were mostly pathetically emaciated wraiths, but a few were obscenely overweight. The odor in the still, dead air was overpowering: part industrial disinfectant, part urine, part human feces. A synthetic Christmas tree blinked spastically in the claustrophobic room.

Some of the patients had tiny metal radios pressed like cold packs to their heads. A black hussar in a torn pin-striped johnny was discoing around an amputee sleeping fitfully in his wheelchair. Hudson saw broken, gnarled bodies harnessed into steel-and-leather braces. "Metals of honor," the hospital aides used to say when Hudson had been there.

He felt such rage now, such hatred for everything American, everything he'd once loved about his country.

No hospital personnel in sight. There wasn't a single corpsman, not a nurse or nurse's aide, in any of the halls.

David Hudson kept walking—faster—almost hearing a soft military drum roll in his head. He went down a bright yellow hallway, a falsely cheery one. He remembered the surroundings with vibrant clarity now. Almost uncontrollable rage swept through his body.

In the fall of 1973 he'd been admitted to the VA, ostensibly for psychiatric evaluation and tests. A smug Ivy League doctor had talked to him twice about his affliction, the unfortunate loss of his arm. The army doctor was equally interested in Hudson's POW experience. Had he killed a Vietcong camp commandant while making his escape? Yes, Hudson assured him; in fact, the escape was what had first brought him to the attention of army intelligence. They had tested him in Vietnam, then sent him back to Fort Bragg for further training . . . The interviews lasted no more than fifty minutes each time. Hudson had then filled out endless Veterans Administration questionnaires and numbered forms. He was assigned a VA caseworker, an obese man with a birthmark on his cheek, whom he never saw after their first half-hour interview.

At the end of the yellow hallway were glass double doors to the outside. Through the hospital doors, Hudson could see fenced-in back lawns. The fences were not intended to keep the veterans in, he knew. They'd been built to keep the people outside from seeing what was inside: the terrifying, awful disgrace of America's veterans.

David Hudson hit the glass door squarely with his right shoulder and plunged into the sharp winter cold.

Directly behind the main hospital building was a steep frost-covered lawn that ended in threadbare scrub pines. Hudson moved across it quickly. Concentrate, he instructed himself. Don't think about anything but the present. Nothing but what's happening right now.

Two men suddenly stepped out from behind a row of thickly snow-laden firs. One man had the impressive, very formal appearance of a United Nations diplomat. The other was a common-looking street thug with a tough, expressionless face.

"You might have chosen the Oak Bar at the Plaza just as easily. Certainly that would have been more convenient," the impressive-looking man said. "Colonel Hudson, I presume? . . . I am François Monserrat."

The distinguished man's English was slightly accented. He might have been French? Swiss? . . . Monserrat. Carlos's replacement.

David Hudson smiled, showing slightly parted teeth. Every one of his senses was coming alive now. "The next time we meet, it can be your turn to choose a location. At the clock in Grand Central Station? The observation deck of the Empire State Building? Whatever site pleases you," he offered.

"I'll remember that. You have a proposition for me to consider, Colonel? The remainder of the securities from Green Band? A substantial amount, I take it."

Hudson's eyes remained hooded, showing no emotion, not a hint of the seething rage inside. "Yes, I would say substantial. Over four billion dollars. That's enough to cause an unprecedented international incident. Whatever you wish."

"And what do you want from us, dare I ask? What is your final reward out of this, Colonel?"

"Less than you might think. The deposit of one hundred fifty million in a secure, numbered account. Your assurance that the GRU won't pursue my men afterward. The end of Green Band, at least where you're concerned."

"That's all? I can't accept that."

"No, I suppose it isn't all. I have something else in mind . . . You see, I want you to destroy the pathetic American way of life. I want you to end the American century a little early. We both intensely hate the American system—at least what it's become. We both want to set it on fire, to purify the world. We've both been trained to accomplish that."

Hudson's apocalyptic words hung in the chilly air. The European terrorist stared into Colonel Hudson's eyes. Then, François Monserrat smiled, and his smile was hideous. He understood his man perfectly now.

"You're planning to complete this transaction soon, I take it? The final exchange?"

Hudson looked at his wristwatch as if to check the time. He knew precisely what time it was. He was just going through the expected motions. "It's ten-thirty now. In six hours, gentlemen."

Monserrat hesitated, a momentary uncharacteristic flicker of indecision. "Six hours is acceptable. We will be ready. Is that all?"

367

Colonel David Hudson experienced a sudden flash of insight as he stood huddled with the two men. His old charm surfaced, his old West Point charisma. "There is another matter. One more serious problem we have to discuss."

"And what might that be, Colonel Hudson?"

"I realize that no one is supposed to know who you are. That's the primary reason I wanted you here. Why I insisted on it, if you were to get the bulk of these bonds. You see me, I see you. Except for one thing . . ."

"Except what?"

"Next time, I want to see the *real* François Monserrat. If he doesn't come in person, there will be no final exchange."

Having said that, Colonel David Hudson turned away, walked briskly back toward the VA hospital, and disappeared inside.

His revenge, his fifteen-year odyssey, was almost complete now. The final telling moment was coming for each and every one of them. Deceit! As it had never been seen before. Not since the Vietnam War, anyway.

They had taught him to destroy so very, very well . . . Whatever he wished to destroy . . .

*Manhattan*

In a fashionable and expensive part of New York City, Vice President Thomas More Elliot walked at a quickening pace along the rim of the East River, directly behind the United Nations complex.

There was the customary parade of joggers running along the concrete promenade. A spinsterish woman looked as if she were contemplating suicide. A slender young model blissfully walked her dog.

He was alone and troubled that morning. There were apparently no bodyguards for the vice president of the United States. No Secret Service men were anywhere in sight. There was no one to protect Thomas Elliot from possible harm.

The walk alone was something the vice president did infrequently, but it was something he needed to do now. It was a fundamental human need to be alone. He needed to be able to think, to be able to see a complex and challenging plan in its entirety.

He desperately needed to piece together the real reason why he was here, alone.

He paused and stared into the sluggish wintry gray river. Smoke drifted lazily upward on the other bank. He thought about his childhood, then, as if those comforting recollections might put everything in perspective. The casual rise of smoke reminded him of those autumnal bonfires on the grounds of his family home in Connecticut. How could that small boy, whose face he saw in memory, have come all this way? All the way to this present, seminal moment in American history?

Vice President Elliot placed his gloved hands in the deep pockets of his overcoat. Green Band was almost at an end. Out there, in this vast city, the terrorist François Monserrat, the New York police, and Colonel David Hudson and his men were rushing toward their personal rendezvous with destiny. Meanwhile, other powerful forces were slotting quietly into place.

He frowned. A barge crawled over the oily surface of the river. Dirty washing hung on a rope, and smoke rose upward from a blunt funnel. He thought he saw a shapeless figure move aboard the barge.

Colonel David Hudson was to have his moment of destiny . . .

As was he, the vice president of the United States.

In a very short time, when the considerable dust had cleared on the brief reign of Justin Kearney—a disillusioned man who hadn't been able to come to terms with the strict limitations of his power, a man who would resign his office in the wake of an economic crisis, who would probably be exiled to some rustic estate and live out the remainder of his days writing heavily censored memoirs—when all the dust had cleared, Thomas More Elliot, like Lyndon Baines Johnson twenty-odd years before, like Gerald Ford a little more than a decade ago, would step up to the presidency of the United States.

Everything depended on the final act of Green Band.

# Chapter 39

THE VETS CABS appeared suddenly. They paraded single file out of an abandoned warehouse garage in downtown Manhattan. The cabs were assimilated into normal traffic flow until they branched onto Division and Catherine streets, leading toward the East River and FDR Drive.

Each of the cabs had been equipped with PRC-77 transmitter-receivers, known in Vietnam as "monsters". The PRC units automatically scrambled and unscrambled all transmissions. There was no practical way the New York police could intercept messages traveling back and forth among the cabs.

There were six cabs, which could carry fourteen heavily armed Vets: an assault platoon with rifleman-snipers. M-60 gas-operated machine-gunners, a thumper man with an M-79 grenade launcher, and a communications operator.

The most spectacular touch in the commando raid was that the ground-attack force had air support. Two Cobra assault copters would be backing the Vets if any combat action started on the street.

David Hudson, who scouted and studied the street from the lead cab, was beginning to feel an unexpected sense of release. It was almost over. Finally, revenge. Finally, dignity.

He experienced some of his old combat sensations from Vietnam, only this time with a difference. A big, important difference.

This time they were going to be allowed to win.

A New York police detective, Ernie "Cowboy" Tubbs, who had been dragged unceremoniously out of bed to join the manhunt, saw one of the cabs go past on Division Street. Then he saw two more Vets cabs.

He turned to his partner, Detective Maury Klein, a short man in a black tent of a raincoat. Tubbs said, "Christ, that's them. That's Green Band. Bingo, Maury."

Detective Klein, who was addicted to Rolaids and Pepto-Bismol, peered sorrowfully through the windshield. His stomach was already killing him. "Jee-sus Christ, Ernie! Half those bastards are supposed to be Special Forces."

Tubbs shrugged and swung their late-model Dodge out from behind the line of yellow cabs. Only a single car separated them from the rearguard Vets cab. "We've spotted Green Band!" Tubbs rasped into the hand mike on his dashboard.

Maury Klein uneasily cradled an American 180 submachine gun in both arms. The assault gun looked terribly out of place inside the Dodge, a middle-class family car. The American 180 fired thirty rounds per second. It was almost never used in city fighting for that reason.

"This sucks, man. *Sucks!*" Marty Klein continued to complain. "Bar on a Hundred and Twenty-fifth Street, I tangled with one Green Beret Special Forces dude. That was enough for me, forever!" The notion of mixing it up with ex-Special Forces veterans seemed like one of the worst ideas he'd ever had in his police force life. Maury Klein was a vet, too, class of 1953, Korea.

At Henry Street there were only a few traffic lights working. There was almost no other traffic. An eerie, dockside feeling pervaded the steamy gray area of lower Manhattan.

"Looks like they're going to the FDR Drive for sure . . . Entrance is down here somewhere. Right around Houston."

"North or south?" Ernie Tubbs yelled to his partner.

"I think both ways. South for sure. We'll see it here any . . . there! That's it."

Just then Tubbs spotted the dilapitated ramp to the south lanes of the drive.

The Vets cabs were approaching fast from both directions. The first cabs were already rattling up the crumbling stone and metal ramps.

Tubbs flicked on his hand mike again. "Contact! All Panther units. They're getting on the FDR! They're heading south! Over."

Suddenly the rear Vets cab veered sharply. It tried to cut Tubbs off.

"Son of a bitch!"

Tubbs swerved left with skillful, near perfect timing. The unmarked police sedan continued to shoot up the half-blocked entranceway that didn't look wide enough anymore.

"Jesus Christ, Ernie! Watch the walls!"

The Vets cab, meanwhile, had finished its tailspin. It was blocking off every police car except one, Tubbs's, which had somehow slipped by. "Son of a bitch! Son of a bitch!" Detective

373

Tubbs yelled as he fought the unmarked car's steering wheel for control.

"All units, all units! They set a roadblock on the FDR! Repeat. There's a roadblock on the FDR! Over."

The single police sedan was now screeching into teeming traffic, filling all three narrow, twisting lanes of the FDR south. A car slammed to a jolting stop behind. Horns blared from every possible direction.

The police car was hemmed in tight by two of the cabs. The black barrels of M-16s were jammed out both windows of the cab to their left.

Ernie Tubbs couldn't breathe. He was bottled in at fifty-five miles an hour. One of the M-16s fired a round. The warning shot flared over the sedan's roof like night tracers in a battle zone.

A Vet in military khakis and black greasepaint screamed over at Tubbs. His voice was muffled under the traffic whistle, but Tubbs could hear every word.

"Get off at the next stop! Get the fuck off this road! . . . Everybody but the driver, hands up! I said hands up! Hands up!"

Closing on the next exit, Tubbs spun his wheel hard right toward the guardrail. The unmarked police car shot at a seventy-degree angle toward the off ramp.

It bumped hard over loose plates, sending off sparks. The patrol car went up on two wheels and threatened to turn over. After a moment during which gravity seemed an indecisive force, the car finally bounced back onto all four wheels. It shimmied down the off ramp, then stopped dead on the bordering city street.

"We lost 'em! Over." Ernie Tubbs screamed into his radio transmitter. "We lost 'em on the FDR!"

Detective Maury Klein finally whispered, "Thank fucking God."

Inside 13 Wall Street, Carroll heard the news that Green Band had been spotted. He raced down the steep flights, taking two and three steps at a time to the street. Everything was happening at once. Total bedlam. Squad cars were screeching up and down Wall Street and Broad and Water.

Carroll was carting an M-16 rifle, which felt weird bouncing against his body. Flashback time—he was an infantry soldier again . . . But this was downtown Manhattan, not Vietnam.

His coat flew open as he ran, revealing the Browning as well as a heavy bulletproof vest. His heart was as chaotic as the street noise.

A radio squad car he passed relayed the latest information on Green Band. "They're moving at about thirty-five miles an hour. Six vehicles. They're all regular Checker cabs. All are heavily armed. They're proceeding east."

It's a setup for something else, Carroll suddenly knew it.

What, though? What were the Vets going to do now? What was Colonel David Hudson's plan? How was he going to escape the tightening dragnet?

A silver-and-black Bell helicopter was waiting in a Kinney parking lot. A few weeks earlier the parking lot would have been filled with the luxury cars of inveterate Wall Street workaholics. A rate sign announced $14.50 plus NYC tax for twelve hours. The police helicopter was whirring like an outsize moth. It was ready to fly.

"M-Sixteen and a Bell chopper." Arch Carroll winced as he jumped inside the hot, cramped helicopter. "Christ, this brings back memories. Hi, I'm Carroll," he said to the police pilot.

"Luther Parrish," the pilot grunted. He was a heavyset black man with a leather flak jacket and clear yellow goggle glasses. "You ex-'Nam? You look like it. Feel like it." Parrish snapped a thick wad of gum as he talked.

"Class of 1970." Arch Carroll purposely played it a little combat cool. The truth was, he hated choppers. He hated seeing the goddam things. He didn't like the idea of being suspended in air with nothing to rely on but slender blades that furiously slashed the air.

"How 'bout that! Class of seventy, too. Well, here we go again, sports fans. I take it you don't much like airplane rides?"

Before Carroll had a chance to answer, the copter jumped straight up from the parking lot. The ascent left Carroll's small intestines somewhere behind. The chopper pierced the smoky city afternoon, hugging the dusky walls of nearby buildings and cleverly avoiding swift winds sweeping off the river.

As the copter swung out wide toward the East River, another Bell joined in from due south.

"No, I'm not real crazy about helicopters. No offense, Luther."

Adrenaline flowed wildly through Carroll's body. Down below, he could see traffic streaming on the FDR.

The police pilot shouted over the roaring rotors. "Beautiful day, man. You can see Long Island, Connecticut, almost see Paris, France."

"Beautiful day to get shot in the fucking heart."

Parrish snorted a laugh. "You been to 'Nam all right. Let's see, we've got two, maybe three, armed patrol helicopters on them right now. Pick up more help once we find out which borough they're goin' to. I think we'll be fine."

"I hope you're right."

"You see them down there? Little toy taxicabs. See? See right there?"

"Yeah, with little toy M-Sixteens, toy rocket launchers," Carroll said to the pilot.

"You talk just like ex-infantry. Ironic-type shit. Makin' me all misty eyed."

"Still infantry from the look of things. Except I'm afraid we're fighting the Green Berets today."

The black pilot turned to Carroll with a knowing look. "They're *bad* dudes all right. Definitely Special Forces." He nodded as if to a secret beat. He almost seemed proud of the Vets bravado. Their urban street-fighting style had hit a chord.

A thousand feet below, the FDR Drive was a delicate ribbon of silver and shiny jet black. The Vets cabs looked intensely yellow down there. As the lineup of cabs crossed the Brooklyn Bridge, the two helicopters swung high and wide to avoid being seen. They actually disappeared briefly into low-flying clouds.

Carroll's shirt was already soaked through. Everything seemed to be happening at a distance. The world was slightly fuzzed and unreal. They were going to solve Green Band, after all.

On the Brooklyn side of the bridge, he could see that traffic was heavy but moving. The steady *whoosh* of cars, an occasional bleating horn, traveled all the way up to the cockpit.

"They're getting off at the exit for the Navy Yard! This is Carroll to control. The Vets convoy is exiting at the Navy Yard! They're proceeding northeast into Brooklyn!" Carroll screeched into the microphone.

At that same instant, a deafening explosion jarred the under-belly of the helicopter with a jolt that rattled right through Carroll's bones. His head cracked hard against the metal roof, and sharp bolts of pain stabbed behind his eyes.

Then a second jarring blast struck the cockpit.

Splinters of glass flew in all directions. Star fractures cob-webbed across the windshield. Everywhere, metal was ringing with gunshots. Glaring red flashes were angrily ribboning the sky.

"Ohhh, goddamn, I'm hit. I'm hit," Parrish moaned as he slumped forward.

A machine gun chattered loudly off to Carroll's left. He caught a brief glimpse of floating, blinking red lamps on the right and the hulking shapes of two choppers he hadn't seen before.

Christ! Two Cobras were attacking.

The sky filled with bright, jarring yellow orbs of light, with roaring fire and billowing black smoke. The companion police helicopter had disintegrated before Carroll's eyes. Within sec-onds there was nothing left of the chopper but leaping gold-and-orange flames. Nothing but an eerie, fading afterim-age in the sky.

Carroll could see that Luther Parrish had been badly hit. Puddles of blood were collecting from a wound on the side of his head. The electric circuits in the cockpit seemed to be completely out.

Heavy machine-gun fire suddenly welled up from below. The pilot moaned and grabbed his legs. The helicopter had begun to fall, to somersault and plummet.

Carroll crazily fired his M-16 at one of the attacking Cobras. The red light winked derisively—then the copter calmly disappeared from sight.

Carroll froze. The police helicopter suddenly flipped over. It was upside down. Blood was rushing, swirling through his head.

The helicopter was now in a deadfall, sailing and spinning into the Brooklyn Navy Yard below. A flat black rooftop, with a water tower mounted on it, suddenly loomed at the copter's windshield. Carroll could see them skimming over an expanse of shadowy factory buildings a block long, at least. They missed a smoking industrial chimney by inches. Then the copter's tail was clipped off by a high brick retaining wall.

A deserted grid of avenues and streets appeared through the windshield as the chopper cleared the last building. Cars were parked in long, uneven lines up both sides. Carroll was familiar with helicopters from his many trips in Vietnam, though not how to fly. Reflexively he grabbed at the controls.

He was beyond all fear now, beyond anything he'd even felt in combat or police action. He was in a new realm—a place where he was acutely conscious of everything around him.

This was it, he thought. He was going to die.

The helicopter's belly cleanly sheared the rooftops off half a dozen parked cars. Carroll covered his face and shielded Parrish as best he could.

The helicopter struck the street on a side angle. It skidded, bounded violently, then issued a grinding shriek. Sparks, plumes of intense red flames, flew in every direction. Whole sides of parked automobiles, headlights, and bumpers were effortlessly cut away. A fire hydrant popped out of the sidewalk.

The helicopter plowed to a tearing, screaming, crunching halt against two crushed cars.

A man in a factory security uniform came running down the deserted street, zigzagging crazily toward the unbelievable accident. "Hey, hey! That's my car! That's my *car!*"

Carroll cradled the badly wounded pilot. "Grab hold. You just hold me," he whispered, hoping the man wasn't already dead. "Just hold me, Luther. Don't let go."

He began to half carry the hulking NYPD pilot away from the burning helicopter wreckage. His eyes nervously searched the skies for the attacking Cobras, but he could see nothing.

The choppers might as well have been a nightmare. The nightmare of Vietnam all over again. *But it was happening right here on the streets of Brooklyn.*

And now Archer Carroll was out of the grand chase. He had lost Green Band. They had eluded him again.

# Chapter 40

THE VETS CABS proceeded northeast, then almost due east across Brooklyn. They were moving inexorably toward François Monserrat and the appointed end of Green Band. Everything was precisely on schedule.

Erect and alert behind the wheel, David Hudson was experiencing a moment of unusual anxiety. It all had to do with being this close to the end. They were less than seven minutes from the rendezvous with Monserrat.

Nothing could distract David Hudson from Green Band now. He would concentrate as if he were entering a combat zone. Nothing must look even mildly suspicious . . .

François Monserrat's soldiers could be watching the streets from neighborhood rooftops and darkened apartment windows. If they spotted the unexpected attack force, the final massive exchange of Wall Street securities would fail. Green Band would fail.

Like an advance scout in 'Nam, Hudson noted everything. A

knot of black youths was easing out of Turner's Grill. Their voices carried—low, guttural sounds in syncopated street rhythms. He checked and rechecked the squat, cheerless brick buildings as he drove closer to the agreed-upon meeting place.

Hudson drove slowly on until he found a parking spot farther down the slope-shouldered Bedford-Stuyvesant side street. Very nonchalantly he climbed out of the car. He continued to look around the quiet neighborhood, searching for any sign of danger. He finally popped open the cab's dented and scarred trunk. The Wall Street securities were there in ordinary-looking gray vinyl suitcases.

Hudson hoisted up the bags and began to walk as rapidly as he could toward a red brick factory at the next corner. He was certain he was being watched. François Monserrat was somewhere nearby. All of his senses and instincts corroborated that warning signal. This was to be the moment of reckoning. Hudson's Special Forces training to be matched against Monserrat's years of experience, his years of meticulous deceit.

Hudson shouldered open the heavy wood front door of a building that housed shabby apartments and a small Italian-American shoe factory, the Gino Company of Milano.

He pushed into a dark hallway, where trapped cooking smells immediately assaulted him. The musty scent of old winter clothes hung in the air. The meeting place seemed appropriately isolated, but almost too mundane.

"Don't turn around, Colonel."

Three men with long-nosed Magnums and Berettas drawn, stepped into the dim corridor.

"Move right up against the wall . . . That's good. Right there. That will be fine, Colonel Hudson."

The leader had a cultivated Spanish accent, more than likely

Cuban. François Monserrat ran the Caribbean and most of the terrorist activities in South America, Hudson remembered. At the rate he was going, one day Monserrat was going to run the entire Third World.

"I'm not armed," Hudson said quietly.

"We have to search you anyway."

One of the men positioned himself about three feet away from Colonel David Hudson. He pointed his gun between Hudson's eyes. It was a popular gunman's trick, one Hudson himself had been taught at Fort Bragg. At close range, shoot out the eyes.

The second man patted him down, quickly and professionally. The third man searched the suitcases, slashing them carefully with a knife, looking for false siding, a false bottom.

"Upstairs!" the terrorist who held the gun finally commanded Hudson. He spoke like a military officer, Hudson noted.

They began to climb a steep and creaking flight of stairs, then another flight. Were they leading him to Monserrat? Finally, the enigmatic Monserrat himself? Or would there be more deception?

"This is your floor, Colonel. That blue door straight ahead. You can just walk inside. You're most definitely expected."

"Point of information? I have a question for you, for all of you. Curiosity on my part." David Hudson spoke without turning to face them.

An impatient grunt came from behind . . .

The Lizard Man. Past interrogations. Special Forces training. Hudson's mind continued to churn at a furious rate.

All to prepare him for this very moment? For this and no other?

"Do they ever tell you what's really happening? Has anyone bothered to tell you the truth about this operation? Do you know what this meeting *really* is? Do you know why?"

David Hudson was introducing some element of doubt into all of their minds, petty doubts and confusion, paranoid unease he could use later, if he needed to.

Deception.

"Don't bother to knock, Colonel." The man in charge calmly spoke once again. "Just go right in; you're expected. Everything you try to do is expected, Colonel."

A slice of dull yellow light emanated from the fourth-floor tenement room as David Hudson peered inside. He paused at the doorway's edge.

He was about to confront the mysterious and dangerous Monserrat. He was about to end Green Band's long mission.

The Vietcong's Lizard Man had taught Hudson an essential lesson in Vietnam: Play games in which your opponent wasn't given the rules. This was the principle behind all successful guerrilla warfare, Hudson believed.

Colonel David Hudson versus Monserrat.

Now it would begin, and end.

"All blue-and-white units! We've picked them up again . . . We've got our friends Green Band!"

NYPD cruiser radios echoed brassily above the noise of whining police and hospital emergency sirens at the helicopter crash site near the Brooklyn Navy Yard.

"They're moving into a residential neighborhood. Bedford-Stuyvesant. It's right in the heart of the fucking ghetto. They're traveling on Halsey Street in Bed-Stuy. Over."

Arch Carroll sagged heavily against the open front door of

one of the half-dozen police cruisers that had arrived after the accident. Crime scene technicians were already swarming onto the fire-lit street.

He wasn't sure if he'd heard the radio report right . . . Green Band appeared; Green Band disappeared. Which was it now?

Carroll tried to clear his head as he listened to the minute-by-minute updates squawking over nearby police-cruiser radios.

He felt numb. He was beyond pain.

Parrish was carried on a litter into a waiting EMS ambulance. KIA, Carroll was almost certain.

"Carroll? You're Arch Carroll, aren't you? Do you want to go with me? I'm heading to Halsey Street. It's about ten minutes from here." A police captain, a plump, white-haired man Carroll knew from a saner niche in his life, came up to him.

Carroll knew he appeared badly dazed. He felt far worse than that, but he nodded. Yes, he definitely wanted to witness the end. He had to be there. Colonel David Hudson—Monserrat—Archer Carroll—they all had to be there. Everything had led to this point.

Seconds later he was uncomfortably hunched up in a patrol car. He felt sure he was going to be sick. Hammers of fear were tripping off in his head.

The cruiser lurched into motion. The flashing cherry-red light began to revolve. The siren of the speeding car warbled above the Brooklyn rooftops.


This was the master terrorist Monserrat.

This was François Monserrat.

David Hudson could not believe that what his eyes told him was true.

Monserrat? . . . Or was this more incredible deception? The

highest manifestation of deception? He felt the familiar electric tingling in his fingertips, his arm, his legs.

He watched the mysterious dark-suited figure come toward him. He noted the two gunmen in the shadows against the far wall.

"Colonel Hudson." The handshake was quick, firm. "I'm François Monserrat. The real one this time." A thin smile played at the corners of his mouth. It was the most confident and assured look that David Hudson had ever witnessed.

Monserrat's smile dimmed immediately. "Let's get down to business. I believe we can complete our transaction quickly. Look at what he's brought, Marcel. *Rapidement!*"

A man in a dark suit stepped inside the room at Monserrat's command. He was perhaps sixty and had the pallid complexion, the weak eyesight, of someone who spent much of his life looking through microscopes and magnifying glasses. He bent low to examine the securities Colonel David Hudson had brought with him.

Hudson watched closely as he rubbed the individual trading bonds carefully, testing their texture between his thumb and forefinger. He smelled selected bonds, testing for fresh ink, for any unusually pungent odors, anything that would suggest recent printing. He worked extremely fast.

Nevertheless, each minute passed with excruciating slowness.

"For the most part, the bonds are authentic," he finally said to Monserrat, looking up.

"Any problems at all?"

"I have a slight question about the Morgan Guaranty, perhaps about the smaller Lehman Brothers lot. I think there are possibly some counterfeit papers in those stacks. As you know, there are *always* some counterfeits," he added. "Everything else is quite in order."

François Monserrat nodded curtly. He seemed uneasy now. The terrorist picked up the plain black telephone on the table. He dialed a telephone company business office, gave a four-digit number, then spoke to someone who was clearly an overseas operator. Seconds later the terrorist was speaking directly to someone obviously known at a bank in Geneva.

"My account is Number four-eleven/FA. Make the agreed-upon deposit into the account . . ." A few minutes later Monserrat hung up.

Then the phone rang, and Colonel Hudson received a confirmation that the money had indeed been successfully transferred in Europe. More than two hundred million dollars had gone out of the Soviet accounts into special accounts opened by the Vets in London, Paris, Amsterdam, and Madrid. Vets 28, Thomas O'Neil, the Customs chief of Dublin International Airport, had come through once again. The Green Band plan *was* perfect.

"Colonel, I believe our business is concluded. You seem to have won each round. This time, anyway." Monserrat executed a cold deferential bow.

As Colonel David Hudson stood up from the table, he felt that a terrible weight had finally been lifted. He was free of an obsession he'd carried with him for almost fifteen years.

At that precise moment, he was silently counting down to zero.

Green Band was almost at an end.

Almost, but not quite. Just one more twist, one final element of surprise.

Deception, at its best.

A game in which Hudson alone knew the rules. An amazing game called Green Band.

Less than forty seconds remained . . . Two pistols were drawn in the room . . .

Concentrate. David Hudson eased himself toward a controlled calmness.

Talk to them. Keep talking to Monserrat.

"I have one question before I leave. May I? May I ask one troubling question?"

Monserrat nodded. "What harm? You may ask anything. Then perhaps I have a question."

Colonel Hudson watched Monserrat's eyes as he spoke. He saw nothing, no emotion there. No affect. The two of them were close in so many ways. Killing machines.

"How long have you been with the Russians? How long have you been one of their moles?"

"I was *always* with the Russians, Colonel. I *am* Russian. My parents were stationed in middle America. They were among the hundreds of agents who came here in the late 1940s. I was taught to assimilate myself—to be American. There are many others like me. *Many* others. They're all over the United States right now. Waiting, Colonel. We want to destroy this country financially, and in every other way."

Fourteen seconds. Twelve seconds. Ten seconds. Colonel David Hudson kept counting in his head, kept talking in a monotone to François Monserrat. His heartbeat remained low. He was still in complete control.

"Harry Stemkowsky . . . Do you remember a man named Stemkowsky? A poor crippled sergeant? One of my men?"

"One of the casualties of war. Your war. Your war, Colonel, not ours. He wouldn't betray you under any circumstances."

As he reached three in his countdown, Colonel David Hudson took two fast, unexpected steps to his left. Both Russian terrorists awkwardly swung up their pistols. They were too late.

Hudson tucked his chin down hard against his chest and dove headfirst through a glass window, crashing into the factory section of the building.

At that precise moment, the entire building shook with the first savage round from the M-60s, which completely pulverized the tenement's fourth floor.

Flash fires broke out simultaneously in three separate areas of the factory. Bright orange-and-crimson flames strained to reach the stained yellow ceiling. Huge panes of glass buckled, then burst from their casements and crashed to the cement below. Everywhere, the old struts and supports of the building were beginning to sag, warped by the rising heat, the hungry reaches of the licking flames.

M-16 rifles coughed and rattled everywhere.

The Vets attack force was under way.

David Hudson waited in a combat crouch behind heavy factory machines. The thick smoke from the fire was friend and enemy at the same time. The billowing smoke and flames made it impossible for Monserrat and his men to locate Hudson, but it also made him vulnerable, exposed to sudden attack from any side.

Colonel Hudson heard the sound he'd been waiting for. The whirring of the helicopter rotors was unmistakably loud and clear.

The Cobra had arrived on the rooftop exactly as they'd planned it. Everything was perfect, right to the final escape.

Colonel David Hudson allowed himself a trace of a smile. Just a trace.

"Get the fuck out of my way! Move it! Move it! *Move, move, move!*"

A roaring, unbelievable firefight had erupted. Arch Carroll saw rows of flat rooftops shooting flames as he pushed and elbowed his way through the crowd gathered on Halsey Street. Ghouls, he thought. The worst kinds of ambulance chasers.

He winced. His left arm was numb, and something was wrong with his lower back; contact with the pavement sent jarring pains up his spine.

None of the neighborhood people—leather-jacketed teenagers, sullen young women, small grinning children—seemed to realize that this violent spectacle was real.

"Get back! Damn it, get back!" Carroll yelled hoarsely as he ran. "Get inside with those kids! Get back inside your houses."

Expectant, wide-eyed faces were crowded into every available apartment window. Farther down Halsey Street, hundreds of neighborhood people filed out into the cold, rainy afternoon. They were staring toward the explosions, enthralled by the blazing fire, the sudden jolting volleys of M-16 rifle and pistol shots.

Carroll continued to run in his clumsy crouch, moving in closer to the gunshot-riddled building.

A police bullhorn suddenly boomed out. It thundered over the cacophony of gunblasts and piercing human shouts. "You there! You, running! Stop right there!"

Carroll ignored all the voices. He kept charging forward. His steps weaved as he struggled with pains that attacked his body. As he reached the fiery building he heard an even more familiar and terrifying sound. A Cobra was hovering over the factory roof. The same helicopter that had shot him down was back. Green Band was here.

Arch Carroll vaulted the building's stone steps. He took the stairs three at a time, and with each leap he thought he could hear the rattle of his own loose bones flying about in his body.

A heavyset man suddenly burst out of the open doorway directly in front of Carroll. The man looked Spanish or maybe Cuban. He was holding an 870 riot gun.

Carroll's gun was set on rapid-repeat. A full round of .30-caliber bullets flickered into the unfortunate terrorist's face and throat. He reeled back inside the doorway.

The smoke, forcing itself out of the broken first-floor windows, choked Carroll. He managed to keep running and swiftly entered the building, almost tripping over the body of the dying gunman sprawled inside the doorway. The man gazed up at him with a surprised look in his eyes.

Instinctively Carroll hugged the wall. Cheek tight against the cold, peeling plaster, he gasped for breath. His head was spinning at an unbelievable speed.

Cobra helicopter? How did they manage a Cobra? Getting a Cobra just wasn't possible . . . Green Band was waiting upstairs, and that didn't seem possible, either.

A heavy, grated iron door opened slowly onto the tenement rooftop. Columns of smoke, scattered by the wind, temporarily blurred David Hudson's vision. He was no more than forty yards from the waiting Cobra.

Colonel Hudson walked cautiously at first, then he began to trot like a victorious athlete toward the waiting helicopter. He'd done it. They had all done their jobs almost perfectly. The Green Band mission was finally over. The sudden exhilaration of victory was unbelievable to savor.

Hudson never saw the second figure on the roof until the skillful assailant was on top of him. He'd been careless. For once, just once, he'd forgotten to check, to double-check, every possibility.

"You can stop right there, Colonel."

Face and shoulders still obscured in shadow, the figure appeared cautiously from behind the water tower. One hand held a Beretta. Then a face came into the light. François Monserrat stood fully exposed before Colonel David Hudson.

Monserrat laughed a laugh of triumph. "My congratulations, Colonel. You nearly accomplished the perfect crime."

Once inside the burning tenement, Carroll was unsure which way to go. He choked on a thick gust of smoke and felt violently sick. His lungs chafed as if they'd been rubbed with sandpaper.

Crackling reports of M-16s and booming incendiary bombs rang out. He could still hear the sharp repeating sound of the rotors of the Cobra that had landed on the rooftop. Monserrat and Colonel Hudson were inside the building . . . *Get up there*, his mind commanded him.

Carroll coughed and gasped as he struggled up the sets of steep, winding stairs. Flames curled all around him, throwing off searing heat. The pain in his legs was unbearable now. Something was terribly wrong with his back.

A heavy metal door blocked his way at the head of the stairs. Carroll put his shoulder into it hard, and it shrieked open. He had finally reached the rooftop.

The crimson taillights of a U.S. military helicopter sparkled impressively in the haze of smoke. Colorful, slashing streaks were thrown across the dark asphalt toward Carroll.

The Cobra was being readied for takeoff. The rotors were spinning. It was a familiar war-zone scene.

Somewhere in the smoke shrouding the rooftop, Carroll heard voices. They were strident and angry. They came from off to his left, beyond a high brick retaining wall. He could hear them quite clearly.

"You see, you must see that governments of the past are no longer viable. The currently elected governments are mere illusions. They are ghosts of a sentimentalized reality. You must understand *that*, at least. There *are* no more democracies." The first voice was filled with the unbearable tension of the moment.

The second voice was harsh, but the wind muffled the exact words. Whatever the second person had to say was whipped away by the roar of the chopper.

Carroll pressed closer to the voices. They became clearer now.

"I love this country," one of the two shouted above the wind. "But I hate what it did to the veterans after 'Nam. I hate what some of our leaders did. But I still love this country."

Carroll saw them both then.

Colonel David Hudson. The same man who was in all the FBI and Pentagon photographs . . . strikingly handsome, tall, blond . . . "the consummate military commander," according to his classified records. America's carefully programmed Juan Carlos.

And the other . . .

Dear God, the other.

At that moment Arch Carroll felt something precious and vital collapse deep inside him. It was much worse than physical pain. He remembered the first time he'd experienced the horror of death—his father's death in Florida. He remembered so well the feeling on the night Nora had died in New York Hospital.

His mouth was dry, and he was afraid.

Nothing could have possibly prepared him for this awful moment. Not even all his years as a policeman.

The man Colonel David Hudson had addressed as Monserrat was Walter Trentkamp . . . But the shadowy face Carroll saw was not the Uncle Walter of his youth, his father's trusted friend. This man was a ruthless stranger.

Carroll's world wheeled around him. His sense of reality left him. He closed his eyes and raked one hand over his smoke-blackened face. Burning tears were pushing, pressing, against his lids.

Uncle fucking Walter. It was the worst hurt, the worst conceivable betrayal, of his life. How could this have happened?

He thought about everything Trentkamp had been privy to in the past. He reviewed his own long investigation of Green Band. Trentkamp knew every detail he'd learned at each maddening turn.

Had Trentkamp dispatched him on the early wild-goose chase? Why? Well, he knew the answer to that. So he could control Carroll. So he could carefully control the DIA's terrorist group. Talk to me on this one, Archer. Let me know what you find out. Will you promise me that? François Monserrat had enlisted Carroll to help him find Colonel David Hudson and the Vets.

Talk to me, Archer . . .

Promise me, Archer!

Walter Trentkamp had sat in on the highest-level meetings in the White House, always observing, always studying. What incredible self-confidence and gall. How many years had this been going on? How many fucking years? . . . François Monserrat! The most ruthless of the world's terrorists was none other than Walter Trentkamp. Hard for him to believe. Yet it was true. Walter Trentkamp was an obscenity.

The rage that Carroll felt ripped through him. He'd been used. Just like the Vets, he'd been used, his trust violated.

Carroll carefully moved toward Trentkamp and Hudson. The blinding rage inside him now heightened. He struggled against the overwhelming urge to fire his Browning. To pull the trigger. To shoot to kill. *And what are you, please tell me, mister?* But he knew, he had always known, he was more than just a trained killer.

Carroll was ready now. He stepped out from behind the shadowy retaining wall. He spoke in a powerful whisper.

"Hello, Walter. I wanted to keep my promise. I did promise to talk to you about everything I found out."

Trentkamp's face registered only brief surprise. Monserrat quickly surfaced, supremely confident, indifferent to Carroll.

"It was never anything personal, you understand. You were my *reshenie*. That's a Russian word. You were my solution to a problem. Nothing more than that. My mission is total Soviet domination. We have an interesting face-off. The world's premier terrorists. America's very own terrorist hunter. All of us in check for the moment. A powerful snapshot of history, no?"

Archer Carroll raised his Browning. Colonel David Hudson . . . François Monserrat . . . himself. None of them could win. Carroll wasn't even sure what "win" meant right now. *And what are you, please tell me, mister?*

"How do you live a life made of nothing but lies?" He edged closer to Hudson and Trentkamp. "Nothing but fucking deceit and lies."

"I don't believe in the same truths you do. It follows that I don't believe in the same lies. Don't you realize that *you're* living with lies, too? Your own people have deceived you again and again . . . Everyone has lied to you, Archer. Your government is the greatest lie of all."

Only his instincts counted now. Colonel David Hudson rigidly held on to that.

He had a flashback of the prison camp in North Vietnam.

Monserrat was like the Lizard Man. He was the same kind of enemy.

Instincts.

Reflexes.

Survival.

Monserrat was concentrating on Carroll . . . "Everyone has lied to you, Archer. Your government is the greatest lie of all."

A silent scream rose from Hudson's throat, and at that moment, his arm chopped upward in a short, powerful arc. Monserrat's elbow shattered with a sickening crunch. The Beretta dropped. A harsh, ugly growl, like an animal's, escaped from his twisted mouth.

A needle-thin knife was now in Colonel David Hudson's hand.

Assassin.

Monserrat was better than the Lizard Man. In spite of the blow to his arm, he moved quickly away from Hudson and the knife.

David Hudson followed as if he were Monserrat's shadow. The flashing stiletto lanced forward.

Monserrat raised his hands to shield his face. The stiletto sliced down his arm. He never cried out, simply moved into a martial-arts crouch. He was ready to fight back, to crush his enemy.

Colonel Hudson screamed as he feinted one move, a second move, *then* struck again. The silver blade shivered forward with ferocious accuracy.

Hudson twisted the blade, then immediately pulled away. In rapid motion the stiletto was thrust forward again. It slashed Monserrat's throat. Still Monserrat kept coming.

In one superhuman effort, Monserrat reached for his throat. Then he stared at the blood gushing into his hands.

The terrorist suddenly went limp. There was a brief look at Hudson. He opened his mouth as if to say something, then slumped to the asphalt roof.

Carroll watched the bitter struggle in horror, the last convulsion of François Monserrat. He trained his Browning on Colonel Hudson now. His finger tightened around the trigger.

It was then that he heard the distinct *click* of the automatic weapon. It came from directly behind him. Carroll whirled around.

Four men in tattered khaki green were surrounding him. Their M-21 rifles were pointed at him.

They looked like soldiers. They were Vets. This was Green Band.

Here was everything he'd wanted to know—only now Carroll didn't want to know.

Outrage!

Walter Trentkamp's tall, imposing figure now looked very small to Carroll as it lay on the ground in a pool of blood. The hard gray-green eyes as empty in death as in life. *Christ! Christ!*

Carroll suddenly began to shout at the top of his voice.

"Who are you, Hudson? *What the hell do you want? Who sent you to Wall Street?*"

Outrage!

Something hard exploded against Carroll's head. He staggered, almost fell. The Bronx street fighter in him refused to go down. Goddamn! Them!

Arch Carroll thought he was going blind. The pain in his head was unbearable. Streams of blood coursed down his face.

"Who are you, Hudson?" One final, maddening question formed on his lips. He took another lunging step toward Colonel Hudson, toward the body of François Monserrat—of Walter Trentkamp.

He was struck again with tremendous force.

A terrible mashing noise echoed in Carroll's head. He was falling, then, collapsing against his will. He heard himself moan.

The revolver crashed down hard again.

He gazed up and saw Colonel David Hudson. Carroll tried desperately to speak. So many questions to ask. Everything was blurry now. He tried to get up. He had to make the madness stop. But Archer Carroll now felt himself falling into a tunnel. It was dark and desolate.

# Chapter 41

*Manhattan*

WITH A SHAKING hand, Anton Birnbaum poured miserly portions of aged Sandeman port for himself and for Caitlin Dillon.

He felt a thousand years old. He had a piercing headache from his recent sleeplessness and mental hyperactivity. Now, in the thin daylight that streaked his apartment, he went to the window and peered into the streets of his beloved New York. *What in hell was happening out there?*

Caitlin Dillon, whose head also reeled from the hours of intense concentration without sleep, took a cigarette from her purse and started to light it. Then she changed her mind. Her throat was raw, and there was a heavy pressure behind her eyes. What she needed, she knew, was a long sleep. Both she and Birnbaum were waiting for final news of Green Band, news from Carroll. Caitlin now understood what it was like to be a policeman's wife. She didn't know how those women could bear it.

"We know some of what we need to know," Birnbaum said. "Two years ago, in Tripoli, François Monserrat met with important leaders from the Third World. In particular, he met key leaders from the Middle Eastern oil-producing countries. The heads of their military forces were in attendance there as well." Birnbaum walked away from the window.

"I'm convinced that they planned a cunning new way to disrupt the economic system of the West. Their plan called for the cartel to ultimately gain control of the entire American stock market."

"They already had enough economic leverage to definitely influence the market," Caitlin said quietly. Her head pounded. A jackhammer was drilling mercilessly in the recesses of her skull. She thought about Carroll, who was out there right this moment in pursuit of Green Band. Why hadn't they heard anything?

"That spring, our newly elected president learned of the frightening Tripoli plot. More important, the Committee of Twelve must have heard about Red Tuesday. Only they moved much faster than President Kearney could in Washington."

The old man's eyes became cold. "Caitlin, I believe they created Green Band to counter Red Tuesday. Effectively, the Committee of Twelve has stolen billions from the Arabs. Green Band is the very finest and most dangerous group of men you would ever want to meet. Now they're selling them back their own funds. This has been an economic world war. The first of its kind—unless we include the 1970s oil embargo."

Caitlin thought that if it had been anyone other than Anton Birnbaum making these accusations, outlining these

400

hypotheses . . . But *it was* Birnbaum. And he was serious about everything he was proposing . . . Why hadn't she heard from Carroll yet?

"How does Hudson fit in? What's his part in this, Anton?" Caitlin asked.

"Ah, the enigmatic Mr. Hudson." Birnbaum allowed a tight smile to cross his face. "I've given great thought to Colonel Hudson. Either he's in the pay of the Committee of Twelve . . . or they're ruthlessly using Hudson and his veterans group. It wouldn't be the first time, would it? It wouldn't be the first time these men were used by those who wield great power in this country. Either way, we'll know in a few hours. We'll know the truth soon, won't we?"

As he arrived at the designated address, Colonel David Hudson felt exactly the way he'd always known he would—if they had won in Vietnam. The adrenaline, the magical excitement of victory, was pumping, rushing furiously through his body.

This would certainly be the safest house he'd ever used, Hudson thought as he reached York Avenue on Manhattan's fashionable East Side. He entered an elegant glass-and-grill-work doorway just beyond the corner at Ninetieth Street.

Billie Bogan's apartment was located on the river side of the starkly modern building, a building that apparently had paper-thin ceilings and walls, because Hudson could hear a piano playing as he approached the doorway on the fifteenth floor.

The lovely music surprised him. He hadn't even known that Billie played.

David Hudson hesitated before pushing the doorbell. Warning alarms were going off again. It was all perfectly natural.

One didn't stop being a military terrorist and saboteur overnight.

Billie answered the door seconds after the first ring. She was wearing a pink T-shirt that said WINTER across her chest. She had on tight black French jeans, no shoes or socks. She looked stunning and exotic, even now.

"David."

Her brilliant blue eyes passed from puzzlement to undisguised pleasure as she saw who it was. She wore no makeup; she didn't need it.

She reached out and pulled Hudson toward her. She held him tightly. David Hudson ached to have his arm back—to hold her in both arms just this once.

"Was that you playing the piano?" he asked.

Billie pecked at his cheek and gave him an extra hug. "Of course it was me . . . You know, I think the piano is the reason I ultimately escaped from Birmingham. As I found out about Mozart, Brahms, Beethoven, I was convinced there had to be more than the dreary dullness I was used to. Come inside. I'm so happy to see you. It's so *good* to see you." She kissed him again.

David Hudson smiled more willingly than he had in a long time. "I'm happy to see you, too. I feel like I'm home at last," he said.

Once inside, they talked. They held each other. They stared into each other's eyes for a long time. Hudson told Billie about his past, talking with the speed of a man who had observed vows of silence for too many years. It all came tumbling out—West Point, the horrors of Vietnam, his early, abortive career in the army.

He told her everything, except about the past year, which he was tempted to tell her as well. How his brilliant revenge had become his sweet victory. A material reward— millions of dollars for himself and the other Vets. He wished he could share it with her, share everything right now.

Under the tent of a brightly striped wool blanket, with the windows thrown half-open, they made love once, and then again. Hudson was still learning to feel, and the vigorous lovemaking helped enormously. She brought him closer and closer to climax . . . right to the delicious edges. But he couldn't make it over.

Finally, the most debilitating wave of exhaustion swept over David Hudson. He felt shaky. He was sliding headlong toward a tranquil dream state. The warning alarms still hadn't completely stopped, but now they almost seemed a natural part of him.

One moment, he was softly stroking Billie's thick blond hair, touching the elegant oval of her face. The next, he was falling into sleep. His eyes closed gently.

Billie lay awake in the large brass bed, watching the ember glow on a filtered American cigarette. She sighed quietly.

Sometimes she surprised even herself with her ability to effortlessly create a lie, in perfect context, consistent with a whole world of other lies . . . Deception.

Her being able to play Chopin, and fitting that so naturally into the Birmingham, England, framework was an inspiration. But then again, wasn't that precisely why she was here with the great Colonel David Hudson?

She rose silently from the double bed, tossing off rumpled designer sheets. She was certain it would take a miracle to wake Colonel Hudson, even with a cannon.

She returned to the bedroom with a Beretta. A blunt-nosed silencer was attached to it.

She knew better than to hesitate for even a fraction of a second. She swung her arms up stiffly. She moved to fire the revolver into his lightly pulsing temple, just below the blond hairline. She hesitated a moment too long.

The sleeping body jumped forward. Colonel David Hudson's eyes blinked open, and he fired through the covers. He fired again and again and again.

Warning signals were shrieking in his head. Terrible pain screamed out at David Hudson.

Deception—forever—deception.

Everywhere. Even *here*.

The Committee of Twelve, the American Wise Men, did not want David Hudson to live. They had easily recruited him after the disappointments of Vietnam, the disappointment in knowing his early promise in the army could never be realized. He'd been their agent provocateur for crises around the world. They had been so intelligent, every bit as smart and precise as he was. They'd sent the girl, of course, his escort. They'd known about Vintage, about his habits. They'd used him so well.

Finally, Colonel David Hudson understood.

# Chapter 42

*Brooklyn*

CARROLL SLOWLY OPENED his eyes and sat up painfully. All around him were crashing sounds, police and U.S. Army personnel, blinding bright lights, flashing, running shapes. Faces peered down at him. Who were these people?

"What happened?" Carroll finally asked. "How long have . . . What happened to the body? A body was over there!"

A uniformed New York cop knelt down beside him. Carroll had never seen the man before. "What other body are you talking about?"

"There was a body there, over near the Cobra. Walter Trentkamp of the FBI was killed right over there."

The policeman shook his head. "I was one of the first up here on the roof. There wasn't any other body. You know, you've got a small watermelon growing up on top of your head. You *sure* you're all right?"

Carroll stood up clumsily. Everything was spinning. "Oh, yeah, I'm fine. Tiptop shape."

Arch Carroll, grasping the bricks in the wall for support, started down the winding metal stairs.

Somebody had taken Walter Trentkamp's body away.

"Hey, buddy, you ought to get yourself treated! Have somebody look at your head. There wasn't any body up here."

Carroll hardly heard the policeman's words. He wanted to go home. He needed to go home, right away. He thought about his kids and about Caitlin.

He thought about Caitlin's meeting with Anton Birnbaum and wondered what might have transpired there. He was worried about the people he loved . . . There wasn't any body on the roof . . . Sure thing—this was all a dream, a horrible nightmare.

He didn't know how he managed the first wild minutes of the drive to Riverdale. Maybe it was practice—all those half-drunken nights of his recent past. Maybe God *did* look after babies and drunks. But there was a time coming when God might make him abdicate his responsibilities, his watchfulness . . .

What then?

The familiar lights of the old house in Riverdale were glittering brightly. As he drove up his street, Carroll remembered a time when his father and mother would have been there, a time when everything had seemed so much saner in America . . . when Trentkamp was Uncle Walter, for God's sake.

Walter Trentkamp had been his father's friend for all those incredible years. Had his father ever begun to guess anything? Had his father ever sensed the horrifying betrayal coming from Trentkamp? We had all been so naive about foreign governments back then. About our own government, as it was turning out. Americans thought of democracy as the world's one superior political system. We felt that we understood the parameters of our government's power. We understood *nothing*, Carroll now saw.

Trentkamp and the KGB had been so brilliant at fooling everyone. Walter Trentkamp had been so confident. He'd never hesitated to use Carroll. What better conduit for information? Walter's hubris was startling, but his modus operandi was consistent. As Carroll thought back now, he remembered that Walter had spent time in Europe after World War II. He recalled "fact-finding" trips to South America, to Mexico, to Southeast Asia, while Carroll had been serving there himself. It was no wonder they had never been able to identify Monserrat. *They hadn't been looking in the right places.*

No one had thought to look in New York or Washington. Why would anyone suspect the living legend? Walter Trentkamp had no respect for American intelligence, and he had been absolutely right. His ruse, the classic misdirection, had been perfect—the lifework of a master spy, a Donald Maclean or a Kim Philby.

Arch Carroll's eyes were watering again—only now it was because he was so glad to see his kids. They all jumped up and ran to him as he stumbled inside the house. Then the Carroll family was hugging and kissing. They were squeezing their father as tightly as they could.

"We have to get out of here fast," Carroll whispered to Mary Katherine. "We have to move out of the house now . . . Help me dress them. Try to explain as little as you can. I have to call Caitlin."

Mary Katherine nodded. She didn't even seem that

surprised at the news. "You go call Caitlin now. I'll outfit the troops."

Two hours later the Carrolls, the family of six, and Caitlin Dillon quietly checked into the Durham Hotel on West Eighty-seventh Street.

Carroll's initial plan was to stay there for a night, maybe a few nights, until they could decide how to work with Anton Birnbaum, how to work with the New York police. Life was suddenly full of treacherous false bottoms. Was there anyone he could trust?

Once they were alone together in the hotel, Caitlin and Carroll fell into an embrace. They shared a long, tender kiss that neither of them wanted to end. Caitlin pushed against Archer Carroll with a fierce, undisguised need. There was no more reason to hide anything, to hold back her feelings.

"I love you so much," she said.

"I love you, too, Caitlin. I was afraid today. I thought . . . that I might never see you again."

They made love in the hotel room, and it was all passion, definitely not Lima, Ohio. Then a second time, Caitlin and Carroll gently held hands—almost as if they might never do this beautiful thing again. Almost as if they would never share their love again.

"I hated it when you were out there after them," Caitlin whispered as she lay beside Carroll. Her breath was like feathers on his cheekbone. "I've never felt so afraid. I don't want to feel that way ever again."

Carroll brushed her hair from her face. She was so unbelievably precious to him. "I told Walter Trentkamp that I planned to quit once Green Band was over. I haven't changed my mind."

Caitlin stared deeply into his eyes. "There's a catch, though."

"Yes, there's one catch. Green Band isn't over yet."

There was so much terrifying evidence to be considered and studied. There were classified files from the FBI and Pentagon; there were also taped statements from Birnbaum's highly placed contacts in Washington and Europe . . .

They just had to get to the right people with what they knew, with the truth.

Who were the right people, though? Whom could they trust? The newspapers? Television stations? The New York police? The CIA?

The Committee of Twelve seemed to be everywhere. Were they connected with the police, the CIA? Did they somehow control the newspapers and TV?

It was all so unbelievably shitty.

During the first agonizing hours in the hotel, Carroll and Caitlin read every major newspaper report. Twice that afternoon Carroll took cabs to the large stand in Times Square that carried out-of-town newspapers. He and Caitlin read and reread everything written about Green Band. They searched desperately for a faint shadow of what they knew to be the truth.

There was none that they could find. *Nothing* had been reported about secret intragovernmental groups. *Nothing* had been reported about a terror plan called "Red Tuesday." Or about Walter Trentkamp. Had the body been spirited away by the Twelve? . . . Nothing was said about Colonel David Hudson's Special Forces training at Fort Bragg, North Carolina. In the news, Colonel Hudson was described as a "Jackal-like provocateur," the renegade mastermind of Green Band. Hudson was depicted as an obsessed man still looking for some justice, some personal meaning, years after Vietnam . . .

It all sounded so plausible, if you didn't know any better.

409

Early on the morning of December 22, Caitlin and Carroll had some visitors at the hotel. The visitors were Anton Birnbaum and Samantha Hawes.

The best and worst part of the Green Band investigation had begun. The tension and pressure were even more relentless than before. For the past twenty-four hours Carroll's stomach had been doing an uncomfortable dance.

A picture of Green Band was finally emerging. If not a complete portait, it was at least an outline, a foreshadowing of the truth. The story was certainly different from anything reported in the newspapers or on TV.

"The Twelve, the American Wise Men, are descended from our own OSS, America's intelligence team during the Second World War," Anton Birnbaum said in a voice that seemed to grow weaker each day. "The route is serpentine, but it can be followed . . . The existence of the Twelve goes back to the younger Dulles, his reluctance to surrender his wartime intelligence machine to the politicians. When the OSS was transformed into the CIA, the Twelve began to meet outside official circles. They were still probably the most powerful men in Washington. At first they gave counsel, then they took things into their own able hands . . . The original OSS was probably the best American intelligence unit ever.

"The Twelve still smugly believe they are the elite. They're *convinced* they are doing the country a grand service, guiding us through the Cuban missile threat, the time of the assassinations, Watergate, now Green Band. Every year, each decade, they become more and more powerful."

Birnbaum was looking pale and brittle. At the outset of the

morning, he'd told Caitlin that he was fearful of a heart attack or stroke if he continued at this pace. "The Red Tuesday plan could have incited another market crash, the worst since 1929. Green Band worked to stop that, at least. The Committee members also managed to profit from the results. The companies they control have already made hundreds of millions of dollars."

Samantha Hawes had more information about Colonel Hudson. She'd managed to retrieve some of the missing Vets files during the past few days.

"David Hudson was approached by at least one Committee member when he was still in the army, while he was at Fort Bragg after Vietnam. General Lucas Thompson, his old commander, approached Hudson first. General Thompson knew everything about Hudson's POW experiences. He knew about Hudson's training at Fort Bragg, too. Army intelligence had prepared Hudson to be their Juan Carlos. They backed off when Hudson lost his arm. Well, the Committee had plenty of uses for Colonel Hudson and his special skills . . . Another interesting note—Philip Berger of the CIA ran Hudson's original commando training at Fort Bragg. Several Committee members have spoken at veterans affairs over the past few years. The connections are there, the manipulation is feasible. The Committee needed a paramilitary group, and they used David Hudson."

Carroll had read the missing FBI and Pentagon files that Samantha Hawes had brought with her. "Hudson was given a lot of help with Green Band, probably more than he needed. The help came in the form of Wall Street information, and precise tips about what we were doing inside number Thirteen. That's why he was able to play so many cat-and-mouse games. He also had Pentagon files on all potential candidates for Vets. As it turned out, Hudson chose men who'd served with him in Vietnam. The Committee promised him millions as a reward once the Green Band mission was completed."

"Yes, only half the Vets are dead now," Birnbaum said. "The rest are missing. Colonel Hudson is missing. Where is David Hudson now, I wonder?"

Caitlin had been unusually quiet for most of the session. She had retrieved the necessary financial backup information. She was still angry. She felt used by this grandiose Committee that believed it was above the government, above laws.

"We're beginning to make progress," she said in a quiet, businesslike manner. "But we are still faced with an over-whelming problem. Can we trust anyone but the people right in this room? Do we take our information to the newspapers? Do we go to the director of the FBI, Samantha? Whom can we tell this story to?"

There was silence in the room. They were all beginning to understand the frightening power of a select few. Whom could they trust?

The cover-up was almost as clever and masterful as the Green Band plot itself. The cover-up was brilliantly executed.

For another twenty-four hours the Carrolls managed to live in cramped quarters in the West Side hotel. So far, they had no other choice. Whom could they trust?

Late at night, Carroll and Caitlin stayed in the smaller of the two bedrooms. They lay in each other's arms, passing the long, eerie hours exploring each other's bodies. They were realistic enough to know that something nightmarish might still happen—that they might never be together like this again.

"Hudson said something up on that rooftop," Carroll whispered as he stroked Caitlin's hair. "He said that he loved his country. You know, I still feel that way myself. I almost feel close to Hudson in a strange way."

Caitlin and Carroll made love again that night, and it was more tender than it had ever been. They fell asleep holding each other, like children during a storm.

At six o'clock on the morning of December 24, Caitlin found that she couldn't sleep anymore. She finally got up.

When she switched on the tiny portable radio, she heard the news that finally broke her heart.

"Anton Birnbaum, advisor to several U.S. presidents, was killed on Riverside Drive near his home early today. The elderly, still-active financier was struck by an unidentified hit-and-run driver . . . Birnbaum was eighty-three years old at the time of his death."

Caitlin shook Carroll's shoulder. "Oh, Arch, wake up. They killed him," she sobbed. "The Committee killed Anton this morning. They've killed him. What's going to happen to us? Oh, poor Anton."

Carroll mumbled and cursed as he got up from bed. He threw on his clothes, then hurried down to Broadway, where he bought the *Daily News*, *The New York Times*, and the *New York Post*.

All the front-page stories about Anton Birnbaum contained respectful eulogies. They also contained substantial, and what Carroll took to be purposeful, lies. At best, the newspapers revealed only a small fragment of the truth.

At the news kiosk, he read the articles with trembling

413

fingers. It was as if nothing had ever happened. There was no high-placed traitor in the FBI. There was no Monserrat and no mention of the whereabouts of Colonel David Hudson.

Trudging back to the hotel, Carroll saw two men following him.

There was no way anyone connected with Green Band could live.

# Chapter 43

*ESCAPE.* IT WAS the only possibility that remained.

On the night of December 24, Arch Carroll, Caitlin Dillon, the four Carroll children, and Mary Katherine locked hands and walked rapidly down Columbus Avenue. There had to be some way for three adults and four small children to escape a surveillance team. The New York crowds would provide temporary safety.

Columbus Avenue was buzzing with holiday music and festive bustle. The energetic crowd parted reluctantly for the hurrying family. Carroll wondered how he could protect Caitlin, Mary K., the kids—when he knew that professional gunmen were following them.

"Can we please stop running, Daddy? Please? Please, Daddy. Just for a minute? Please?" said Lizzie as she was being dragged along. Up ahead, Caitlin and Mary Katherine had the other three children bravely in tow.

Carroll stopped and wrapped his arms around his little girl.

He whispered soothingly against her cold, red-rimmed ear. "Please, baby, please be good. Just a little longer, sweetheart."

Carroll was almost certain he knew what was going to happen next. He gazed north, then down the bright lights of Columbus Avenue. His weary eyes brushed over colorful signs that said Sedutto, Diane's Uptown, Pershings, Cantina.

Columbus Avenue had changed dramatically since he'd last been above Seventy-second Street. The area had once been crowded with Spanish food stores as well as transient hotels and Oriental rug dealers. Now it was a trendy, self-conscious version of Greenwich Village.

He glanced over his shoulder again. The same persistent pair of men was still following. He was sure they had been joined by others. There seemed to be five men following the Carroll family.

Where in the name of God do we go from here? Somebody help us.

Carroll was sweating, even in the chill night air. He was so tired. He wanted to go to sleep right there in the middle of crowded Columbus Avenue.

This is happening. Whether I choose to believe it or not, this is happening.

Escape.

He had one desperate prayer. He was bursting with fear. He could see the same emotion on Caitlin's face. Mary Katherine was very pale, her usual ruddy color gone. He reached out for Caitlin and held her tight.

"Listen to me. Listen closely." He whispered something to her that made her cry. "I love you so much, Caitlin. Everything *has* to be all right."

"Oh, Arch, be careful. Please be careful."

Then Carroll gently pushed her away. He sent Caitlin and his sister and the tangle of children running in the opposite direction, across Seventy-second Street. Away, far away from him.

"Daaa-ddy! . . . Daa-ddy!" Carroll heard his babies' cries as he raced away. He ran as fast as he could along the clogged sidewalk.

Suddenly powerful arms grabbed him. A hand clamped down hard, twisting into his face. Searing pain ripped through his eyes.

They were attacking him in the middle of New York City, in one of the most crowded, residential areas of the city. They had come for him in full view of a hundred witnesses . . .

They didn't even care about the witnesses anymore.

"Get the hell off me! Get off me, you pieces of shit!" Carroll's shouts rose above the honking horns, above the city's deafening street rumble. "Somebody, please help!"

They were injecting him. Some kind of long needle pierced his trousers right into his leg.

They were killing him right out here.

On West Seventieth Street in New York City.

"Somebody help! Somebody fucking help!"

There were obviously no secrets anymore. There was no bullshit pretense that this was a police bust, that they were New York detectives.

"Get off! . . . *No needle . . . noooo!*"

Arch Carroll roared. He screamed and fought back savagely. He clawed at them with his remaining strength. He was sure he broke a jaw. His elbow smashed hard into a forehead, and he heard a bone snap loudly.

Then he was being dragged into a dark blue sedan. He was

being held upside down! He looked back as they pulled him out of the staring crowds.

He was still hanging upside down when he saw the second car arrive, saw Caitlin and his sister and the kids being snatched away.

No one connected with Green Band could live. The Committee, the American Wise Men, couldn't allow that.

"*Not the kids!* You goddamned bastards! Not my kids, not my kids! . . . No, *please*, not my kids!"

# Chapter 44

*Virginia*

THOMAS MORE ELLIOT'S palms were unpleasantly dry and cold. He suppressed a nervous tic that was starting to pulse in his throat. He finally stepped out of the dark blue stretch limousine and into the chill Virginia winter air. Dead trees were silhouetted against the gray skyline, and in the distance there was the sound of bird hunters' gunshots.

He turned and walked up the fieldstone steps that led to the large double doors of an imposing thirty-room country house. He paused before going in and sucked air deeply into his lungs.

Inside, the cavernous front hall was badly overheated. He felt a trickle of sweat run along his collar. His footsteps echoed on the marble floor as he crossed to a great curving flight of stairs that led up to the floors above. It was not a house that Thomas More Elliot enjoyed. Its very size, its history of late, made him uncomfortable.

When he reached the landing, he came to an ornately carved walnut door. It shone so deeply from years of meticulous care that he could almost see his own indistinct reflection in it.

He opened the door and walked in.

A group of men sat around a long, polished oak table. They were dressed mostly in dark business suits. Some of them, including General Lucas Thompson, were retired military and naval commanders. Others were influential bankers, landowners, proprietors of TV stations, and highly respected newspapers.

The man at the head of the table, a retired admiral with a shining bald head, waved at the vice president. "Sit down, Thomas. Sit. Please.

"A year ago," the admiral continued once Elliot had taken a seat, "we met in this very room. Our mood that day was one of some agitation . . ."

There was a polite ripple of laughter.

"We debated, I'm sure we all remember, the complex problem posed by the so-called Red Tuesday plan, the plan that was hatched—if that's the word—in Tripoli by the oil-producing nations . . . There were rather heated arguments that day."

The admiral smiled. Thomas Elliot thought he resembled a rather smug school principal on award day at a private academy.

"On that day we reached a decision—unanimous, finally—to create what we called Green Band. I believe the name was something I suggested myself, a name with both financial and military connotations."

The admiral continued in sanctimonious tones, "We are here today to confirm that the paramilitary operation called

Green Band was a success. We created temporary panic in the economic system. A panic we were able to control. We took hundreds of millions of dollars back from the oil-producing cartel. We brilliantly usurped the terrorist plan known as Red Tuesday. The world will find Jimmy Hoffa before they ever locate the body of François Monserrat ... And with the destruction of Green Band and the inevitable death of our volatile associate, Colonel Hudson, the file should be closed on this unfortunate episode in our history ... We are making *every* effort to make certain that it is."

Thomas Elliot shifted on his chair. The atmosphere in the large room was changing subtly. The men were beginning to loosen up, to move toward a celebratory atmosphere, one that was muted, quiet, and, most of all, tasteful.

The admiral said, "In approximately two weeks, Justin Kearney will dramatically resign his presidency ... He will be remembered chiefly as a scapegoat for the economic near tragedy ... More important, though"—and here all eyes in the room turned toward Thomas More Elliot—"Thomas Elliot will ascend to that office ..."

There was an outbreak of mild applause. Elliot looked around at the eleven men. His own presence brought the number to an even dozen.

The twelve men who effectively ran America, the American Wise Men.

"Later," said the admiral, "there will be champagne and cigars. For the moment, Thomas, our dry congratulations to you, and I think to everyone in this room ..."

The admiral looked reflective for a moment. "In a few weeks, for the first time, one of us will occupy the highest office in the land. And that means our control is tighter, more sure than

421

ever before . . ." He looked down the row of men. "Which means we will no longer need to contend with a president who doesn't think the way we do . . . someone who imagines his power is independent of what we bestow."

Thomas More Elliot stared off into the gray light that lay against the window. His throat had become suddenly dry. He reached for the water pitcher on the table. He was about to say something that would not contribute to the general mood of contentment in the room. But that couldn't be helped. Somebody had to deliver the news.

"I have heard from our people in New York City. A man called Archer Carroll is in police custody there. I have been told that he is talking . . . that he's telling his story to anyone who will listen . . . and that certain media representatives are paying very close attention to what he is saying."

Thomas More Elliot sipped his tepid water.

"What does he know?" the admiral asked eventually. "Everything," the vice president said.

# Chapter 45

AT SEVENTY-SECOND STREET, Police Sergeant Joe Macchio and Patrolwoman Jeanne McGuiness were driving out of the woods of Central Park when they spotted the scene.

"This is car one-three-eight. Please give *immediate assistance* at Seventy-second Street and Central Park West!" Patrolwoman Jeanne McGuiness, a tall, skinny woman with an impassive face, was already speaking into the car radio. The red police bubble on top of the cruiser had begun to revolve slowly.

Up ahead, traveling at maybe fifty or fifty-five miles an hour, was a dark blue Lincoln. That *wasn't* the problem.

The problem was some suicidal or homicidal maniac trying to wiggle out of the shattered backseat window. He was halfway out. Holding him inside were two other men.

"Look! Look there! The second car behind!" McGuiness

pointed straight ahead. Inside the second car, children, a host of screaming kids, seemed to be fighting and struggling to get out.

"Son of a bitch!" Joe Macchio growled. He had been dreaming of Christmas, and something of the peaceful spirit had created a glow in him. Now that was all gone.

Macchio and McGuiness left their police cruiser. With revolvers drawn, they cautiously approached the two sedans, which had now stopped at the southwest corner of Seventy-second. Other blue-and-whites, sirens screaming, were already racing up Broadway.

"We're federal agents." A man in a dark business suit burst out of the lead sedan. He was confidently holding out a portfolio wallet and an official-looking badge.

"I don't care if you're the commander in chief of the United States Army," Sergeant Macchio croaked in his most convincing street-cop voice. "What the hell's going on here? Who the hell's this guy? Why are these kids screaming like somebody's being murdered?"

A second dark-suited man stepped out of the trailing sedan. "I'm Michael Kenyon of the CIA, Officer." He said it calmly but authoritatively. "I think I can explain this whole thing."

Carroll was still half-in, half-out of the back window of the sedan. He was groggy, almost out on his feet. He hollered at the two police officers. "Hey! Please!" His speech was slurred. "My kids . . . they're in danger . . . I'm a federal officer . . ."

Sergeant Joe Macchio couldn't help himself—he finally started to laugh. "Not that I think this is funny, pal. But *you're* a federal officer?"

Ten minutes later the situation wasn't any closer to being solved. Several more police blue-and-whites had arrived. So had cars from the New York FBI and more from the CIA.

There was a buzzing cluster of police officials on Seventy-second Street.

Two EMS ambulances had pulled up, but Caitlin and Mary Katherine wouldn't let them take Carroll to Roosevelt Hospital or anyplace else without them.

Caitlin was yelling at the policeman, telling him that she and Carroll were part of the Green Band investigation team. She had proof in her pocketbook.

The CIA agents had lots of impressive proof that they were who they said they were. The arguing continued on the corner, getting more heated with every passing moment. It began to draw a curious sidewalk crowd.

Mickey Kevin Carroll finally sidled up to Sergeant Joe Macchio, who had walked off to try to think the whole crazy thing out.

"Can I see your hat?" Mickey Kevin asked. "My dad's a policeman. He doesn't get to wear a hat, though."

Joe Macchio looked down at the small boy and finally offered a tired smile. "And which one *is* your dad?" he asked. "Is your dad here now?"

"*That's* my dad." Mickey Kevin pointed at the man peacefully slumped, seemingly sleeping, on the EMS cot, looking like Crusader Rabbit.

"He's a policeman, son?"

"Yes, sir."

Well, that settled it for Sergeant Macchio. "That's what I needed to know, son. That's what I needed to know for starters, anyway."

Sergeant Macchio stooped down and handed Mickey Kevin Carroll his hat. Then he hastily walked in the direction of the disturbance that had closed down Seventy-second Street, not

425

to mention the downtown lanes of Central Park West and the park road.

"Tell you what we're gonna do, eh!" Sergeant Macchio clapped his hands for a little old-fashioned order and attention. "We're gonna sort this all out down at the station house!"

At that news, the entire Carroll family started to do a very odd thing; at least Sergeant Macchio and the rest of the New York cops thought it was peculiar. The kids started to balls-out cheer and clap for the NYPD.

The cops weren't used to that. A couple of the older patrolmen even started to blush. They'd almost never been treated like the arriving cavalry before, like the good guys.

"All right, *all right*, now! Everybody pile into the wagons. Let's get this show on the road. See who's been naughty, eh?"

Photographs of the scene were snapped by somebody from *The New York Times*, also by a free-lance photojournalist who lived across the street in the Dakota. A shot of Mickey Kevin wearing Macchio's hat was featured in *Newsweek* magazine.

Eventually the *Newsweek* shot of Mickey Kevin appeared framed on the mantel in the Carroll house. Lizzie, Mary III, and Clancy all complained loudly about favoritism. Arch told them to shut their yaps, they were all family, weren't they?

# Chapter 46

*Washington, D.C.*

A DIRECT LINE to the president of the United States signaled through at six o'clock on the morning of March 7. Clustered inside the Oval Office were most of the members of the National Security Council. Not one of the high-ranking officials could believe what was happening now.

A prerecorded message came over the telephone wire: "The White House is scheduled to be firebombed this morning, in a matter of minutes . . . This decision is irrevocable. This decision is nonnegotiable. You are to evacuate the White House immediately."

Inside a telephone booth, less than a mile from the White House, Colonel David Hudson pushed down the recording machine's stop button. He stuffed the compact recorder into the pocket of his fatigue jacket. Hudson laughed out loud.

Washington waited, but the White House was never struck

that morning. Instead, the home of General Lucas Thompson was firebombed. So was the home of Vice President Elliot, the homes of Admiral Thomas Penny, of Philip Berger, of Lawrence Guthrie . . . twelve homes in all.

David Hudson finally climbed into a light green touring van. He drove west out of the serene and strikingly lovely capital. No more nightmare voices screeched inside his head. *Finally, there was an end to deception.*

A deadly conspiracy is working against
Detective Lindsay Boxer and soon
she could be the one on trial . . .

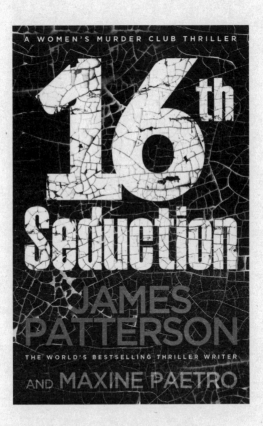

Read on for an extract.

THAT MUGGY MORNING in July my partner, Rich Conklin, and I were on stakeout in the Tenderloin, one of San Francisco's sketchiest, most crime-ridden neighborhoods. We had parked our 1998 gray Chevy sedan where we had a good view of the six-story apartment building on the corner of Leavenworth and Turk.

It's been said that watching paint dry is high entertainment compared with being on stakeout, but this was the exception to the rule.

We were psyched and determined.

We had just been assigned to a counterterrorism task force reporting back to Warren Jacobi, chief of police, and also Dean Reardon, deputy director of Homeland Security, based in DC.

This task force had been formed to address a local threat

by a global terrorist group known as GAR, which had claimed credit for six sequential acts of mass terrorism in the last five days.

They were equal-ethnicity bombers, hitting three holy places—a mosque, a cathedral, and a synagogue—as well as two universities and an airport, killing over nine hundred people of all ages and nationalities in six countries.

As we understood it, GAR (Great Antiestablishment Reset) had sprung from the rubble of Middle Eastern terror groups. Several surviving leaders had swept up young dissidents around the globe, including significant numbers of zealots from Western populations who'd come of age after the digital revolution.

The identities of these killers were undetectable within their home populations, since GAR's far-flung membership hid their activities inside the dark web, an internet underground perfect for gathering without meeting.

Still, they killed real people in real life.

And then they bragged.

After a year of burning, torturing, and blowing up innocent victims, GAR published their mission statement. They planned to infiltrate every country and bring down organized religion and governments and authorities of all types. Without a known supreme commander or national hub to target, blocking this open-source terrorism had been as effective as grasping poison gas in your hand.

Because of GAR's unrelenting murderous activities, San Francisco, like most large cities, was on high alert on that Fourth of July weekend.

Conklin and I had been told very little about our assign-

4

ment, only that one of the presumed GAR operatives, known to us as J., had recently vaulted to the number one spot on our government's watch list.

Over the last few days J. had been spotted going in and out of the dun-colored tenement on the corner of Turk and Leavenworth, the one with laddered fire escapes on two sides and a lone tree growing out of the pavement beside the front door.

Our instructions were to watch for him. If we saw him, we were to report his activities by radio, even as eyes in the skies were on this intersection from an AFB in Nevada or Arizona or Washington, DC.

It was a watch-only assignment, and when a male figure matching the grainy image we had—of a bearded man, five foot nine, hat shading his face—left the dun-colored apartment building, we took note.

When this character crossed to our side of the street and got into a white refrigerator van parked in front of the T.L. Market and Deli, we phoned it in.

Conklin and I have been partners for so many years and can almost read each other's minds. We exchanged a look and knew that we couldn't just *watch* a suspected terrorist pull out into our streets without doing something about it.

I said, "Following is watching."

Rich said, "Just a second, Lindsay. Okay?"

His conversation with the deputy was short. Rich gave me the thumbs-up and I started up the car. We pulled out two car lengths behind the white van driven by a presumed high-level terrorist known as J.

I EDGED OUR sharklike Chevy along Turk and turned left on Hyde, keeping just far enough behind J.'s van to stay out of his rearview while keeping an eye on him. After following him through a couple of turns, I lost the van at a stoplight on Tenth Street. I had to make a split-second decision whether or not to run the light.

My decision was *Go*.

My hands were sweating on the wheel as I shot through the intersection and was blasted by a cacophony of horns, which called attention to us. I didn't enjoy that at all.

Conklin said, "There he is."

The white van was hemmed in by other vehicles traveling at something close to the speed limit. I kept it in our sights from a good distance behind the pack. And then the van merged into US Route 101 South toward San Jose.

The highway was a good, wide road with enough traffic to ensure that J. would never pick our Chevy out of the flow.

Conklin worked the radio communications, deftly switching channels between chief of police Warren Jacobi and DHS deputy director Dean Reardon, who was three time zones away. Dispatch kept us updated on the movements of other units in our task force that were now part of a staggered caravan weaving between lanes, taking turns at stepping on the gas, then falling back.

We followed J.'s van under the sunny glare on 101 South, and after twelve miles, instead of heading down to San Jose and the Central Coast, he took the lane that funneled traffic to SFO.

Conklin had Jacobi on the line.

"Chief, he's heading toward SFO."

Several voices crackled over the radio, but I kept visual contact with the man in the van that was moving steadily toward San Francisco International Airport.

That van was now the most frightening vehicle imaginable. GAR had sensitized all of us to worst-case scenarios, and a lot of explosives could be packed into a vehicle of that size. A terrorist wouldn't have to get on a plane or even walk into an airline terminal. I could easily imagine J. crashing his vehicle through luggage check-in and ramming the plate-glass windows before setting off a bomb.

Conklin had signed off with Jacobi and now said to me, "Lindsay, SFO security has sent fire trucks and construction vehicles out to obstruct traffic on airport access roads in all directions."

Good.

I stepped on the gas and flipped on the sirens. Behind us, others in our team did the same, and I saw flashing lights getting onto the service road from the north.

Passenger cars pulled onto the shoulder to let us fly by, and within seconds we were passing J.'s van as we entered the International Departures lane.

Signs listing names of airlines appeared overhead. SFO's parking garage rose up on our right. Off-ramps and service roads circled and crossed underneath our roadway, which was now an overpass. The outline of the international terminal grew closer and larger just up ahead.

Rich and I were leading a group of cars heading to the airport when I saw cruisers heading away from the terminal right toward us.

It was a high-speed pincer movement.

J. saw what was happening and had only two choices: keep going or stop. He wrenched his wheel hard to the right and the van skidded across to the far right lane, where there was one last exit to the garage, which a hundred yards farther on had its own exit to South Link Road. The exit was open and unguarded.

I screamed to Conklin, *"Hang on!"*

I passed the white van on my right, gave the Chevy more gas, and turned the wheel hard, blocking the exit. At the last possible moment, as I was bracing for a crash, J. jerked his wheel hard left and pulled around us.

By then the airport roadway was filled with law enforcement cruisers, their lights flashing, sirens blowing.

The van screeched to a halt.

Adrenaline had sent my heart rate into the red zone, and sweat sheeted down my body.

Both my partner and I asked if the other was okay as cop cars lined up behind us and ahead of us, forming an impenetrable vehicular wall.

A security cop with a megaphone addressed J.

"Get out of the vehicle. Hands up. Get out now, buddy. No one wants to hurt you."

Would J. go ballistic?

I pictured the van going up in a fiery explosion forty feet from where I sat in an old sedan. I flashed on the image of my little girl when I saw her this morning, wearing baby-duck yellow, beating her spoon on the table. Would I ever see her again?

Just then the white van's passenger door opened and J. jumped out. A voice amplified through a bullhorn boomed, *"Don't move. Hands in the air."*

J. ignored the warning.

He ran across the four lanes and reached the concrete guardrail. He looked out over the edge. He paused.

There was nothing between him and the road below but forty feet of air.

Shots were fired.

I saw J. jump.

Rich shouted at me, *"Get down!"*

We both ducked below the dash, linked our fingers over the backs of our necks, as an explosion boomed, rocking our car, setting off the car alarm, blinding us with white light.

That sick bastard had detonated his bomb.

# Also by James Patterson

### ALEX CROSS NOVELS

Along Came a Spider • Kiss the Girls • Jack and Jill •
Cat and Mouse • Pop Goes the Weasel • Roses are Red •
Violets are Blue • Four Blind Mice • The Big Bad Wolf •
London Bridges • Mary, Mary • Cross • Double Cross •
Cross Country • Alex Cross's Trial (*with Richard DiLallo*) •
I, Alex Cross • Cross Fire • Kill Alex Cross • Merry
Christmas, Alex Cross • Alex Cross, Run • Cross My
Heart • Hope to Die • Cross Justice • Cross the Line

### THE WOMEN'S MURDER CLUB SERIES

1st to Die • 2nd Chance (*with Andrew Gross*) • 3rd Degree
(*with Andrew Gross*) • 4th of July (*with Maxine Paetro*) •
The 5th Horseman (*with Maxine Paetro*) • The 6th Target
(*with Maxine Paetro*) • 7th Heaven (*with Maxine Paetro*) •
8th Confession (*with Maxine Paetro*) • 9th Judgement (*with
Maxine Paetro*) • 10th Anniversary (*with Maxine Paetro*) •
11th Hour (*with Maxine Paetro*) • 12th of Never (*with Maxine
Paetro*) • Unlucky 13 (*with Maxine Paetro*) • 14th Deadly Sin
(*with Maxine Paetro*) • 15th Affair (*with Maxine Paetro*) •
16th Seduction (*with Maxine Paetro*)

### DETECTIVE MICHAEL BENNETT SERIES

Step on a Crack (*with Michael Ledwidge*) • Run for Your Life
(*with Michael Ledwidge*) • Worst Case (*with Michael Ledwidge*) •
Tick Tock (*with Michael Ledwidge*) • I, Michael Bennett
(*with Michael Ledwidge*) • Gone (*with Michael Ledwidge*) •
Burn (*with Michael Ledwidge*) • Alert (*with Michael Ledwidge*) •
Bullseye (*with Michael Ledwidge*)

## PRIVATE NOVELS

Private (*with Maxine Paetro*) • Private London (*with Mark Pearson*) • Private Games (*with Mark Sullivan*) • Private: No. 1 Suspect (*with Maxine Paetro*) • Private Berlin (*with Mark Sullivan*) • Private Down Under (*with Michael White*) • Private L.A. (*with Mark Sullivan*) • Private India (*with Ashwin Sanghi*) • Private Vegas (*with Maxine Paetro*) • Private Sydney (*with Kathryn Fox*) • Private Paris (*with Mark Sullivan*) • The Games (*with Mark Sullivan*) • Private Delhi (*with Ashwin Sanghi*)

## NYPD RED SERIES

NYPD Red (*with Marshall Karp*) • NYPD Red 2 (*with Marshall Karp*) • NYPD Red 3 (*with Marshall Karp*) • NYPD Red 4 (*with Marshall Karp*)

## DETECTIVE HARRIET BLUE SERIES

Never Never (*with Candice Fox*) • Fifty Fifty (*with Candice Fox, to be published July 2017*)

## NON-FICTION

Torn Apart (*with Hal and Cory Friedman*) • The Murder of King Tut (*with Martin Dugard*)

## ROMANCE

Sundays at Tiffany's (*with Gabrielle Charbonnet*) • The Christmas Wedding (*with Richard DiLallo*) • First Love (*with Emily Raymond*) • Two from the Heart (*with Frank Costantini, Emily Raymond and Brian Sitts*)

## OTHER TITLES

Miracle at Augusta (*with Peter de Jonge*)

# FAMILY OF PAGE-TURNERS

## MIDDLE SCHOOL BOOKS

The Worst Years of My Life (*with Chris Tebbetts*) • Get Me Out of Here! (*with Chris Tebbetts*) • My Brother Is a Big, Fat Liar (*with Lisa Papademetriou*) • How I Survived Bullies, Broccoli, and Snake Hill (*with Chris Tebbetts*) • Ultimate Showdown (*with Julia Bergen*) • Save Rafe! (*with Chris Tebbetts*) • Just My Rotten Luck (*with Chris Tebbetts*) • Dog's Best Friend (*with Chris Tebbetts*) • Escape to Australia (*with Martin Chatterton*)

## I FUNNY SERIES

I Funny (*with Chris Grabenstein*) • I Even Funnier (*with Chris Grabenstein*) • I Totally Funniest (*with Chris Grabenstein*) • I Funny TV (*with Chris Grabenstein*)

## TREASURE HUNTERS SERIES

Treasure Hunters (*with Chris Grabenstein*) • Danger Down the Nile (*with Chris Grabenstein*) • Secret of the Forbidden City (*with Chris Grabenstein*) • Peril at the Top of the World (*with Chris Grabenstein*)

## HOUSE OF ROBOTS SERIES

House of Robots (*with Chris Grabenstein*) • Robots Go Wild! (*with Chris Grabenstein*) • Robot Revolution (*with Chris Grabenstein*)

## OTHER ILLUSTRATED NOVELS

Kenny Wright: Superhero (*with Chris Tebbetts*) • Homeroom Diaries (*with Lisa Papademetriou*) • Jacky Ha-Ha (*with Chris Grabenstein*) • Word of Mouse (*with Chris Grabenstein*)

## MAXIMUM RIDE SERIES

The Angel Experiment • School's Out Forever • Saving the World and Other Extreme Sports • The Final Warning • Max • Fang • Angel • Nevermore • Forever

## CONFESSIONS SERIES

Confessions of a Murder Suspect (*with Maxine Paetro*) • The Private School Murders (*with Maxine Paetro*) • The Paris Mysteries (*with Maxine Paetro*) • The Murder of an Angel (*with Maxine Paetro*)

## WITCH & WIZARD SERIES

Witch & Wizard (*with Gabrielle Charbonnet*) • The Gift (*with Ned Rust*) • The Fire (*with Jill Dembowski*) • The Kiss (*with Jill Dembowski*) • The Lost (*with Emily Raymond*)

## DANIEL X SERIES

The Dangerous Days of Daniel X (*with Michael Ledwidge*) • Watch the Skies (*with Ned Rust*) • Demons and Druids (*with Adam Sadler*) • Game Over (*with Ned Rust*) • Armageddon (*with Chris Grabenstein*) • Lights Out (*with Chris Grabenstein*)

## GRAPHIC NOVELS

Daniel X: Alien Hunter (*with Leopoldo Gout*) • Maximum Ride: Manga Vols. 1–9 (*with NaRae Lee*)

For more information about James Patterson's novels, visit www.jamespatterson.co.uk

Or become a fan on Facebook